Praise for Catherynne M. Valente's Previous Books

YUME NO HON

"An allegorical fantasy whose dreamlike threads reach into Shinto and Western myth, mathematics and physics...Those who admire literary craft and rich language will most appreciate this sublime tale."
—*Publishers Weekly*

"An internal landscape painted with thoroughly poetic turns of phrase . . . packs a great deal of punch in its fleeting short chapters."
—*Booklist*

THE LABYRINTH

"[Valente's] poetic prose shimmers. . . . Readers who luxuriate in the telling of a tale and savor phrases where every word has significance will enjoy the challenge."
—*Publishers Weekly*

"Line by line and page by page, *The Labyrinth* contains more beauty than all but a very few books published this year . . . it is precise and undeniably original."
—SFSite.com

Also by Catherynne M. Valente

YUME NO HON
THE LABYRINTH
THE GRASS-CUTTING SWORD

Poetry
APOCRYPHA
ORACLES

The Orphan's Tales,

Vol. I:

IN THE NIGHT GARDEN

Catherynne M. Valente

THE ORPHAN'S TALES: IN THE NIGHT GARDEN
A Bantam Spectra Book / November 2006

Published by
Bantam Dell
A Division of Random House, Inc.
New York, New York

Interior illustrations by Michael Wm. Kaluta

Book design by Glen Edelstein

Library of Congress Cataloging-in-Publication Data
Valente, Catherynne, M., 1979–
The orphan's tales: in the night garden / Catherynne Valente.
p. cm.
ISBN-10: 0-553-38403-1
ISBN-13: 978-0-553-38403-1
I. Title.

PS3622.A4258 O77 2006   2006048425
813/.6 22

Printed in the United States of America
Published simultaneously in Canada

www.bantamdell.com

BVG   10 9 8 7 6 5 4 3

For Sarah, who,

when she was very young,

wanted a Garden

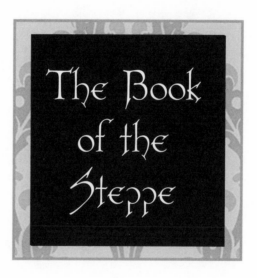

The Book
of the
Steppe

PRELUDE

ONCE THERE WAS A CHILD WHOSE FACE WAS LIKE THE NEW MOON SHINing on cypress trees and the feathers of waterbirds. She was a strange child, full of secrets. She would sit alone in the great Palace Garden on winter nights, pressing her hands into the snow and watching it melt under her heat. She wore a crown of garlic greens and wisteria; she drank from the silver fountains studded with lapis; she ate cold pears under a canopy of pines on rainy afternoons.

Now this child had a strange and wonderful birthmark, in that her eyelids and the flesh around her eyes were stained a deep indigo-black, like ink pooled in china pots. It gave her the mysterious, taciturn look of an owl on ivory rafters, or a raccoon drinking from the swift-flowing river. It colored her eyes such that when she was grown she would never have to smoke her eyelashes with kohl.

For this mark she was feared, and from her earliest days, the girl was abandoned to wander the Garden around the many-towered Palace. Her parents regarded her with trepidation and terror, wondering if her deformity reflected poorly on their virtue. The other nobles firmly believed she was a demon, sent to destroy the glittering court. Their children, who often roamed the Garden like a flock of wild geese, kept away from her, lest she curse them with her terrible powers. The Sultan could not decide—after all, if she were a demon, it would not do to offend her infernal kin by doing away with her like so much cut grass. In the end, all preferred that she simply remain silent and far away, so that none would have to confront the dilemma.

And so it went like this for many years, while thirteen summers like fat orange roses sprang and withered.

But one day another child came near to her, though not too near, hesitant as a deer about to bolt into the shadows. His face was like a winter sun, his form like a river reed. He stood before the girl in her tattered silk dress and shabby cloak which had once been white, and touched her eyelids with his sweet-scented forefinger. She found, to her surprise, that she endured his touch, for she was lonely and ever full of sorrow.

"Are you really a spirit? A *very* wicked spirit? Why are your eyes dark like that, like the lake before the dawn?" The pretty boy-child cocked his head to one side, an ibis in midstream. The girl said nothing.

"I am not afraid of you!" The boy stood his ground but his voice broke hoarsely. The girl continued to stare at him while the willow trees wavered in the east wind. When she spoke her voice was the low hum of cicadas in the far-misted hills.

"Why not?"

"I am very brave. One day I will be a great General and wear a scarlet cloak." At this there was almost a smile on the girl's pale lips.

"And you have come to slay the great girl-demon who haunts the Garden?" she whispered.

"Oh, no, I . . ." The boy spread his hands, feeling suddenly that he had shown very bad form somewhere along the way.

"No one has spoken so many words to me since I saw the winter snows through a warm window draped in furs." The girl stared again, impossibly still. All at once, a tiny light stole through her dusky eyes and she seemed to make a decision within herself. "Shall I tell you the truth, then? Tell you my secret? You of all the children who wear ruby rings and smell of olive soap?" Her voice had gone so quiet it was almost without breath.

"I asked, didn't I? I can keep secrets. My sister says I am very good at it, like the King of the Thieves in the nursery story." There was another long silence, as clouds covered the sun. And the girl began to speak very softly, almost afraid to hear her own voice.

"On an evening, when I was a very small child, an old woman came to the great silver gate, and twisting her hands among the rose roots told me this: I was not born with this mark. A spirit came into my cradle on the seventh day of the seventh month of my life, and while my mother slept in her snow white bed, the spirit touched my face, and left there many tales and spells, like the tattoos of sailors. The verses and songs were so great in number and so closely written that they appeared as one long, unbroken streak of jet on my eyelids. But they are the words of the river and the marsh, the lake and the wind. Together they make a great magic, and when the tales are all read out, and heard end to shining end, to the last syllable, the spirit will return and judge me.

"After the old woman vanished into the blue-faced night, I spent each day hidden in a thicket of jasmine and oleander, trying to read what I could in a cast-off bronze mirror, or in the reflections of the Garden pools. But it is difficult; I must read them backwards, and I can only read one eye at a time." She stopped, and the last was no louder than a spider weaving its opaline threads.

"And there is no one to listen."

The boy stared. He looked closely and could see wavering lines in the solid black of her eyelid, hints of alphabets and letters he could not imagine. The closer he looked, the more the shapes seemed to leap at him, clutch at him, until he was quite dizzy.

He licked his lips. They were all whispers now, the two of them, conspirators and thieves. The other children had all gone, and they stood alone under the braided whips of a gnarled willow.

"Tell me? Tell me one of the tales from your eyelids. Please. Just one." He was terrified that she would rebuke him and run, like the hound which is often beaten. But she only continued to look at him with those strange, dark eyes.

"You are kind to me when no one else will come near. And my tales are all I have to give as thanks. But you must come away from the open Garden, into my hiding place, for I would have no one else know. You would surely be punished, and they would take my mirror and my knife, which are all I own, and lock me away to keep the demon spirit from hollowing their fine house."

And so they crept away from the yellow-tinged willow, across the endless rows of roses. They ducked under an arch of chestnut blossoms and were suddenly enveloped in a bower of white petals, the perfume touching them like hands. Red branches had thatched themselves into a kind of low roof, and there was ample room on the soft, compact earth thatched with leaves for them both to sit.

"I will tell you the first tale I was able to read, from the crease of my left eyelid."

The boy sat very still, listening like a silk-eared hare deep in the forest.

"Once in a far away there was a restless Prince, who was not satisfied by his father's riches, or the beauty of the Palace women, or the diversions of the banquet hall. This Prince was called Leander, after the tawny lion that bounds across the steppes like a fearful wind. One night he crept out of the vine-covered walls of the great Castle like a hawk on the hunt, to find a quest and silence the gnaw of discontent in his breast . . ."

The Tale of the Prince and the Goose

NOW THE **PRINCE** STOLE INTO THE NIGHT, THE shadows wrapping around him like slippery river eels, and his footfalls were black and soundless on the pine needles. He journeyed through the Forest, stars flooding overhead as though they had burst through some gilded dam, having no particular plan except to get as far from the Palace as possible before the sun rose up and his father's hounds were set on his scent. The trees made a roof of many tiles over his head, a scented mosaic studded with blue clouds. For the first time in his young life, the Prince felt a fierce kind of happiness, rimmed with light.

As dawn swept up behind him like a clever thief, he

rested against the trunk of a great baobab, leaning his head against the knotted wood. He breakfasted on cheese and dried meat he had stolen from the kitchens. The salt of the meat was more delicious than anything he had ever tasted, and he slept for a few hours under the sky which bloomed in the colors of wisteria and lilies.

Traveling on, it was not long before he came to a little hut in a pleasant meadow with a thatched roof and a well-made wooden door, round with solid brass studs. The chimney smoked cheerily, smelling of sage and cedar. Milling around the house was a flock of gray-feathered geese, circling like cirrus clouds, ethereal and wild. They were very fine animals and beautiful, squawking and ruffling their feathers under the curling eaves of camphor and fresh straw.

Now the Prince was young and resourceful, but not very wise, and he had taken only a little food from the kitchens and a few apples from the orchards. He had assumed that he could forage easily, for the whole world must be as fertile as his father's lands, and all trees must be as full of jeweled fruit, all animals as docile and savory, all peasants as agreeable and generous. It was beginning to be clear that this might not be the case, and his stomach growled noisily. He resolved to replenish his pack before he went further. There were, after all, so many geese, and certainly whatever warm and festive creatures dwelt in that fine hut, they would not even notice if one of the long-necked animals disappeared.

The Prince had been trained to hunt and sneak from his earliest childhood, and he crept silently on well-muscled thighs from his hiding place. He stole behind a great plow and waited among the high summer grasses, searching for the right moment, controlling his breathing and slowing his hammering heart. The midmorning sun was hot on his neck. His hair crawled with sweat, trickling down into his collar, but he did not move at all until, finally, one of the lovely geese wandered away from the pack, peering around the blade of the plow and fixing him with wide black eyes. Her gaze was very strange, endless and deep as the autumn moon, pupilless and knowing.

But swift as a sleek wolf, the Prince escaped her gaze. He caught her slender neck in his hand and snapped it, the sound no louder than a twig caught underfoot. He rose from the dry grass and moved back towards the tree line, but the geese had noticed that one of their number was missing, and sent up a great alarm, terrible and piercing.

The door of the hut flew open and out stomped a fearful woman, a flurry of streaming gray hair and glinting axe blade. Her face was wide and flat, covered with horrible and arcane markings, great black tattoos and scars cutting across her features so that it was impossible to tell if she had once been beautiful. She wore a wide leather belt studded with silver, two long knives glittering at her hips. She screamed horribly and the sound of it shook the cypresses and the oaks, vibrating in the air like a shattered flute.

"What have you done? What have you done? Awful, awful boy!—Villain, demon!" She screeched again, higher and shriller than any owl, and the geese joined her, keening and wailing. Their howls gouged at the air, at the rich red earth, a sound both monstrous and alien, full of inhuman, bottomless grief. It dug at his ears like claws.

Finally, the woman quieted and simply shook her great head, weeping. The Prince stood, stunned, more chagrined over his lack of stealth than her rage. She was, after all, only a woman, and it was only a bird. She was dwarfish and no longer young, and he knew he had nothing to fear from her. He clutched the bird's corpse behind his back, hoping his broad chest and arms would hide it.

"I have only just stumbled upon your house, Lady. I meant no offense." The wretched woman loosed her awful scream again, and her eyes grew hideously large. He had not noticed their yellowish cast before, but it was certainly there now, feral and sickly.

"You lie, you lie! You have killed my goose, my beautiful bird, my child! She was mine and you broke her neck! My darling, my child!" She broke into bitter weeping. The Prince could not understand. He drew the goose's body from behind his back to hold it out to the crone.

But in his fist he held not a bird, but a radiant young woman, small and delicate as a crane poised in the water, long black hair like a coiled serpent winding around his hand, for he clutched her at the root of the braided mane. She was clothed in diaphanous rags which barely covered her shimmering limbs. And her long, smooth neck was neatly broken.

The tattooed woman ran at him, swinging her axe like a scythe through wheat, and he dropped the girl's body with a horrible thump onto the grass. When she reached him, she stopped short and breathed hard into his face, stinking of rotted plums and dark, secret mosses. She lifted her axe and cut off two fingers on the Prince's left hand, licking the spray of blood from her cracked lips. He could not run, the blow was so sudden and complete, but only cry out and clutch his maimed hand. He knew if he bolted from her he would lose much more than a finger. He promised the crone a thousand thousand kingdoms, the treasures of a hundred dragons, babbling oaths like a child. But she would have none of it, and slowly moved her free hand to one of the long knives.

"You have killed my child, my only daughter."

She laid her ponderous axe on the damp earth and drew, with one long, sinuous sigh, the bright-bladed knife from its sheath—

The girl paused, and looked into her companion's eyes, which were like deep marshes at sunset.

"Don't stop!" he choked. "Tell me! Did she kill him then and there?"

"It is night, boy. You must go in to dinner and I must make my bed among the cedar boughs. Each to our own."

The boy gaped, grasping frantically for a reason to stay and hear the fate of the wounded Prince. Hurriedly, he murmured, "Wait, wait. I will go to dinner, and steal food for us like the brave Prince Leander, and creep out under cover of night like a hawk on the hunt, and stay the night with you, here under the stars, which are bright as crane feathers in the sun. Then you can finish the story." He looked at her with a hope whose fierceness was brighter than any torch now lit at court.

She was quiet for a moment, head bowed like a temple postulant.

Finally, she nodded, without looking up.

"Very well."

In the Garden

As the last harp strings of crimson sighed into the silent westward darkness, the boy returned, clutching a handkerchief filled to bursting. He clambered into the little thicket and proudly laid out their feast. The girl sat as she had when he left her, still as one of the calm profiles of the Garden statues. Her strange quiet unnerved him, frightened him. He could not hold her dark gaze, her wide, almond-shaped eyes ringed about with their strange markings.

Instead, he glanced awkwardly at the steaming food. On the little square of silk lay a glistening roasted dove, fat peaches and cold pears, a half loaf of buttery bread covered in jam, broiled turnips and potatoes, a lump of hard cheese, and several sugared violets whisked away from the table garnish. He drew from his pocket a flask of pale watered wine, the great prize of his kitchen adventures.

The girl made no move, did not reach for the dove or the pears. Her crow-feather hair wafted into her face, borne by the warm breeze, and all at once she began to shudder and weep. The boy did not know where to look, did not wish to shame her by witnessing her tears. He fixed his eyes on the shivering boughs of a distant cypress tree, and waited. By and by, the sniffling ceased, and he turned back to her.

Of course, he understood that she had never eaten so well in her life, as she had never been welcome at the Palace dinners—he imagined that she had lived on the fruits and nuts of the Garden, foraging like a beggar. But he could not understand why plenty would make someone weep. His hands were soft and scented with rose oil, and his hair gleamed. He had known nothing but the court and the peculiar adoration it bestowed on beautiful youths. But he was a child of nobility, and would not embarrass her with displays of compassion.

Wordlessly, she tore a wing off the coppery dove and delicately mouthed the meat. With a small, ornate silver knife hidden in the folds of her plain shift she sliced a pear in two. As she extended one pale green half to the boy, he wondered vaguely how she had come upon such a handsome knife. Certainly he had nothing so fine, and yet her dress, such as it was, was threadbare and her fingernails dirty. A thread of fragrant juice ran down her chin, and for the first time, the girl smiled, and it was like the moonrise over a mountain stream, the light caught in a stag's pale antlers, clear water running under the night sky. When she spoke again, the boy leaned forward eagerly, shoved his thick, dark hair back from his face, bit into a ripe peach and stuffed a bit of cheese into his mouth, mechanically, without noticing the taste. Her large eyes slid shut as she spoke, so that her eyelids and their mosaic covering seemed to float like black lilies in the paleness of her face.

"The wild woman drew her long knife from her belt and held it for a moment, almost playfully, at the Prince's smooth neck, a sliver of breath before the fatal cut . . ."

THE TALE OF THE PRINCE AND THE GOOSE, CONTINUED

"LET ME LIVE, LADY," HE WHISPERED, "I BEG YOU. I shall stay here and be your servant; I will take the place of the bird-maiden and remain loyal to you for all of my days. I will be yours. I am young and strong. Please."

He did not know what moved him to make such an offer, or if he meant to keep his promise, true as law. But the words ripped from him as though the woman had put her fist into his throat and seized them for her own.

Her eyes blazed like clouds filled with a thousand tiny seeds of lightning. But they held now a calculating gleam, and indeed, in another instant the knife had vanished from the Prince's throat.

"Even if I agree it will not save you," she hissed, her voice like a great toad singing at dawn. "But I will tell you the tale of my daughter and how she became winged. Then, perhaps, you will see what it is you offer, and we shall discover whether or not you prefer death."

But she did not speak. Instead, she tore a long strip of mottled fur from the collar of her tunic and bandaged his hand. Her touch was practiced and much softer than he expected, almost, though not quite, tender. From a pouch at her waist she drew some withered leaves, among which he thought he could recognize bay and juniper. She pressed them into his ruined stumps. Tightening the poultice, she examined her work and judged it fair.

"First, I am not blind. I can see that you are young and strong, and there is no doubt I can use up your youth and vigor like well water. This is not the question. Can you listen? Can you learn? Can you keep silent? I wonder. I believe you are a spoiled brat with no ears at all."

The Prince bent his head, penitent. Already his hand had stopped its thick throbbing, and he said nothing, judging that nothing was the best shield he could fashion against her. The crone sat against a large stone and rolled a few musky leaves between her gnarled fingers . . .

THE WITCH'S
TALE

I CAME FROM THE NORTHERN TRIBES, THE STEPPE-
women with their shaggy horses and snow-clotted braids.
I'm sure you've heard stories—we were monsters, we were
unnatural, we deserved what we got.

Among the unnatural monsters, I was more monstrous
and more unnatural than the rest. They called me Knife.
When I was young and my strength was taut as a bow-
string, I was the best rider of all the young girls. I had
many necklaces of jasper and wolf-tooth, three fine hunting knives, a strong bow that I could draw into the shape
of the full moon, a quiver full of arrows fletched in hawk
feathers, and a wildcat hide from my first kill. All around

me were the wild, honey-colored steppes, the fat deer we hunted, and the sleek, brown, fragrant horses I loved. They ran like ripples in a mountain lake. I ran alongside them, and rode astride them, and I slept against their flanks.

I was happy, the sun was high. I had enough.

My sisters were all older than I, my brothers away fighting on the borders of our country, and so I was free, and feral, and my smile was often too like a snarl. One day Grandmother Bent-Bow, whom everyone called Grandmother but who was truly mine, and had the ugliest face I knew, like beaten bark, called me to her under the new moon. She told me that she had found a man for me to marry. I loved my grandmother very much, but I did not care to be married. I was a muscle-knotted mare; I needed no mount to slow me down. But Grandmother's word was the closest thing to law we had. Monsters, you know, cannot appreciate the niceties of commandments carved in stone.

And so, even though I was very young, I stood in her beautiful deerskin breeches, with my proud wildcat hide on my shoulders, and wed the man she had chosen. He was dark, with very bright eyes, and we hunted together—at first only cutting meat side by side, but slowly we became one hunter, leaping onto heavy-boned deer with twin knives flashing. We smiled and snarled and smiled again under a sky blazing with stars, like milk spilled across a black hide.

When I was not hunting with him, my sisters Sheath and Quiver—for daughters come always in threes among us—and I raced each other, practiced the songs of our tribe and the twanging songs of our bows, and from Grandmother we learned magic. I braided her silver hair while she taught us secret things—monstrous things, unnatural things. Under the Snake-Star and the Bridle-Star and the Knife-Star, my own namesake, Grandmother prickled my face with delicate tattoos and called me her best girl, called me initiate, and horsewoman true.

We grew, we hunted, we laughed. I was happy. But though I did not know it, the sun was getting lower in the sky.

One day your father's army—

Stop gaping, boy. Did you think I did not know who you were the second you crossed onto my land?

One day your father's army came screeching up from the south like a prairie fire. He wanted our fat herds and strong horses. He wanted the heads of monsters on his wall. He wanted to clean his kingdom of unnatural things, things which squalled and crept and darkened the corners of the light.

I had never seen anything like his soldiers. They wore armor like scales, with towering smoky plumes, and they shone like a thousand clouds on horses black as demons. I shot all my arrows into those clouds, and all of Sheath's arrows, which were fletched with crow feathers, after a man cut her sword arm off. From a ruin of her blood and dark, wet insides, I pulled her blade and tried to swing it into the gut of one of the clouds, but I was never much use with blades, no matter my name, and he was on top of me before my blow had even begun its arc.

He was a filthy man—and when a scrabbling creature who spends her nights squeezed between horses under no kind of roof calls a body filthy, you can be sure it is no ordinary dirt-stench. Leather-lashed beard bristling with lice and blood, he picked me up by the waist, hauling me up onto his warhorse. To shut my cursing mouth, he smashed my face with an armored fist. The glove floated before me, silvery and oddly beautiful, and then my forehead split and glutted red.

What sort of monster was I? I could not even hold my own against one knight; I could not even get a sword into one hollering pig. I looked up through a sheet of tears and blood and clay-slick dirt to see my new husband racing after us, screaming like a wounded wolf, and your father with his raven plume riding behind him. The black-feathered rider rammed a colossal blade through his poor chest with as little thought or effort as squeezing a fly from the air with two fingers. I saw the bits of bone and gore fly forward; I watched my husband spit blood onto the grass and kneel as if in prayer before he went face-first into the blood-whipped mud.

I tried to stop crying and pressed my face into the comfort of the strange horse's flank—at least it was a horse, at least its sweat and hide were not so different from my own long-legged friends'—smelling for the goodness of my family in those thick, powerful haunches.

We rode south.

The sun had disappeared.

That first fist of many marked my face, knotted my forehead into scar like a sailor's rope. The rest, though, is my doing. We rode for a long time. I lost track of the days. The sour smell of the filthy man and his starving horse enclosed me. There was hardly enough to feed the knights and the women, let alone those poor beasts, who should have been oiled and loved and held while they slurped clear water.

After a few days Quiver managed to kill herself by leaping into a river;

the current like a breath of night carried her far from me, who should have caught her and held her face to mine. She was the oldest, yet I live and she is dead.

I knew before we arrived at the Palace what would happen to me. Even monsters are not stupid. I would be a slave, meant for the pleasure of your father and his grime-bathed soldiers. I would be dressed prettily, and oiled like a whore. Slavery did not disturb me; escape would be simple enough. But I would do nothing for their pleasure, and I would not be beautiful for them. They found my grandmother's tattoos, those beautiful dark lines snaking over my face, to be *exotic*.

My hatred burned black and furious as an iron furnace. And so one night when my friend the filth-monger had fallen into a drunken sleep I took his dagger from the sheath at his side. It was a lovely weapon, with a straight, clean blade that shimmered like the water of Quiver's grave. I placed it at my cheeks, and drew the knife twice, three times, down across my face, slashing the flesh and obliterating forever whatever beauty a monster owns.

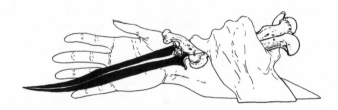

Of course the men were enraged when the morning came and my face was as thickly smeared with blood as if I had covered it in a crimson hide. I was taken from the tent and thrown into the train of true slaves, the miserable lot which were destined for mines and quarries. I truly believed this would be my place, too, cutting rocks and scooping metal from the mountains, and I exulted—what is easier than running off when those mountains are all around and welcoming? I felt as though I was within a fox's skin, full of tricks and victory. But I was mistaken.

The Palace reared up before us like a stallion, heavy and fierce—and to my shock, I was not sent beyond it, to the gold-riddled hills, or the limestone-swathed valleys, but dragged inside. Down, down, down, down a thousand stairs and through a hundred gates I was led by rough hands, and thrown into a tiny cell dank with sweat and years. Ah, I thought then, this is my punishment for spoiling a soldier's war prize.

I howled. I screamed and screeched like a flock of frenzied owls, clawing at my hair and the stone floor until my fingers shredded into uselessness. I lay on the floor like a child, curled up and weeping, my escape made impossible, my life to be spent in this place, a hundred nights from my snowy, windblown steppes. It was then that I heard a chuckling voice from the darkness, familiar and roughly sweet, rubbing my cheek like wolf's fur.

"Are you quite finished, girl?" it asked quietly. I looked into the murky air, into the corners of the room, where I expected to see piles of bones and old hair—instead, my grandmother sat cross-legged, clothed in rags and laughing.

"You needed to storm a bit, I know, but it is just getting indulgent now. Haven't I taught you anything?" She opened her skinny arms like beaten bark and I fell into her. I do not know how long she held me, how many times I died and was resurrected and died again. But when I looked up into her face, she was stroking my hair and smiling. "It isn't so bad, dear, they might have killed you."

"This is worse," I grunted. With a sound like a hand against a horse's side, my grandmother slapped me hard across my mangled face.

"No. You are alive. Your sisters are both dead. Why are you feeling sorry for yourself, you rotten child? I think I have spoiled you." I was stricken, and I stared like a dumb animal.

"They have brought me here because they think they can break me, or use me, or both," she mused. "After all, I am a very special slave. I belong to their silly court wizard now, with his hat and his rabbit tricks. I have decided to be happy about it—they will leave me here long enough that I know who is in charge and who is not, and then I will be brought before the King to show what a good dog I am. I will be more than close enough to him to cut his throat." She smiled brilliantly, full of cheer. "So we have little time to talk, for me to tell you what you need to know, so that you can decide to be happy about your fate, too." She pursed her lips together, examining my savaged cheeks. "It is good that you ruined your face, because it brought you to me, but also because beautiful women rarely work strong magic."

I watched her and listened, her words closing over me like a pool of cold water, rocking me and cooling my flushed skin. Her eyes glinted like an owl's, and her face was calm as the moon.

"Now, you listen. Before they come to separate us, I must tell you the story of my apprenticeship, so that you can come to know what I know, what you would have learned on your own, and your sisters too, if the

King had not landed on us like a rock dropped from a great height. As it is, you must take what you can from these old bones."

The girl stopped her tale with a press of her gentle lips, looking off into the night with eyes of shadow and woven web.

"You stop and start like a stubborn tortoise," the boy said flatly, "always pulling your head in just when I want to hear more. It is very frustrating."

The girl smiled wanly, as though she meant to apologize, but could not quite manage it. She licked her lips delicately, forlornly tasting the last vestiges of the roasted dove.

"But I must rest a little. We can sleep for an hour, then I will continue." She paused, blushing to the tips of her temples. "You can lie beside me if you want; it gets cold here at night."

She made a space in the long grass and the boy awkwardly lay against her. For long moments, neither of them slept, stiff and tense against each other as though the one had not slept every night of his life beside a brother or a sister, and the other had not spent every night of hers in blossom bowers and tree hollows. He watched her, the wind rustling her hair like river rushes, until finally, she was asleep, and then, the softening of her limbs a kind of permission, drifted away himself.

But it was not very long until he was shaking her awake, thirsty for her stories as a beggar in an endless desert.

Grandmother's Tale

THE TALE OF MY LONG YEARS OF STUDY IS TOO
much to impart to you in this small, dark time we have together, my child. What I will tell you is the story of a single
night, the last night of my formal apprenticeship, the last
night of my girlhood. It is a good story to tell here in the
shadowed corners of the earth, in this deep-within-deep
place, where the sun falters.

My mother died in a horse raid when I was very young,
and her mother had died in childbirth, and so when I
came of age there was no one to teach me, to show me the
secret ways, to give me a place in the tribe. Instead, I was
sent away, packed into a cart with hides and jewelry to pay

for my fostering in a neighboring village, to be taught by the witch-woman of their people. My hair was thick and red, then, bright as a fire ripping through the steppes. My limbs were smooth and hard as hooves—the jangling cart bouncing across the wide emptiness between villages hardly affected me.

When I arrived, my mistress seemed to me fierce and beautiful and terrifying. Thurayya was very strict—she distrusted my foreignness, my red hair, and my simple name, and most of all my stubbornness. For one year I did nothing but serve her; sweep her hut, polish her blades, carry her water, comb her horses. She said nothing to me. I slept outside the hut, under the stars and cushioned by dry grass. Only in the second year did she allow me to sleep beside her, and begin my education. Is this the proper way to teach a girl? I don't know. But I could not bear to bring you up, or Quiver, or Sheath, that way. Perhaps I am not, in the end, as strong as my old mistress.

The first night of that second year, I lay stiffly against her old, musty skin, her sharp bones and stringy white hair turned almost my own shade by the last embers of fire, and without looking at me, she suddenly spoke.

"Listen, Bent-Bow, you little goat. See if you can't learn something besides milking yaks . . ."

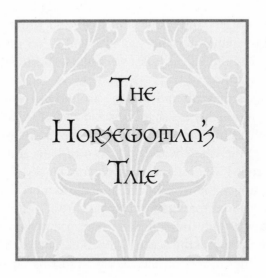

The
Horsewoman's
Tale

OPEN YOUR EARS, AND LET THE SKY IN.

In the beginning, before you were the spark in the dream of a lice-shagged goat and a lonely farmhand, there was nothing but sky. It was black, and vast, and all the other things you might expect a sky with nothing floating around in it to be. But the sky was only a sky if you looked at it slantwise—if you looked at it straight, which of course, no one could, because there wasn't anyone to look any way, it was the long, slippery flank of a Mare.

The Mare was black, and vast, and all the other things you would expect a horse the size of everything to be.

After a long while, the Mare chewed a hole in herself, for reasons she has kept as her own. The hole filled up with light the way a hole in you or me would fill up with blood, and this was called a Star. They were the first, true children of the Mare, made of the flesh of her own body. And because she liked the light, and the company, she chewed other holes, roughly in the shapes of Badgers and Plows and Deer and Knives and Snails and Foxes and Grass and Water and suchlike, and so on until the Mare was ablaze with holes, and all the holes were Stars, and the sky was not very empty at all anymore.

Now, the holes were up and walking around like you and me by this time, and one, in roughly the shape of a Rider, climbed over the Mare and she became full, as full and huge as a horse the size of everything can be, until she foaled the whole world in a rush of light and milk and black, black blood from the most secret depths of the sky. The grass and the rivers and the stones and women and horses and more Stars and men and clouds and birds and trees came dancing through the afterbirth of the Mare, and swam happily in her milk and stopped up her secret blood, and the world was made, and the oceans washed the shore, and the Mare went cantering into the corners of herself, which just barely showed through the burning field of her Stars, and lay in a pasture neither you nor I could guess at, and chewed her favorite Grass-Stars in peace.

Now the holes which were Stars were still full of light, and still walking around the sky, awkward as three-legged dogs. Without the Mare, the black was just black, and not a flank, not a hide, not a thing with smell and salt and fur. Naturally, this frightened the holes, since up until then they had always had the smell of the Mare in their noses and the feel of her at their backs. A few of the holes looked down on all the things which had come out of the Mare before she went off away from them, and thought that it seemed less terrible and dark than the sky—and besides, there were things like themselves there: badgers and plows and deer and knives and snails and foxes and grass and water. And even horses, which were like the Mare they remembered, only much smaller, and of many different colors.

And, my mange-ridden little goat, there they lived, just like you and I do, while the less brave of their brothers and sisters stayed up in the sky to light their way. And they were teachers and students and mothers and daughters and brothers and uncles and crabby old men. And they couldn't help it: everywhere they walked they carried their light, the light which, you remember, wasn't really light, but the Mare-blood of the first days of the world.

Now, in the beginning, they were so full of this blood-light that everything they touched went silver and white with it—it flowed out of them like sweat and all kinds of things were wet with it. But as time went on, there was less of the light to spill, and they began to be afraid that they would lose the last thing the Mare their mother had ever given them. But they were more afraid of the great black motherless sky, and would not leave the world again. So they went away into little clutches, like flowers growing in rocks, into the caves and the hills and the rivers and the valleys, far off from anyone else, and touched only each other, for between them the light only pooled, and rippled, and did not leak from their bodies.

But after the Stars hid themselves away, the things they touched were still where they had left them, full of light, the light which was blood, and they glowed with the silver and white of it. And these things were special, flea-bed mine—where they were stones or plants they passed their light into deeper stones and into their seeds, and where they were people, they passed the light to their children, which diminished just as it had when the Stars first touched the world and the blood went out of them. It was not long before no one could tell what had been touched in the first days and what had not. The light was buried and secret.

But it was not gone. In many things and many people it is still glowing, deep down in their guts, and this, my scraggly, milk-bellied kid, is what magic is.

GRANDMOTHER'S TALE, CONTINUED

I LISTENED TO HER STORY, AND IN MY SECRET heart I thought she smelled sweet, of blood and milk and hide, like the Mare herself, and I allowed my body to inch, ever so slightly, closer to hers. She said nothing more that night.

I grew under her frown for many years like a sleek colt, learning to find the glowing thing in my gut, to control its light and strength, to be its bridle and bit. The world moved under me like a flowing field beneath amber hooves, and I could feel the blood-light in me pulsing, its life in my body like a newborn—and I had to deliver many, my girl, both under Thurayya's direction and alone.

I exulted in it, the pooling of light in my heart. I learned to make it into medicine, and spells, and charms, to push it out of me and fashion it into shapes. How many nights did I spend with her under the lightning and the black clouds, her hair streaming like frenzied serpents, her thin arms extended towards the raging sky? I learned without the light, too: the way of animals, and the way of the steppes. I learned how to deliver a colt who has become strangled in its mother's womb, and how to catch and milk the shaggy cattle that chewed the prairie grass. The time went quickly, when I was young, and I loved my mistress, and there was so much yet to know.

But one night Thurayya came to me and the moon crowned her with silver and black.

"Bent-Bow," she hissed, "goat-of-my-heart. You must come with me now. For once in your life, do not question me."

I opened, thought better of it, and closed my ever-busy mouth, to take my pack and follow the thin shape of the witch away over a long meadow which bordered the village. Her form swayed ahead of me, blurred, as the miles we crossed began to carry me into a half-dream, the sky and the cutting winter air skimming along past my cheeks.

After some time we approached a monstrous cliff, rising up like a great bear ahead of us. She drew me up next to her and embraced me, a thing she had never done. When she pulled away her craggy face was wet with tears.

"You have been my best student. I am proud of you. But I cannot go with you tonight. I have never done this thing—it is not my right. It belongs only to you, and had there been any woman of your family left to bring you here, we would never have met. After tonight, if you come back to the village, it will be the end of your time with me. You will be a full well: enough silver water within you to return to your own people and ladle it out to them, to guide them, and teach them. The rest of your education will be the private learning women like us work for all our days, when you will become both teacher and student, mistress and apprentice. You will return pregnant with knowledge to bear to your tribe, and your power will grow like a child, and you will spend the rest of your life in labor. But you must pass this night first, and emerge again. Then you will be ready, my beautiful, beautiful daughter. My beautiful little goat."

She smiled brightly, her lips curving like a scimitar, and pointed to a gaping hole in the cliff wall. I kissed her cheek awkwardly, looking into her shining eyes. I was determined not to show my fear, to possess it and enter it, to dwell within it until it disappeared into my calm, quiet belly. I turned away from Thurayya, from my life with her and my youth, and entered the mouth of the cave.

Soon I could see nothing; darkness like hands pressed in on me. I made a place for myself on the cool, compact earth, listening to the slow, lazy rustle of bats far overhead. And I waited, bounded in blackness.

The Tale of the Prince and the Goose, Continued

KNIFE'S FACE WAS LIT BY THE REDDENING SUN, HER nose casting shadows on her scars, her eyes deep and impenetrable as snowy mountains. Well water glistened crimson and saffron in wooden buckets that lay scattered around the house like wildflowers, reflecting the blazing sky. The Prince rested on his heels, ran his hand through thick black hair, now marshy with sweat. He started, as if out of a spell, and looked sharply at the old witch.

"Well," he blurted, "what happened then?"

The woman cackled huskily. "Then the pretty Prince came inside the hut, for it was becoming night, and kneaded dough for the terrible, ugly witch's bread."

This was nearly too much for the Prince, who had tried very hard to keep his dignity thus far. To now work in this deformity's kitchen like a scullery maid? Leander of the Eight Kingdoms, the Two-Blooded Border-Lord, Son of Helia the Radiant, would absolutely not bake filthy, thin peasant's bread in this wretched place. He had promised to serve her, yes, but he had meant to do so in some manly fashion which involved the slaying of some things and the rescuing of others. Bread needed to be neither slain nor rescued.

He opened his noble mouth to say so, but the chill stare of the witch stopped his words like a noose about his neck. Her teeth gleamed horribly bright under cracked lips, and seemed to lengthen and twist into clashing ivory knives. In a moment the vision had evaporated, but the Prince was now convinced that bread-baking was a most estimable and agreeable work, and that perhaps kneading was not too dissimilar to slaying.

Though he had to duck to enter the hut, it was more comfortable and spacious inside than he could have expected, a fire licking at gnarled hawthorn logs in one corner, bound books lining the walls. Knife turned as he removed his fine leather boots.

"Excuse the doorway. My people have always been small."

Bundles of dried herbs and once-bright flowers hung like stalactites from racks on her ceiling; gray, red, brown. He saw withered peach blossoms, dusty lupines, roses and bundles of mushrooms like roses, angelica and buckbean and bladderwrack, coltsfoot, rue, and mallow—and there his knowledge of botany, with its princely limitations, failed him. Glinting black furs covered the floor like autumn leaves. Great terra-cotta jars and mystifying chests with copper and silver locks, innumerable walking sticks of every material, and bolts of strange, deeply hued fabric were strewn about the borders of the wide central room, and a massive table of shimmering wood dominated the area near the fire. It was, all in all, everything he had been led to expect from a witch's house.

On the table were heaps of inchoate dough and ceramic pots of fragrant spices. The witch gestured towards it and a low chair. She turned to a large iron stove, her muscled back obscuring whatever task lay unfinished on its steaming surface. There was a long silence, stroked by the soft, slushing sounds of the Prince's hand slowly, awkwardly pounding dough—for he kept his wounded fist at his side, so that his seeping blood would not stain the loaf. The pain had nearly left the stumps of his fingers. After a time, Knife looked up from the stove, shaking her gray hair like a foal, and spoke into the rough-hewn wall.

"You have your mother's hair, you know, all those long curls like strips of bark. Not the color of course, but the heft of it." Her voice was rough and pained. The Witch turned from her work and moved to the table with two clay cups of steaming greenish-yellow tea.

"Willow bark and wild mint," she grunted, picking at the woodgrain, her face caught and silhouetted by the firelight. "And a bit of her eyes, though your father is there, too, black, reflecting nothing."

The Prince's breath stopped, and words rushed to his lips only to die strangled on his tongue. His whole body seemed to struggle with itself, until suddenly he was crying softly, salting the bread, his young shoulders shuddering.

"Please," he begged, "how can you know anything of my mother? No— do not tell me, do not speak of her. Never speak of her." He dried his eyes with the dirty cuff of his sleeve. "Tell me what happened to your grandmother in the cave, tell me old Star-tales no one believes anymore, but do not ask me to remember my mother."

The Witch swallowed her tea.

"In the cell, Grandmother rubbed at her temples and drank a little of the polluted water left us in a decrepit iron jug. I waited patiently, still a good student. At length, she began again . . ."

GRANDMOTHER'S TALE, CONTINUED

IT WAS DARK, OF COURSE. THESE SORTS OF THINGS always begin in the dark. I leaned with my back against the rock wall, feeling the slight damp, the thick air of that stone womb which was blacker than black.

Ages passed. Or minutes.

I looked into the shadows, their substance, their limbs, their weight. At times, I felt at peace and watchful, as though I sat on the giant lip of a blue-black lily, its fat flesh curling underneath me, so perfect that no part of me could not be a part of it, and my body was changed, converted into its charcoal and gloom. At other times, I felt cold and alone and very small. But I felt the tiny, struggling light inside me, and it was warm as a fire at my feet. It spread through me as though I was a sieve of silk, left me clean and pure in that silent cavern. I sat with palms upturned, trying to hold the curve of darkness like a great hanging belly, thunder-black and written upon with swarthy symbols, all alive and breathing and swirling in the violet long-past-sunset.

I think I must have nearly fallen asleep, when suddenly my flesh sparked and shivered, and a thing began to coalesce out of the hematite air. I could not, at first, see anything at all but a length of deeper black amid the blackness. Its edges seemed to shimmer with light, a heat lightning crisping the edges of a shape, glowing like an afterimage. I was afraid, granddaughter, of course I was afraid. I cowered into the curve of the cavern, shaking like a newborn fawn.

At length I perceived a long head and flowing hair, luminous eyes round as moons. It seemed a part of the stone, a part of the night, a part of nothing I had ever come near to knowing. My eyes rolled in my head and sweat slicked my skin. My heart beat so fast I felt as though I had swallowed a hummingbird.

Finally, the outlines of the shape, rimmed in white fire, became clear and distinct.

In a moment it was utterly familiar to me, the long curve of black neck, the smooth haunches and velvet fur, a thick tail in a hundred braids brushing the cave floor, breath puffing from her great nostrils like pipe smoke: a horse beyond fantasies of horses, beyond any guess at size or hope of beauty, her ears seeming to brush the ceiling like stiff feathers, their twitchings carving some arcane verse on the rock. Scattered around her hooves lay charred jawbones and shoulder blades, and sternums like scepters.

The Mare watched me calmly, snorting occasionally and blinking her incandescent eyes. There was no sound for a space that seemed like a thousand winters joined at the snowline.

I still could not say where the courage came from, from what hidden place in me it sprung up and gurgled brightly, but I stood on clamoring legs and reached out my little hand to the creature, avoiding the rattling bones in their protective ring. I stroked her nose and the sides of her lightless face—and granddaughter, I cannot even now describe the softness of her flesh, the gentle glide of my hand over her thick, gleaming fur. Her skin was the texture of new cream, the shade of a crow flying high in a moonless night. She was beautiful and terrifying, savage and pure. Her eyes wheeled like suns and her great heart thundered against me. I buried

my face in her mane and breathed the scent of wild earth and a burning sky. There was no other world but her.

And suddenly, without warning, that great head turned like an opening door and the black Mare bit into the flesh of my shoulder with blazing teeth, tearing muscle from bone. I screamed uselessly into the echoes, and blood surged from the wound like a river through a red canyon, gushing warmly onto my breasts and hands. I flailed against her, beating her flank with my fists, but the teeth only ground harder into me. I think I must have fainted then, and as I fell against her body I expected nothing but death.

When I came around I lay once more against the rock wall, drenched in my own blood as though I had been caught in a rainstorm. The Mare had disappeared. I wept bitterly—though she had sunk her teeth in me I missed them, I felt empty without their light burning into me. She had done no more than she had always done—chewed a hole in flesh. And the edges of her hole longed for her, after she was gone. Her absence filled the chamber like a voice.

In her place was a much smaller creature, not at all commanding or terrible, sitting on its haunches, eyes sparking in the returned blackness. When it saw I had revived, it padded across the earthen floor and stood directly in front of my face; a handsome red Fox with a splendid furry tail. He smelled of burnt grass and copper filings, and his fur crackled with a baleful kind of rusted light.

To my surprise, he bent his inquisitive head and began licking the blood from my wound. He closed his polished eyes as he worked, long, rough passes with his pink tongue, prickling and horribly painful. I bit my lip and did not whimper, though the brush of his fur against my tortured skin was agony. Slowly the scarlet ebbed from the pale. But he was not finished with me. The little Fox opened his mouth and spoke quite clearly.

"Press some of the goldenseal and dandelion root from your pack into the wound, then use bay leaves to bind the poultice. It will help. But it is important that you do not stop the blood flow entirely. My mother has prepared you, but you will need the blood of your body."

I obeyed numbly. When I had finished, the Fox bent to sniff at my shoulder and check my work. I watched him carefully, and as he inclined his head I lashed out and gripped his bristling throat in my fist. Through his struggles against my strong hands and his snapping snout trying to reach me, I hissed at him through my own sharp teeth.

"Now, tell me what is going on here, Fox, or I shall have you skinned and in my pack with the bay and the dandelion faster than a lion can swallow a mouse."

The Fox snorted and sputtered like a petulant child, and after some sniffling and snorting, and after realizing I would not let his neck out of my hands, replied with injured dignity:

"You, little *girl*, are not supposed to *touch* me, you are not supposed to *assault* me or ask me *questions*. It is not *done*. But you touched the Mare, and that too is forbidden. I can only hope the pain of her bite was extreme. That she endured your hands on her! Filthy! They are so dirty, you are so dirty and dark, and you touched her, you touched me!"

I let him go carefully, moving backwards from his furious form as he rubbed his nose and his throat and washed his fur with desperate strokes of a pink tongue. I smiled with what I assumed was bravery and nodded with what I imagined to be a casual air. "Fox, I think I have been good, and suffered quite enough to know what is happening to me in this place."

The Fox hooted in derision, a strange noise coming from his delicate russet snout.

"Oh, you think you have been *good*, do you? You think you have *suffered*? You know nothing at all, stupid as a goat." He drew himself up on his haunches. "I am the Servant of the Black Mare. That was my mother you *fondled*, wicked child. She who invented words, and yet does not speak; she who brings dreams and visions, yet does not sleep; she who swallows the storm, yet knows nothing of rain or wind. I speak for her; I am her *own*. This was not your test, human child; that lies beyond. Pain is no test. In my mind you have already failed; you dared touch her who carries the Moon in her Belly, who foaled the Stars in the Beginning of the World. But she allowed your unclean hands on her, and still blessed you with her sacred Teeth, so there must be something in you which was born in her."

The Fox pawed the earth fretfully, imploring me with his eyes. "*Why* did you do it? Why did you have to *stroke* her as though she were your mount, your little pet? Oh mother mine, would you have *ridden* her? Even . . . even *I* have never been permitted to touch her, in all my years of service, never *once* . . . Terrible child, why could you not have kept your hands to yourself?"

The Fox trotted towards me again. In a crimson flash he cruelly raked his claws across my left breast, splitting the flesh like a ripe plum. I could have sworn there were tears in his little black eyes, catching in his golden fur and whiskers.

"There," he snarled, "that is for your trespass; that is *my* mark. I am the Servant! I walk alongside the Mare; I have drunk her milk and hunted with her! I chewed the tiny Grass-Stars in their hundreds and thousands by her side! And I will not heal *that* one for you!"

I breathed hard, genuinely afraid now of the little animal, his hackles high, both of us panting in the dark. I clasped a hand over my new wound, blood dripping through the sieve of my fingers. The Fox seemed to compose himself, his fur returning to its usual sleekness.

"I have wasted half your time already, idiot girl." His eyes glazed over, retreating into ritual. "But you will not pass your tests, so it hardly matters. Go further in, filth-child, into the second chamber, which is the Wolf Cave, and from there to the Cave of the Seven Sleepers. There lies your test. Pass these chambers and emerge a woman. Or die within them. Remember, pain is not a test. Knowledge is not enough. Many have gone before you, little one, and none have ever spoken of their trials. It is forbidden. You may take nothing but your own body; your pack must stay here. Go, with the blessing of the Mare, and acquit yourself as well as a brat like you can."

With that, the Fox snapped his needle jaws once in my direction and walked towards the far end of the cavern, right through the stone wall, disappearing as though he never was. I was still bleeding, and though a few of the leaves and powders from my pack helped, there was a dark stain on my dress. I smoothed my hair and stood, firmer now, looking for the entrance into the second chamber. And of course, where the Fox had vanished with a flourish of his beautiful tail, there was now a small hole low in the rock, the color of fresh blood, hardly big enough for me to squeeze through. I walked towards it, trying to tell myself that I was at ease, serene as the moon on a crane's feathers.

The girl closed her large eyes as she spoke, so that her eyelids and their mosaic covering seemed to float like black lilies in the paleness of her face. Frogs sent emerald notes up into the air, and owls sang in low gleaming strands, resting in black branches, veiled in the violet breath of jacaranda flowers. Under their harmonics, her voice sighed back and forth. The girl drank from the wine flask, running her fingers over its engraved surface. The wind rustled her hair like petals on a lake.

Even though they had rested, as she spoke the boy had again drifted into a shallow sleep, and the story's words wove in and out of his mind like a needle drawing silken thread. His head lay on the girl's lap, and she stroked his soft black hair as she continued, at first timidly, then with a growing tenderness. The stars overhead burned like court candles. The moon was high, full as a blown sail, riding softly through the rolling blue clouds, cutting through their foamy sapphirine flesh with a glowing prow. Shadows fell in long minarets on the gardens, the courtyards, the lemon trees and olive, the acacias and the climbing vines, the bone white lilies and the sleeping Palace. The girl's voice was like river rushes rubbing together in a warm wind, winding through the cobbled paths.

Grandmother's
Tale,
Continued

I CROUCHED AND WRIGGLED INTO THE HOLE,
into the slick rock, which became mud as quickly as ice
becomes water. On my belly I dug into the earth like a
worm—I could barely breathe for the dripping dirt; I
could barely move for the press of the slippery cave. I told
myself I was not afraid of dirt, dirt is dirt, and holes always
empty out somewhere. I told myself that while dirt which
was only dirt slithered into my mouth and my nose and
my eyes, and all I could taste was earth, and I could see
nothing at all.

But I emerged—you always emerge, eventually—on
the other side, into another cavern with another earthen

floor. It was too dark to see the other side, the rock walls narrowing upwards into a skinny crack through which I could see the cascading moonlight and hear the fall of a soft rain somewhere in the distance.

I should have known, I should have known from the moment my foot touched the cave floor. I could hear a storm terribly far off, the drip of water off thick pine needles and the drinking grasses, the sucking mushrooms, the soggy moss. It rang in my ears like bells on a horse's saddle, the silver, slight glistening of rain on fat green leaves, and the slippery smell of damp, rotting flowers. But the haunch of sky I saw through the opening in the cave-roof showed a clear night, full of hard, bright stars.

The rain fell in some place so far off that it did not even disturb the air above me. But my ears and my nose struck on it, like a blade sparking under a hammer. I trotted quickly around the dim room, examining and investigating, trying to sniff out the test before it leapt out at me. I should have known—but it felt so natural to press a wet nose into the corners of the rock, to canter and bristle and snap my jaws together in the dark.

I looked for a second door, but there was nothing, though one side of the rock face was curiously polished, a deep amber color that reflected the room and the moonlight—and me. I saw a flash of gray and white as I passed it, and stopped suddenly, my heart spinning around in my throat. I saw my image in the stone.

Staring dumbfounded at me from the shining cave wall was a very large and very handsome gray wolf. Great shaggy ears twitched, and my tongue lolled between frighteningly fierce teeth. My eyes sparkled black and my fur was the shade of shadows cast on water by the moon, starry-white and silver, every shimmer of silver from stone to snow, glossy and pale over powerful legs, down to the tip of my extremely long and proud tail, which I thumped grandly on the earthen floor.

All in all, my granddaughter, I looked very fine. I howled just to hear it, bouncing off the walls like an arrow of green wood. It was so loud I jumped at my own voice. Yet I was still alone in the room. I trotted back and forth as though I had never had to manage with only two legs. Nothing was more natural than my new loping gait, the balance of my tail, the catch of my claws on hidden roots and rocks. I padded around on my new paws, the quick thud of them quickly replacing the ridiculous idea that I had ever been a girl and slept in a soft bed. My thoughts became wolfish, itching to be released into the night to hunt and run with these strong limbs over the fields. My heart was flooded with the memory of bounding through feathery snow with my pack, nursing my beautiful gray pups in a warm den, tracking hares and deer over green mountains, prowling through farms filled with fat pigs and helpless spring lambs; wordless and fierce, without the endless sweeping of huts and hearths. But then—what is a hut? What is a hearth? It became terribly difficult even to remember my name, and then to remember that I had one, and then to remember what a name was. It was like going to sleep, covering myself in a warm blanket which was a body, and I was so tired, you know, so tired.

You must understand, Knife-of-my-heart, how the thing that changed me takes the mind as well as the body, how it swallows up everything into itself.

But as that night seemed to trickle by and nothing at all happened, I curled into a ball of gleaming fur in the center of the cave and fell asleep, lost in the blackness of endless night and dreams of hunting and eating, always eating.

Looking back now, I think I hardly slept at all—wolves don't need a night's full sack of sleep. I startled awake though there was no sound to disturb me, and saw three tall figures standing a polite distance away.

The first was a white wolf with sloping ears and gentle eyes the color of rain, her fur gleaming nearly blue, like the new moon on snowy branches. Her tail waved slowly behind her, a stream of ice, drawing patterns in the soil.

The second was black as midwinter's night, his eyes of storm clouds cut with lightning, fur thick and dark as the depths of a mountain lake.

The third was every shade of gold as I was every shade of silver, from the white of flame to deep bronze, flowing and braiding together like liquid fire. Her eyes were the same flickering color, leaping and sparking.

My mouth was horribly dry and I could not swallow. It took all of my newfound wolfness not to bolt from their terrible faces. I struggled and grasped for my reason, my girl-self in the mounds and layers of wolf. They spoke then in unison, their muzzles shaping the words strangely, but beautifully, a growling gentleness.

"Welcome, little dog. Which of us will you have?"

I tried to speak, but it was impossible. I stuttered and gasped and yelped, trying to form words out of my silky muzzle and dagger-teeth. My silver brow furrowed with the effort.

"Child," the white one said, her voice was the wind off the mountains, welcoming and sweet, "you must choose. If you cannot manage to speak, you may simply come to one of us, and touch our fur with your nose. We are wolves, after all; we do not overvalue speech."

"She doesn't understand, sister." The black one interrupted, his words like saplings felled by bronze axes. He turned to me with brittle, proud eyes, and spoke slowly, as if to a very stupid and stubborn horse. "A guide, little dog. You have to choose one of us as your guide. You *must* know how these things are done." The black beast snorted, clearly too bored to continue.

I looked at them, tall and terrible, the white and the black. And the third, the soft and rippling gold one, who had not spoken, but whose tail swayed lazily from side to side, her calm eyes like jeweled moons. I padded over to her and pressed my wet nose into her neck like a field of daffodils. Her fur smelled good, and sweet, which was all I could think of—that she smelled right, and smelling, after all, is everything. I could swear she smiled at me. And when I pulled back from her warm-smelling body, the other two had gone. She looked at me with eyes like the spaces in a honeycomb, and glanced away past me, where her pack-mates had gone.

"We got so lost, you know," she whispered.

I didn't understand—how could I begin to guess?—but I pushed my snout up under hers reassuringly, and shut my eyes, washed in her smell. She growled deep in her throat, though not a threat-growl, a soft pup-growl that rattled in my bones.

"We never meant to get so lost . . ."

The Wolf's Tale

IN THE FIRST DAYS, WHEN WE CAME WALKING OVER
the first grass, we burned it, no matter how lightly we tried
to step. It went up in long white rows of flame, and even
we were afraid of it, afraid of what we could do to this
place. We tried to walk on stone only—mute, dead stone,
you understand, and mute, dead grass, not the living blade
and rock that—oh, it doesn't matter. Our feet killed it,
whatever we touched, and we huddled in fear of the fires
that we couldn't stop.

But whether the grass got stronger or we got weaker, it
was not long before we just left scorch marks. Black and
ugly, yes, but there were no more holocausts in our tracks,

and we began to explore the world that the Mare had left for us when she left the sky.

I was as young as we all were. We named everything; we named ourselves. The Bee-Star, which was so bright and small and happier than any of us—that little sun yellow speck who never had to kill grass or stone just to walk from one place to another—called me Liulfr, and whenever he buzzed around my ears I heard the whirr of my name in his wings.

It was more confused than you might think. There were so many of us—but so many more of them. The Mare's real children were so much wilder and more numerous than we were, the ones that came flying out of her body still clung with moon-grease and sky-spittle. We were just holes, after all, holes filled up with light, and deep in our secret hearts we worried that we were an accident, nothing more than puddles who stood up and gave each other names, and the lightless creatures which could walk (so easily, so easily!) were the only things that were meant to be born.

So we watched them; we followed them and tried to imitate them. Some of them looked like some of us—holes in the shapes of men and holes in the shapes of animals and holes in the shapes of plants and tools and stones—and naturally we clung to those that seemed most like us; but above all things we tried to imitate men and women, who seemed the most *intended* of all the things that came out of the Mare, who came out speaking and naming and plowing and stomping, just as we had.

But they were afraid of us, of how we burned, and how we set to flame what they thought was good and beautiful. They called us ghosts and worse, but we couldn't leave them—they had been inside the Mare, after all, and we had never known that, never known what she looked like from under rib and heart. We wanted to know; we wanted, in her absence, to love what had been part of her.

And yes, we saw our light passing into them, into the men and the plants and the tools and the stones, and many of us left then, went into conclaves of like-with-like, Rose-Stars with Bee-Stars and Worm-Stars with Snail-Stars, determined to keep safe and whole.

But some of us, like whipped dogs following behind a cruel master, kept near people, and tried to look like them, for we had discovered, just as they had discovered how to seed a field and leave one part fallow, that just because we had been chewed into a certain shape did not mean we had to keep it. It always hurt the first time, to shiver off the shape our mother gave us, but it got easier. It was the biggest thing we knew how to do, but we were learning.

We were just children, and we played with the world like blocks and dolls, like blocks and dolls, but our siblings did not want to play with us.

And so it was that the Manikarnika met their fate, and we learned a thing we could do that was much bigger and more terrible than changing our skin.

I would like to say I knew them, and I did, in the sense that second cousins in a large family know each other—which is to say hardly at all. They were not like me—they were Stone-Stars, while I was a Wolf-Star, and they changed to women, while after a few experiments I stubbornly kept the paws and the tail that my mother gave me.

But there is not one among us who does not know this story.

The Manikarnika were seven sisters, and when they were gnawed from the flesh of the Mare, they were Stones. Jade and Granite and Opal, Garnet and Shale and Iron Ore and little Diamond, pale as a milk-soaked paw.

They were horrified when they tried to roll and clatter on the dead stone and burned it, melted it, fused it together into glittering, molten rivers. When they learned to walk on two legs, they avoided the mountains like sickness, refusing to harm anything that was so like their first bodies. I tell you this so you will know they were gentle, that the burning was not what any of us meant—but accidents will breed accidents, you know. We couldn't help it. They couldn't help it.

After the first of us started to dim, and the first of us went into exile beyond the swamps and hills, the Manikarnika stayed. They were not jealous of their light, and were determined to show us that we could live in the world the Mare had made, that it was meant for us as well as for her true children.

To show us this, they went to the villages of men, and asked to be taken in, like beggar-women, dressed in rags and poor as empty plates. They were sure they would be welcomed, and we would see that the second litter of the Mare would call us sisters and brothers and even wives, and there would be family between the first and the last. Of course their light still spangled all around them, but who could refuse a beautiful girl who barely owned her own dress no matter how brightly she glowed? Who could refuse seven?

The first house they went to was the palace of a King—such as palaces were in those days, which is to say the large mud hut on a hill above smaller mud huts. The King sent his men to see to the commotion at his door, and they found there the bone-ragged Manikarnika: Jade and Granite and Opal with their many-colored, speckled skin, Garnet red as blushing, Shale and Iron Ore gleaming silver and bright as water, and little Diamond, small and pale and delicate as the slenderest strand of a spider's web. They clung together pitifully, and asked to be brought inside the mud-brick walls, to be fed and clothed, to be loved.

The King's men shuddered at their strange light, and bolted their wooden gates against them.

Undeterred, they went next to the cluster of small mud huts and knocked at the door of a poor widow's house. Surely, her husband dead and her children grown, she would take them in and call them daughters. The old widow opened her hidebound door and saw there the Manikarnika: Jade and Granite and Opal with their smooth, polished arms, Garnet sharp-elbowed, Shale and Iron Ore darkly glinting, and little Diamond, clear as morning. They huddled together mournfully, asking to be let in out of the cold, given soup, given warm arms and soft words.

The widow shuddered at their strange light and began to weep for all her lost ones, and in her weeping let the hidebound door fall shut against them.

But they did not give up. They went out beyond the mud huts to the mud-haired people who moved from place to place across the open steppes with wagons and horses and sleds. They went to one of the tents, unremarkable as any of the others, and called out to the young girl who lived there with her new infant. The girl opened the flap of her tent and saw there the Manikarnika: Jade and Granite and Opal cool as wind-smoothed snow, Garnet hot as sun-battered sand, Shale and Iron Ore freezing till their toes were black, and little Diamond, light and sweet as rain. They leaned one against the other, exhausted, and asked to be let in from the wild, covered in fur and given milk.

The girl laughed and said that she had plenty to spare. The sisters smiled like seven dawns breaking, and triumphant they lay down, curled together with the nomad girl on the floor of a plain tent. And they were happy, and the ground beneath them was only a little darkened with the weight of their light.

By morning, they were dead.

THE
WITCH'S TALE,
CONTINUED

IN THE DUNGEON, DUST AND STRAW COVERED THE
dank floor and no slanting sliver of light crept in. There
was no sound but the soft dripping of water from damp
ceiling to damp floor. Scraps of unfamiliar meat and
swamp brown water had been pushed under the door—I
had heard nothing but my grandmother's voice. She put a
withered hand on my head, stroking the thick hair with a
gentleness practiced on dozens of children. I looked up at
her cracked lips, her cracked face. In the deep shadow I
curled into my grandmother's lap, trying to spread my
meager, ragged dress over her painfully thin legs. She
smiled down at me and shrugged off the cloth as though

it meant nothing to her, and though her lips were split and spotted with dried blood, her face was lit like a festival lantern. I wished that I could be as brave as she was, that whatever strength she had earned in the cave had been mine, too.

I handed her the beaten jug of dirty water from near the door, trying to be happy in serving her, as I used to be. But she refused it and with hands broken and bloodied by whoever had dragged her here, she worked at the leather knots of her robe until she could peel the filthy cloth away from her shoulder. The flesh there was mangled and pitted, a long, twisting scar that punctured and poisoned her brown skin. I stared.

"So that you know what I tell you is true." She chuckled as she bound up her dress again.

"I . . . I didn't doubt . . ."

My grandmother touched my cheek lightly. "No, no, of course you didn't. You were always a good girl. And so, you see, I have broken my promise. I disobey the Fox, and tell you all these things I was meant to keep secret as a green-eyed baby in a brown-eyed man's house. But I have never much cared what that old red beast thought. And do you know? Now, the Mare comes to me in my dreams, and I do ride her, I ride her over the blanched steppes, with the sun gold and hot on our backs."

She didn't need to say it—I felt it, deep in my stomach, that the Mare would never come for me, and I would never feel that hide between my calves.

Grandmother Bent-Bow coughed like an arrow striking a tree. "Forgive me, little Knife, that I haven't spent this time rocking you in my arms and singing the songs of our mothers. It is too important that you learn what I suffered in the cave; we both know that you will never face those tests. There is no one now to guide you to the cave-mouth, no one to kiss you and call you their best and prettiest goat. There will never be anyone to take you home when it is over, shaking and shivering in rough blankets, no one for you, and no one for the child you are carrying, as tiny within you as a mayfly on the slow river. So instead of a sweet reunion with your old grandmother, you get a lesson, and you had better learn it, and learn it well."

My breath caught, knotted like new yarn in my dry throat. I had not even known that my belly had taken a child from the body of my husband before he died. But in that moment I knew she told the truth. I fought to keep still at her side. Shakily, I whispered, "I am listening, Grandmother. I am trying to walk with you and learn your steps."

Her wrinkled eyelids slid closed and as she spoke they quivered, as though tiny wolves were leaping beneath her skin.

The
Wolf's Tale,
Continued

THE YOUNG GIRL WOKE HER CAMP SCREAMING. MEN
came running—they opened her tent to find her huddled
against her baby, sobbing, covered in light.

Light dripped from her hair, down the bridge of her
nose, from the lobes of her ears. It trickled into her
mouth, splashed her child's forehead, pooled sickly between her breasts. Pale and bright as the whites of a
maiden's eyes, it drenched the front of her hide-dress—it
spattered the walls and soaked the earthen floor of the
tent into glowing, churning mud.

Around her lay seven stone bodies, and they did not
glow, or shimmer, or gleam. Jade and Granite and Opal,

dark and hollow as old trees, Garnet leeched and empty, Shale and Iron Ore pale as paper, and Diamond, little Diamond, nothing left of her but a cicada shell, crystalline, clear, and nothing left within her, not even dead bone.

They had come, the girl wept, in the night. The King's men who had known what had come begging at their door, known and called it strange and wicked. They had held her arms behind her while they cut open the pitiful sisters, who did not even cry out while the light was let out of them—and it sprayed from them like blood, she cried, and she tasted it as it spurted warm over her face, and it tasted of sweet water and clover. They opened the throats of the Stars and when they left, she tried to hold her hands against the wounds, but there were too many and she was not strong enough, and who among them knew how to heal a thing that is drowning in its own light which is blood which is light?

The tribe was afraid and uncertain of what to do, but they washed the light from the poor girl, and took the seven stone bodies out into a great field waving with poppies, and gave them what funeral rites they knew.

And so it was that the Stars learned that we could die, the biggest thing we could do, and those who were left vanished from the world, into the crevices and secret places of the earth, terrified as rabbits.

It was not long after that that the girl and her black-eyed baby looked into the sky through the gaps in the still-wet ceiling of her tent and saw new stars there—seven of them, clinging together like sisters.

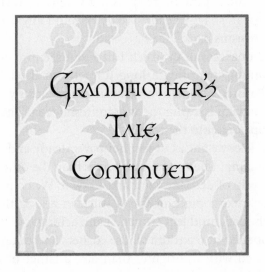

Grandmother's Tale, Continued

LIULFR THE WOLF-STAR HAD NOT MOVED ONE OF her golden muscles while she spoke. Her voice had not lifted up nor dipped down. She just stared straight ahead.

"We do not know where they go, the ones that die. Where we go. Their bodies stay here and new stars peek out of the sky, but where are *they*?"

What should I have said to comfort her?

"That girl, that poor nomad girl, had been nearly drowned in light, the light of seven bodies. She had choked on it and her baby had sputtered in it—no other thing had ever known so much. Her children and her children's children were nearly mad with it, and as time went on, they began to seek us out, though each child had less and less of the Manikarnika's sheen on them. They came and they came, predictable as tides, and now you come—granddaughter dangling at the end of so many granddaughters, one after the other like a chain of folk passing a bucket of water between them. A little more spills out whenever it changes hands." She shook her great, shaggy head. "We don't mind anymore. It is almost like having our cousins back."

The polished quartz wall in which I had first seen my wolf-self slowly melted into nothing, revealing a long tunnel into the black earth. She sighed with exhausted resignation and nudged me gently with her snout like a mother showing her pup the way to fresh water. The mingled light of our fur disappeared into the wall.

Liulfr trotted silently ahead of me, her paws steady and sure. She flickered like a brass lamp. The tunnel was longer than the other, so black that I had to stifle a yelp of despair when first I saw it. We crept on our bellies through the rock like a piece of bread stuck in a long throat, forepaws scrabbling on the soil, hind legs crouched and aching.

The throat opened into a room whose corners and rafters were washed with light, scoured with it, brighter than day, a lather of light like soap rubbed furiously in the hand. I could hardly see, the change was so sudden, and in the center of it, the wolf-creature like a sun, gently blazing.

The cavern was not empty. Seven biers were laid out in curving rows, each bearing a woman, asleep or dead, fourteen slender hands closed over fourteen frozen breasts. Their hair swept over their pedestals as though it had grown a thousand years; their limbs were covered in jewels, more than I had ever seen together, piled up like apples at harvest. Piles of jade and granite and opal, of garnet bright as blood, of shale and iron ore, and of diamond, tiny diamonds glittering like snow.

In the Garden

WAKENED NOW, THE BOY CHEWED SLOWLY ON AN APPLE CORE, MESMER-
ized. Wolves bounded gracefully through his mind, nosing the wind. He
stretched his long arms, yawned, and pulled from his pack a rich red
blanket edged in gold thread and embroidered with lilies. He wrapped it
around his shoulders and edged gingerly towards the girl, as a man
would move towards a skittish colt. They huddled together under their
scarlet tent, and she lowered her lashes earthward when his hand
brushed her knee, snatching the water flask and drawing it in. They were
very close; he could smell the musk of her hair, cedar and jasmine.

The first lights of dawn, luminous and blue, filtered down through
the fine fabric of leaves, writing in rose and silver shadows on their skin.

It is very still, the world at dawn, under its glittering net of dew. In
their little thicket, the pair of children who were very nearly finished
with childhood sat dry and warm, and the girl's voice had fallen as silent
as a cat's paw on pine needles. The infant sun brushed the boy's hair
from his face with a shimmering, cherubic hand. He did not move from
the girl's side, but it was nearing light, and his sister would be rising
soon, her face growing stormy at the sight of his empty bed.

"I have to go," he rasped finally. "I have to get back before the household wakes up."

The girl nodded, suddenly shy, drawing back into herself after all this long night of spinning out her heart like flax, straw into gold.

"But I will come back," he reassured her, "as the flocks of river birds do, at sunset. I will bring us another supper and you will tell me all the rest about the grandmother in her cave."

He touched her face, and his hand on her cheek was soft as a hare's paw. The girl smiled into his palm, and nodded. Her luminous eyes lifted and long lashes closed briefly, exposing the swirling black of the birthmark covering her eyelids, inky and deep, a night without stars. The boy marked that he did not find it un-beautiful, now that he knew her a little. He dipped his tousled golden head a little, to meet her eyes as they slid open again.

"I will come every night, to hear your stories. Every night," he declared quietly, and ran into the striations of mist covering the gardens, catching in the jasmine and aster, and the apple trees.

The girl bent to the remains of their evening meal and gathered together the flasks and crusts of bread to feed the crows and gulls. She then rose from her little bower, shaking a few errant petals from her hair in a shower lit by the strong red-gold beams of the day.

When the sun had lain down in the west and covered itself with long blue blankets, and the girl sat cross-legged under the silver-lavender jasmine branches, she saw the boy's eager shadow racing across the thick emerald lawn to her. He burst into her thicket, industriously setting out her dinner. She had been sure he would not come.

He brought dark bread and pale cheeses, a slice of roasted lamb and a cluster of berries bulging with juice, several small roasted potatoes, a cold green apple and a slice of chocolate, precious as myrrh.

"I thought I would leave the wine tonight, so that I do not steal off to sleep again," he admitted bashfully, extending his water flask instead.

"No, no, it's all right, what you brought is more than enough," she assured him with a nervous laugh. They fussed with the food and did not speak, the boy as eager for her tale as a bear seeking salmon in the frothing river. As she ate, her face grew brighter, as though she were a small sun, rising just as the great golden one went down.

"How did you live all these years in the Garden?" The boy munched on a fat chunk of apple.

The girl looked around. "The Sultan has more than enough fruit trees to feed one child, and the water in the fountains is clear and clean. I have had enough. The Palace throws away more than I could ever use. Once in a while there is even an amira's old dress tossed on the refuse pile. And when the winters have been harsh, the birds have brought me mice and rabbits. I am cared for. The Garden raised me; it is my mother and my father, and mothers and fathers always find a way to feed and clothe their children."

"The birds . . . ?" The boy was incredulous.

She shrugged. "All creatures are lonely. They are drawn to me and I am drawn to them, and we warm each other in the snow. You should know better—weren't you drawn, too? And I feed you my stories like morsels of meat roasted in a fire."

The boy blushed deeply, turning his eyes away from her. They finished their meal in silence.

Finally, when lamb and fruit had been eaten, sweet water had been drunk, and each of them had found a comfortable place in the flower thicket to lean on their sides, heads bent inwards like conspirators, the girl spoke, and her voice filled up the boy like cream splashing in a silver bowl.

Grandmother's Tale, Continued

FROM THE LONG, UNMOVING SHADOWS BEYOND THE
last of the seven bodies, my silent guide made a small,
rustling sound with her beautiful tail.

"We brought them back here, from the field of poppies
and old, sodden wheat. They weighed nothing at all, like
carrying moths. And we kept them here, where my dark
brother and my pale sister and some few others came to
hide ourselves. What else was there to do? There are no
graveyards for us, no rites, no songs, no fires. We had their
shells in our hands, and we didn't know what to do, we
just didn't know." Liulfr nosed the faceted face of the one
buried in diamonds. Her voice was a whisper thick as wet

wool. "The new stars up there, the stars that flare up when we die, they're just markers. It's not them. This isn't them. We don't know where they are. You look up into the sky, little girl: it's a mausoleum, and those new, bright lights are tombs, but *they* are not there. But they are not here, either."

The Wolf-Star fixed me with her yellow eyes. I padded quietly across the room and sat down heavily before the jewel-girl, pale and dead. I was not sure what was expected of me. It was very warm, the light rubbing against my hindquarters and nuzzling my fur lazily. The glassy wound at the diamond-woman's throat seemed to grow in my vision, like a second mouth grinning horribly below the first. I nosed at it and it was neither warm nor cold, but hard, nothing like flesh.

Beneath my silver fur the wound the Mare had made throbbed, and the smaller cut from the Fox just below it stung like the quick needle of a wasp. Liulfr simply watched me, offering no help at all. This, then, was my test. I got to my paws and half climbed over the poor girl, half kneeled on her slippery drift of gems. I put my muzzle to my chest and gnawed open the space between the wounds, so that the scabs broke and they flowed freely into each other, one long, deep gash: a hole chewed in flesh, the first bite of the world.

The blood came dark and ugly at first, and I was dizzy—dizzy and so hot in that close, dark room!—and it splashed on the empty corpse like ink spilled over a mirror. But after a long while it began to flow clear, and then filled with a gentle light, soft and sweet-smelling as sugared pears in a copper dish, cold, so cold, and the color of the moon. Half faint, I wearily pressed my bleeding breast hard against the woman's cut throat.

I thought she would wake up. I really did. I thought that all in a rush she would gasp and cry out, her back would arch like a drawn bow, her eyes would suddenly open, and she would cough. She would draw ragged breaths, and all those diamonds would clatter to the floor as she finally bolted upright, face beaming bright as morning.

She did not move. The light trickled out of me and into her, and I watched it foam at the bottom of her back, like a cup of water tossed into a deep bathtub. The shadows draped the room, and the blood which was light slowed and stopped.

Gently, with all the weight of breath, the dead woman on the bier closed her fingers over my paw.

That was all—she did not open her eyes or sit up and ask for water. Four fingers just lifted and fell again, closing me in a grip which stone might envy.

The Wolf-Star leaned over us. "We always hope—it would be an answer, anyway. But they never wake up. I suppose after all this time it would be strange if they did." Liulfr closed her eyes and began to wash me, to clean my wound in the wolfish way, with her long tongue, rough as marsh sand. With each stroke my body pulsed, vibrating under her like a plucked harp. I could see only her golden fur, shimmering candle-wise, though I could feel the Stone-Star's fingers on my fur, cold and lifeless. She lapped up the light like milk, slurping at it, sucking it from the gash in the Manikarnika, carefully collecting every drop.

Finally, she closed her long, silky snout over my shaggy breast, gripping my chest in her jaws and pinning me to the diamond girl, teeth pressing my ragged skin.

I could feel it, rushing all through me like a burst wine barrel, the light and blood that poured out of her jaws, finding its circuit in me, doubled back brighter and harsher and more terrible than before, searching out a wave to ride into my bones and belly, great, rolling tides that filled me up like a water-horn. I was glutted with it, light from the Wolf's mouth and the jewel's body, the jewel's body and mine, light old and unspeakable as the sky. I choked, moaned, even screamed emptily into the cavern as they pushed it through me—for this is *work*, granddaughter, the change of light; it is pushing a boulder up a mountain, or a mountain up a mountain. She opened and filled and sewed and opened me again. And how many hours I lay helpless and quivering between them I cannot say. They took the dim, whittled light I had in me and returned it to me, blazing like nothing I had ever known.

When finally I felt the Wolf's jaw release me, I started as if out of a dream, every pore thrumming, open, shaking. I was a woman again, I could feel it: five fingers on each hand, teeth flat and thick, long hair grazing my waist like a paintbrush.

Liulfr touched my face with her wet nose. "What we have given you is yours, but it does not belong to you. We don't mind it, we have never minded, but light is a thing with limits. You must understand that when a Star gives it she is diminished." She shut her eyes against my cheek. "I have been here for you and your mothers for a long time; I am the source you come to; I am the well from which you drink."

For the first time, the Star seemed to me to be less bright than the cave walls. She was just an old wolf, her fur bare in patches, her eyes milky and misted, her muzzle going gray. But then she smiled, as much as a wolf can smile, and I was once more surrounded by her light and warmth, which was—was it? I could not tell—only a little less than it had been before.

"You changed when you entered the cave. We did it for you then. It is a great magic, almost," and here she paused, stealing a glance at the woman with colorless curls, "the greatest of all. Metamorphosis is the most profound of all acts. When your light comes from our hands, and not from your grandparents and their grandparents back and back and back, to that poor girl in her tent clutching a baby to her breast, you can be like us, at least a little like us, and it is only a simple thing to change the outline of a hole." The Wolf-Star swallowed hard. "After all, a hole is nothing but space." After a silence deeper than a dungeon, she stood back, straight-spined, and stared down at me, speaking carefully through her silky muzzle.

"But you are not one of us. For you, this thing is irreversible except by death, and not only the flesh is altered. Only the strongest of you can resist the collapse of the soul into the form; the mind is lazy, it naturally imitates the body. I have known none of you yet who can remain human when they wear another skin. But the thing is yours to do, if you should wish to do it."

The cold, clear hand of the jewel-girl released mine, and it had all the life of a scrap of paper blowing across an empty street. Without a word, the old gold-pelted Wolf led me back through the two doors and into the great open arena of the first cavern. It seemed a century ago that I had bent under the Mare's teeth there, that she had made her hole in me.

"Go, Star-daughter. There is much work for you to do."

I knew I should not, but I could not keep myself from it. I knelt and put my arms around her great, shaggy neck, burying my face in the smell of her, of cedar and wet rock, of snow just fallen. "You never know," I whispered, "maybe the new Stars aren't just markers. Maybe they *are* the Manikarnika. Maybe they went home."

Liulfr shook her head against my skin, and the fur was like the crackle of heat-lightning. Her voice was tiny and soft. "No one goes home. A hole is nothing but space. We are accidents, and there is no grace for us."

She pulled back and gave my cheek the briefest of licks. The Wolf-Star padded quietly away from me, vanishing before she found the far wall.

Stumbling out into the lightening world, my eyes stung by the first darts of sunlight, I sat heavily on the grass, exhaustion slamming into me like a stone wall.

And the Fox stood a few feet from me, watching me with cold eyes.

"Some who deserve failure do not achieve it," he sniffed. "Some who deserve nothing are given the world. So, here it is, woman. The world. Go into it, but do not ever speak of what has passed here. It is forbidden to all with tongues to utter it. We want to stay hidden; we have chosen this place, and power granted can be lost. Do not think you have seen the last of me, nor ever that you are now my equal. Liulfr is hopeless and old. A filled hole is *not* empty space, and we were all full, so full of light. You are a thief and a vampire, and if I had my way you and your daughters would have no more of our blood."

As the sun crept on lion's feet over the green hills, it illuminated his fur, bristle by bristle, until he was so bright I could not look. And then he was gone, and the light shone through the place where he had been.

Out of the Garden

WHEN MIDNIGHT LAY OVER THE TWO CHILDREN LIKE A SERAPH'S BLUE arm, the boy gingerly laid his head on the girl's lap, letting her voice cradle him. He pretended he did not hear her breath stop when he shifted, or the quaver in her voice like a single mislaid thread in a beaded gown.

But as soon as his head touched the rough fabric of her dress, a terrible crunching sound was heard as strange feet trampled the earth outside their little thicket. The girl screamed, an awful, high-pitched sound like a crane shot through with a silver arrow. The boy leapt up, drawing his pathetic little dagger, determined to protect his secret prize. But as ghostly hands ripped apart the sweet-smelling briars, he recognized that the danger was far worse than any witch or arcane spell.

The boy saw, framed in jasmine boughs like a fiery mandala, the wrathful face of his sister, her eyes filling with accusations like a judge's scroll.

"I've caught you now, you vile little rat!" she crowed triumphantly. "You'll be punished! Consorting with the demon girl!"

"She's not a demon!" he blurted, not at all meaning to—Dinarzad was fearful as a lion in heat. The girl breathed quick and hoarse, unable to move. "She's not! You leave us alone!"

Something of the wolf and the cave must have seeped into him, like spilled ink, for he never before had had the courage to say such a thing to her. Dinarzad swooped into the thicket like a crazed harpy—the boy could almost imagine feathers puffing from her skin—and seized him by the hair, dragging him away from the now weeping girl though he kicked and cursed like a grown man.

In his vision, the girl retreated, a moon slipping behind cobalt-rimmed clouds. The light was draining from his world; all he could see was her eyes, huge and dark as forest owls, staring after him.

When they reached the gates of the Garden, the boy bit his sister savagely on her perfumed arm and she stopped, slapping him hard across the face—so hard it split his lip like a pine branch. He spat blood onto the earth.

"You may think you are a man now, little brother, but men do not go near wicked devils like her. Do you want to bring her curse on the whole family? You spoiled little whelp! I'll whip you till morning!"

Defiant as a rooster crowing at sunset, the boy bellowed back, "Yes! Yes! I *am* a whelp! I am a wolf with teeth like pirates' swords and I'll tear you into as many pieces as there are jewels in the Sultan's vaults! She is not a demon—and I am going back to her. Right now." He crossed his arms over his young chest and felt pride surging in him like the Star's blood.

But Dinarzad blazed. Her eyes grew dark as molded dungeons and she gripped his arm, tightening slowly.

"No, little brother. You are not going anywhere."

The boy woke in a dark, foul-smelling prison.

Dinarzad held a child in each arm, twins bawling their identical hearts out. He was trapped with her in the royal nursery, amid the tortured cries of dozens of infants, more terrible than horned demons at their forges.

Dinarzad, almost a woman grown and ready to be married out of the household, spent her evenings caring for the Palace children, and she ruled them all with a fist stronger than any iron smelted by mortal man. She was a vengeful goddess and her will was absolute. Tonight she was tending the youngest, and for his trespass the boy was tied to her skirts and this wretched room. It was worse, he was certain, than any old dungeon in a King's castle, and there was no hope of escape as long as his sister's eyes were fastened on him like scorpion's pincers.

But the gods are not always unkind to small boys, and fate was to intervene in the pink flesh of a colicky princeling. Not yet understanding its royal duty, the poor thing simply insisted on his mother's arms. Thus Dinarzad was compelled to deliver the squalling child to the appropriate bedroom.

"If you so much as move a toe from one flagstone to the next," she warned, "I will lock you away until you rot. One brother will not be missed amid the dozens."

And with that, she swept out the door, rose-colored silks trailing behind her.

Of course, the boy had disappeared out the north window within three heartbeats.

The bower looked as though a battle had been fought there, pitch tossed from battlements and soldiers in formation crushing all underfoot. The white blossoms were in tatters, hanging like peasants' rags on snapped boughs. Their supper had been strewn everywhere, and he saw that he had dented his water flask against a gnarled root when Dinarzad had snatched him away. The ruin of the flowers touched him most, the oleander torn petal from petal, scattered onto the dirt. The place where he had heard tales that still burned like lamp oil inside him was destroyed, ransacked like a fine house.

And the girl was nowhere in sight.

He searched over all the hiding places he knew in the vast Garden, through the hedges and rose trees, the lily ponds with their ululating bullfrogs, the olive groves and the borders of the fruit orchards. She was gone, disappeared, and all the stories with her.

The boy sat down heavily on the rim of a bronze fountain, whose water trickled gently into the night. He put his golden head in his hands, reproaching himself for lack of care, that he had let himself be caught, found missing. He was an impossible thief and even more hopeless protector. But then, he thought to himself, Prince Leander was also caught, so perhaps he could be forgiven.

He looked up in his despair, and the moon floated through his sight like a great paper lantern. And as the clouds passed over it, a single wild goose arced over its vast face, tracing a graceful path in the night. He heard it call, lonely and foreign, like a jade flute, and sighed deeply.

The goose sounded again, this time very near him, and the boy realized that it was no bird which called to him, but the dark-eyed girl, who was hiding behind a slender young cedar not far away. His heart flew upward like a duck taking flight from a still pond, and he ran to her, stopping just short of clasping her in his young arms. She looked bashful and embarrassed, her black eyes downcast.

"How did you learn to call like the wild water birds?" he asked eagerly.

"I told you. I have fed them and talked with them since I was a child—there was no one else. They . . . sometimes they spread their wings over me on winter nights when it is very cold, and we rest together under the hard stars."

The boy again resisted the urge to embrace her, and instead clapped her on the shoulder as he had seen his father do with his comrades.

"You told me, but how could I believe it? Someday you must teach me!" he announced. "But first, the story! Continue the story! I must know what happened to the Prince now that the Witch has finished her tale!"

The two stole away from the fountain, which was, after all, a poor hiding place. They ducked into a grove of sweet-scented cedars and the girl settled in.

She smiled up at him, a strange, feline grin.

"You are wrong, though. The Witch had hardly begun . . ."

The Witch's Tale, Continued

GRANDMOTHER FOLDED HER ARMS LIKE AN OLD stick-bug, smiling her thin smile and stroking my hair. I still remember her voice, and how it wrapped around that dark cellar, clawing at the walls and licking into the massive locks at the same time that it softened my fear like a spinner wetting thread between her lips.

"So you can change like that, even now? Right now?"

"Yes, I could."

"Could I do it?"

"You will never go to the cave now, my love. You will never touch the light inside Liulfr, or inside the dead Star. You will be a witch of leaves and grasses, at best: you will make love-potions and cold-cures and gout-softeners for those who can pay you, and look up at the sky, and tell a young girl whether her husband will have light or dark hair, and deliver her baby when the time is right for it, and you will bury her when the time is right for that, but that is all."

I swallowed that, chewing on it like a strip of hide. Finally, I grunted. A weak witch was better than no witch at all.

"Could you do it to another person?" I asked suddenly.

Grandmother's eyebrows knitted, as if she were trying to work out a strange set of hoofprints. "I don't know. I think I could, I . . . I suspect there's a way it could be done. But I wouldn't like to be the one to try it."

"Do it now, then!" I cried, grabbing at her skinny hands. "Turn into a mouse and crawl out through the lock, or a bird and fly out through the window grate. Bring back a key and let me free, and we'll go into the steppe together, and eat deer, and never think about this place again."

"Poor little Knife, you can be dull and blunt as a rock, sometimes," she said kindly. "If I became a mouse, I would scurry out and think of nothing more pressing than getting cheese into my little gray belly. I would forget you, and we would never eat deer together again. Besides, I have a killing to do before I can think on mice or birds. And you have a birthing."

The Tale of the Prince and the Goose, Continued

THE WITCH STOPPED SPEAKING. NIGHT STREAMED through the Witch's windows like bolts of silk. Thick and black, it coiled around them both. The Prince was uncomfortable and cold, his hands covered in bread flour, but he did not dare complain.

The Prince no longer heard her at all, and his hand had begun, again, to bleed. Blood trickled into the bread, but he did not see it. The crackling fire leapt like trout, scenting the hut with green branched sage and sweetgrass smoke. The Prince's eyes watered, though he did not know whether it was the stinging air that wrenched the tears from him or the buried memory pierced by her casual mention of his mother. The memory had paced back and forth in him for hours, a flash of yellow hair and a flutter of wings beating at the back of his brain.

And it all was becoming so strange and hard to follow, the path he had taken to this house through the forest, the braided words spilling like ink from this gnarled woman's mouth, the throbbing fear waiting in him, that at the end of all this storytelling, he would still have to suffer her punishment for his killing of the goose—and the memory, the memory, brushing his heart with its awful gray wings.

In truth, lost in her tale, he had nearly forgotten that there ever was such a pearl-feathered creature as that dead bird, that he had ever snapped its neck in the morning light. But he looked down at his flour-speckled hands, washed in the flicker of fire and shadow, and glimpsed drops of blacker blood among the white dust and within his own wet wound, and remembered. It was only a moment ago, wasn't it, that he had left his father's Castle like a fugitive, determined never to return? And now he was a prisoner only a few miles beyond the borders of the kingdom, his adventure cut off before it had begun. He was lost as a trapped hare, lost in the mire of this hissing voice, of the hut shadows and the fire and the corpse of the goose-girl, crumpled against the wall, near the hearth to keep her flesh warm.

And now she had uttered his mother's name, and those old, forbidden syllables layered her tale, which had nothing at all to do with him, of course, but somehow his mother's memory was a rough lever, and with it the Witch slowly broke him open, inch by bone. He had hardly heard the last sliver of the long tale, so sunk in sorrow, its waters swirled around his chin.

The Witch cocked her head to one side, watching her guest with mild curiosity. Quietly, she took his hand in hers and pressed her palm against the bloodied fingers, stilling the blood. She rubbed some sweet-smelling root against the stubs of his fingers—it prickled cold against his raw flesh.

"Grass and leaves," she snorted. He tried a wan smile, but it refused to come. The Witch narrowed her feral eyes at him.

"What is it, boy? My servant, yet you cannot even listen to me for an evening? Instead you wrap yourself up in your own troubles like a bolt of wool, and moon after me to take them off your shoulders."

"My mother," the Prince mumbled, "you said you knew my mother."

"And you told me not to speak of her," she grunted. "Very well, then, shall we stop and listen to the murderer beat his breast and spit out his woe onto my floor? Your mother is dead and your father has all but erased her from the memory of the world. Is it necessary to know more than that of the poor woman?"

Her voice had cracked dangerously at the end, and the Prince started at it, marveled at the things which must have passed in the kingdom without his knowledge, to find exiled deep in the forest a woman who had known the dead Queen. Oh, the name of his mother was written neatly on the genealogical rolls and trilled in country songs which mostly praised her long and yellow hair—but that same name was forbidden within the rooms of government, and within any room his father might hazard to step. Yet the Witch knew her.

She rubbed her long bony fingers, a sound like branches rasping together in the wind, and grinned up at him again, under the gray and greasy curtain of her hair.

"You think I am so wicked, don't you? A monster. Unnatural. How cruel of me to keep you here and rattle on about my dead grandmother whom you care nothing about. To hold back the doom I keep in store for you and tease you about your mother. I am telling you all this for a reason, you curdle-brained child. Didn't you ever have a tutor? I am teaching dead, dull history—so that you will understand why your feet carried you *here* instead of towards some other broken old woman's hut, and what you ended when you snapped my daughter's neck. Don't keep looking at me with that same idiot stare. Listen, or you will comprehend nothing, not even your mother. Shall I just kill you now and have my revenge? It would certainly save breath, and at my age every breath is named and numbered. I entertain you at the expense of not a few figures in that scroll of sighs, boy; do not test me." She paused, grimacing as if she truly were tallying the accounts of her lungs. "And never assume that a woman is wicked simply because she is ugly and behaves unfavorably towards you. It is unbecoming behavior for a Prince."

She slurped her tea noisily. When she spoke again, her voice had softened from a dagger point to a smooth, hand-warmed pommel.

"But I can see that you are in pain, and that is the province of monsters. You drag your mother's corpse with you—it leaves a great furrow in the earth. If it is important enough to very rudely interrupt a woman who already owns two fingers she did not have this morning just to exhume those old bones, I will listen to you instead. It matters nothing to me. Believe me, it will not go easier for you if you come to feel warmly towards me because you have unburdened your soul. We have all the nights the world has ever made ahead of us. Speak of the dead in the dark, boy, and I will take her body from you, if you want to be rid of it."

The Prince looked up at her, hunched as though whipped, his ribs creaking within him, as though chipped by thousands of tiny blades. He could not breathe, his heart slammed against his chest, his throat flamed. He wanted to tell her what he knew, his soul scorched itself black in the effort, but he could not speak.

And the Witch was laughing at him.

But it was not a vicious laugh; rather, the old hag's chuckle had gone sad and soft and sorry.

She leaned in, her movement like a door closing. "You tell him her name. You tell him, when you see him again."

She placed her leathery hand on his forehead, and the other over his lips, cradling his head between her hands like a beloved doll. He wanted to loathe her touch, to spit at her, but as soon as her dry flesh touched his, peace flowed over him like a rippling river, his muscles unlocked and his breath returned. Her hands on him were like the paws of a bear on her cub, strong and cool. When she let him go, he was wide-eyed and straight-backed, his forehead cool.

"Grass and leaves?" he whispered.

"Quite so," said the Witch.

And with a smooth throat he let fall the words that had long since rusted in him:

"My father killed her." He shook his head. "It seems like an easy thing to admit, now, but no one speaks of it. No one. I was only a baby when she died, but my nurse told me the way of it, over and over like a lullaby. She was determined that I hold this thing inside me like a heart—something irremovable and constant. She would hold me to her, and whisper the same story, endlessly repeated. I remember her hair, like a forest of straight, white birches all around me, and her dark eyes above . . ."

THE NURSEMAID'S TALE

YOUR MOTHER WAS MORE BEAUTIFUL THAN THE
summer sun, little one. They'll tell you she weren't, that
she were ugly as a frog's gullet, but it's a lie. Yaya tells the
truth to her boys, always and always.

All of gold she was, her hair, her skin, even her eyes, like
a lion's. She was called Helia, and that's as good a name as
any I've heard.

Your father guarded her, jealous as a jackal, and kept
her in a tower room. But her reputation as a beauty for the
books filled the countryside. He weren't married to her
too long before you were born—that's usually the way of
it when the wife looks like a lion or a sun—and when you

came out of her, easy as nothing, she loved you terribly. You were as dark as she was light, the tiny little moon to her sun. I was her maid then, and she was full of light. I tell you, darling-duck, it hurt to look at her sometimes, when she stood at her tower window with you at her breast, and her hair all filled up with fire. I used to wonder if she gave you milk, or if the sun just emptied into your mouth through her teat.

But one night she was not in her tower. You were almost a boy and the fat was still on your cheeks, then. You waddled about her empty room— your father didn't even give her a chair, I swear it. She stood all day, and lay on the stones to sleep, and I never heard the woman complain. And I can't say, since I'd have no way of knowing, what she did that strange night (the rich don't tell us but how they like their ribbons tied and their tea brewed, and Yaya doesn't mind, it's their way), but in the yellow morning your father's anger clouded up heaven and shook the thatch from the ceiling.

He and his old fortune-teller blustered about the Castle, full of their own huffing wind, blaming me for letting her free, as though a Queen ought not to do as she pleases. He seized me by the arm hard as an iron cuff and we raced up the rickety staircase to the tower where your mother stood, as calm as can be, and you a-sleeping in her arms with not a care in your head. She looked at your father with the glance of a tiger with a full belly, her golden eyes all bright with hate and happiness.

I won't forget that look, not for all the apples I could eat. Helia hated the King, and that's the truth; you ask him when you're grown and see if he calls your old Yaya a liar. You woke up with a cry when your father ripped you from her and shoved you into my arms, just before he hit your mother so strong that she spat a tooth onto the floor—how do you like that? But she didn't hardly blink, and that awful look never left her eyes. He hissed at her, and it was a strange, black, dark thing he said:

"Woman, you will not make me a fool again. I should have cut your throat when I first saw you."

"Probably true," purred your mother. And then the King smiled, and I began to be afraid that there was something secret and rotten in my master—but I said nothing. A servant never says nothing unless she's asked, and who ever asked Yaya a thing but when the supper was coming?

"Do you remember?" he spat. "With your death I instruct your son."

She grinned horribly at his purple face and whispered just as sweet as cream, "And he will learn, oh husband mine. He will learn."

She died the next morning. I couldn't guess why or for what crime, but she was executed like a thief caught with a slab of butter. I was there, in the courtyard, and I held you close, and like a good nurse I turned your face away at the last moment.

It was before dawn, in the sleepy gray, and your father pulled poor Helia out of the Castle, in a plain white shift with her hair streaming like fire in the fog. The batty old conjurer was there, in his fine blue robes, but he never spoke a word—a servant never says nothing unless he's asked—just smiled softly all the while. The King tied your poor dam onto a pile of fresh-cut logs and tied her to it with rough-hewn ropes. She didn't struggle, not even when the ropes were so tight her wrists bled. But when she saw you, well, no mother is so strong she doesn't care if her babe sees her burn. She wept, then, and screamed, trying to reach out to you, her little chick a-peeping away in the morning, though she never begged to live, no, not once.

I wanted to help her, Yaya did, but I would have burned beside her, and you would be all alone with no one to love you and stand up between you and the rotten thing in your father.

The King drew a long knife and hacked off her magnificent hair, handing the length to his addle-brained Wizard. They stood over her for a moment, and your sire's face was dark as dirt. Then, he lit the branches of ash and oak with a great crackling torch, and she was still screaming, but it had a terrible, terrible keening sound, like a song, a frightful death-song that came out of her bones, and you cried even harder, so scared you were by that screeching, singing noise. The fire licked at her feet and caught her dress; it lit up her head like an angel's.

Now, your Yaya wouldn't lie, no matter what they tell you at dinner, so listen when I say what I saw. When the fire had wrapped her all up in red, through the wriggling flames I saw your mother *change*. Her hair went from gold to black and the shape of her body wobbled in the scald, looking now like the Helia I knew, and now like someone else, someone ugly and horrible and dark as anything.

They'll tell you Yaya is off her head and drinks too much bad red beer, but I think the Wizard saw it, too, and his eyes went angry. He rushed us all out of the cold, saying that someone would come clean up her bones, but that the baby shouldn't see—I told him right out if he didn't want you to see he ought not to have dragged you out of bed to watch, but he ignored me like that ragged old stork always does.

But, dear-as-dumplings, her crying followed me, clawing at my back, and behind the cries, behind them I could swear I heard rustling, and flapping, and fluttering, and it only got louder, louder and louder until I had to hold my hands over my ears as we ran from her, from your mother, burning like meat.

The Tale of the Prince and the Goose, Continued

"Is that all?" the Witch asked, her tone bored.

The Prince nodded dumbly, though something small and calculating had entered his heart, as though he had caught the scent of a stag in the brush, a stag he was sure to catch, if he could creep silently enough. Knife arranged herself on her fur-covered stool and began again.

THE
WITCH'S TALE,
CONTINUED

TIME RAN ALONG LIKE A LEOPARD WITH EIGHT LEGS
in those cells—we could not see it, could not hear its passing, but it crept by on those spotted paws and ate us whole
just the same. I grew round as a harvest moon, though my
limbs were like birch twigs and my cheeks sunk in my
face. Hunger and darkness watched over us like worried
nurses.

And one night I lay down among the mildewed straw
and the scurrying, squeaking rats to give birth to my child.
My grandmother held me in a nest of her limbs, bracing
me against the stone walls, her face pressed against mine,
whispering while I whimpered and wiping away my

dirt-blackened tears. She rubbed my swollen belly with her wrinkled brown hands in a swirling motion like the patterns of birds migrating.

The pain was its own world, its own landscape drawn in red and black and flashes of sobbing white. I screamed—but everyone screamed in the prisons. I cursed everything I could think of—but curses are common in jails as gangrene. My hair was matted to my skull with sweat and my bare feet slipped on the floor as I kicked and thrashed like a sick bullfrog. My body ate itself, tearing its own bones apart. I cried and cried. I clutched at Grandmother and she clutched at me, trying to calm me down, nuzzling me like a wolf cub in the snow.

I couldn't feel her, I could only feel myself coming apart.

But my daughter was born, perfect and whole, with a shock of black hair and calm black eyes. I held her in my arms, her wet, shaking little body, born in the darkness far from our home. Smiling into her face I rocked back and forth, beyond words, beyond despair.

And then my grandmother's voice slid into me like a needle drawn through linen.

"But we cannot keep her, Knife, you must know we cannot keep her."

I shrank away and drew my daughter tightly to me. Grandmother hushed me and began to move her hands over me again, to make it better, as if I were a child with a stubbed toe.

"She would never survive. The King would have such a tiny thing killed, even if she did not starve to death in this place. She cannot stay with us. You know it, you just don't want to know it—no mother would."

I am so ashamed of my tears that night, hot and thick, dripping like candle wax from a thousand temples, but they would not stop.

"No, no, she's mine, I love her already. If you loved her, you wouldn't ask me to give her up. I won't give her up, I won't." I looked up helplessly. "She doesn't even have a name! How can I?"

Grandmother's eyes creased with pain, a book read too often, and by rough hands. She shrugged, knowing how stubborn I could be, and for the first time went away from me in the dark, and huddled in a far corner of the cell, hugging her knees to her chest on a pile of mold-greened bones. After a while, I heard her snoring.

After all her talk, the next weeks in Grandmother's silence were like being plunged into cold water without a chestful of air. She would not speak to me, and I was, for the first time, really and truly imprisoned. We squatted in our separate corners like prizefighters. I nursed my baby girl as best I knew how, her fierce little mouth tugging my breast, her fierce little cries tugging at my ears. She tired me, oh, how she tired me! I could only nap, like a sick cat, awake and asleep, awake and asleep—flagstones are no cradle, and they are no bed, and I had no horse milk to teach her the taste of them, and no steppe grass to teach her the feel of it. She would never know any of the things I knew.

And her black eyes were always open in the dark. Her skin was always pale and clammy, and she shivered so, she shivered so in the damp. She was thin and chilled, thin as a window, and I wept while she suckled, rocking back and forth against the slimy wall. She never cried at all. She just watched me with those hollow black eyes.

"Aerie," I sniffled one night, into the shadows where Grandmother hunched. "I'm calling her Aerie."

"That's a hopeful name, for a girl who will probably never see daylight, let alone a high nest between snowy mountains."

I stroked her soft cheek, which had no color at all, just a shallow grayness beneath the skin. She turned her mouth to my finger, and for the thousandth time, I began to cry. I was so weary of crying, by then. My milk and my tears spilled out of me every day and I thought every day that I must have no wetness left in me to give, but every day I wept again, and nursed again.

"I can't, Grandmother, I can't. You want me to put her down like a horse with a shattered knee and I *can't*. Even if it would be better for her, I couldn't, I couldn't even keep myself from going to her the moment she cried—her cry is a hook and it catches me in the throat."

"Oh, little one, I would never ask you that. How could you think I would? Not for nothing have you heard me rattle on like a tortoise shell blown from stone to stone. What we can give her is better than that, and certainly better than what we will manage for ourselves. Knife, let me have her; trust that the tale I told was to a point. You want to call her Aerie? Well enough. We'll see what we can do about getting her one."

She had to pry Aerie from me like a jewel from its setting, and she smiled, sad and small, at her great-grandchild's slight weight in her arms, touching her for the first time since she took the child from my body. Grandmother laid the baby out on what rags we could gather, to protect her from the cold floor. Aerie began, then, finally, to cry, sucking great icy breaths and sobbing to the rafters.

The old woman began to prepare herself—for what I could not think—shutting her eyes like veiled doors, and instructed me to do the same.

I saw no point. All I had was the power to kill a few deer and ride a horse, bind up a rotted limb and set a bone. If we weren't going to kill my child, I had no help to offer. She told me what I am. Grass and leaves. My tiny girl continued to wail; it disturbed the worms and roaches and spiders that crawled happily over our cell. I ached to reach for her, to wrap her again and hold her to my breast, no matter how dry and exhausted that breast might be.

Grandmother let her fingers fall over Aerie's solemn face. "I'm . . . I'm not sure this is going to work, you know." She cleared her throat. "I have never done it, and the Wolf never told me if it was allowed. A hole is nothing but space, but a filled hole is a Star. I am full, and she is empty. That should be enough."

I had never heard my grandmother doubt a single thing under the red sun. If she had said that one rabbit should be enough to feed the world, I would have nodded and set about stripping its fur.

Grandmother bent her head to the floor as if in prayer, and slowly thumped her skull against it, over and over, harder and harder. I tried to catch her and pull her up but she shoved me aside and kept at it, slamming her face into the stones. A dark, wet mark spread beneath her, and the sound of her bone hitting rock grew thick and ugly before, finally, she stopped and raised up her face again.

It was bloody, yes, but among the black streaks of blood were streaks of silver, streaks of light, like gray growing in a young woman's hair. It covered her cheeks and ran trickling over her eyes, dripping from her chin. She touched her finger to the soggy mess that had been her forehead, and seeing the light on her fingers, bent her brow to my daughter's mouth.

Aerie did not seem to understand at first, but the silver and the black dribbled into her mouth, and she had never needed much prodding to suckle. She fastened her mouth to Grandmother and patted her tiny hands against the old woman's hair with a hungry baby's glee. The light went into her, and the blood, all together, and in the dark, my daughter glowed.

Grandmother pulled away, and wiped Aerie's mouth like any other child's. She put her hands on her poor, pale body and clamped her eyes shut, breathing hard and harsh, grinding her fingers against my child's flesh as though she were shaping her like clay.

Slowly, Aerie changed. Her feet warped with moon-colored light and seemed to melt, her arms flattened like sheets of paper without ink. Feathers grew like silken hair on her body, first the curling down and then the strong gray feathers of flight, tipped black at the edges, the color of silver thread spinning on a crystal wheel. Her mouth, silent, as if in wonder herself, bent into a graceful beak, which snapped in a kind of awe at the empty air.

Only her eyes were the same, the watchful gaze colored like stones at the bottom of a lake.

She hopped up, my girl, now a pretty gosling, and nuzzled my palm with her soft head. She was still so small. I bent and kissed her feathers, feeling my heart wither like a dead hawthorn within.

We carried Aerie to the barred window and, balancing on a pile of bones to reach it, squeezed her little body through the gaps.

"There are hundreds of flocks of geese in this country, Knife. One will care for her until she is grown. It is for the best. We will not manage nearly so well. Go, little bird."

Aerie looked at me for a long moment, her black eyes glittering in the frosted wind. Then she turned and hopped from the half-buried window into the deep grass. It was dark and the stars were burning their holes in the black. I watched her go, out of one darkness and into another.

Three days after we watched Aerie stumble away over the fields, the great iron doors which separated the damp dungeon from the court glistening in candlelight were flung open with such force that they cracked the stone foundations. Grandmother and I were seized by rough hands that bruised and tore at us as we were carried up and up the spiral staircases on which I had been borne downward into hell—so long ago it seemed another woman. Our eyes could not adjust, everything was washed in white and yellow.

And so, when we came before the King, we could not look directly at him at first, so bright was the sun glinting off his golden crown and jeweled jacket. This, of course, was what he wanted. Later I would learn that he rarely wore the regalia for audiences. A tall man announced the King, a tall man whose hair was twisted, knotted, falling slate-gray to his hips. He wore a wide, bolted iron collar that brushed the fabric of his blue and brown robes.

"You have been brought for judgment before His Royal Highness, King of the Eight Kingdoms and Steward of the Eastlands, Autokrator of the Unified Tribes, Lord of the Thousand Caves, the Sacred Vessel who owns all above and below earth. This is your Arbiter."

By then I could see in the glare the coldness of the King's eyes, like ice beneath ice. The herald had a cruel mouth, and he turned it on me, pursing his thick lips as he surveyed my emaciated form. Grandmother was stiff as a bristling hound beside me; she recognized him as her would-be master—Omir, the court Wizard who stood ever at the King's ear. Before I ever came down the stone stair, he had tried, and failed, to bend her into the shape he wished, as though a woman were a stubborn plank of ash wood.

"You have"—and his voice, his voice was like oil sliding on silk, sinuous and sickening— "You have committed treason, my clever, clever girls. Not a minor feat when locked in a room underground, but you've managed it. You have engineered the loss of the King's rightful property. What's more, the property in question was not a prize won in war, but born right here within His Highness's borders—within his very walls!—and clearly his legal chattel."

The Wizard rubbed his long fingers as if they hid some secret ache. Grandmother looked at him levelly, her voice empty of fear as a hollow egg.

"Why do you not come near to me, Omir *Doulios,* and tell me how my great-granddaughter is the property of this wallowing pig?"

The Wizard seemed to flinch, but he quickly smoothed his face over. "How close, old woman? Close enough for you to slip a knife under my ribs? I think not. I need not even offer evidence—your admission of a great-granddaughter is enough." He looked at me with a hot stare that clung to my skin and held me limp in its grip. "The dam has foaled—where is the colt?" I tried to speak, to protest, but Grandmother silenced me with a squeeze of her hand on mine.

"You will not get what you desire this way, either. It is not for you," she hissed. And at this the Wizard did step closer.

"I will not get it, you dried up old soup-bone. I will take it."

But his one step had been enough. With a cry like a bear run through with a spear, Grandmother laughed at him, drawing a silver knife with a hilt of bone from her tattered dress. The knife cut true, and slid redly across the Wizard's neck.

The Tale of the Prince and the Goose, Continued

THE FIRE HAD GUTTERED TO NOTHING AND THE Prince sat in darkness, staring at palms he could not see. The Witch touched lightly the knotted scar on her forehead, the line that twisted and looped like a sea serpent. She smiled grimly, her mouth knotting upward in just the same line.

The accusation lay between them on the table, fat and hideous, black-spined and full of smoke. The Witch said nothing, and he tried not to look at the corpse which lay covered in soot and dew, leaning against the fireplace like new-cut wood.

"I didn't know," the Prince whispered. "I couldn't

have known. How could I? She *was* just a bird. I didn't mean . . ." He had
ruined the only thing his precious quest had touched.

The Witch covered his shaking hand with hers. Her voice was soft and
kind, as soft and kind as a Witch can manage.

"If you had meant it, my beautiful boy, I would have eaten your liver
and smiled through the meal."

Prince Leander looked up at Knife with a sudden passion. "But there
has to be a way to bring her back! There has to. You are a Witch. I am a
Prince. In all the books, where there is a Witch and a Prince there is a way."
He seized the edges of the table and leaned close to the crone. "Tell me
how to do it and I will save her. It is what a Prince *ought* to do, to save
maidens. I beg you, send me to the farthest ice cap, or the widest swamp,
but I will go if it means her life."

The Witch smiled, a real and tender smile, as from a grown wolf to a
whelp.

"Maybe. As you say, it is the main thing Princes are good for."

The Witch was silent. She collected the dough from the table, flour and
blood and tears and all, and slid it into a hulking oven.

"How did you escape from the Castle?" the Prince asked suddenly, wary
as a cat.

"I was banished," she replied shortly, pushing the misshapen loaf farther onto its iron grille.

Leander could see the rest of the tale piling up like fat parchment scrolls
behind Knife's eyes. But just as plainly he saw that she had told him all she
wished to tell.

"All you must know is the evil your family has done to mine. She was
the last of us, the last child of that poor girl who crouched in her tent
while men butchered stars. Now that she is dead there will never be any
more of us. That is a truth you can hold like a sun-baked brick in your
hand. It has weight, it has heft. To save my daughter you need no more."

"So there is a way. What must I do?" The Prince fixed her with that sin-
cere gaze which all Princes possess.

The Witch grunted, squinting at him through the low light. "She must
be wrapped in the skin of the Leucrotta under the new moon. Then it is
possible, though not likely, that she will be restored." The Witch waited for
a response, but none came. "Really, boy. Have you never seen the outside
of the Castle walls? The Leucrotta is a terrible beast who lives in the
Dismal Marshes. He is the color of clotted blood, part stag and part horse,
of a size that dwarfs both, a mouth that stretches ear to ear, and instead of
teeth it has twin rows of solid bone. It is very fearsome, I assure you."

"I am not afraid!" cried the Prince, nearly tripping over himself to show his willingness to brave any challenge to rescue the beautiful bird-maiden and redeem his family name.

"Wait, boy. You do not understand. Let me tell you a tale of another Prince who went to face the Leucrotta . . ."

The Other Prince's Tale

ONCE UPON A TIME THERE WAS A HANDSOME PRINCE who went to rescue his innocent sister from the fell beast.

The Leucrotta snapped his spine with one crack of its jaws, and wore his head and hands on its antlers for a fortnight in celebration.

The Witch sat back with satisfaction.

In the Garden

THE BOY GIGGLED. HE SAT PRIMLY ACROSS FROM THE GIRL NOW, NOT nearly brave enough to attempt to touch her again. She laughed, too, a low, quiet sound in the dark. Her eyes drifted up through the cedar boughs, black hawks darting towards him and away again. They were nervous now, skittish and afraid of Dinarzad's thunderous steps which surely were not far off. There was no supper to distract them, only the two, eager to tell and eager to hear, awkward and unsure, terrified of discovery.

In the night, which cantered towards morning like an eager mare, he inched closer to her, and urged her not to stop.

The girl drew her breath inward and began again, with her voice of waving willows bordering a dark lake.

The Tale of the Prince and the Goose, Continued

WHEN LEANDER LEFT THE HUT IN THE MORNING half-light, the Witch gave him a knowing grimace and kissed his cheek with her leathery lips. It was an awkward gesture, and he did not look her in the eye. But her hand fell to his, and unwrapped the leaves from his stumps. He was not very surprised to see that they had healed over entirely, new skin pink and warm, the fingers severed neatly at the knuckle, with no blood or scar to be seen.

"Grass and leaves," he said, smiling.

The Witch winked.

And so, the Prince left her, having found a Quest after all. He chased its tail into the high mountains tipped with snow like wise men's beards, and down to the sea, laid before him smooth as a dress. He did not mind the difficulty of the terrain, being, after all, a soldier, though it was more tedious than he had thought a Quest would be.

For instance, he had not guessed how much of the body of a Quest was simply *walking*. He walked until three pairs of shoes were ruined, cursing his lack of a horse. He stomped over every imaginable landscape from dank fen to pleasant farm to alpine ice. And yet, no one greeted him in the villages through which he passed. No one shouted with great joy that the Prince had blessed their village with his presence—what an honor to have you, Sire!—no one insisted he feast at their table—only the best of the harvest for you, Sire!—no one begged to be regaled with a song of his adventures—oh, do tell us of the terrible Witch, Sire!

In fact, no one took much notice of him at all—innkeepers were surly, tavern-women taciturn and rather getting on in years, milkmaids were unfriendly, wide-calved, and attached firmly to the flanks of their cows. After a time he looked not very different from the lowest peasants—covered in grime, face sour as a priest on Tuesday, and entirely without well-made shoes. All in all, it was nothing like what he had been led to expect.

One evening as the sun was counting up the day's gold in the west, Leander ducked into a seaside tavern in the north part of the country with a peculiar sign above the door—a great fist strangling a fish. He laid a few coins on the bar and rested his burning feet against the damp floor. He sucked down a bitter, watered-down ale that tasted of leather and warm bile. It was a filthy place, with dozens of dark, cowled faces peering out from what seemed like far more than four corners. At least in this, he had found, the tales were accurate: Disreputable strangers abounded, as numerous as whitecaps on the sea.

The bartender was a great hulk of a man who looked as though some giant had simply dropped an armful of limbs into a heap. He brandished a thick rag like a sword, and the rusted iron of his eyes dared anyone to order a drink. His hair was the color of sandy shoals that trapped the hulls of ships; his hands were the size of well-wrought drums. He smelt of lamp oil and brine.

He glanced at Leander under his heavy eyelids and said nothing as the young Prince grimaced at his mug. He didn't mean to turn up his nose at the house brew, but the stuff was so foul his face contorted without consulting him. The bartender scowled and spat. But Leander had gotten quite tired of his brusque reception in these wretched little towns. He glared at the barkeep.

"Do you know who I am?"

The slab of skin behind the counter studied the wood grain of his bar. "Yes," he grunted, "but you'll not get a better ale on account of it." The Prince rolled his eyes.

"That is not why I asked, good sir. It is," he struggled for the right word, "fine as the water of the wells at my own house. But all I have met have been rough with me since I set out for the Dismal Marshes, and I have very little time to find what I seek. If only the townsfolk would be *kind* to me, would smile and bow and point out the way like the markers on the dusty road. But they will not. I guessed you knew me, yet you said nothing of it, nor offered yourself as helpmeet. Why?"

The man shrugged, and his body seemed to quake like the shifting of continents. "I know some things. Some things the common folk don't. They likely don't know you from the King's cows. And if they did—" The tavern-keeper's eyes glinted like the hull of a ship in morning light. "Your father is less than loved here. They'd like to take their taxes out of your hide, if they could manage it. They'd like to take back the babies that disappear into the tower of that sorcerer. Barring that, they'd like to kill you as payment for them. I'd not stop them, myself. Best if you don't make yourself known. You're *awfully* far from home. What does your name mean here besides a foreign tyrant? Not to mention, it isn't the habit of us *peasants* to be helping strange travelers. I'd rather have a dog with your pedigree, catch my meaning? And that's more words than I've said to a customer in a month, so take them well and get on your way."

The abashed Prince picked at his mug. He was becoming used to humility, to being shown that he was a fool. This alarmed him, of course, but this was hardly the place to show his courage and breeding.

"Will you tell me, at least, how to find the Dismal Marshes? I fear I have become quite lost. And," Leander gulped like a caught trout, "is it possible you know of a cobbler with a good pair of boots to sell?" The barman glanced over the ale-stained bar to peek at the princely toes poking out of the Prince's ruined shoes like worms out of a bait-sack. He grunted again.

"Once, when I was a young man, I went to the Marshes. I'll tell you the tale, if it'll clear you from my chairs."

The great-shouldered man straightened like a child reciting lessons, and when he spoke his tale, his voice became deep as the sounding of the sea on stone, and his words lost their slur. The Prince was transfixed, for by now he had become an excellent listener.

"My name is Eyvind. No reason for you to have heard it . . ."

The Tavern-Keeper's Tale

IN MY YOUNGER DAYS I WAS A BEAR.

This is nothing to gawk at. Bears are quite common in
my country, which lies as far to the North as the deserts lie
to the South. All my land was covered in snow, and peopled with a proud tribe of pale-furred bears, who governed it well and wisely. When we moved over the ice we
were like a wave that is gone before the foam touches the
shore.

I was one of the white bears, and I was very happy. I
loved a she-bear, and she was the finest of all our fishers.
She could dip a silky paw into the rushing glacier melt
and seize twenty salmon at once, holding them up like a

bouquet of wildflowers. Her eyes were large and dark and they danced like the lights that often painted the night sky. She was a novice astrologer, but she could already read the Stars as easily as letters. When she stood on her haunches she was taller, even, than I.

In the Land Where the Snow Does Not Melt, the hours of our days were simply filled, with fishing and hunting, with the rearing of cubs, with watching the Stars. My people were always very great astrologers, though rarely consulted by you folk. Once in a very great while a *Versammlung* was held—a Congress of the Bears.

And so a Versammlung was called the day I and several other young bears were to announce our chosen mates. Such things are dependent on the Star-motion, and the Congress must be consulted. Seal fat was laid out like a glistening carpet with great slabs of salmon, pinker than a cub's paw in the first hour of his life. Hundreds of white foxes had been killed in honor of the Star-gods, and I had made a cloak of their fur for the offering.

A Versammlung is something to see. The bears come across the glaciers like blocks of living ice, and their eyes flash brighter than a glimpse of seal flesh in the cold water. By the time they had all arrived, the Stars had already begun to shine in through the curtain of sky. I bowed before them. It always pays to be polite when one is asking for a favor. Besides, I was sure that they would approve my choice—she was after all the pride of the Land Where the Snow Does Not Melt.

"*The Stars whisper on their sky-floe,*" one bear began.

"*Bless them in their cloud-hunt,*" I answered. All these things are ritual—no one says a word that has not been spoken a thousand times before, a thousand thousand times, and even the first of those was a repetition of words that came before.

At this the rest settled in, ripping into the seal flesh with great relish.

After all had eaten and were rolling back on the snow, a great, woolly bear came forward. I knew him; he was called Gunde, quite the fiercest of us.

"The Stars whisper, brother. A great horror has occurred far away to the South. The red summer fire which is called the Harpoon-Star told me. One of his sisters—murdered. A Snake-Star, beautiful and green, and she is dead." The bears sent up a terrible howl of mourning, piercing as a bone-needle. I shivered.

"We weep for our sky-aunt; we mourn for the flesh that vanishes. It is a wicked omen. The shape of the Stars is confused—the signs of the Black Seal and the Caribou-Beset-by-Wolves are conjunct. The Great Paw is in retrograde. We have taken the augurs. You may not take a mate in this dark time, which must be a time of grief for all who still love the Stars. We are sorry, brothers."

I howled, long and low as a buried horn. How was it right that a death in the forest could deny me my heart on the ice? I dredged the frost with my claws.

"Perhaps in another year, when the Constellations have removed their veils of black and gray . . ." Gunde wanted only to comfort me, but I could hear the lie in his tender growls—the Stars never stop grieving. They had denied me my bride once and for all. Never would they be moved in their judgment. As we were taught long ago, the Stars cannot retrace their orbits.

"I care *nothing* for the death of the serpent-god." The Versammlung gasped at my blasphemy. No one but I in my rage would have dared to show a callused paw to their names. "If you will not grant me my mate, I will take her and we will travel to another sea, where the snakes and stars do not command."

A soft step sounded behind me, and I could smell her icy fur before I could see her, those clear black eyes looking down at me with pity.

"No," she whispered, and her voice was like the slide of a cub's belly on the ice. "Did you think I spent all my days looking down at the ice? I see the sky like any bear, and better than most. I saw that the sign of the Fox-That-Is-Hard-to-Catch dipped below the horizon out of season, and that the Moon darkened like whale's blood on the glacier. Then, when the Hunter's Knife rose in the South, I knew that the clouds were full of grief. It is not meant to be, Eyvind. And more—the Molted-Antler is in the Third House—you will have no mate, not now, and not ever. Not I nor any other. What is written you cannot un-write. Smile as best you can and hunt with me, fish with me, but do not ask me to your den. You can curse the Stars, but I will not."

"Beautiful beast, choice of my heart!" I wept openly in the sight of all my warriors, unable to believe that I would be denied something so obviously fated. "No," I suddenly cried, "I will not smile. I will travel to the forest of the South and avenge the death of the Star-sister, the serpent-god. I will right the wrong done to her sacred flesh and I will win the favor of the Harpoon-Star, He-Who-Pierces-the-Underfur-with-His-Light. He will give me my bride. I have fought a thousand battles against fierce tribes of wolves. So, too, will I win this battle and call her my victory."

My love just shook her great white head and padded heavily away across the snow.

I left the rest shuffling on the ice. I went immediately. I took nothing. I did not once look up at the Stars for guidance. I heard none of my brothers' protests, nor my bright-tailed bear's tears falling like first snow on the frozen earth. I thought then that I knew the right path, that it stretched out before me so sure, so sure and straight that I could not help but follow it. My paws would find it easily, since this must all have been written long before. Why else would the snake-god have died, except to be avenged by me?

As you can see, I was a very stupid bear.

I journeyed south from the glaciers no one of my kind had ever left. I ate salmon from the stream, I bandaged my paws when they bled from the incessant walking, I spoke to nothing, since there was nothing to speak to. In the deep nights I watched the Mother's-Milk glow white against the sky, winding through the Stars like an unspooled thread.

The world is wider than any one bear can fathom. It gobbles distance like a hungry cub. I could not, after a full cycle of the moon, understand why the land had not yet become the burning jungles of the Southern Kingdoms, why the sun did not glower red, why the Stars had not shifted into Constellations of which I had only heard legends: the Scorpion, the Lion, the Serpent. I still moved through a landscape of cold wind and mountains like broken teeth. At this rate my love would be a grandmother, gray in fur and tooth, before I could have her.

When the moon had become full for the third time since I set out, and rode the sky like a great whale, full-finned and gleaming, the earth did, abruptly, change. It became wet and full of green things; water ran freely here, in sluggish streams there, grass-colored and strung through with amber. I did not match the world anymore. My white fur stood out like a tear in the green hills. Tall reeds sprang up everywhere, thin and golden, and eels snapped their long bodies in the water. I could see great copses of tamarind trees with their red roots gnarling, cypresses bruising the sky with their branches, briars and brambles like a human woman's long hair.

Waterbirds dipped their beaks into the glistening creeks, their feathers shining like untrammeled snow.

All I had known was the pure and unbroken white of my home, the pale horizon going on and on forever. The Dismal Marshes were beyond my heart's experience. I could smell the thickness of the air, the dank smell of growing things twisting in the earth, the softness of rain and fruit on the trees. My fur rippled, both afraid and awakened.

As I stood with my paws gathering mud, one of the massive waterbirds broke off from the flock and leapt towards me, half walking on his thready legs, half flying. He was bright green, the color of the grasses around him; some of his feathers were such a rich shade of it they were nearly black. His eyes were flashes of sudden rainstorms. His beak curved earthward like a scimitar, and quite as sharp. He was so bright I had to squint, my eyes already weary of so much color. He was clothed in the colors of the sky after the Sun has fled, rimmed in light.

The bird stopped up short very near to me, flaring his great wings and stamping his feet. I could smell his flesh, like salt fish and rich soils.

"Well, I say," he began in a svelte voice, "this *is* an oddity. I shall have to call upon Beast at once! One does not keep such a thing to oneself; it is *quite* rude. Come then, don't stand there gawking like a hatchling! You may come to luncheon and discuss what, exactly, we are going to do with you."

Spluttering, I moved to catch up with him, splashing in silt and green water up to my knees, as he was already sprinting far ahead in his peculiar half-flight across the marshes.

"Wait!" I called, and my voice boomed out over the swamp, scattering cicadas and kingfishers in its wake.

"Waiting, waiting, lady-in, gentlemen-out, wait for water and meet the drought!" the great heron sang out over his emerald shoulder, and ran even faster. He was a blur of green and blue, and I could not keep up.

But as I stopped, panting, fur soaked in sweat, I saw a massive, gnarled hall of tamarinds which arched up to make a thatched roof of leaves, and the bird leaning against the doorpost.

"How *do* you hunt even the smallest mouse, Eyvind? Really!" And he ducked inside, leaving me to be stunned at the sound of my own name from this bizarre creature's mouth.

A little lunch service carved from cattails and willow roots sat on a small table in a room any gentleman would be proud to call his. The tamarinds had coiled around each other to make three chairs and an array of cabinets, tables, and twisting staircases that vanished into a filmy mist, which hung over the room like a well-apportioned ceiling. I could not believe that I would fit in the little hall, but it seemed to suit me exactly, and as I watched, the red-tinged branches shifted and sighed to make a long ridge on which I could rest.

"They are so considerate, my tammies," the Heron said fondly, as he dipped his beak into a small cup and slurped with relish. I sank onto the fragrant bed with a heavy sigh, my muscles burning like lamp oil. Only then did I notice that we were not alone.

A huge creature the color of dried blood stood calmly in a corner, drinking from a large bowl of oak leaves. The rear of the hall had swelled tall and wide to accommodate him. His red antlers tangled rather horribly around themselves, and as he slurped at his tea, I could see that his teeth were not teeth at all, but a bright ridge of solid bone.

"Beast! This is the one of whom our Brother spoke! Is it not thrilling that he has come *directly* to my Marsh?"

"Yes, Your Majesty," the scarlet beast replied in a musical voice. His eyes twinkled with laughter like the fall of leaves on the water. "We do so rarely get such . . . *august* guests."

"Majesty?" I asked, unsure of what impossible kingdom the Heron could rule.

"Of course. I am the Marsh King. This is Beast, who is a kind of courtier of mine, you might say. It is a sad state for a King to have but one courtier, but he is quite a good one."

"How kind of you, Eminence," the beast intoned, with the slightest flavor of gentle mockery in his voice.

"Think nothing of it, my good friend! Now, we must to business, for there is not much time."

I was so bewildered at this point I could say nothing at all. But I forced my tongue to work in the dry cavern of my mouth. "How can you know my name? Who is this Brother of which you speak? I do not understand you."

"Oh, no one expects you to, dear chap!" the Marsh King assured me in a tenderly condescending voice. Beast winked at me with one crimson eye. The Heron continued, "You keep your counsel and the gods keep theirs. My Brother is the Harpoon-Star, who came to visit us some months ago and announced your coming. Sit still and I shall tell you of his audience."

The Tale of the Harpoon and the Heron

Laakea the Harpoon-Star burned black the marsh grass as he came. The smell of it, scorched bread and copper filings, heralded him long before his light appeared over one of the hills. In great circles it scalded, crisped, sizzled. Each step sent up hisses of steam as he walked through the Great Marsh, frogs and eels yelping in wordless terror as the fire of his heels lapped at their oily bodies. I felt the song of the grass steaming before I could see him—it had been many years since my brother had left his hermitage where he hunted moons like quick pale stags.

You'll forgive the flowery talk, won't you? Our family

does so love to be told they are beautiful. Vanity is an old and venerable habit.

He was white, of course; his sort of Stars—the small and hot-burning ones—are always white. His hair fell like a newly washed sheet, long and flat to his waist, and his skin faded into the pale horizon, the shade of paper turned to ash. A great spear was slung over his shoulder by a strap of white serpent-hide; golden eyes panted beneath colorless lashes. He was barefoot; in fact, he wore no clothing but a bleached cloth over his angular hips, and his thighs were covered in arcane tattoos, the symbols of the Star-tongue. Yet even the ink of these markings was a strange silver that showed only when touched by the trailing marsh mist.

I embraced my brother awkwardly as he entered my hall, sending twigs into tiny conflagrations. I did not, of course, wish to burn my tammies, but the proper affection must always be shown to visiting family. I tried to make the usual pleasantries and invitations to drink, but he would not have it.

"I have news. It cannot wait. Will you for once allow me to speak my piece without interruption?"

I blushed with great dignity and abashed grace. Settling myself to listen, I gratefully mused that Beast was out engaging one of the Princes that come into our realm occasionally, and so there would be nothing to disturb Laakea in his tale. He was not overfond of Beast—Stars care only for their kin. At any rate, they are dreadfully formal creatures, and Beast would be bored.

Removing his spear from his shoulders he sighed heavily, and his voice echoed through the trees like clouds across the face of the moon. "A terrible thing has occurred—a man has killed our sister, the Snake-Star of the South." He waited for my reaction, but the black Ibis-Emir had already winged north to tell me of her death, to weep his great sapphire tears into my hands. Seeing that I was not surprised, Laakea pressed on.

"I did not realize she had tarried so long in that damned kingdom, that blighted land of festering winds and towers that bruise the sky with iron fingertips . . ."

THE STAR'S TALE

I CONFESS THAT I WAS MUCH CONSUMED WITH MY hunt, for I pursued a great rarity—a Firebird, as a wedding present for my poor, wretched sister—and I tracked him over many a hill and river-carved valley. You know how we can be about things which sparkle and shine. We imagine they will put back something of what has been lost.

Firebirds are overfond of red fruits, and I had hoped to lure him with crimson seeds gathered from the Ixora, the Torch-Trees of the desert—very difficult to harvest, but the Firebird's favorite delicacy, bright and soft as a cherry, with a pit cased in flint and iron, to light the new tree aflame. Some Firebirds, it is said, even nest among the trees, and return there to lay their eggs in the ash like salmon swimming upriver.

I waited in the salt flats that border the Tinderbox Desert, and the Ixora that fire the night to keep the sky warm for the sun when it has gone below the earth. In the twilight I could see their orange branches flickering, snapping, sparking up like the camp of a thousand soldiers. I saw no Firebirds, but I was not concerned. They are secretive, and the forest of Torch-Trees is wide. I spent weeks searching out the guttering, dying ones, and collecting the juice-filled rubies as they dropped. I combed the ash of those already dead, but found no flaming eggs.

Finally, I had strewn the salt with cherry seeds—they were bright as drops of blood; surely the Firebird would swoop down to snatch them up in his bronze beak.

I waited for three nights, and the Firebird did not come. But on the third night I forgot him entirely. An appalling phantasm caught me on the flats and all thought of my quarry vanished.

Three of our sister's handmaidens—you know them, of course; sweet little serpent-girls they are, their hair all flowered with jade grass-snakes and emerald vipers—stumbled through the sand, clutching each other for the strength to stand. Their holy vestments were torn as if by a great claw, hanging from their thin bodies like curls of new paper. I turned my head aside to give them modesty, for they were as near to naked as makes no difference, and their pale leaf-light skin was desert-scalded to scarlet. They moaned and screamed in such pitiful tones—a choir of anguish echoing in the desert canyons. I took this at first for simple cries of pain, but it was a lament, a lament and a requiem. They clutched me by my face and turned me towards them, forced me to witness their shame.

Brother, they were so horrible to see I can hardly tell you of their faces—their wounds were a tapestry of broken flesh. And yet even this had not sated the men who dared lay hands on their sacred bodies, but their tongues had been cut out by rough knives, and only ragged stumps remained to form words. One took a strange object from her sister and pressed it miserably into her parched mouth.

"Ssspear-brother," she hissed, "our mistresssss is ssslain, dead, dead and gone. Thisss is what the men who took her did to ussss. They were pig-demonsss, they mauled our bodiesss with cloven hoovesss. We have walked all this way from her grave to find some part of her family. Pray put usss to death so we may not sssuffer longer than it was necesssssary to deliver our messsssage."

I looked on, nauseated, as the second of our sister's maidens took the object from her sister's mouth and pushed it into her own. "We have traveled far to find one of our kin to take the burden of knowledge from usss. We are not sssuicidesss; you have to help ussss. But in return we will help you. We are sssseerss, we know what isss to come, we sssee the flux of time like water poured from one cup to another. You musssst go now, to the North, and prevent vengeance from falling into the handsss of one who would pervert what our missstresss has already done in her own name, one who would erase her holy work only to ssscribble over it with his own. Ssshe has died; ssshe has risssen—in his bumbling he will rob her of those things, all a ssshade can own." She took the lump of pink flesh from her mouth and gave it to the last of the sisters.

"Holy seers, what is this misshapen thing you pass from mouth to mouth?" I asked with trepidation—such terrible magic was at work here I hardly dared speak. The Stars leave divination to those tied to the earth; we do not dabble in the future. Why would my sister have broken with tradition so?

"We ssstole it from the Basssilissk," whispered the third oracle pitifully, "it isss a tongue, ssso that we may ssspeak to grant you thisss warning. Were we to hunt down *three* monssssssterss? We are sssiblingss; we ssshare among usss."

The third sister was clearly the eldest, and the bearer of the clearest vision. She closed the one eye that remained to her and spoke without inflection the prophecy they had journeyed so far to disclose.

"You must sssee the Marsssh King. A creature of sssnow and claw will come to him, begging to avenge our missstress in order to incur your favor. He musssst not be allowed to purssssue thisss. Sssnakes sssee to their own; ssshe doesss not require thisss *animal*'sss asssssistance. If he should stand in her place, her death will be wassssted—his path musst divert from herss in our sssight. He will only cause her death to be wasssssted. Her coilsss are still in motion, and the Quessst of the creature will bring ruin on her plansss. Do you undersssstand, Sssspear-Brother?"

I nodded my assent in the traditional manner, pressing my forehead to hers and accepting their burden. With this, the three of them in one movement collapsed onto the soundless sand, their fall as silent as snakeskin on the dunes. They were quite faint, hunger and sun and burning forests having leached all but the last of their light from them. The Basilisk's tongue rolled out of the third sister's mouth and onto the hot gold of the earth. Their eyes rolled up in their heads, and their mouths formed pleas I could not hear, but understood well enough.

But I could not do what they asked—even a bird must know that.

Death is the wall we dare not look behind, and no Star has ever killed another. I would not be the first murderer of my kind.

Instead, I gathered up the blood-drop cherries from the sand. What good could they be now? My sister could not marvel at the color and the light of the Firebird. One by one, I carried woman and fruit into the Tinderbox true, and laid them out beneath the Torch-Trees. In their blazing light, the maidens seemed to glow as they must have when my sister took them in.

I cut deep into the Torch-Trees' ashen trunks with my harpoon. The bark is quite black and hard, calcified into iron by the constant fire. But within, within there is nothing but ash and a thin vein of boiling sap, as the trees consume themselves from the inside out. Only when they have burnt themselves to nothing will they drop a seed, the precious seed, and the clever gardener will catch it as it falls, while the tree crumbles into white ash and nothing more, so that the seed will not burst and flare the moment it cracks on the hard desert stones.

Of course, I had a sack bulging with the volatile little things, and no need of waiting till the Ixora died. Carefully, I peeled them and conserved the wet, sweet fruit, piling the flint-pits carefully as an apology to the tall tree, so that when it died for true a veritable jungle would grow in its place. With equal care I broke the sap-vein deep in the ash and dribbled the waxy, scalding stuff onto the mashed red cherry-flesh.

All this I smeared into the mouths of the three oracles, and then—forgive my arrogance, Brother Heron!—I cut into my own arm and let the pale light of my body flow into the searing medicine, into their mouths. We know of no greater sacrament, and I knew of no other thing I could do for them.

It was hours before they could sit up, and I was well healed by then. They did not thank me, still black in their misery, but the snakes of their hair hissed sweet and comforting in my direction. Wading in their sorrow like drunkards, they moved off into the desert, past the trees, swaying from side to side, clutching each other.

As they passed my cairn of seeds, the youngest of them kicked it over, and they vanished in the flash of spark and thick smoke.

The Tale of the Harpoon and the Heron, Continued

He had finished his tale.

"Oh!" I interrupted, "the poor Basilisk! Has he no tongue at all now? What a wretched fate! He sang so beautifully last Equinox when I visited his caves!" Laakea glared sternly at me, making it quite clear that the happenstance of my friend the Basilisk was of no concern to him.

"So you understand, Bird-Brother. When the creature comes, you must stop him."

"How to stop a creature on a Quest? What do you expect me to do? Spoil the hospitality of my hall?"

Laakea snorted. "I do not care. Kill him. Lock him

away in a tree trunk. I trust in your wisdom. But I must bid you farewell. Much have I neglected in my journey to your marsh—I must attend to the funeral rites of our sister."

"It is not the place of any of us to interfere in the Quests of men. They insist on them—they are as fond of Quests as of their own hearts."

"Who is to say it will be a man?" Laakea answered, bored as a babe.

With this the white-clad Star left my hall, scorching the grass once more as he walked southward, sending up veils of mist that dissipated like a memory when he had gone and not even his footfalls could be heard.

The Tavern-Keeper's Tale, Continued

"SO YOU SEE, MY DEAR LAD, THE DILEMMA." THE
Marsh King crossed his reedlike legs in a curiously fey gesture. "In no way can I allow you to do what you intend. It
is not *personal*, of course. It is best in the end to let women
see to their own vengeance. Those who meddle are seldom
thanked—take my dear Harpoon's story as exemplum!
Now. I don't suppose I can convince you to scurry on
home and be a good bear from now on?"

I shifted on my paws and murdered my tears where
they stood. "I cannot simply give up! I will go on, whether
or not you tell me the truth. If she can contrive her own
revenge from the grave, perhaps she can grant me the

small thing I ask. Why would the gods conspire to rob me of a mate? Is it such a terrible thing to mate?"

"It is, in fact, quite insignificant," the Marsh King said gently. "The gods, if you insist on calling them such, do not conspire, but events themselves order the world like a pack of cards, and there is little you or I can do to change the cut of the deck. We must learn to accept personal loss gracefully. Duty is a *noble* word, after all."

I stamped in frustration and the branches of the hall shook wildly. "There must be a way! I have begun a Quest! Quests do not simply *end*. You win or you lose; it is not just suddenly *over*."

"I believe that you have, so to speak, put your finger on it. I see that it is not possible for you to accept that, this time, you simply lose. It is because a Quest is not a natural thing for your kind—nor mine, for that matter. A Quest is a thing for men. It is their invention, their monstrous pet, their addiction. They own all the rights in perpetuity. Every step you take, my dear Eyvind, you are robbing men of their most dearly bought treasure. It is sad for them, that they have only the machinery of Questing to sustain them. But they are a sad race. We must weep for them, but not too much. And we certainly must not take on their ridiculous penchant for self-destructive behavior. Therefore, I have devised a way to prevent you from reaching the land of my late sister and yet preserve a small chance for you to achieve the end you desire. I shall make you into the very model of a Quest—I shall make you a man."

My mouth gaped. Horror shuddered through my fur and sweat dampened my great white jowls. "A man? Why must you punish me so?"

"It is not a punishment, you sorry beast," the Marsh King scoffed. "You took on a Quest, which is a thing only men—and exceedingly stupid men, usually—do. So you must become a man if you wish to continue on that doomed path. It is all really very simple and nicely symmetrical, if you think about it. And a man is not *such* a hideous shape to find oneself in."

"But if I am a man, the Snake-Star will not listen to me; Stars run from men, they hide away from their sweat and their stink. I can never see my beloved again! She would run from me herself, she would think me a hunter. I could not bear to see her run from me, and—"

"Oh, calm yourself. I did not say it would be permanent. You know, you might consider that a mate is not *strictly* necessary to survival. Look at Beast and me! We live together quite happily in blissful bachelorhood and we are not at all bothered by the lack of great, galumphing girl-bears about the house."

At this, Beast looked up from quietly playing a game of bark-piece backgammon against himself. "Mmm? Oh, yes, quite happily. Except for the flies, you know. His Majesty does tend to diet on a rather eclectic selection—quite nauseating to watch." He settled back into the game, which he was earnestly but decidedly losing.

"Well," the Marsh King pursed his beak politely, "at any rate, your manliness need only last for a relatively brief period. I have already discussed this in detail with some of the lower Stars—white dwarfs and the like. I shall bundle you up tight as a mitten in a human skin until," and here he cleared his long blue throat dramatically, "the Virgin is devoured, the sea turns to gold, and the saints migrate west on the wings of henless eggs."

"In the Stars' name, what does *that* mean?" I gasped.

"I haven't the faintest idea! Isn't it marvelous? Oracles always have the best poetry! I only repeated what I was told—it is rather rude of you to expect magic, prophecy, *and* interpretation. That's asking quite a lot, even from a King." He appeared quite flustered, feathers blushing up into an indignant violet. "Just, well, keep a lookout for that sort of thing, don't you know. Sea turning to gold. Hard to miss, I'd say. Rather. Lucky to have such obvious signs. I should think you would be grateful. Now hold still, and let us get on with our business."

"Wait! I haven't agreed to anyth—" I meant to protest further, but I found my tongue no longer worked entirely well; it was short and stumpy and stuck to the roof of my mouth. Horrified, I glanced down at my mighty and beautiful paws only to find wretched, pasty feet covered with a scraggly down, stuck ridiculously at the bottom of skinny legs. With one touch of his wing, the Marsh King had made me hideously, but certainly, a man.

Yet the sovereign had changed as well. He was no longer a tall and regal bird with a respectably threatening wingspan, but a bent old man with a long beard that flashed all the colors of the swamp—green and brown and a brackish gray. He appeared somewhat fishlike, with sallow, damp skin and a wide, pale mouth.

"What is this?" I mumbled as best I could with my worthless tongue.

"Eh? What? Of course, I *am* sorry, I should have explained. When you were an animal, I appeared as a suitably noble animal. As you are now a man, I appear to you as a grandfatherly old type meant to inspire the proper respect from your new breed of creature. It is a courtesy I extend. Think nothing of it."

"But Beast?" I inquired helplessly, for the scarlet-hoofed creature was quite the same as before.

"Beast is just Beast. He is always Beast," came the monarch's bored but affectionate reply.

Hearing his name, the courtier's crimson head bobbed pertly. "Just Beast," he assured me.

The Marsh King raised himself up and ushered me out the door with the air of a host who has just realized he is one guest away from a comfortable nap.

"Off you go then, Eyvind, my boy—and ho! now you really *are* a boy! Splendid. We shall see you again, I have no doubt. Run along! Fare thee well and all that rot!"

The Tale of the Prince and the Goose, Continued

Eyvind's body relaxed. He heaved his great mass onto a stool and sighed. "And I've been a man ever since. I got old and got fat until I looked something like a bear again, what with the gut and the hair. It doesn't do any good. I'm not a bear. I try, but I'm not. I'm still waiting for the sea to turn. It never does. I stay close to the Marshes, hoping that it's true that Kings don't lie. I don't have much hope; after all, your father is a King. The Marshes aren't more than a week's journey north of here. The days, they have their way with me now. Maybe I'll just die serving beer to brats in this filthy tavern."

The Prince stared at the surface of the bar, the loops and whorls of the wood like a fingerprint. "I am sorry for you," he mumbled.

Eyvind's face purpled. "I don't need your pity, boy. That's a useless load. I'll give you a pair of walking boots with no promise they'll fit if you carry a message—you ask that no-good bird when I'll be getting my own back. I'm sick of waiting."

"The . . . the Marsh King, you mean?"

"Stars, boy, you're thick as a cub still sucking at its dam. Yes, the Marsh King. A week's walk north and you'll be knee-deep in mud and eels. Now take these and be off before I charge you rent for that stool you're ruining." He tossed a muddied pair of greasy black boots several sizes too big for the young Prince onto the bar and disappeared with a final grunt into the back room.

Leander took the boots gingerly and slipped out of the tavern, his face burning under the stare of the bedraggled patrons.

He set out north as Eyvind had said, and indeed, at length he came to the Dismal Marshes, their borders a clear and sodden green, full of the stink of rotting grass and bone. He easily picked up the scent of the Leucrotta itself, which was indeed very like blood, coppery and sharp. The Marshes were wide and smoke-colored, jade over polished wood, the sluicing paths of swamplands with their rattling cattails and poised egrets. The water shimmered like necklaces laid over one another, and beneath the water he could see fat eels and the flash of fish.

In fact, the Prince found the Marshes very beautiful, but every step sucked at his oversized shoes until the going was so slow that he thought he might very well be stuck there, save that he knew he must return to the Witch by the new moon in order to fulfill his promise. And so he dragged himself through the swamps, mud sloshing around his boots and catching the sheath of his sword in its wet pockets. At each up-step the mammoth boots threatened to catch, but slapped up against his heels at the last second.

In the center of the Marsh there was a copse of tamarind trees, their reddish bark glinting as though embers burned within. He wondered at it for a moment, drawn to their color. But Leander had had enough of magic, and he quite feared to be further delayed by whatever terror dwelt inside. He gave it a wide berth, though it meant wetting his breeches to the waist.

Just as he passed the copse, a shape composed itself seemingly out of the water and grasses, blocking his way.

"Do you insult me by passing through my land without paying me a visit?"

The shape coalesced into an old man whose beard drooped like the whiskers of catfish and whose hair was a great mass of tumbling moss. His eyes were precisely the shade of marsh water, sparkling green and brown in turns. His hands were wrapped in river reeds and his cloak was sewn together from fallen leaves and acorn mash.

He stood calmly, three feet over the nearest cluster of grasses, fine webbed feet resting on air, bemusedly smoking a pipe fashioned from willow whips.

"Well?" he demanded.

The Prince did not splutter, nor grasp for words like a dying trout gulping for water that will not come. He blinked slowly, once, twice, and sat down heavily on a moss-covered boulder.

The specter laughed heartily. "Poor little hatchling. It all gets to be a little bewildering after a while, I'll admit. I am the Marsh King," he gave a courtly little bow, "and you will have come from the Witch of the Glen to kill my friend Beast. Now, of course, I can't let you do that, but I am happy to pass the time discussing it with you, if you would like to have a Discourse on the subject."

"A Discourse? On whether or not I am going to kill the Leucrotta?" Leander replied, nonplussed. The Marsh King's shaggy head bobbed merrily.

"Oh, he doesn't stand on formalities—prefers 'Beast.' "

"Whether or not I am going to kill the Beast, then?"

"Oh, I'm afraid you still haven't got it, my lad. Just 'Beast.' He thinks the 'the' makes it seem as though he puts on airs. Fine chap, Beast is."

"Beast, then."

"Beast."

"And whether I ought to kill him."

"A Discourse is such a fine thing." The Marsh King sighed dreamily. "I recall I had a fine one once, oh, fifty years or so ago. Some other upstanding, earnest hatchling harassing Beast . . . they do come along at a clip these days. Let's have one, shall we?"

The Marsh King's eyes flashed like a glimpse of eel flesh in the shallow water, gleeful and fey.

The Discourse
of the
Marsh King

WHEN THE LAST YOUNG MAN CAME ROUND, HE
was very rude about it, all manner of officious in his gold
tassels and scarlet cape. He didn't visit me either, but
when I appeared, he was amiable enough. Set his cape
down on that rock and crossed his legs, as ready to
Discourse with me as to lop off poor Beast's head.

"Now"—I began at the simplest point, as you'll see—
"why do you want to kill Beast? He's not borrowed your
sword and forgotten to return it, he's not spoiled your favorite sedan chair, he's not bothered you at all!"

"I am a Prince," he replied, being rather dense. "It is the
function of a Prince—value A—to kill monsters—value

B—for the purpose of establishing order—value C—and maintaining a steady supply of maidens—value D. If one inserts the derivative of value A (Prince) into the equation y equals BC plus CD squared, and sets it equal to zero, giving the apex of the parabola, namely, the point of intersection between A (Prince) and B (Monster), one determines value E—a stable kingdom. It is all very complicated, and if you have a chart handy I can graph it for you."

"Ah, my lad," I said, after he had quite spoiled one of my topographical charts with scribbling equations, "but Beast is not a monster. He does not gobble up maidens like cucumber sandwiches. He keeps to himself like any civilized Beast."

"But he is quite ugly?" the Prince insisted.

"I think he is a fine fellow, but some might consider him homely, yes."

"And he smells foul?"

"Well, I cannot argue with you there—one ought not to stand down-wind!"

"And he does have a terrible jaw of bone, and great tall horns?"

"Yes, yes, you've got Beast, all right!"

"Then he is a monster!" the Prince crowed, "and I must slay him at once. The Formula works!"

"Your Formula must result in a great deal of fighting," I mused.

"Oh, yes, when applied correctly mighty and noble battles result! Of course I always win—the value of Prince X is a constant. It cannot be lesser than that of Monster Y—this is the Moral Superiority Hypothesis made famous five hundred years ago by my ancestor Ethelred, the Mathematician-King. We have never seen his equal, in all these centuries."

"Of that I have *no* doubt."

"If that is all, I believe I must be about my Proof," said the Prince, bran-dishing his sword experimentally. "That is what we call a slaying," he ex-plained, giving the blade a great swing over his head. "For each time a monster is killed, the Hypothesis is Proven."

"How jolly of you to give it such a . . . *civilized* name. But I cannot allow it."

"But . . . but . . ." he spluttered, indignant, "the Formula!"

"Nevertheless. This is my kingdom and no violence may come to any-one within my borders so long as I can help it. That, at least, you should understand. Here, my word is law."

"Oh, yes." He nodded. "The Universal Monarchic Algorithm is most central to the Theorem."

"Theorem?"

"Of Proper Conduct."

"Ah."

"I did my thesis on the Monarchic Algorithm," the young man huffed defensively. "If you will not allow violence within your borders—a moment, while I make some calculations"—he scribbled on my beautiful charts again—"I shall call him out—if he is a proper monster he will not refuse a challenge from a nobleman."

I sighed, giving in to the inevitable. "No, that he will not."

"Very well, then!" The Prince marched off humming a mnemonic tune as he went.

The Tale of the Prince and the Goose, Continued

"WELL, MY FINE BOY, LET ME TELL YOU! THAT BOY tried to drop down from the crags onto Beast at the dueling ground—most unsporting—and got his limbs all tangled in poor Beast's antlers. It took us weeks to remove them—and such unsavory work it was. Perhaps you will show more sense. Now then," the Marsh King said, peering at him over abalone spectacles, "do you know any Formulae or Theorems?"

The Prince shook his head.

"Thank the wide-brimmed hat of heaven for *that*. Perhaps that style of government has gone out of fashion.

Yet I fear you will still insist on disturbing Beast at this uncivilized hour."

"I must."

"And why? We have already established through the recitation of a *most* agreeable secondary Discourse that Beast is not a monster." The Marsh King wrinkled his greenish nose in a puzzled way.

"I know." Leander sighed. "But it cannot be avoided. And I have a question to ask of you before I reveal my purpose."

"For *me*?" The Marsh King brightened considerably, his whiskers rising with pleasure. "Almost all the young men come for Beast! I have not had a visitor in ever so long. What is it, my fine, attractive, *excellent* young man?"

"Eyvind wants to know how much longer he must wait for the sea to turn to gold."

The Marsh King furrowed his great brow and peered at the sky. "I can't say that I know a chap by that name," he admitted sadly.

"He . . . he used to be a bear. You made him a man?" The Prince was suddenly embarrassed. The story had sounded convincing as a stone plaque when the tavern-keeper told it. Yet the elderly monarch still *humph*ed and *hohum*ed to himself. At length his face lit up like a festival lantern.

"*Oh!*" he cried. "The astrologer-bear! Of course! Well, you know, not too much longer, I imagine. Perhaps before you get home to your Witch-woman. Perhaps not. I don't exactly keep an *almanac* of such things, you know. And why should I? I am quite the master of my own shape. And now that that is answered, what in the world could you want with my dear friend Beast?"

"I . . . I need his skin. To restore a maiden to life. It was I who killed her, so I owe her the remedy."

"Oh," said the King distastefully, "how vile of you. What a disgusting operation you propose. Absolutely out of the question."

"Now," a deep voice like bellows squeezed by mammoth hands sounded across the Marsh, "my dear friend, you ought not to speak for me when I am not present. It is quite rude."

Across the long swamps came the dark scarlet form of the Leucrotta, antlers blood-bright against the sky. The smell of him filled the saddlebags of the wind—the smell of still pools of blood glittering under the sun, in well buckets and wine casks, china vases and reed baskets, the hot, coppery smell of its wetness, slowly spreading.

But his hide was strangely beautiful, the color of dark, secret rubies and garnets scattered on the snow. And his antlers towered like turrets armed with strong-armed bowmen, forking like a blazing forest. His great jaw hung slightly open, revealing the shock of white bone. On powerful haunches he moved towards the Prince, eyes all pupils, sparking like flint within the endless black.

"Certainly, my dear Monarch, I can take care of my own affairs?" he intoned.

"Of *course*, Beast, I meant no offense. Dispatch him at your leisure."

"Oh, none *taken*, old boy. And I wouldn't *dream* of trampling all over your jurisdiction. After *you*," Beast yielded.

"Oh, no, after *you*." The Marsh King bowed at the waist.

"I insist."

"I won't hear of it."

The Leucrotta looked appraisingly at Leander for a long while. "My skin, you say? I had not heard that it had any *medicinal* value, but if the Witch needs it, I must, as a gentleman and a monster, yield to her." Both the Prince and the King started, shocked at the suggestion.

"But we must have a battle!" insisted the Prince.

"Don't be ridiculous, boy. I would eviscerate you within a minute. Just take the skin and scurry back."

The Marsh King spluttered in consternation. "My *dear boy*! I must protest! The mess it will make in my swamp! And a skin is not a pocket-watch—you cannot simply *hand it over*!" He stamped his mossy foot—which of course made no sound as he remained floating just above the water.

The Leucrotta shrugged. "I expect I shall grow another within the month."

And with that he bent his great crimson head to his chest and tore his hide from his body like a child peels a ripe apple, all in one long, spiraling stroke.

"You know," he said thoughtfully, as the pile of skin beside him grew, "when the Witch was young we were quite social. How can I refuse that delightful creature? She was beautiful in her day, I must tell you—the scars and tattoos, the way her face was mangled was most divine. The deformity of her features was as lovely to me as summer's first fruit, hanging red and perfect on a dew-bright branch." Beast sighed dreamily. "Such, well, what you would call 'ugliness' is so rare, one finds so little of it expressed as it was in her." He looked pointedly at the Marsh King, who was, if elderly, still handsome in a stately sort of way. "The way her tattoos reflected her scars, in a marvelous symmetry of black ink and punctured white skin—

were I but a troubadour I would have composed *such* songs to her beauty. And the way her hair flashed! Like my own skin burning in the sun!"

Beast was paring the last of his skin from his hooves, the pile beside him enormous and deep scarlet, like leather in the shop of a master tanner. Beast himself sat quite comfortably, even redder than before, his muscles shining with pinpricks and rivulets of blood oozing out of him, dribbling like paint onto the swamp grass. The wind pulled at his exposed flesh, but he seemed to enjoy its ghostly fingers on his great haunches.

"Fear not, my little faun," he assured the Prince, "it is not at all painful. Rather brisk, in fact. I would suggest that the two of you try it, as a fortifying tonic, save that your anatomy is . . . unequipped, shall we say."

The Prince looked on, horrified, at the hulk of the Leucrotta, sitting happily before him and bleeding freely from his massive musculature. He began to gather up the skin into his pack.

"Will you not stay to hear of how I knew the Witch?" cried Beast, hurt filling his voice like a winesack. "After I have done *exactly* as you asked? Didn't your mother teach you to be kind to monsters who completely fail to gobble you up?" Leander's face colored abruptly and an awkward silence descended, a woolen shadow settling over the trio.

"Perhaps not," conceded Beast, "but sit beside me and listen, and all will be well, you'll see."

The sun was still high in the wind-wracked clouds, with time enough before the hours became his enemy. In order not to be turned into anything untoward by the Marsh King, the Prince sighed his acquiescence.

THE LEUCROTTA'S TALE

SHE RESCUED ME, THE LITTLE MINX. I WAS BATtling, as luck seems to frequently have it, a Duke's Son of the Eastern Duchies, the sort with ornate armor of silver and ivory. Terrifically impractical, of course, but they always were dandies, the Duke's boys. I had already gored him through the left side with my antler, but had unfortunately missed all the vital organs, and the ferocity of his blows became as great as twelve wolves who share a mother. He was desperate, the poor thing. But in his desperation he managed to slide his blade just under my ribs, nearly to the hilt.

The highborn scoundrel ought to have done his

research. My heart is not near my ribs, as with humans—it would scarcely fit!—but deep in my belly, and his thirsty blade had not come close. Nevertheless I found myself in great extremity, stuck with his grotesquery of a sword and him ready to hack off my head.

But in the moment of his triumph, which must have been so sweet in his young mouth, an arrow shot from the trees with the speed of a heron which has sighted a fish, and buried itself in his shoulder, the force of it flinging him from my writhing body. A radiant thing leapt from the oaks, clad in mangy, marvelously lice-ridden furs, her hair a violent briar. Her thighs were strong and smooth enough, I suppose, but her face was beautifully destroyed, hacked to pieces by some master artist, and painted over with thick black marks. Her smell would have killed a herd of antelope, had they happened by—rancid sweat and stringy meat and starvation, metallic and sharp. I inhaled her delicious perfume like the steam from cooling cakes.

The fabulous apparition sprang onto the offensive Duke's Son, pinning him to the mossy earth. She landed astride him, panting harshly while she sniffed at his armor like an animal. I imagined the stink of her breath longingly—I was sure it would have that peculiar combination of rotted spinach and boiled egg underlaid with maggoty wood that I so often dreamed of.

"What are you doing?" she rasped, baring her teeth. "No animal is killed in my wood. It is my law—all men of this kingdom know it."

I was surprised to hear her speak so well—perhaps I had hoped for too much in imagining yellow teeth and a language of grunts and hisses. Nevertheless it gave me enormous pleasure to see the Prince squirm in fear like an infant pig.

"I—I apologize! I'm sorry! I didn't know—I . . . I am not from this country!" he protested to no avail, as she ground her body further into his, causing his pretty armor to pierce his skin. He howled in a most satisfactory way.

"Ignorant," she whispered, pain lacing her voice like a dress, "an animal has a *soul*. It might even, on the inside, be something quite other than a monster. Who are you to kill it before you even know what it is?"

"No one! No one! I'm no one!" He began to cry in earnest, now, huge tears dribbling out of his feeble face. Strange, he felt no fear of me, but beneath this human woman he was weak, and blubbering so loudly as to shame even a plain piglet.

She rolled her eyes. "Even nobodies shall not be killed here. But swear to me that you will give up Questing and devote your life to the Princess you no doubt have left at home with nothing to do."

"I swear, I swear!" And at this concession the woman stood up, leaving the Duke's Son inconsolably weeping, the grass beginning to wet his tunic.

"Oh, mightn't you kill him a *little*?" I suggested with my best and most courteous voice. Her eyes turned towards me, caves the depths of which could not be sounded.

"It is my law," she answered tonelessly. "I do not know you. Why are you in my forest?"

"What, precisely, makes it your forest? Have you a Deed?"

"No. I have simply claimed it. Men have learned better than to question that."

I wriggled with excitement at the gravelly abrasion of her voice. "I am not a man, as you can see. I am Beast, *Leucrotta Furialis* by species. I was called out by this whelp here. I thank you for your help; it was most kind."

"No more than I would have given any animal in need." She slung her bow, a fine ash one she had obviously hewn herself from some lucky sapling, over her shoulder. "I am the Witch of the Glen. All things that breathe within my wood are under my protection. Don't take it as a personal favor. If you both understand me, I'll leave you."

"Wait!" I trotted closer to her, so as to give her full view of my color and height. "I must repay your brave deed. I shall perform any task for you, fair, *fair* lady."

Ignoring the wails of the Duke's Son, who had not risen, but sat swatting miserably at the arrow in his shoulder, she looked appraisingly at me, raising one shaggy eyebrow.

"Would you kill a King for me?" she asked quietly.

"Certainly, my lamb." I bowed slightly, extending my forelegs. "But I am not precisely *inconspicuous,* so as to enter a Castle unnoticed, nor equipped with weapons so as to do much damage other than to, well, eat him, which I surmise would be less than satisfactory for you, as it results in the shocking lack of a body. I think *I* am perhaps not the monster for that task." I looked meaningfully at the wretched Prince, who by now had seen his own blood, and appeared to be about to faint.

A smile curled across her face like a rapier whipping against the side of an opponent. It was wonderfully hideous.

"Well, boy, what do you think? Would you like to kill a King in exchange for my sparing your life?"

"Oh, yes," he sobbed feebly, "if it would please you, only don't shoot any

more of your arrows into me! I have a *horror* of sharp things! I only
Quested at all because my father called me a coward and sent me off after
the famous Leucrotta! He wants the skin, you see. For assassinating."

I agreed heartily. "It is possible, my sweet peach, to make a great many
vile things with and from my skin. I hear it fetches high prices on the black
market in all the best sorts of places."

"But you will do this for me?" She would not veer from her course. "You
will go to the Palace and put a knife in the King?"

"Yes! Yes!" The Duke's Son had staggered to one knee, to make the traditional gesture of fealty to the Witch. "Only, which one?"

"The *King*, boy. Who else? In the Palace."

She was impatient, of course. For witches, there is but one King and
one Palace—the one who has wronged them, and the house in which he
lives.

In fairness, Kings are often quite as dense, calling themselves sacred vessels and masters of all things above and below when in fact they command
a few patches of lonely dirt with even lonelier houses sitting upon them.

"You will know it," I added helpfully, "for it is bordered by the two
rivers, one white and one black."

"Yes, yes, mistress, I shall go and accomplish your task. Only—I was not
only sent to kill the Leucrotta. There is a maiden in a tower—" At this the
Witch spat, again rolling her marvelous eyes.

"Those revolting creatures are always getting themselves locked up.
If only they would stay that way," she growled. The Duke's Son blushed
deeply as a girl caught naked.

"Nevertheless, she has been imprisoned by a terrible Wizard of these
parts, and I am charged to rescue her—if I complete your Quest, who will
complete mine?"

With an exasperated snort, the Witch bent, removed the shaft, and
dressed his wound without response. Seeing her work well done, she finally spoke, her voice thorny with delicious irritation.

"I loathe this habit of Quest after Quest. It is useless and shabby as a
secondhand crown. But I would do many things I loathe if it earned the
death of the King, and perhaps more for the Wizard of whom you speak. I
will take on your Quest myself and release the brat from her shack."

She murmured something to the horse and fed it a bit of apple she had
hidden in her pack.

"Go," she ordered the lad, "and kill *nothing* but the King. Return to the
Glen when your murder is complete."

The Duke's Son scampered off. I heard much later that he caused a great scandal by killing some poor, inoffensive monarch in quite another part of the world.

But I was left with an unpaid debt, a pauper before a jeweled queen.

"But as for my part," I purred, "I am still your own Beast, to do with as you like."

She considered for a moment. "Is your skin really a tool of assassination?"

"Undoubtedly, my little lemon tart. It is quite a unique appendage—I grow new ones each month like a fruit tree. Cut into strips and combined with certain ointments of belladonna and hyssop, it can cause paralysis in men born under the sign of the goat. Soaked in an infusion of yarrow and fennel with a dash of Manticore blood, it will cause a woman who has conceived under a new moon to miscarry, or the resulting child's heart to stop in its sleep at the age of seven. Yet that same child, wrapped in a blanket of the skin, will revive, so long as it forever after keeps the skin against its own. This is a particularly good trick, as the child will drop dead should it lose the skin, even if he or she should live to one hundred and seven by its grace. Ground into a powder with a handful of ants from a common hill and a measure of pickled salamander liver, it will cause a man overfond of public speech to swallow his own tongue at a banquet in his honor—there are many applications, each peculiar to the man or woman it is meant to harm. It is utterly devoid of noble uses, I am told. But I have not researched the matter properly, so I could not say. It is, of course, in demand for these properties, and not for warmth or shelter." I was suitably proud of my skin, for it made me an Exotic Animal, rather than simply average. The Witch furrowed her excellent brow, which was the exact texture of curdled cream.

"Then my price is twofold. One day I will require your skin. You must give it to me without question or hesitation. Agreed?"

"It is an honor, my crumpet, my plum. I shall await your summons. And in the meantime, I shall trumpet your beauty to the corners of the earth, so that all may know what I have learned: that a jewel dwells in the Glen, and she is beyond all rubies that the earth can press into life."

The Witch laughed, a sound like a saw cutting across rusted iron.

"Two, you must help me get this girl free—it is a silly task but the sooner done the sooner we are rid of her. Will you come with me?"

I suppressed the sudden desire to dance with glee. "With profound pleasure, my honeycomb. In fact, we may accomplish this all the sooner if you would," I could hardly contain my eagerness, "deign to ride upon my back."

"Is there always such camaraderie between monsters?" she mused.

"We must look out for each other," I answered softly, "for we are a small and dwindling band. Didn't you know?"

"I have not always been a monster," she murmured.

She climbed onto my back with the ease of a whisper, as though she had ridden me for a decade. For a moment I heard her breath catch strangely, as if in recognition of a lost love, or a child long dead. She wound her hands into my mane with great tenderness, and if I am not mistaken, actually put my mane to her face and breathed in my smell.

"It has been years since I have sat astride a horse," she marveled. I protested that I was not a horse at all, but she did not seem to hear. "The place most maidens find themselves caught is to the northwest of here, in the center of a nameless forest, in a nameless tower."

It took less than a day to arrive there, and I reveled unexpectedly in the sensation of a rider, of her small weight like a branch of holly and her gruff company. It is a pleasant thing to be tame, to recognize a rough-carved voice. I shall not say it will not happen again.

The tower itself was solid black stone, hewn from one great block of obsidian, so that it mirrored the forest around it in a dark, rippling mockery of its green beauty. The sky overhead was a uniform gray, like the metallic flesh of a cannon, and sullen clouds dragged themselves west. The fragrant pines and birches would not grow near the tower, which stood in the center of what once must have been a meadow, but was now only a circle of leached grass, dead and white. The thing tapered, as towers do, to a sharp point, giving the impression of a great arrowhead rising from the earth. Its architecture was unnatural, beyond even what magic can build, and I could smell the blood of children in the gently waving grass at its base. It was a coldly terrible place, but the Witch seemed undisturbed by it. She dismounted and strode to the foot of the tower, and called up to its wicked heights.

"Woman! Come out! I have—" She looked down at the bloodless grass, embarrassed. "I have come to rescue you," she finally said, as if admitting that she were covered in boils. I was momentarily distracted by the delectable image of her covered in boils, but my reverie was rudely broken by the appearance of a head at the top of the tower.

It was crowned in hideous golden curls which fell in long braids down the side of the parapet, and possessed of eyes blue as a drowned eel, set in a face which was smooth and plague-rosy. The maiden's bosom heaved in a most gauche fashion, bound far too tightly into a white dress which showed nothing of any interest to me. She was quite a spectacle, this

maiden. Most distasteful. Perhaps she locked herself in the tower to save the world the sight of her ugliness. Certainly beside my ravishing Witch she was a toad, a wart, a pustule.

The creature pursed her lips curiously and spoke with a voice sweet as spoiled milk. "Certainly. Come up."

A black arch appeared noiselessly in the flesh of the tower, a lightless curtain parting to reveal nothing but further and deeper darknesses. With a knowing glance towards me, the Witch entered the fissure, and I trotted in behind her.

"I know the dark well; it and I have become fast friends. If the old man seeks to frighten me this way, he is a great fool," she whispered.

We ascended quickly, the liquid stone of a murky staircase sliding beneath us. I followed her scent in the black, the trail of her body heat lighting my way. For a long while there was no sound but our breathing, and the pattern of our feet on the rock like rain in a forest. It was not unpleasant.

As suddenly as we had entered the womblike shadows, we left them behind—stepping into a round room at the top of the tower which held the maiden in its center like a jewel in an iron ring.

"Welcome," she intoned. "My name is Magadin."

Her voice echoed in the chamber like an arrow glancing off its target. We could say nothing at first, so stunned were we at the girl's appearance. Her head, which we had seen from below, was the picture of pearl-edged royalty, gilded and cool-skinned, repulsive to me but beautiful by mortal standards. Yet the rest of her body was terrifying and marvelous—her hands were covered in thick russet fur, tapering to jaundiced claws; her hips twisted into a deer's delicate haunches; and turquoise wings jutted painfully from her shoulder blades, splitting the skin and drawing blood in great swathes. Her feet sparkled green as underwater opals, webbed and slime-filmed like a frog, yet her legs beneath the gauzy dress were silver as a fish, smoothly coated in translucent scales. Feather-fine fins sprouted from her heels. Her breasts, which below had seemed milky and unblemished, were actually furred in the patterns of a white tiger, dark and feral stripes beginning to show across her delicate collarbone. A wolfish tail thumped unhappily behind her, having torn through the beaded fabric. The ends of her braids appeared to be slowly flapping, the veined surface of dragonfly wings shining through her curls.

Worse, all around her were severed heads mounted on the walls, what once were maidens, each in various stages of metamorphosis: One was half covered in serpent-hide, her hair hissing violently; another had lost her mouth, a beak twisting out of her face in its place; another's eyes had shrunk terribly, and dark hair covered her batlike features. The menagerie of beast-princesses ringed the chamber, watching us with eyes that seemed not entirely dead.

"You see," the maiden admitted quietly, "why I have not been rescued yet. Why nothing guards the door. They come by the dozens, pretty knights all in a row, and run like frightened squirrels when they see what I am."

I saw pity coalesce on the Witch's face, and she took the maiden into her arms tenderly, as the girl wept great red tears, which fell on her dress like some unspeakable wine. "Tell me what he has done to you," she said softly, stroking her veined hair.

"He is trying to *change* me," Magadin squeaked, her voice cracking like a wounded hawk, "as he tried to change *them*. He took me from my father's house . . ."

THE
BEAST-MAIDEN'S
TALE

I WAS BORN FAR, FAR FROM HERE ON MIDWIN-
ter's Night, in the middle of a storm that tore the tiles
from the roof and flooded the sky with clouds blacker
than chimneys. I drew first breath in a tall tower wrapped
with ivy and lilies like waxing moons, all of gray stone
shot through with quartz. Wind battered at the windows;
the sky boiled with thunder. The midwife placed me in my
mother's arms, wide-eyed and wondering. She smiled at
me, her face tired and white, full of sorrow, and died with
her finger clutched in my tiny hand.

When the wild milkwoods and chestnuts had bloomed
twelve times and withered, my father married again, a

woman of radiant face and hair like a river of fire, her body like the living sun entering our hall. Her name was Iolanthe. She was a young widow with vast lands, and had two daughters of her own, Isaura and Imogen, somewhat older than I, each more proud and beautiful than the other.

I see you smile, Witch. You think you know how these stories go.

But they were not like their exotic mother; they were exceedingly dull and stupid, their only worth lying in the golden shades of their practiced curls. They were little golden birds, chirping and empty-headed, always together, clutching each other's little pink hands. I quickly became my stepmother's favorite, quick and clever as I was. She was an imperious woman, and my father obeyed her every whisper as eagerly as a colt its master.

I adored her.

Obviously, my new sisters hated me.

My only notions of my own mother were stories my father had told me of that last smile, soft and sad. These melted like tea steam in the face of Iolanthe who blazed so brightly, whose laughter lit the chandeliers, whose great dark gowns swept majestically along our halls, filling the house as my mother's ghost could not.

After a time it became clear that she favored me even over her own children, who grew purple-faced with hate and envy. For my part, I cared nothing for the simpering fools. My stepmother was my world; she had enchanted me completely. I took on her mannerisms, became haughty and fierce, but captivating to all. I was the wonder of the Palace, my father's pride. I grew up and grew older, more beautiful and wiser, devouring our libraries with delight. I was dark where my stepmother was light, pale as a winter wind where she was rosy as summer dusk.

On my sixteenth birthday, when such things usually occur, a herald announced at every door in the land that the royal Wizard sought some worthy young girl as his apprentice, and that all families of suitable blood were to present their daughters at some appointed day and some appointed time. Of course, we were all thrilled as lambs with a mouthful of alfalfa—each of us certain we would be chosen, and our days filled with riches and power.

Iolanthe heard the summons, and her face darkened. She was heavily pregnant then; her black gown rippled loose behind her. She closed the door after the well-meaning herald, and forbade all three of us to try for the apprenticeship. Instead, she took me up the stone stairs to a high tower, all wrapped with ivy and lilies like waxing moons. She leaned into the heavy door and it ground open, showing a room now filled with decrepit books and ancient scrolls. Nevertheless, it remained, my birth-bed and my mother's deathbed, facing the long, tapered window, smooth and cleanly white, as though it had never tasted our blood.

"My daughter," she began, her voice like water over river stones, "for so I hope I may call you, my own girl, as though I had given you life in this room where your true mother died. I wish that I had, and saved you those years of loneliness. My own blood, as you know, did not fare so well." She shrugged, raising her eyes to the ceiling with exasperation. "They are lovely girls, and I raised them as best I could. Perhaps I indulged them. They will make good marriages to enrich our lands, but though they will be your father's heirs, they can never be mine. That does not mean, how-ever, that I will stand to see them shipped off to a filthy Wizard with a col-lar of iron."

Her eyes glinted with fury like campfires on a winter's night. Without tensing or moving from her chair, she made a quick gesture at one of the shelves, and a heavy, scarlet-bound volume flew obediently into her long, white hand. I gasped, goggle-eyed, and her dark, musical laughter filled the air.

"Didn't you know? All stepmothers are witches. It is our compensation for remaining forever an intruder in another woman's house. That, daughter mine, is an estate lonely beyond description. Even this," she touched her belly warmly, "will not earn me peace. It is a son to till the fields and battle infidels, and yet still your mother will be the Lady of the House, and I only a tenant. Everywhere, your mother's shade outranks me. I call you my daughter and it freezes in the air, it angers her beyond endurance. But what can she do, the poor wretch? She is long dead, and I live. Daughter, daughter, daughter," she chanted throatily, as if challenging the dusty breeze. "In this, at least, you can be my true and devoted child. If you want to know magic, I will teach it, and I will teach it without a collar. You can learn the secret things that lie in these volumes and in my own breast. When you are captive in a husband's house, it may pass the time."

"But why do you object to the Wizard? Isn't the magic he would teach as good as yours?"

Iolanthe ground her teeth. "I thought you were a wiser child, Magadin. Did it never seem odd to you that he wants a girl, when most will take only students of their own kind, girls to women and boys to men? Or that he wants an apprentice at all, when he is a slave, *doulios,* marked by his collar as one whose power has been sold, son back to father back to father, as long as there has been any strength in his blood? He can do nothing without the leave of the King; they are bound together. And I will not barter away any of my girls to that place."

"And you are not a slave? A *doulios*?"

"No, my girl, that I am not."

And so, over the weeks before the appointed day, as the apple groves yielded their musky ciders, I learned from her—small, halting things. Mostly I read her books. I rarely saw my father or my stepsisters, cloistered as I was in my birth-tower, my fingers acquiring the ink stains of a clerk and my clothes growing plainer and less colorful as I tired quickly of the brocades and ribbons that enchanted my sisters. When my brother was born, I stayed in the tower, my hair all dusty and uncombed. They called him Ismail; I took no interest. When she recovered, my stepmother and I spent our hours with heads bent together over concoctions and pleasant, trifling charms, and I was happy. I was sure true knowledge would come later.

Deep in the blue-tongued winter, the Wizard's day came, and I was to meet the payment for that happiness.

I hid in the stairwell as Iolanthe told me, while Imogen and Isaura were secreted away in a tall armoire. My sisters held each other in terror, huddled side by side like tender fawns left in the bower by their doe. They did not extend their arms to me, but shut the doors abruptly. I folded myself up under the stairs. We were not to squeak, we were not to sneeze, and she would tell the messenger that her daughters had caught chill and died in the frost. I peered through the cracks in the wood to watch my stepmother lie for us.

But it was no messenger who came, but the Wizard himself, his blue and brown robes streaming behind him, his long hair twisted and gray, a heavy iron collar hanging around his neck like a noblewoman's jewelry. He seemed not to notice it—and he carried a second one, alike in weight and color, in his veined hand.

"There are three girls in this house, yes?" he said imperiously, looking down his aquiline nose at my stepmother. She bent her shining head in grief.

"My daughters all perished in the first snows. A chill took this house; I was lucky to keep my child, so many died—"

"Oh, stop it." He interrupted, his voice cutting across hers like a ship slicing through a foamy wave. "I don't have time for this. There are three children in this house, and if you do not produce them, I certainly can. I can hear two of them scratching at that great closet like hungry little mice.

Want to come out, hungry mice? I won't hurt you, and if you are good girls, I may give you a nice cheese."

The armoire cracked open. My sisters were nothing if not curious, curious and stupid. Hesitantly, the golden-curled girls stepped out of their hiding place and clung to each other, staring shyly at the floor.

Iolanthe's face showed nothing. She bent even lower, nearly bowing to the tall man. "I meant no dishonesty, you must believe me," she wept, and genuine tears splashed onto the flagstones. "What I told you was true— the frost took my eldest daughter, who was dearly beloved in this house. I could not bear to have either of my other girls, clever as they are, risk trying for your honors—I could not lose them, too!" My stepmother actually crumpled into a heap at his feet, crying pitifully and clutching at his boots for mercy. I could almost laugh, but I was not as stupid as my sisters.

The Wizard seemed to believe her, as he drew her up to her feet again and wiped the tears from her face. "There, there. You are very ugly when you cry, you ought to try not to do it. Let us see about these two lambs of yours, shall we?" He held up the iron collar and Iolanthe flinched ever so slightly. "It is a simple test. Each of them will try my collar, and if it should be fortunate enough to fit one of them, she will come with me and learn all sorts of wonderful things and live a life that even a queen would envy. That *does* sound nice, doesn't it, girls?"

My sisters nodded, but they trembled with fear like leaves blown across an empty street. He approached them as a man will approach a horse he wishes to break, and his long, pale fingers settled first on Imogen.

"Please, sir," she whispered, "I don't want to."

"Well, little girls must learn to do things they don't wish to do. It is the way of the world," the Wizard said comfortingly, and opened the latch of the gray collar, fastening it around her neck.

It hung loose, limp as cabbage, around her collarbone.

"See? That wasn't so awful. You are far too weak to be of any use to me. Next!"

Isaura nearly vomited on his feet. "Please, sir," she begged, "I don't want to."

He chuckled and did not waste his breath on an answer. He clasped the collar around her slim little neck, soft as a swan's.

It was so tight she could hardly breathe, and I saw that the collar was special, that it chose, and not the Wizard, for it shrank around my sister's neck like a fist until she cried out and began to claw at it in desperation.

With an exasperated sigh, he removed the collar in one swift movement. "Let this be a lesson, woman. Lying nets nothing, just as spoons catch no fish."

He turned on his heel to go, and I saw relief ripple through Iolanthe's body. But my sister—oh, Imogen, you little viper!—my sister cried out after him.

"Wait!"

She glanced at Isaura for reassurance, and for a moment seemed to think better of herself.

"Yes? Is there something, little love?"

Imogen squeaked, and could not speak. Isaura let go of her sister's hand and stepped forward as though reciting lessons.

"Mother lied. Magadin didn't die—nobody died. She's under the stairway, hiding like a *rat*."

I believe that at that moment Iolanthe might have throttled her own child to death. But she did not protest; what protest could she offer?

Isaura bounded across the room with glee and threw open the wooden hatch that covered the space under the stairs.

"Hello!" she crowed.

"How could you?" I hissed.

"We are tired of your airs and your stupid black fingers and your secrets. You are a *beastly* girl. No one wants *you* here any longer."

"Yes!" cried Imogen in her piping voice. "We hope that horrid collar does fit you, and you go away and never, ever come back! It's what you deserve!"

"Why?" I asked, still crouched in my hiding place.

"You *stole* her from us!" Imogen cried out miserably, like an infant bird falling from the nest. "She is *our* mother, not yours, and you took her away! We were happy before we came to this awful place! And now she has another baby—she will forget us completely!"

She wept bitterly, but Isaura did not shed a tear. She snatched me by the wrist and pulled me out of the dark, sending me stumbling to the Wizard's feet. It was only then that she and Imogen saw their mother's stare, cold as gallows. Imogen cried harder, and touched my sleeve imploringly. "I'm sorry, I'm sorry, try to understand . . ." she whispered. Isaura pushed her aside.

"Try it on. Try it on and rot, Magadin," she hissed.

I drew myself up before the Wizard, who grinned like a jungle cat who has just made a meal of a particularly fat vole. He held out the collar but, with my stepmother's eyes burning on my skin, I refused to bend my neck towards it. He pursed his dry lips and stepped forward, clapping the thing around my throat with alarming speed.

It fit so perfectly I hardly felt its weight. There was no sound in the hall, but I saw Isaura smile into her sleeve. The Wizard checked the joints of the collar and gave me over to his men, dropping three silver coins into Iolanthe's hand in exchange for me.

As I was pushed out of my house, I heard behind me the soft thump of my stepmother collapsing onto the tile.

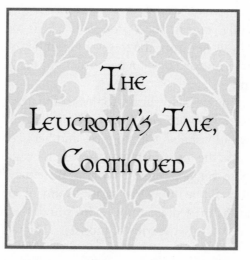

THE
LEUCROTTA'S TALE,
CONTINUED

"SO YOU SEE HOW IT IS," THE BEAST-MAIDEN SAID.
"There was no apprenticeship at all. He locked me up here
without even taking me to the Palace, and here I have been
for fifty years and more. Each fortnight he comes and
forces me to drink terrible concoctions, he rubs unguents
over my body, causes the lightning to burn my veins. He
keeps me young and strong, for I have lasted longer than
any of the others, and he has never had so likely a subject.
He cannot lose me to hag-hood. But it is not working, and
soon I will be hung on the wall like the rest, and he will
begin again with some other maid. I will be forced to
watch her die as they watch me."

The Witch raised up the maiden's face and smoothed her tears away as though she was erasing a canvas. She smiled at the helpless girl, her face lighting like a midsummer fire. "He once held me prisoner to discover the same secret—the old man is obsessed with it—and I escaped. So shall you. Never put your faith in a Prince. When you require a miracle, trust in a Witch."

"There is nothing you can do," I protested. "She is too far gone; even I can smell that. Throw her from the tower and put her out of her misery." But the Witch only chuckled deep in her throat, the gurgling of a hundred mountain streams.

"I have made it my specialty, Beast, to thwart the magic of this particular man. I have grown since our last meeting; he only wallows in the depths of his few filthy skills." She stopped, and her eyes grew sad. "I am afraid I cannot erase the beast from you, however. I cannot make you the girl you were. These things cannot be undone, once they have gone so far. In the old days it could be done, and easily, by any of my mothers before me. But much has happened. I cannot rejoin you to the tribe of maidens. But I can welcome you into the tribe of monsters. You will live; you will be rescued."

The beast-maiden's eyes grew large with the weight of bitter tears. "But without my beauty, what am I? I cannot marry this way, and surely by now my father and stepmother are dead. I am as stupid as the day I left her; in fifty years I have learned nothing that would make her proud of me. This is all I am, a maiden in a tower, and for that sad race there is no salve but a Prince, hung around their necks like an anchor in epaulets. What else is there for me?"

"Nothing," a voice growled from the shadows. One of the heads curled her lips backward into an *O* of hate. "You are ugly now; no one will have you!"

"You'll stay with us and like it, dog-daughter!" The beaked head cawed laughter, smacking her gums.

"Good for nothing but the circus!"

"Maybe the wife of a farm goat, eating garbage in the pen!"

"Queen of the dung flies!"

"Empress of monkeys!"

The heads cackled together, spitting and snarling. A few simply wept without words. The Witch scowled.

"Don't listen. They are already dead. The Wizard gave them voice to torture you—they long ago escaped this place."

"We're not dead, little Witch! Try your parlor tricks somewhere else! She's ours!" The heads pealed off into laughter again.

"Where could I go?" Magadin asked pathetically. "How could I live?"

"Beast owes me," the Witch answered. "He will take you to the sea, where you can find work on the ships anchored there. Or you can take one to lands far away, where no one can follow you. If I am not mistaken, he thinks you very lovely now." She grinned knowingly at me.

"Certainly, my dove," I replied with dignity, "the fur much improves what I saw from the foot of the tower. I have friends in the seaport of Muireann. With me at your side no one will refuse you. You are one of us, now. I assure you, we are gentler to each other than the wretched race of maidens. I will watch over you." The woman seemed to acquiesce. Her eyes lit like yellow candles.

"Now," said the Witch, "you cannot go anywhere bleeding and broken like a bird who has fallen from her tree."

She took the maid's face in her hands, winding her fingers in Magadin's dusk-honey hair, and closed her lips softly over the beast-girl's mouth.

All the muscles in Magadin's tortured body seemed to relax. The wounds caused by the sprouting of her wings healed in a breath, feathers covering the ruined flesh. Her tail became healthy and full, while her fierce claws receded a bit, into a civilized length. The fluttering wings at her braid tips melted into the rest of her hair, darkening it to a burnished bronze and thickening the mass into a leonine cascade. Her legs straightened slightly so that she could walk again, though they kept their rounded doe-shape, and the fish scales did not disappear from her calves. Her skin took on a rich, even tone, and the stripes on her flesh grew darker, more vibrant, seeming to become their own natural shade rather than a stain on her skin. Magadin was altogether a radiant beast now, her transformation complete, yet forever unfinished. I approved greatly.

But the heads howled in loathing and horror, their taunts dissolving into spittle-filled gibberish. As they parted, the two women glanced at each other in triumph and walked towards me hand in hand, ignoring the thrashing heads entirely. The maiden's deer gait would always be strange, like a foreign dance, but she was smiling. The three of us left the tower as swiftly as foxes, emerging onto the snow-dead grass as the tower began to shake with the rising screams from within.

The Witch never looked back, but gestured carelessly towards the black monolith with her left hand as she and Magadin climbed onto my back. The tower promptly shuddered like a coughing crone and crumbled into the earth.

In the Tower

Visions of shorn skins and beast-maids milling in his mind like harem girls, the boy left the cedar grove and the girl, who now slept on the bed of pine needles, exhausted by the telling of her own story. He thought he could see the bright pale eyes of wild birds in the branches, like pearls strung on threads of darkness, waiting for him to leave so they could tend to her.

As he stole back into the Palace without a sound, he was quite confident that he had acquitted himself perfectly—even the Prince could not have been so stealthy. But as he shut the door to his own bedchamber, a brazier flared, flooding the room with amber light like a fruit dashed against the wall.

Dinarzad sat among the furs of his bed, a long slender stalk of straw in her hand. She held it aloft, still smoldering over the torch.

"Well." She chuckled. "You can't blame me. I gave you fair warning." She moved then, quick as a fly-bound spider, snatching him by the forearm and dragging him up a long staircase. Without another word she flung him into a small tower room, and turned the key in the great lock. The room was bare save for a tiny bed and wind-washed flagstones, illumined by the sapphire-ringed fingers of dawn, which pried at the window.

The boy yelped in frustration and kicked the meager bed. He let a few furious tears fall like blows onto the cold floor. All was truly lost now—there were not even linens on the bed with which to fashion a rope. He was a stupid child after all, stuck in a tower like the deformed maiden, when he should be roaming the marshes like the Prince. It was all wrong, upside down, unnatural. The boy punched the stone wall in mute anger, and instantly regretted it, rubbing his bruised knuckles as his eyes watered in pain.

Outside the tower keep, Dinarzad closed her almond eyes and took a deep, jagged breath, harsh as a sword drawn across a thick chain. She knew she would be punished terribly for letting him sneak out in the night. Her welts had not yet healed from the last time a child escaped from her nursery. But she was the Sultan's daughter, and no amira of her standing would let terror or wounds show to anyone. She banished her tears as she strode down the polished steps, the key tucked into her robes. But when she crawled into her own bed, she began to weep silently under the wolf pelts, her tears wetting the down pillow like rain on the snow. She wished for nothing but to sleep past her punishments and wake to a Palace with no children for her to look after, no whips tipped in lead, and no prized brothers to mock and loathe her.

When the girl woke and the great wings had moved from her pale body, she saw the dark-haired boy had gone, and she let hot, secret tears fall into the black earth.

The night was full of weeping.

Dinarzad brought the boy supper in the tower the next evening, just as rose and flame were beginning to divide the sky between them. She said nothing, punctuating her exit with the slow rolling of the iron key in the lock. The boy did not eat it all, though he was hungry. He set aside some of the dense, sweet bread and onions, saving the apples like gold ornaments in useless hope.

The boy leaned against the tower wall, seething. He tried to reconstruct the story in his mind, but it kept getting confused, bleeding into itself like watercolors. Aerie seemed to have the girl's strange eyes, and he could not even recall something so simple as the color of Beast.

Standing on his toes, he stretched to reach the window-sill and peer into the Garden below, to spy at least the top of a cypress under which the girl might be lying. The trees stood high before him like quill pens in pots, wafting slowly in the night wind. And they were beautiful, because she might be resting under one of them.

Except that she was not, for she stood in the manicured grass at the foot of the great gray tower, staring up at the helpless boy with eyes wide and dark as an owl's throat.

The girl watched him silently. It was not beyond the realm of possibility that she would climb up the craggy stones and ivy to rescue the boy, though she had certainly never heard of such a thing. For a moment, she let herself be filled and warmed with knowing that he had looked for her.

When it was fully dark, she hooked a toe into one of the cracks between stones and began to climb.

The boy heard her scrabbling up the ivy and nettles that clothed the tower. He was excited to know she drew near, but ashamed that it was again she that had hunted and tracked him. He should have jumped, he decided. A broken leg was not *such* a tragedy.

Of course, it did not matter. The girl was here, and that meant she must like him a little. It was not just that she wanted to tell her tales; it must be that she missed him, too. This thought rose up in him like a blinding sun. Embarrassed, he snuffed it out, showing her his most welcoming, yet dignified, face.

But when she pulled herself onto the sill, glistening with sweat, she would not come inside, only perch in the window like a half-tamed parrot. She was afraid, of him perhaps, certainly of getting caught. Up till now he had taken the punishment, but if she were found in the Palace, it was very likely she would be killed. His breath caught with the realization, with admiration for her bravery. Once again, she had outdone him.

"I . . . I know you wanted to hear the rest of the story . . ." she whispered, and somehow he felt ashamed of it, for the first time, as though he were taking something precious from her, and caring for nothing but the gleam of the prize.

Nevertheless, the girl began to speak again, and her voice filled the room like a copper bell. The boy closed his eyes.

The Tale
of the Prince
and the Goose,
Continued

"I WAS TRUE TO MY WORD," SAID BEAST. "AFTER THE
Witch left us in her Glen, I brought Magadin to the village
of Muireann, and arranged to have her hired as a sail-
mender on one of the great ships. All told she has done
well enough for herself, considering. Of course, there remained the last leg of the two-fold price the Witch exacted
for my life. You must see now, that I am bound by my
word of honor to give over the skin. Now my debt is
done."

The Marsh King spat and snorted a loud *hrumph* from
his perch in the air. "I think this is all most unpalatable!"
He accused Beast with eyes that flashed like eels snapping

their tails. "You *liked* that horrid human! You thought she was beautiful! It's unnatural! I think you *loved* her! How disgusting—you know the other monsters would never stand for it. The beast-maid is one thing, but a *human woman*? At any rate I think you like *her* better than *me*. I don't recall you ever giving *me* your skin, even when I wanted to kill that wretched salamander who annoyed me so last spring."

Beast was immediately conciliatory, jostling the Marsh King with his head, which smeared the monarch's wiry beard with thick blood. "Poppet! You know I like you best of all. I chose to be your courtier—I could have chosen anyone. She was nothing, a momentary infatuation—not even infatuation! An aesthetic admiration, that's all! Don't be angry. You mustn't begrudge her, when there is so much trouble ahead."

The Marsh King seemed to cheer up slightly, sniffing a little. Suddenly, he started and brusquely strode away from the Prince.

"Well, lad, I suggest that you have your prize and ought, to put it politely, to clear off. Matters of state to attend to, don't you know." The pair promptly left Leander sitting in the swamp with his breeches soaked through and a skin which, if it had not to begin with, was beginning to smell.

By now it was nearing evening, and the Prince guiltily decided that, since Eyvind was soon to come into whatever adventure had been stored up for him, he needn't *actually* return to the tavern to deliver his message. After all, it had probably already occurred, whatever it was. He resolved to send a message-boy when all of this was over.

This almost quieted his conscience.

And so he made his way home, discovering the second truth of Quests, which is that, mysteriously enough, the path homeward is a great deal shorter than the path deedward. The sun slips easily through the sky, as if on a golden rail, and earth seems to positively skip by under one's feet. Adventures rarely occur on the home trek, as if fate wills the loyal and successful Prince to the bed at the end of his duty. It was almost pleasant to walk back to the Witch, except that guilt and fear gnawed at his stomach like starved mice.

So it was that when the Prince returned to the Witch's hut, he trembled, but had, at least, the same heavy boots given to him by the tavern-keeper, which had not failed him. It was perhaps an even trade. It was the last night of the full moon, and darkness lay on Knife's little farm like a thick-fingered hand. The milling geese were now quiet, and the plow stood in

the half-light of the stars like a skeleton. The door of the hut was ajar, and Leander, the Leucrotta skin tucked neatly away, bent his dark head and crossed the threshold.

Knife was not in the vast kitchen, though the hearth still glowered stubbornly, despite having long since been neglected. But behind a second door she lay curled up on a great bed, with the gray geese surrounding her, fashioning a blanket the color of waves over her gnarled body.

Leander knelt quietly at her side and pressed the red bundle into her hand. She turned her head in mid-snore and grimaced.

"So, you're back." She sighed, propping herself up in her strange feathered bed. The birds rearranged themselves, regarding him with dozens of beady eyes. "I suppose that makes you a good Prince, as Princes go. But you're early. The dark moon rises only an hour before dawn, and it is not yet time to give my girl her second birth. And there is one thing more to tell."

She shifted, and the geese moved with her, stretching their long necks to lay their heads on her, to touch her in any way they could. Silver wings like crossed arms covered her chest.

"I told the first part for myself, so that you would know what was. This I tell for you, so that you will know what is to come."

The
Witch's Tale,
Continued

THE KNIFE CUT TRUE, BUT NOT DEEPLY. THE Wizard did not even spare a hand to staunch the blood from his own wound. It was a thin scarlet line under his chin, above the collar's iron rim, but only one line among many on that leather-thick expanse of flesh. In one fluid motion like wind moving from one willow to the next, he caught my grandmother's hand, snapping her wrist in his grip, and thrust her own knife into her belly.

Grandmother stood still, surprised, looking at the knife's bone handle jutting like a new limb from her body. And then suddenly she choked, and bright blood erupted from her white lips. She collapsed into my arms as the

Wizard ducked into a small room behind the throne, servants in tow, looking after his shallow wound.

And through all this, the King had said nothing, nor moved, but watched it with a falcon's curiosity. He did not take his cool eyes off me for a moment. Grandmother lay like a child in my arms. She smiled wanly, and the blood kept pouring out of her, deep, dark blood from the depths of her, thick and black until it was not, until it was silver and pale, flowing over my hands, over my lap like a little brook of fresh water. I was soaked in it, and Grandmother reached up, her hand dripping with the stuff, and put her fingers into my mouth, so that the light trickled down my throat.

It tasted of nothing at all.

"You see? I can fill you up after all. You are all of us now, all that is left, drenched with blood and light like our long-dead grandmother in that terrible tent. You are strong enough to buy our vengeance for us. With my death, I instruct you."

She smiled, just the faintest shadow of a smile, and died, with a noise in her throat like dried beans rattling in a gourd. There was nothing left in her; the blood-light had seeped into me and she was a shell, a hole, empty space.

I did not weep; I would not let them see it. I took the knife with its thick bone hilt from her flesh and clutched it tightly in my bloody fist.

And as I looked up at the King in all his jewels, for a moment I could see a shape just behind him—a pair of black eyes glittering amid bristled red fur.

It was the Fox, and he was laughing.

I could never discover what they did with my grandmother's body, but it was removed from the hall as though it were kitchen rubbish, a pile of apple cores and pig fat. The stains were scrubbed from the floor when the Wizard returned, his throat bandaged.

The King had never taken his unblinking eyes from me, and now I stood before him in rags which had once dreamed of being white, covered in the dark glut of her blood, my face streaked with it as though I had painted myself for war, or marriage. The Wizard pushed back his braided gray hair from his creased, high forehead and addressed the King.

"That leaves only the girl, my lord. I will take her into my tower, if I have your leave."

But the King raised a silky hand, dismissing the suggestion. I stared hard at him as his eyes ranged over my body, clawing at me, trying to gain entrance. For he had conceived a terrible lust for me in his heart, and I could see it grow like a bristled boar behind his gaze.

"You have your tower, Omir. And I have mine." His voice was quiet and utterly cold, a foul wind through the feathers of a dead crow. I saw the understanding that I had gripped like a new blade at the moment I saw him watching me dawn in the Wizard's pale eyes. It was a thick-tongued silence as the three of us thought furiously, each to gain his end.

Finally, the Wizard won through, and spoke in a brusque tone that excluded me as wholly as a doubled fist.

"My lord, may I speak to you in private for a moment?"

The two retreated to the opposite end of the great hall. But the ears of my people are keen, and I heard them as clearly as my own horse snorting in a field of grass.

"My King, I have a thought which may achieve all our ends. You want the Witch-woman. I want whatever power her grandmother might have taught her. Why satisfy only your lust? Why not *marry* the creature?" The King was silent—one could almost hear the tick of calculation echo in the rafters.

"But she is a barbarian," he reasoned. "She is worthy of my use, not my hand."

"But lord," the Wizard insisted, "to marry her would show the conquered tribes that you are to be trusted, that you are a good and just ruler. To win their trust is the only way to quiet the savage bands. Make her Queen and they will adore you for it. Even monsters are given fair hand by the new King, they will whisper. And everyone knows those tribeswomen are fertile as cows. She'll bury you in sons. I only ask, humbly: The nights she does not spend with you, give her over to me, so I may extract what I can from her before she dies, whether from your ministrations or mine.

"Let me tell you a tale to make clear my meaning . . ."

The Wizard's Tale

ONCE, IN A FAR-OFF KINGDOM—OF COURSE, NOT nearly so magnificent as yours, my lord—there lived a Raja by the name of Indrajit. He was a fine ruler, strong and just as an arrow through the heart of a thief. His conquering Hand was laid out on the fields and farms like a cloud that brings blessed rain. None refused his rule, and no voice was raised against the power of that most sacred Hand.

But still he sought to bring the light and glory of his just rule to the far reaches of the countryside, an ambition not unknown to you, my lord. He looked beyond the great river that flowed like a bolt of silk through the fertile kingdom. And so he led his famed Royal Guards, who as legend told it had sprung up from the earth when Indrajit slew a monstrous boar in the hinterlands and the beast's teeth fell to the ground and shattered. From those teeth came the hundred and forty-four warriors ever after known as the *Dentas Varaahasind*—the Teeth of the Boar. They were bound utterly to Indrajit, whose slaying of the monster had given them life. The boar-soldiers were fierce and terrible, and their loyalty was pure as snow on the carcass of a kill. They carried shields made from the vast shoulder blades of the wild pigs of the mountains, which grew in that time to be as large as the vaults of the Raja's treasure house. Their armor was covered in the blood-red skin of these boars, and they wore necklaces of the long, curving teeth that had given them birth. They painted their faces in pitch and sharpened their teeth with blacksmith's tools, so that the sight of them was like seeing a demon horde rising up under the moon. The country loved the Raja, as subjects should, but they lived in cold terror of the Varaahasind.

Indrajit one summer led his loyal band across the sparkling river to a small monastery, which he wished to conquer and use as an outpost for the bringing of his just reign to the South. The temple was, curiously, peopled entirely by women, and it was dedicated to some heathen serpent-god draped in jewels. When the women saw the Varaahasind approach, and heard their ghastly battle cry, which was like to the screaming of a boar pierced with an ash spear, they did not shriek or run, but gathered close around the icon of their god, shielding the green-bronze metal with their veiled bodies. A few of the women did show their fear, and fainted dead away, but their limbs were held up by the other acolytes.

Touched by their devotion, Indrajit did not sever their ungrateful breasts immediately and feed their bodies to his men. Instead, he pulled them aside and simply smashed the statue into jagged shards with the pommel of his massive sword, famed in all regions as an invincible blade. Still the women did not cry out as women ought to do. Instead, one of them, with eyes as black as the lightless throat of the serpent, looked at the great King and said:

"That was ill-done. You will walk under Her curse now, for the length of your days, which will spool out onto the earth like a hideous thread."

Indrajit was not so touched by their devotion that he broached the disrespect of a woman. He ordered his men to take the women out into the forest and cut out their tongues, so that they would never again speak to their betters, leaving them to wander and beg. But he was fascinated by the woman who had spoken so defiantly to him, whose name was Zmeya.

He, as any King would, wished to teach the recalcitrant wench her station in the world.

But he also birthed a powerful lust for her in his heart. She was, after all, very beautiful in her white veils, and her black eyes were so deep they seemed to have no pupils at all. Her hair fell past her waist in long black curls, and it shone most curiously in the summer sun, like the smooth skin of a salamander, and her skin brooked no blemish, nor tolerated a less than perfect contour. She did not lower those disconcerting eyes from the King, even when he bound her hand and foot. He carried her slung over his copper-studded saddle to his Palace to be his Queen.

She was only one of a thousand wives, of course, and even more bound concubines. But in marrying her he hoped both to sate his lust and to incur the good fortune of her god, and thus she was more prized than any of the wretched mares he harvested from his own country. But he could not house her with the perfumed harem, lest she incite the poor beasts to rebellion. Thus Zmeya was kept in a room all her own, accessible only by a passage from the Raja's bedchamber. Before she entered that vaulted space, she turned to Indrajit and spoke to him for the second time.

"I will consent to this marriage of my free will and swear an oath not to wage battle against you within your walls; I will bear you seven sons and seven daughters, and they will all grow to be great warriors and beauties famed throughout the wide world. I will avert from you the wrath of the serpent-god and protect your house. But you must grant to me this condition."

Indrajit burned for this woman, with her strange hair and lithe limbs. He would certainly grant her this thing if he could have her without a struggle.

"On the third day of each new moon I must be free to do as I wish, and you must swear an oath on the body of the Boar whose flesh gave you your sworn warriors that you will not attempt to see me or come near me on that day. Fear not, I will not leave the Castle nor try to escape you. This is my condition, and it cannot be altered."

The Raja agreed with a voice of crimson velvet, and Zmeya spoke no more.

Years went by like blackbirds in the night, and indeed, the strange-haired woman gave birth to seven sons and seven daughters, each with the same black eyes and thick curls as their mother. Truly, they seemed to be nothing like their father at all, but took their blood only from Zmeya, who never seemed to grow older nor less beautiful. Even when the children were fully grown, each stronger and more radiant than the last—and, true to her promise, all the girls were great warriors, and all the boys beauties—she stood among them as a sun among candles.

And the King, being a King, kept his word. He busied himself with subjugating the continent and managing the affairs of state. But his suspicion grew, as each child looked less and less like him, that she spent her new moons in adultery and sin. She was, after all, a heathen and entirely uncivilized. She could not be trusted. Indrajit grew purple in the flesh over this fear, made himself ill with it, until he could no longer restrain himself, but resolved at the next new moon to spy upon his barbarian wife and catch her at her crime.

And so it was. It was not difficult, since her chamber was connected to his. He crept down the hall as silently as only a practiced assassin can, and put his eye to the cracks in the wooden door.

What he saw was a vision from the dream of a demon. The room was washed in the sickly light of the dying moon, and it was a mass of writhing snakes, fourteen serpents in their outlandish skin, purples and blues and greens flashing phosphorescent in the night, great curving lengths rising up the stone walls and hissing in some unnamable tongue. They seemed to be every color, iridescent as a dragonfly's wing, and thick as a man's body. The dead light of the night-sky seemed to feed them, and they danced a terrible dance in the shadows.

And in the center was a serpent so vast it made the others seem like bait for a child's fishing line. Her girth was as a Palace column, and her skin flashed in all the colors of a rushing stream at sunset, glowing with a white fire. Her eyes gleamed black upon black, with no pupils at all, and when she saw the peering eye of Indrajit at the door, the serpent queen threw her long body into tremors and screamed like the grinding of a granite stone into a blade.

"Betrayer!" she cried, and shimmered as though he was seeing her through a wash of heat, becoming again Zmeya with her flying hair, and each of the smaller snakes became the seven sons and seven daughters. They all looked at him with identical accusing eyes, hatred flaring like a blue flame in each.

"You swore," she cried, throwing open the door with such strength that it shattered against the wall, "you swore this time was mine. And now all is lost for you, wretched Indrajit. You came to my temple and destroyed it like a glutton presented with a roasted bull all for himself. You took me in rough ropes to this black-halled palace. All I asked was one day without your stinking pig-breath on my neck. I gave you all of these children—"

"Demons!" he bellowed, full of horror.

"Children! My children, my beautiful hatchlings. They are perfect! You did not take the time to discover the nature of our order before you ruined us. I do not worship the serpent god—I *am* the serpent god! I sat in the sky when the earth was nothing but air. Once a month I return to my old form to bathe in what thin, distant light I can glimpse, and they with me, for you touch me and touch me and take me from myself, so that I have nothing left with which to nurse them. I have given you a litter of demigods, Indrajit, who would have filled a thousand books with their deeds. Now they are nothing and you are damned."

Indeed, the children seemed to be fading, tears coursing down their cheeks as their bodies became transparent, and then vanished as though blown by a fell wind.

Zmeya looked with a terrible grief upon them. "They are so delicate at this age, like cobwebs in a banquet hall. We so rarely have children, we hardly know how to keep them alive. I tried so hard, but you left me with nothing, and they perish so easily, little bubbles popping in the sun. A hole is only empty space, and I couldn't fill them up, I couldn't do it. If their feeding is interrupted, if they are kept from the sky-mother's light, they fade like morning steam on the river. You have killed all your best heirs, Raja. And you have brought your own doom down to you like a child's yellow kite."

At this she lunged at him, sighing again into her serpent-self. But Indrajit signaled and in a breath twelve of the Varaahasind were at his side, and the Captain had sliced off the serpent's ponderous head with a clean stroke of his blade.

It was the decree of the Raja that a great feast was to be held for the Varaahasind that night. The body of the great snake was dressed and quartered, and sent down to the bubbling kitchens. Each of the men was to eat his share of the succulent meat, so that Zmeya could never return, trailing that doom behind her. And Indrajit himself would eat her swollen heart, and so take the strength of the serpent-god into his breast, and spread his reign across the sea.

The
Witch's Tale,
Continued

"YOU SEE," THE WIZARD CAJOLED, "BECAUSE HE took his enemy to wife, Indrajit was eventually able to take all her power from her. Make her your Queen and let me have her but once a month, like Zmeya, and between us we will feast upon all that is in her."

Again, there was a long and calculating silence. At length his tumblers and locks must have seized upon an agreeable equation. The King seemed to half agree.

"But I cannot marry her with her face mangled with paint and scars. It would not do to appear in audience with *that* beside me."

"I understand. For me, too, it is her power and not

her flesh that draws. The wild people are, to say the least," he sniffed, "fragrant and lumpish. But this is no trouble at all—I can change her so that she will appear to all, even you, as beautiful as the risen sun. I have learned that much, at least."

The King looked at me across the long ivory hall.

It was dawn when they moved me again, this time into the Wizard's chambers, where he bound me hand and foot with nettle-ropes and wedged a knotted gag into my mouth. I lay on the cold floor, looking at the tables filled with books and candles that had expired long ago, spilling their waxy blood onto the pages. He was preparing some vile-smelling liquid in a glass kettle, to change me, no doubt, into some unnatural beast. I wondered uselessly if Grandmother had been frightened when the change came over her. I could not tell if I was—my blood surged, but I was calm as an underground lake.

"It is a fine hour for me, Knife. The imbecilic King wants to rut with you—let him have his way. I doubt you will enjoy it. But you will enjoy my affections far less. I have gotten the better bargain."

He pursed his thin lips as a deep red infused the kettle. "After all this time, and all those useless women spoiling my beautiful tower, you fall right into my lap, with all the knowledge I need to complete my work. It makes one believe in providence. Almost." He tapped the side of a vial which bubbled thickly and smelled of rotted tobacco fields. "Change, my little barbarian, is the nature of the universe. He who controls the process of change is next to the gods in his might and glory. Metamorphosis is the most profound of acts. Without it, nothing grows, nothing evolves, nothing expands. But should I simply wait for nature to take her pitifully slow course, bending me to her will? Preposterous. Since I was apprenticed in the Southern Kingdoms I have striven to control my own changes, kept myself alive and strong, though I served the old King before my master, and the Raja himself before that. I have strained, through all those reigns, to discover the secret whereby I may alter myself according to my own designs. The mind, you understand, must have sway over the body. It is the province of gods to fashion their forms to their will, and through you, my little wolfling, I will become as bright as any Star. It is all about control. Who has it, and who does not." The Wizard dropped a handful of clumped herbs into his salivating brew and turned to look at me, a calm gleam in his depthless eyes.

"Of course, when one is not naturally inclined, one finds ways to exert control which are less . . . elegant." The man seized a rat which was scurrying across the floor and wrenched four teeth from its squirming body, dropping them into his vial, where they sizzled. "For instance. The King wishes to believe himself powerful and in control of his destiny—it is the wish of all beings, in the end. But I control his actions as surely as if he were a doll in the hands of a cherubic child. You recall the story I told him? I told him only half—the half he needed to convince himself to keep you. I wanted you exactly where you are, so I told him just enough to present him with an excuse. Would you like to hear the rest?"

I sagged miserably and moaned beneath the filthy cloth which bound my mouth.

"Of course you would. You'll listen to anything I wish to tell you, won't you? Where were we? Oh, yes, Zmeya was dead and resting comfortably in one hundred and forty-five satisfied stomachs . . ."

The Wizard's Tale, Continued

THE PALACE OF INDRAJIT THE TERRIBLE SLEPT peacefully that night, dreaming the blood-rich dreams of righteous murderers. But when dawn broke like a windowpane over the steel-tooth mountains, a strange thing occurred.

The Varaahasind, bringers of death, began to go mad.

At first it was nothing anyone would notice. The soldiers, after all, had always behaved barbarically, decorating their huts with the limbs of slaughtered maidens, painting their faces with boar's blood. Madness would have to be strong as paired oxen in them to be marked out from their usual custom.

And so it was that morning found a lieutenant at his bath, calmly shaving his ornate beard, which curved down to his collarbone like the tusks of a great pig. He was delicately cutting it with the edge of his sword, eradicating the symbol of his glorious manhood. It was against the code of the Varaahasind to shave that proud beard, the penalty death by exposure—yet this man removed it so cleanly that his face was like that of a child, smooth as a moon.

The next week, a captain was found in an ivory tub, singing some wordless psalm full of hideous vowels—worse, the tub itself was filled to its gilt edges with wriggling green snakes, thick as a woman's waist, which wound around the captain in reptilian ecstasy.

And finally, on the third day of the new year, the second in command of the fell troops lost his ability to speak. He spat and hissed obscenely, his body contorting with the effort of uttering even the slightest sibilant syllable. When the court physician calmed the poor man sufficiently to open his mouth, it was revealed that his tongue had become forked, a deep split through the thick flesh.

At this pass, the King and the Commander of the Varaahasind began to fear for their own minds, and called a certain magician to them, in order to divine the source of the malady.

I was young then. I had just taken the collar under Indrajit. For the first time I was not just Omir, scrabbling on a farm for roots out of the earth. I was Omir *Doulios,* and if others spit that word as a curse, I wore it like a crown. It meant I was more than a potato or a turnip or a beet covered in mud. Even a slave is better, even a slave handed master to master until he dies. I wore the iron collar as easily as a necklace. It clasped my throat from chin to chest, a symbol of my servitude, polished each morning to a high shine, glinting like a sword held to my neck. I was forbidden to perform magic except in the service of Indrajit, and even then not without the observation of other craftsmen, as if I were a common cobbler. But it was better than a damp parsnip and a damp wife. And so, when I was brought for the first time before the Throne of Teeth, excitement filled my blood, after long months of boredom and the waste of my talents.

"Omir Doulios, lowest of slaves, you are come before us to solve the riddle of the lunacy which plagues my men. The speed with which you accomplish this task will directly determine how long you will live once you have left our presence," Indrajit intoned peremptorily, without waiting for the speech of introduction I had painstakingly prepared. The Tusk-Crown flashed and glowered in the torchlight, distorting my vision. Yet, I thought, perhaps this was better. For, of course, I had already deduced the root of their sickness, being the wisest of all my brothers and sisters in slavery. I had a morsel to dangle before his porcine nose, and it might purchase me that which then I most desired.

"My most noble King," I began quickly, "I can answer your riddle for you in a moment, without consulting a book or an oracle, if you will but grant me the price I ask."

I could see his rage flare at such impudence as mine, but his fear won some great battle within his breast and he nodded his assent, which could not be withdrawn.

"The solution is simple. You have killed and eaten a Star, which the simple-minded call gods. Her presence within you and your men is trying to assert itself, to re-form into the shape of the Great Serpent."

"And what is it you ask in return for this simple solution?"

"My freedom, King, what else?"

Indrajit's brow furrowed like a field after a storm, and when he answered his voice was thick and angry.

"We have given our word, and it is unbreakable. But for such a reward you must also give us the cure for this cancer, to end the malevolence of our former wife within."

And at this I trembled, for I could not admit that such a thing was perhaps beyond my power. The stupid King had committed a crime from which he could not escape. Had he but consulted me before cannibalizing his concubine, I could have devised much more delicious tortures for her, for which none could be held culpable. Punishments have always been a specialty of mine.

I calculated quickly. The paramount thing at that moment seemed to be to give him something, anything, a path to follow. My lord Indrajit was at a loss without a clear plan, orders laid out on parchment and signed in ink made from the oil of crushed sapphires. He was never very original in his thoughts, and the only plans which made sense to him involved great amounts of blood, and never his own. Given these variables, a course presented itself, which did have some slim chance for success, but more important, would appeal to his innermost heart, engorged as it had always been on the blackest of vintages, stamped from rotted grapes.

"My most honored lord, Zmeya-within is driven in a blind passion to punish the men, the pieces of her former body separated only by a scrim of flesh. But if you were to put your sworn band to death, the sliver of her within you should sleep, become dormant, and your just and mighty reign may continue."

For a long time the Raja said nothing at all, but seemed to slump in his great enameled throne, which was encrusted with teeth of many creatures and jewels as dark as the most secret blood of the conquered. His wide face moved unfathomably, a tectonic drift of features, as he considered the murder of so many men. I felt reasonably certain that it was not the number which troubled him, but whether or not they would submit to summary execution. These were no peasants, and only he knew by what underworld alchemy they had come to life.

Finally, he spoke, and his voice was like the closing of a marble tomb. "Send messengers, Omir Doulios, to gather the men in the Hall of Voices. I will address them at sundown."

And, easily as that, my audience was over, and my freedom nearer to hand. I have not waited so eagerly for nightfall since I was a child in my mother's arms, barely able to restrain my joy at the winter festivals, and the trees all strung with golden lanterns.

As nights will, the night came. One hundred and forty-four soldiers filed dutifully into the cavernous Hall of Voices, where whispers were amplified into bone-curdling screams. They came in all of their battle finery, perhaps sensing that it was a momentous evening, boars' teeth swinging freely from muscled necks and leather breastplates, some even pierced through noses and ears. Each wore a cloak of pig's hide, boiled and tanned until it was an ugly shade of scalded pink. They had painted their faces with grease and pitch, and combed blood into their hair. They gathered in formation before Indrajit, who stood on a dais above them, with me seated just behind, looking on their coarse faces with serenity and grace.

"Our most loyal servants, who among all our slaves have always been best beloved," he began, holding out his arms to them in a fatherly gesture, "much has fear followed our footsteps, like a graceful hound. But a cure has been found for the madness which has stricken you, and we have come here tonight to administer it."

I am not sure what he intended to do then, and I shall never discover it. For the men suddenly froze as though some black lightning had passed through them, their muscles locked in place, faces contorted in a hidden terror that might have been ecstasy. As one, one hundred and forty-four mouths gaped open horribly, wider than any human mouth. A terrible symphony arose as their jawbones shattered and their heads snapped back. I watched as one hundred and forty-four men spoke with one voice, one awful voice dredged from the depths of the earth, dragging mountains in its wake, echoing in the Hall like an arrow loosed.

"ONLY THE LIVING MAY BE CURED. I AM DEAD. LOOK ON ME NOW, O HUSBAND. AM I NOT BEAUTIFUL? AM I NOT STRONG?"

Indrajit could not understand, at first, but he blanched like a woman and staggered from the throne in horror. "What witchery is this, Wizard? What have you done?"

"It was not I, Your Grace," I stammered, helping him to his feet. But the fell voice erupted again from those broken mouths:

"FOOLISH BOY ON YOUR TIN THRONE. I AM ALL POSSIBLE THINGS. HOW CAN YOU HAVE THOUGHT FIRE WOULD DESTROY ME, OR THE BELLIES OF MEN? BUT THESE THINGS WILL DE-STROY YOU, AND EASILY."

Suddenly, the bodies of the soldiers shook terribly, and their bones rattled like drums in the Hall. Out of their shattered jaws came an unspeakable light, black and pale and green as if the air had been burned. The lights twined together, braiding their smoky brilliance into a monstrous pillar—and as each sliver of light left the body of a Varaahasind, his flesh shuddered and died, vanishing back into the single tooth from which he came. The clatter of teeth falling onto the mosaic floor echoed solemnly, and the pillar grew.

Indrajit trembled. By now even he grasped the situation, and clutched at his belly helplessly, knowing that he carried the last of his wife, and that he could not escape her. The light-serpent towered over him, eyeless, aware. He prostrated himself, the witless fool, and prayed for her mercy. She spoke again, but this time her voice, no longer contained within so many bodies, was a soft hiss of wind and guttering flame.

"I would have given you the world, if only you had been a greater man."

With this, the light enveloped him, and passed through his flesh, and the passing ground his bones into his blood, and when it left him, there was only his crown, rolling mutely on the throne, and all its yellow tusk was burned black.

The light itself seemed to pause and stare at me, all its empty menace focused on my heart, and I feared, for a moment, that I would not be spared, though I had not taken part in the dread feast. I was frozen before the half-woman, and her stare seemed to last a thousand nights.

But a second light entered the Hall of Voices, and I was forgotten. White tendrils shone through the painted windows like pillars of gold, and the new light was so great I could not bear to look at it. It filled the Hall with its carpet of broken teeth as though it had weight, like water poured slowly into a glass. But as suddenly as it had come, it was gone, and a man all in white stood before the white smoke-serpent, carrying a pale spear, with his colorless hair streaming behind him. With a tender expression, he opened his alabaster mouth, and a small, secret shaft of light passed between them, soft as the stars in the spring.

When he closed his bloodless lips, the serpent had gone. Zmeya stood in its place, though not whole, not whole at all. She was hard and clear, as though cut from glass. Great onyx bracelets encircled her arms from shoulder to wrist, in the shapes of restive serpents. She wore nothing but these massive jewels, and her hair was circled in a single, slender snake, whose skin was too many colors to count—yet they were all pale and muted, like a painting which has been splashed with water.

Without a word to me, the pale man lifted her stiff form and carried her from the Hall.

The Witch's Tale, Continued

"SO YOU SEE? IF YOU ARE QUIET, AND PATIENT, you may be able to get your petty revenge after all. It is none of my business. The King is as stupid as he is coarse, and when I have what I want from you, I would consider it a favor if you would kill him, and release me from my service here as Indrajit's death released me then. Hatch your plots in the darkness, for the darkness is all you have."

He turned from his table with a cup of the thick drink, now green and black as moldy flesh. He smiled, a smile which might be taken as tender, or proud, had it been on any face but his. The Wizard hauled me up by my hair and yanked the gag from my mouth. He forced the brew down my throat. It tasted of bile and rotted flowers—roses, perhaps—and there was a dark, musty undertaste that might have been sweat from some unnamable body.

As soon as it was in me, roiling in my belly, he flung me aside and watched with the curiosity of a cat watching a mouse it knows it is about to devour. I screamed and clutched at my skin—a terrible golden cloud had swallowed my vision, and my skin was ripping apart like the pages of his foul books. I knelt on the floor and vomited twice, still shrieking into the stones. He never reached a hand to help me, only watched as my skin was stolen away.

I must eventually have fainted. When I came to he held up a great mirror with a cruel smile of victory on his thin lips.

In the carved mirror stood a tall woman with hair the color of young wheat cascading past her waist in glowing curls, wide gray eyes like pools of clean rain, and milk-skin without the slightest mark. I was tall, my breasts rode high and full, and there was not a knot or rope of muscle anywhere on me—I was as weak and soft as a lamb at suck.

"And now," the Wizard crooned silkily, "we will call you Queen." Seeing my expression, he laughed. "You cannot think I meant for my King to lie with a barbarian! Metamorphosis is my art! Now you are beautiful. Now he can show you to the crowds. Now you cannot return to your people, for they would never know you. You belong to us. We will call you Helia after the great sun which rides the sky and blesses the reign of our King."

"You cannot take my name from me, slave," I said softly, touching that hair the likes of which I had never seen, save on the golden horses of my youth.

"My Queen, I *have* taken it."

I spent the nights by turns with the King and his soundless cruelties—for he hardly spoke a word to me after our hurried marriage in a temple I could not name, when he clasped a belt of gold and jasper around my waist in place of a ring: he seemed to marvel that it fit perfectly. The other nights I was bound in Omir's chamber, while he bled me in order to leech power Grandmother had given me from my veins. He opened me with silver needles and gold, even grotesque thorns the size of a well-muscled arm. But it was not deep enough, because the blood never ran silver. It was not deep enough—or perhaps I had nothing after all. Perhaps I was as empty as a hole in the air.

He would not listen when I told him I was nothing, only an apprentice who would never be otherwise. He had taken the moon from me, and given me only a sun that burned and burned.

But I spent every day in my tower prison. Even when I was pregnant, I had no respite, but lay on the stone flags as though dead, listening to the dripping of my blood into the crack of the floor.

Yet all the Kingdoms rejoiced when I gave birth to my son, named for the lions of the wild steppes. And only then, when I had produced an heir, was I allowed an hour a day when I could hold him in free arms and let my tears fall on his smooth forehead.

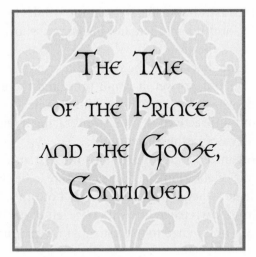

The Tale of the Prince and the Goose, Continued

LEANDER STARED, HIS HANDS SHAKING, HIS MOUTH dry. The birds watched him like an exceptionally slow child who has just learned to throw a ball into the air and catch it without dropping it.

"Helia?" he whispered.

"I would have thought you would figure it out sooner. Nevertheless, all revelations are, in the end, disappointing. Did you think it was by accident that your adventure took you to me? You had hardly to turn the corner and I was there. Surely you expected to get a little further on your way before meeting a Witch? I have waited, just beyond your father's reach, all these years. I knew no son of mine

could be bound up in a Castle all his life and never try to run free. I have
bent all my heart on the thought, as though I were crafting a bow to let arrows fly to you. I did not quite think, though, that your first act once you
arrived would be to murder your sister."

Perhaps it was only then that Leander realized the full impact of the
Witch's tale, and his eyes broke like webs in the wind. He cried in earnest
then, for his sister, and his mother, and his father, whose crimes he had
never guessed.

"But I can bring her back, with the skin, I can bring her back—"

"Yes, yes, my son, but not yet. It is not time, and there is more yet to
tell." She reached awkwardly out to draw him into her—Knife's embrace
was as strange and unpracticed as a tiger embracing a seal. And into his
ear she whispered, voice rattling like cattails:

"Your father organized a great festival for the first anniversary of your
birth. As part of the celebration, the dungeons were to be cleared out—the
remaining prisoners, starved like deer at the bottom of winter, to be
executed—all the poor wretched folk who were left of my tribe.

"I, of course, was not invited to the festival or the execution . . ."

THE
WITCH'S TALE,
CONTINUED

THE COURT GLEAMED LIKE A GREAT ICED CAKE, AND
you were bounced on a hundred shoulders, kissed by a
thousand lips while I lay bound in golden cords in the
tower. But when the night was full as a sail, and everyone
had drunk as much wine as goats will gobble their
bearded nanny's milk, I cut my ropes on a sharp stone
and, tucking the rough blade into my dress, crept out of
the tower, down those old familiar stairs, one last time
into the dark of the prisons where Aerie was born.

They looked out at me, terrified, from their cells. I was a
stranger to them, hideous as a ghoul in all my various

shades of gold. I had to speak softly, to tell them I was not the Queen at all, but their own Knife, and as their knife I would cut them free. They didn't believe it. That ragged child who chewed raw meat and scampered after crows to catch their feathers could not be draped in silk and smell of violets growing in soft moss. They asked me how to tell a doe's prints from a stag's, and how many wildcats I had killed before my marriage, and what my grandmother's name had been, and both my sisters'.

I answered them all. And one by one, I broke their locks until they sat quivering around me like a flock of wild birds. Only some forty of them were left, of all our hundreds of warriors.

"I can't let you go under the King's axe like cattle tomorrow. I can buy your lives at a better price than that. Only . . . oh, I'm not sure I can. The Wizard cut me and cut me and there was nothing. I don't know, but I will try. I will try. Come closer, I think I must be able to touch you—"

They pressed me heavily; the smell of their sweat and dying penetrated me like a slow poison. All those faces, cheekbones sharp and high, all those eyes, all those bony fingers grabbing at me! They did not know what they reached for, only that they reached for me, their Knife, and for salvation.

I closed my eyes and spoke in my heart to the Black Mare, who foaled the stars in the beginning of the world. I begged her for the power to which I had no right, for light which was not mine.

Slowly, I took the sharp stone and dug at my breast, cutting through the skin and into the meat of myself, as deep as I could stand it. And the blood flowed, red, and darker, but not silver, never silver.

I cut deeper, driving the rock into myself until I could hear it scrape the bone. I cried out, and my voice echoed in the dark, an echo of an echo, of all my cries when my daughter was born, of all my cries when I let her go.

Something pale dribbled from me, small drops like pearls. Nothing like my grandmother's wealth of light, but it was there, at the bottom of my body.

With my tribe huddled around me as though my body alone could keep them warm, I bent low and showed them that they had to taste it, they had to suckle at me as a dying woman in the desert will suckle at the blood of her horse to survive.

One by one, they took their few drops, and as they did I became weaker and weaker, for forty men and women can drink a great deal when they are frightened. I was faint and wobbling on my heels, crouched among them, and one by one I took their frail bodies into my hands and shaped them as I had seen Grandmother do, shaped them like clay on a stone table.

They changed, more slowly than Aerie had, since I was so weak, since I did not have the light of the cave and the stars. But the great silver wings came, the beaks lengthened from their lips, their legs disappeared under pale down. One by one, they staggered upright and squeezed between the window bars, into the night scented with festival fireworks, the moon under their wings, honking under the stars.

And I sat in the damp trickle of the dungeon, sobbing and laughing, skin flaming with light, my arms flung out to them as they spiraled up and up and up.

THE TALE OF THE PRINCE AND THE GOOSE, CONTINUED

LEANDER FELT THE HEAT AND WEIGHT OF DOZENS OF black eyes on him. The wild geese that had formed his mother's bed linens stared at him with a disconcerting light, full of veiled secrets. Knife stroked their long necks.

"You know the rest. I was punished; you were taken from me and given over to my maid. But she ran from my pyre and saw nothing. When I was left to burn, my flock came and braved the licking flames to cut me loose and bear me away to the Forest. The poor things—they could hold no part of their own selves in these feathered bodies. They didn't know why they did it, why they were compelled to dive into the fire—some died—but they did.

They knew only that they loved me, and could not be apart from me. And so we are a tribe again, after all."

Leander shut his eyes against the gazes of all those long-necked creatures.

"And now we come to it, my son," she said, crossing her arms over her broad chest. "I told you that you might prefer death to any salvation I might offer. I could not buy my people's vengeance, only their lives. You must purchase a better end than I. When a knife is buried in your father's chest, then I shall count myself satisfied, and you forgiven. You must swear it to me."

He had thought that her price would be more terrible somehow, that he would not already burn with the desire to avenge this hut of birds. He felt no hesitation, only relief that he could, at the last, do something for them. Leander placed his arms over his mother, smelling her wild, sharp scent and feeling her thick bones under his hands. After all he had heard he could not swear other than this, and he murmured his assent. She clapped her hands behind his back and pushed him off of her.

"Well, then, I think the moon has risen, and you may wrap your poor sister in her skin, so she may be whole. Don't forget to keep the skin on her, to tie it close to her, or it will be for nothing. Make it tight, for she will have to break out of it with her own strength, or not at all."

"It is magic. You should do it, not I."

The Witch coughed hoarsely and spat.

"I *will* do it. I am her mother. You will manage the grass and leaves, boy, and I will manage the blood."

In the Garden

THE BOY STARED AT THE GIRL, HER FACE FRAMED BY AN EXPLOSION OF white stars, trailing in the sky like sea foam. Her eyes were shut; she was enchanted by her own voice, which moved back and forth across his skin like a violin bow. If she had asked him to sprout Aerie's own wings and fly from the tower, he would have leapt from the window, if it meant she would never stop speaking.

Mesmerized by her cloaked eyes and the waterfall of her shadowy hair, he ventured once again to lie beside her on the wide stone sill, and place his head in her lap, like a young lion in a tamer's trance.

The Tale of the Prince and the Goose, Continued

LEANDER LOOKED AT HIS SISTER'S CORPSE, WHICH despite his long travels had not changed at all, had not even begun to rot—she still bore the same pale skin and silver hair, flawless and fair. When he put his hands on her, the flesh was cool, but it had not yet grown hard.

The Prince wrapped her in the scarlet skin as his mother told him. He made sure her hands were folded against her chest, and her hair pulled away from the sticky skin. He tucked her feet up and pulled the red stuff under her. When he tucked the last corner into itself, the whole fleshy shape became hard and round as an egg, shining like a malevolent star on the summer grass. He sat against a knotted oak, sweating.

Knife knelt on the dark grass, setting a bundle wrapped in cloth at her side. Her bones creaked like windows pried open in winter. She stroked the egg, and leaned against it, putting her arms around the thing and crooning quietly to it. She shut her eyes and the Prince thought, for a moment, that she wept—but surely not, surely not.

She pulled a long knife out of one of the sheaths at her waist and held it across her lap. She stared at the moon's shadow on the metal. "The skin is good, my boy, you did very well. But it didn't kill her, so it is not enough only to wrap her up in it and wait for her to wake up. Not enough. The slave never cut deep enough, never enough, and I managed to gouge myself that deeply just once. This time pays for all—deep enough to bring her back, deep enough to fill her egg with a yolk of starlight, deep enough for my girl to come home."

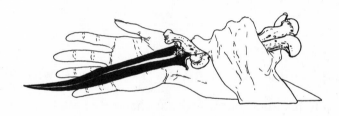

Leander did not understand for a moment, being, as most Princes are, reluctant to see things which were not written out plainly before him in three kinds of ink. But when she raised her blade, he knew what she meant, and he lunged forward to stop her, but she was much faster than he, and sank the knife in her chest before he could wrench her hand away.

"Enough," she barked, and with a horrible sawing motion, laid open her heart over the scarlet egg. The blood flowed into the skin, dark as dungeons, dark as geese eyes. And then it came, the light, first in drops and then in a sickly stream, soaking into the egg like cream strained into a glass. It became white with blood-light, and glowed lantern-bright. Knife slumped against the slick surface and slid to the grass, her body empty as a hole in the sky.

Soon, the light had drained entirely into the skin, and it was dark again, red against the shadowy grass. After a few moments, a terrible sound began to issue from the skin-egg, scratching and weeping, a muffled breathing which was getting fainter. Leander wanted to rip the egg open; he wanted to fall to the ground and mourn his mother. Caught between them, he did nothing, but watched helplessly, his feet knotted to the ground.

With a great crack like the splintering of a palace column, a white hand squirmed out of the egg, clawing for purchase on its slick surface. A girl emerged, her hair strewn with shards of the crimson shell, wet and bright with egg fluid. She pulled herself up with painfully thin limbs. When she stepped onto the grass, she caught sight of her slender foot and froze. She held out her hands, staring dumbfounded at them. Then she spied him standing beneath his tree.

Aerie opened her human mouth for the first time, and screamed so loudly and so horribly that nightingales fell dead from their boughs.

She could not stop screaming. Her chest rose and fell swiftly, and her cries filled the night. Leander rushed to her and she collapsed into his arms, still staring at her hands. He didn't think she could speak; what language could she have, after all? He whispered gently to her—it's all right, you're safe, it's your brother, it's all right—and as she began to struggle against him, he tied the remnants of the skin around her small waist like a lady's sash. She slashed at him with her nails, gibbering and screaming. Only when she saw the body of the Witch did she quiet, and strain towards it. Still holding her fragile form, he helped her crawl towards the crumpled crone.

Aerie stumbled to Knife on limbs that she could hardly use, crying a single word that told the Prince that she knew language and more, the thing the spell was not meant to encompass—she had been awake within the bird body since her first day of life.

Aerie fell into Knife's arms, whimpering in a low and grinding voice: "Mama, Mama, Mama . . ."

They lay together on the wet earth, and Knife did not wake.

Still, Aerie would not move. Her fingers curled into her mother's hair, Leander's hands curled in hers. One by one, the wild geese hopped out of the door of the old hut, waddling over to Knife and the ruined egg-skin. One by one, they laid their pearly heads on her body, all finding a place for themselves on her still-warm skin. One by one, they closed their eyes, not to be parted from their mistress at the end. Knife seemed to float in a sea of wings, and each bird's silent death took her further from her children.

Leander let go of his sister's hand and opened the cloth bundle that sat beside the limbs which had once been Knife. Inside lay a loaf of bread, lumpy and ill-formed, an ugly reddish color baked into the crust. It was not soft, nor did it seem as though it would taste good, but Leander understood—it was his own loaf, kneaded by his broken hand, his blood and tears folded into it, over and over. It had always been meant for this morning. He broke it in half, leaning a shaking, staring Aerie into his arms and slowly pressing tiny morsels into her shuddering mouth. She grimaced, but swallowed as if starving, and he, too, ate a few pieces of the strange food, its tang bitter on his tongue.

After a long while, they walked from their mother into the moonlight.

Aerie stood at the well, washing her new hands until they bled.

Her brother approached her slowly and took her hands in his. They were slick with red, running with it, and her eyes were wild.

"Aerie, Aerie, you're hurting yourself. We have to start for the Castle. With luck we can slip in tonight."

She shook her head violently, dark hair still splashed with silver light, so that she looked like an old woman with gray in her black strands. Her voice was like a crushed tuning fork, the dust of a harp splintered on a desolate shore.

"I am. *Not.* Going. Not there. Not to the birth-nest."

"Knife asked us—"

"Mother!"

"Mother asked us, she made us swear."

"You."

"All right. She made me swear. So, I am going. Are you abandoning her now that she's dead? It's my father, not yours. What's the matter?"

"Abandon her? *Abandon?*" She struck her chest with her fist. "My mother! My flock!"

"Yes, but this is what *my* flock does. The flock of Princes. We go on Quests. We make vows. And sometimes, we kill Kings. It's our duty."

"Not mine. You're not my *hatching*. Not my *duty*." She spat the last as though it were dredged from the bottom of her belly, thick with sludge. She looked at her brother, her eyes raking up and down his shape. She seemed to calm herself, to collect her mind. "You are alone," she whispered. "I am alone. Mother was alone. It never changes. I'll tell you, tell you why. When I was not I. When I *flew* . . ."

THE
GOSLING'S
TALE

THE FIRST MOON-CRESCENTS STARVED ME. I HAD
no Flock. I remembered Mother; I knew I was a no-bird.
But I was hungry still; I could not think, I was so hungry.
There were Falcons near the birth-nest. Slave-hunters. I
flew after them, ate scraps from their beaks. They snapped
at me through leather masks, drew blood from my wings,
scratched at my eyes. I was not theirs. Not their *duty*. I
could not fly very well yet, but I learned. I watched the
seagulls and the starlings and the sapsuckers and the
spoonbills: I learned to swoop and bank and speed and
land.

No words, only flying, and wind like a mother.

I went to the Crows, who would not have me.

I went to the Sparrows, who would not have me.

I went to the Hawks, who would not have me.

I went to the Eagles, who would not have me.

I was alone. The geese had all gone south and there were none left to take me with them. No flock; no food. I was still small. I wandered far away from the birth-nest. I slept in the cracks of trees, in the wind off the eastern moon, cold and afraid, afraid of the Falcons, afraid of the shadow of the birth-nest. I cried in my sleep, and my tears were quiet.

There was a morning, once, when I was a year old? Two? Time is different for geese. A bird bigger than anything, bigger than a Falcon, found me up in my tree, my wings pulled up over my head. He pushed at my feathers with his warm beak. I looked up, into his eyes. They were red, orange, white—fire colors.

"Why are you crying, little one?" he said, and his voice was like sunlight on the wing.

"I am alone," I told him, and shivered, fearing his great bronze talons.

"I am alone, too," he said. His feathers were the same as his eyes—the colors of embers, of flames licking at green branches, and his tail was a shower of gold. "If you want to come with me, neither of us will be alone. I will teach you how to catch moles when they peek out to see the sun, and how to steal cherries from orchards without being shot, and where there are fresh wells without dogs to guard them."

I sniffed at the cold air—but the bird was warm and crackling, and I felt no shivering clouds on my feathers. I was hungry; I did not know what a cherry was. So my webbed feet flapped against the bark and I climbed out of the tree and into the wind.

I didn't have anything to say. All I knew about were worms and scraps of meat the Falcons dropped, and that some trees have birds already living in them. The Firebird cleared his throat.

"Are you lost as well as alone?" he asked politely.

"I . . . I think so. I think I had a mother once, and she sent me away, but it's hard to remember. I keep searching for anything that looks like me. The Falcons bite me. The Crows call me names. I can't find anything with gray feathers and webbed feet and a long neck."

"Well, then," he said gravely, "it is doubly important that you learn about thieving, because it would not do at all for you to starve before you find your gray feathers and webbed feet and long necks. Luckily for you, you have fallen in with a Zhar-Ptitza, a Firebird. They are the best of all possible birds, and I am the best of them. You're only a baby, and you will need looking after, at least until the summer comes and the geese come back. For you, my chick, are a goose. At least, I think you are. I've never known one before, not really. But don't you worry, little gray-winged dear, I shall tell you all you need to know. I shall tell you about my best thievery..."

The Firebird's Tale

CALL ME LANTERN—AND DON'T LAUGH. I WAS always gentle, and my mother thought it better to name me after a little sweet flame in a glass than a fire which eats up trees and children and granaries. Firebirds are normally not particularly social creatures, but I was always too fond of family, and I stayed nest-side far longer than other proud scarlet drakes.

I was gentle—but I was also the best thief in my flock, and I could pluck the tiniest mustard seed from the hand of a princess and she would not even know it had gone until she went to plant it in her garden. And so it was that when my cousin was sitting on an ashen nest with a clutch of eight orange eggs—quite a clutch!—and complaining of a terrible need for cherries, the brighter the better, I was begged by all to fetch her some before her sisters pecked her to death in order to buy some measure of quiet. Cherries! And only certain cherries would do, only those sweet and glossy enough to feed the mother of eight.

I loved my cousin, even if her caws pierced my ears—what hen does not have the right to demand strange things when she is at her nesting? I flew off to fetch the fruit.

Now, in a land far distant from ours, which lies in the desert, there was a Sahiba in those days called Ravhija, and her orchards were as famous as her beauty. She spent her twilights tending the trees until each of them bore fruits without blemish or brown, each sweeter than the other, glistening and heavy. I have told you I was a fine thief—but none yet had managed to steal from Ravhija, whose cleverness was as famous as her orchards. It was these cherries my cousin longed for, and so I resolved to be the first.

I am not a small bird, nor are my colors inconspicuous. It is a handicap in my profession, but I use it as well as I can. I easily hopped a low brick wall as the sun closed up its deep blue talons, and the last loyal flash of light hid my plumage from any wandering eye. My tail trailed on the soft red soil as I crept, half fluttering, half walking, through the rows, looking for a tree bright enough to hide me. I passed persimmons, apples, limes and pecans, pomegranates, figs and oranges, tangerines, pears and apricots, avocados like fat emeralds and plums like purple fists. All thick with juice, nested in glossy green leaves, swollen to full size, though surely it was impossible for them to fruit all together, and side by side, though some loved frost and some a burning sky. And cherries, there they were, cherries big as a giant's knuckles, and redder than my own self. I clipped off bunches as I passed, holding them in my gullet like a mother stork storing up fish for her chicks. I swooped up high to snatch the best fruit without breaking the ceiling of leaves and being caught. I was a glimmer of gold in the green, quicker than a blink. It is an easy, practiced grace, and I promise, my bedraggled dear, to show you how to do it.

But I had to find a place to hide until it was dark enough to get back over the wall without Ravhija spying me. And only certain trees will do—in the way of natural camouflage, the Firebird is sadly lacking. But as providence would have it, at the very center of the orchard was the most extraordinary tree I had ever seen. It was made for me; it matched me in shade and fruit, as if that tree had grown me in its branches, and dropped me onto the wind in some distant autumn beyond memory.

It was a pumpkin tree.

Or so I surmised, though all other pumpkins I had known grew from vines sprawled on the earth. The trunk was a deep orange gourd, twisting and winding around itself, tapering from a thick, fat base tangled with sprawling golden roots up to a spindle, deep grooves in the flesh of it gracefully spiraling, up and up. Branches spooled out here and there, yellow and pale green at the tips, each thick as a waist. The whole thing was strung with vines of red and gold, and from these swung massive pumpkins like lamps, each glowing as though it contained a tiny flame. The whole tree was a festival, sparkling in the center of the fabulous garden like a dancing woman in the center of a dowdy crowd which could only stand still.

I flew to it like a lover. *This* tree would hide me, this tree would keep me safe, this tree was so bright that in it I would be as a little brown sparrow. It seemed to burn like the flaming trees of my own desert, yet the light was soft and kind, and the tree was not consumed. No gardener could find me in all that gold. I circled its trunk in delight, and then up to the pulpy peak—but a pain sparked through me, a terrible rip which sent me tumbling from those perfect limbs. I was afraid that I would spill out of myself, that I had been cut open by some wicked trident. I fell—such an ignoble thing for a Firebird!—I fell into a snarl of glimmering roots, and when the daze passed from my eyes, I saw before me two perfect feet, green as new shoots.

Ravhija bent at the waist, leaning down to me, twirling a long, ruby-colored feather, still tipped in dark blood, in her slender hand. "And what, pretty parakeet, do you think you are doing with my cherries?" she asked sweetly.

Ravhija looked just like the pumpkin tree. Her hair fell to her ankles in twisted ropes of wet, pulpy orange, and she was clothed in wide, dusty leaves that clung to every inch of skin, spreading around her face in a wide collar. Her face was ruddy, shining like cut squash.

"Why would you go to such trouble for a few cherries? Cherries can be bought anywhere. Why do you come to steal from me?"

I blushed, as much as a Firebird can blush when we are already half crimson. "My cousin craves cherries—she is at nest with a clutch of eight, if you can believe it—and your fruit is famous. Of course I could buy it, but then I would never be able to say that I stole it."

Her elfin forehead furrowed, and she straightened, still holding my feather against her hip. I stumbled to my feet while she looked up through green lashes at the marvelous tree. She stood that way for a long time, as though she and it were locked in private consultation. Finally, she spoke, her voice all spice and honey and sweet, thick juice.

"It's my understanding that since I have taken a feather from your tail, you are mine to command. Is that how it is?"

Of course she would know that. My luck would have it no other way.

"Unfortunately for me, it is."

"What would you say then, oh mallard mine, if I were benevolent enough to offer a trade instead of compelling you to do what I want?"

"Why would you do that, if you know I can't refuse you?" I asked, still woozy from the loss of my plumage.

She smiled, and her teeth, too, were pale green, the color of pear skin. "Call it manners, gallantry. Chivalry. Call it the fact that I, unlike some, would rather barter fairly for goods than get them by knavery. The weed takes what does not belong to it and gives nothing back but more weeds; the apple tree takes what is freely given to it, and returns cider and pies and tarts and jams."

I wanted to say that it is hardly the weed's fault if its seed is blown into an apple orchard, and anyway, some plants are good whether or not they are useful in pie-making. But I thought better of it. "Well," I answered instead, picking flecks of dirt from my wings, "what sort of trade?"

"The pick of any fruit I own, in exchange for a fruit I do not."

At this I was finally piqued, and all my remaining feathers flushed fiery with interest.

"Would I have to steal it?"

She laughed, and her leaf-dress rustled. "I'm afraid you might. But at least no one particularly owns them, so the theft would be technical at best—in the sense that the harvesting of any fruit is a theft from a tree. I need the seeds of the Ixora tree, which are not unlike cherries themselves, so I would not begrudge you if you took a few for your cousin. The Ixora grow in the Tinderbox Desert, and their branches burn all day and night. But I think this will not be a problem for you."

"No, my lady." I chuckled. "The fire has not been kindled which can harm me." I did not want to tell her yet how well I knew the Ixora, how I had been born in their scalded shade, and how it was in the ruin of one that my cousin even now waited for me.

"Then it is a trade?"

"It is. Will you give me back my feather now, since we are such good friends?"

She looked at the long red quill, and again at the tree. "No," she said slowly, "I prefer fair barter, but one ought never to fully trust a thief. You may have it back when I have my fruit."

I scratched with one claw at the soil around the golden roots. I was caught, well and truly. "I had better be off, then. The desert is far away. But I think I ought to say, before I go, that I have never heard of a pumpkin tree in any corner of the world, and since everyone knows pumpkins grow on vines, I suspect you have done something vicious to it to make it wind up into a tree, and I ought not to trust you, either."

She leaned against the unnatural tree, lovely as it was, and grinned. Before my eyes—little goose, I would not lie to you—she leaned further and further in until she was entirely swallowed up by the orange trunk, and only her green toes waggled outside of it.

"I collect rare things," came her voice, only a little muffled by the pulp, "and that is what got me into such trouble in the first place."

Her head appeared in the high branches, and bit by bit she emerged, the long ropes of her hair popping free and tumbling nearly to the ground, until she sat quite comfortably on a branch between two still-infant pumpkins. "You see," she said with a sigh, "when you become famous for the variety of your produce, all manner of folk appear at your gates, demanding that you satisfy their appetites, however horrid they may be . . ."

THE GARDENER'S TALE

I AM A TREE.

But it is as easy to say this tree is me. I was born when the tree before it dropped seed; I opened my eyes underground and ate dirt, dirt like cake and jam and wonderful water dripping through the earth like honey through a sieve. I was always thirsty.

And one day I came up through the ground in a little green shoot. I opened the shoot as easily as a door, and stepped out into the sun, a child like any other child. But I still slept in the tree every night as it grew, and as I grew. I loved it like a limb, and it loved me like a torso, and we were very happy together.

Once a peddler came by the brick wall with a sack full of marvels to sell. I ran up to him, since I had never seen another person before, and asked his name, his city, his profession, how many brothers and sisters had he, all the things an excited child will ask of a stranger. He was very kind, and invited me to come over the wall and see what he had to sell—and what he had to sell were seeds.

Apples, persimmons, walnuts, lemons, almonds, dates, and yes, cherries, anything you can name and many I certainly couldn't. I wanted to go over that wall the way certain men want to go to war, and others want to go to women. But I had no money, being a tree only lately sprouted. The peddler felt sorry for me, a grubby little orange-haired girl with green teeth and nothing to her name but a few acres of empty mud. He crouched down very close to my face and told me that should I like to come with him and peddle and tinker and barter and do all the sorts of things traveling folk do, he would give me a penny a month, buy me a real dress, and I could have all the seeds I liked.

I thought this was a very fine plan. I hopped over the wall as graceful as a jackdaw—and fell down dead.

Or as near to dead as makes no difference. When I woke, it was already deep in the furrows of night, and the peddler had carried me back over the wall, laid me in what grass he could find, and left a bulging sack of seeds in my hand.

I could not cross the wall, not ever, no more than a tree can cinch up her roots and travel by coach to another forest. This was sobering. I was as curious about the world as any child, and I knew then that I would never see it.

So I planted it. Apples, persimmons, walnuts, lemons, almonds, dates, and yes, cherries. Anything you can name and many I never could. I had all the time in the world; the life of a tree is long. I learned the arts of irrigation and aeration, of the tripartite field and the leaving of the fallow, fertilization and pruning, and the science of grafting. And all the while the pumpkin tree grew, and gave fruit, and wherever I mashed the pulp into the roots of the new trees, they would bear their own fruit all the year. The acres of mud became a forest, an orchard, the loveliest of any that ever grew, and at the center my tree that is me and me that is the tree, and we all grew together, and we were happy.

Eventually, folk came, and they were not kind peddlers with sacks full of seeds for a dirty-cheeked little girl. Oh, some of them were kind enough, wanting a basket of pears or a bushel of figs for one reason or another—but what do I need with money, when I drink rain and eat dirt? Finally, pressed by their outstretched hands, I began to trade. Fruit for seed—if they could bring me a seed I did not have, I would give them whatever they liked. And so my orchard grew even wilder and more marvelous, and more folk came. I learned about the world from their lips, and I was a good student.

Finally, three fortnights ago, a man came to my wall. I did not like his look, but who is a tree to judge the looks of men? An oak may be gnarled, and still have a kind and sap-wet heart. His hair was iron and his skin was hazel-bark, and his clothes were bright red, as bright as any robin who chirps on my apples. His neck, though, his neck was pale, almost blue, as though it had not seen sunlight since it slipped from his mother's womb.

"Good afternoon, Ravhija," he said, and bowed, and I have long since ceased to be surprised when all manner of strange creatures know my name. "I have come with a long list."

I put a hand on my hip, which had long since grown its own fine dress, though I admit I still dream of the muslin my peddler might have bought me. "As long as you have good trades, I'll do my best to give over whatever you need."

"Ah, there it is. You see, I do not trade. I make a policy of it. Why lose perfectly good belongings when it is just as easy to take what you want?" He snapped his fingers and a small blue flame appeared above his palm, crackling and hissing. "I do not believe that a tree needs further explanation. Immolation is a fate none of us would wish for ourselves. Let me in."

Well, what choice had I? Either he would burn it all to the ground, or, if he knew my nature, he would drag me across the wall and plunder us anyway. I walked the rows with him as if he were a landlord, though no one but me had ever set foot in the garden. I tried to fill his list, which was very strange, and full of herbs as well as fruits, and bark and sap and bits of soil as well. I had nearly all of it; I am not famed for nothing.

But the last, oh, the last.

"It should be plain that I do not have an Ixora," I whispered, refusing to meet his eyes and shying from the dancing flame he still held in his hand. "Surely you would see the smoke if I did."

"But I was told that you have everything that grows under the sun. I need the Ixora; without it the rest is useless."

"What do you need all this for?" I asked plaintively, holding back my tears as best I knew how.

"My dear lady, I am a Wizard. It is enough that I require a thing. Some are born with magic floating inside them like a fly caught in a glass. The rest of us are not so fortunate . . ."

The Tale of the Boy Who Found Death

IT SEEMED CLEAR TO ME LONG AGO THAT IT WAS better to be a wizard than not to be one. Better to close oneself into a room not so different from a kitchen and brew the world in a glass pot than to scrabble in the dirt for mean roots and carry milk from bony heifers and scratch at your cheeks until they were blood-run as a butcher's.

I could never stop scratching, you see.

From the time I was born, my skin peeled and paled, sloughing off as though I could not wait to be out of it, and it itched, oh, it itched, and the scratching never really helped, but I had to do it, I clawed my arms and my chest and my neck, my cheeks and even the creases of my eyelids—there was nothing of me that did not burn.

Folk gasped when they saw me, a boy determined to shed his skin, thin bits of flesh wavering on my body like bits of paper blown by a harsh wind. Doctors and witches and even wizards came, but no one could cool my flaming body. Finally, my mother wrapped me in swaddling clothes and tied my arms to boards so that I could not scratch, and propped me against our damp store wall. There I stayed and grew, fed with a pitted spoon: carrot mash and carrot soup, carrots steamed and baked, carrots raw and burnt and beaten into cakes, carrot-blossom tea and carrot-crusted bread. All we grew were carrots in our few fields, and all my days were filled with orange roots, spooned into my peeling mouth by my frightened mother.

I hung on my boards and my skin crawled. My breath became shallow and quick, I could never seem to get enough air. When I was no longer a baby but a young boy, and still hung up on the wall like a portrait of myself, my skin hardened into something like scales and my hair fell out, but still my flesh itched and scalded and still I could not scratch. The lightest waft of carrot-breeze through my window was agony, stealing my breath and cutting through my bandages to sear my skin.

"Death is at the window," my father would whisper to my mother after a meal of carrot-broth and carrot-greens. I looked—but I could see nothing at the grimy window but the sickly moon like a seed in a black furrow.

"He's at Death's door," my mother would whisper to my father when my breath came sparse and whistling as weeds in the root-rows. I looked—but I was bounded in a bedroom, and nowhere near our thick, warped-wood door.

And when I was very sick, and orange vomit trickled from my mouth to pool on the floor, they would shake their heads and say: "Death stands at his shoulder." I twisted to see him, to glimpse his shape behind me, but there was nothing.

Finally, when I was not much older than twelve, it stopped. As though some strange creature had passed its hand over me in the night, my scaly, peeling skin smoothed and my breath swelled up again, and in time even my hair grew back. It was as though I had never been ill, and with a joy in her great as bushels lashed together, my mother unwrapped the swaddling clothes and took my arms down from their boards, revealing a grown boy, one she had only glimpsed when she changed the bandages: dark of hair and eye, with skin like a drought-blasted field, scars already fading, and a stare she could not meet.

They were eager to get me working the land, as I had missed many years of farm-chores, but I would not cease scratching my flesh only to scratch at the earth.

"All these years you have said Death was nearby, and I have seen nothing. Before I give my life to carrots and cows, I will find Death and ask him why he did not want me, when he lived at my house and shared my board for so many years."

My parents looked at each other and feared the illness had made me mad. "You cannot find Death," they said. "Death finds you. Be glad we were passed over and learn to pull roots from the soil so that they do not break."

But I had a child's understanding, and in my heart Death was a tall man in black who perhaps did or did not ride a black lion—I could not decide—and if he had been so near me and seen my suffering, then we would surely be friends, since he already knew me so well. I would ask him why, if he was my friend, he let me burn and did not take me.

They forbade me, and I did the sensible thing: I crawled out of my window in the dark of the world and crept over the sprouting fields. Perhaps they missed me; perhaps they cried. I do not know, and I never returned.

I pursued my goal in a most logical way—I sought out all the places Death was likely to frequent. Sick men and stillborn children, wasting women and plague-houses and hospices, battles when I could find them and walk behind the lines in the supply trains, looking for the direst of wounded soldiers. I even befriended poisoners so that I could be near their victims at the last moment. I was resourceful, and my young body seemed to want to make up the time it had spent suspended. I was strong with walking and clever with the many lies I told so that a child might be allowed in the presence of the dying. It was, after a manner of speaking, an education, and certainly slashed and moldering flesh taught me far more than carrots and rainwater would have.

But I could not find Death.

I asked every doctor and midwife, every soldier and assassin, and they all replied the same: "You do not find Death; Death finds you."

Finally, grown long and taut as a knotted wire, I came in my wanderings to a kingdom whose sun blazed an unimaginable red, whose jungles were damp and squelching, whose King was a terror and whose roads were mud tracks through the green. Not far from the capital, I was wet to my hips with the slapping of wide-leaved bushes and the splashing of silt-gilded water. The road was not much better than the forest, and I was in a foul mood when a stranger strode up beside me.

"Hello, boy," he said, a short, gnomish man in brightly colored robes who had tied his hair back in complicated patterns, and who wore a wide bolted iron collar that obscured all of his neck and the beginnings of his shoulders. His cheeks were very round and his voice rough as old fenceposts. He nodded a greeting.

"Are you on pilgrimage?"

"Of course not, why would you say that?" I barked.

"Pilgrims are the only ones who take this road. I think it makes them feel as though they are struggling in the face of adversity, as the soul struggles against the body, or some such patter."

"Are you a pilgrim, then?"

"Of a kind."

"Well, I didn't know there was another road," I sulked.

"Many and varied, many and varied. And perhaps one day there will be no road in the world which does not lead to our harbors and towers and chapels. One may hope. But if you are not a pilgrim, why do you aim your feet for Varaahasind, the City of Boars, where Indrajit sits on his throne?"

I sighed, and launched into the litany that by then was as familiar as my own tongue in my mouth. "I seek Death. I was at his door, he was at my window, he stood at my shoulder, but I could not see him. He has been the goal of my heart for years and I have walked half the earth in search of him—and do not tell me to wait until he finds me, or that a nice boy like myself should run off and play. I've heard it, and plenty worse."

The man seemed to consider, and his collar glinted in the sun, reflecting the wet green road.

"No, I wouldn't tell you that, not that."

We walked for a while in the muck, until the first blanched-brick spires of the city showed through the thick trees.

At length, he said: "What if I told you, instead, that I knew where Death lay, and would take you there gladly?"

I swallowed hard. "I would ask what you would have in return for such service."

"Only that when you have finished listening to all that Death has to say, you listen to me for a while, and see which of us is the wiser."

Others had claimed to know, of course, and then led me to dark alleys dank with shadows, where I was subsequently robbed or beaten and left face down in innumerable puddles. But I could not afford, on so strange a task as mine, to refuse anyone. I shrugged and followed him into the city, where pigskin canopies shaded thin and winding streets, and the wind smelled of brewing barley. I followed him up through endless red-brick terraces and shining rice-fields stacked one atop the other all the way up thick green hills, rice-fields couched between towers, between barracks, anywhere a pool of water might stand.

Near the top of the hill was a house like an anthill, just beyond the enormous wall that shielded a bulbous and darkly glinting palace from the plain rice-plantings and dusty terraces. The house was large and might have been handsome if it did not so much resemble a man's head half-buried in the earth. The thatch of the roof drifted down like hair, and the windows seemed to watch us, shutters like lids opening and closing fitfully in the hot afternoon.

"This is the House of Death," my companion said, as casually as if he were announcing the house of a baker or a midwife.

We entered a large room not unlike a kitchen, with all manner of things boiling and drying and blanching and bubbling. The short man seemed to forget I was there, monitoring everything that sent steam and scent into the air. I finally cleared my throat and he looked up, startled as a sparrow.

"Oh. Death, wasn't it? Yes, here." And he rummaged behind a large cabinet for a moment before producing a dusty object with a stage magician's flourish.

It was a large glass jar, filled to the brim with dirt.

"You have wasted my time, old man," I sighed.

"Not at all, boy. You wanted Death? This is it. Dirt and decay, nothing more. Death translates us all into earth." He frowned at me, his cheeks puffing slightly. "Are you disappointed? Did you want a man in black robes? I'm sure I have a set somewhere. A dour, thin face with bony hands? I've more bones in this house than you could ever count. You've been moping over half the world looking for Death as though that word meant anything but cold bodies and mushrooms growing out of young girls' eye-sockets. What an exceptionally stupid child!" Suddenly he moved very fast, like a turtle after a spider—such unexpected movement from a thing so languid and round. He clapped my throat in his hand, squeezing until I could not breathe, just like those awful days when I hung on the wall and gasped for air. I whistled and wheezed, beating at his chest, and my vision blurred, thick as blood. "You want Death?" he hissed. "I am Death. I will break your neck and cover you with my jar of dirt. When you kill, you become Death, and so Death wears a thousand faces, a thousand robes, a thousand gazes." He loosened his grip. "But you can be Death, too. You can wear that face and that gaze. Would you like to be Death? Would you like to live in his house and learn his trade?"

I rubbed at my throat, panting. "You're just like the others," I rasped. "You lure me to your house with the promise of wisdom and give me nothing but your fist."

"Oh no, I am nothing like the others. I am a Wizard, Indrajit's man, and I am as true a Death as you will find. Keep wandering after your phantoms if you like—eventually someone will strangle you for a scrap of food and then my lessons on the nature of mortality will be, let us say, unnecessary. Or stay with me and learn, stay with me and one day you will stand over a man as I have stood over you and he will know you to be Death, black of eye and sleeve. You may be stupid, but it is not every child who burns so to become Death's prodigy. I am offering what you want, if you are wise enough to take it."

I stared hard at the floor. "Would I have to wear a collar like yours?" I mumbled finally.

"It is always a choice," he said softly, "and I chose it. Magic is a many-sided glass—"

"My mother says magic comes from the Stars, and I have about as much light in me as our cow."

"Some believe that. Some of us, who find magic in things, in stones and words, in grass and leaves, long ago realized that it is unimportant where the leaves got their power, only that they have it. And of those, some folk, men and women and monsters, decided in days long past to trade their freedom for power. They took a collar, yoked themselves to a ruler. If you want power, you will do the same."

"Magic *is* power," I protested.

"Magic is magic. If you want to boil up cough medicine for local brats and keep your hair from turning gray, you're more than welcome to it, and need nothing but an iron pot. But power, power to control one's fate and the fates of others, real power, and certainly the power to become Death, to be Death writ large in the eyes of the lost—well, a monarch's protection is useful, and their resources go far beyond grass and leaves."

I glanced at the jar of earth and licked my lips. After all this time, Death was at my window again, and at my shoulder, and I stood at his door, and this time I could see, I could see everything he offered.

THE GARDENER'S TALE, CONTINUED

I STOLE A GLANCE AT HIS PALE NECK. MY THROAT was dry as birch bark. "But you don't have a collar."

He leaned very close to me, and his breath was sickening-sweet, like too many flowers covering a corpse. "I stayed in that place for many years, and the plague of my skin never returned. I progressed through lessons as best I could—though I was never a prodigy. What I know was hard-won, and I treasure it with the passion of a lover often denied. And then"—a rush of color lit his cheeks— "and then I saw an extraordinary thing happen in that dark and glinting Palace, a thing I could not forget, though I tried, I tried. I won my freedom, tree-child, and no King calls me doulios now. I have spooled out my liberty searching for a way to repeat that extraordinary thing, and I am near to my goal—I need the Ixora to further my work. But I am tired, Ravhija, I am tired of pounding the earth with my feet. It is unbecoming and I have had my fill of picking through measly gardens for the smallest seed. If you do not have an Ixora, you will have to get me one."

"Sir!" I cried. "If you know what I am, you know I cannot leave the garden! How am I to get a tree that grows in the desert?"

"That is none of my concern. I was resourceful; so must you be. You will get it for me, or I will burn your orchard to the ground." He scratched absently at his pale neck. "I will make all your trees into flaming Ixora, and you with them, for I doubt you will live much beyond the last fluttering ashes of your golden tree. Death will find you, and his gaze will be very black."

He swept away with six baskets of my rarest crops and a promise to return with his dancing blue flame in the fall. He swept away, and I stood helpless at the wall.

The Firebird's Tale, Continued

"What a beastly man," I breathed.

Ravhija nodded miserably, stepping down from her branch. "And the summer is almost through, and I with no Ixora. No surprise, really. I have asked for it in trade, but no man is brave enough to reach into the heart of a burning tree just to pull me out a little berry."

"No man," said I, moved as a rock rolled aside from a cave, "but a bird may, and there can be no bird more suited to the Torch-Trees than I. You do not know how simple a thing this is! The Ixora are my home, and to take a few flinty fruits is as easy as picking corn out of a basket!

Even if you did not hold my feather, beautiful mistress of pumpkins, I would go, and happily, to the desert for you."

With glittering green tears in her eyes, Ravhija kissed my downy cheek, and reminded me to wait until the tree had nearly died before prodding about in the ash. She needed at least three, she said, but I could have all the fruit I wanted when I returned. She clucked behind me like a mother sending her boy to school, pointing out this and that and warning me not to scorch myself, though that last was hardly needed. I nibbled at her ropy hair in farewell—this means affection, gray-cheeked girl.

It tasted just exactly like pumpkin.

It is a long flight into the desert. Many countries are crossed, and their colors are as varied as a jester's coat. I watched them fold and unfold underneath me. One by one, they all turned thirsty, turned empty, turned to sand. But even when one has crossed the line in the earth that separates the green from the desert, there is still farther to go to the white sands and salt flats where the Ixora grow.

I know the land very well.

But once I crossed the last of the green lands, I knew I was followed. Little gosling, I will teach you this, too. It is a quiet, subtle thing, to know when you have an uninvited companion, but any bird should know it as surely as he knows which wind will take him into the clouds, and which down to the water. But I had never been hunted as surely as this. The hunter's footsteps were lighter than breath, and though sometimes I thought I saw him, a speck on the land below me, more often I felt him beside me in the air, and I was unnerved.

Knowing I was hunted, I could not go to my cousin's nest-side and nuzzle her before collecting the cherries. I did not know what other part of the forest might be ready to seed. I circled for days, the strange hunter close behind me, avoiding any place I knew a Firebird to nest. It made for a curling, snarled path through the fiery groves, and I lost many days to it. Finally, circling back to the salt flats, I saw what I wanted, laid out like a feast on the white ground.

I am not a stupid bird. The hunter had laid me a trap that, even had I not been sent by the beautiful pumpkin-girl, would have been hard to resist— what does anyone like better than their mother's own dish? I looked down at the fruit, the dozens of cherries that might have quickened a whole forest, and it was like tearing myself in two to turn away from them. But turn away I did.

And it was strange, but the feeling of being hunted did not follow me into the forest. It was gone, vanished like a breeze in a storm. There was no one around me, whatever had stalked me had lost my scent or given up, and it was no matter which, for I could finally go to my cousin's side, and spill what few cherries I had kept in my gullet onto her nest-stoop like a stork vomiting fish. She pecked at it, but her meal was bitter. She wept and wept and could not stop, her tears like burning oil blackening the sand below her ashen nest.

"Lantern, the chicks," she gasped through her sobs, "the chicks, he took them all."

"What?" I cried. "Who took them? What do you mean, cousin? Your eggs are still there, I can see their colors under your down! Stop crying and tell me what happened!"

Sniffling, she whispered in terror, "A thing came into the desert, and he was all white, and he smelled of scorched bread and copper filings, and he went into every dying tree that might have been a nest, and pulled out the sap, and pulled out the seed." I choked in horror. "And as if that was not enough, he fed the meat to his women, and piled the seeds up like trash." She burst into a storm of weeping again, and her breast shook so hard I feared her eggs would crack. "They kicked them over," she murmured, so soft I could barely hear. "The women kicked them over like a child's marbles, and there were no eggs for them to strike. It will be years before any other hen will lay her nest."

I held my cousin in her grief and reeled in my own. Of course, you could not understand, poor gray-heart. It is our greatest secret, and I tell you now so that you will trust me to never withhold wisdom when I have it to give. My cousin's eggs have no rooster; they are quickened by the dying tree. The flint-seeds spark the new tree, yes, but also the new bird, and the first roots of the new Ixora are born out of the egg with the chick. The flint must have *something* to catch its spark—it must have both feather and bark. We need each other, you see. The Zhar-Ptitza drakes only protect the nest. We are like bees—we cannot mate, at least not with our hens. I have heard that some few once managed to pull eggs from a tree and fire them with their own skin, but even their names are lost to ash now. All my family is mothers, brothers, sisters, cousins, aunts, and uncles—and no fathers. There will never be chicks which are mine. The Ixora is the other half of us.

So you see why it is that I answered Ravhija so readily, even though it meant giving her three seeds which might have been three Firebirds. Why, I would have done as she asked even without the feather. I thought, I hoped that if my cousin could hatch a tree's eggs, perhaps a tree—but that doesn't matter now.

There was nothing I could do. I had to wait. The clutch was born and there can be nothing finer than eight new Firebirds cracking their shells, but they, and I, had to wait until the next crop of Ixora went to ash before their black little bodies could burst into flame, before the other hens could quicken their eggs in the flood of sap, before Ravhija's seeds could be spared.

It was five years before I had what she needed. I flew back over the countries, which changed from gold to green under me, sick and as full of dread as a hive of honey. I told myself that she had found some other source, that she had found the strange hunter some morning at her wall, who happily gave over the little red seeds. Someone, I told myself, will surely have saved her. She will wave happily from her tree, and her orange hair will shine in the sunlight, and she will tell me it was all right, don't be silly, it all turned out well in the end.

But I knew it was a lie. The orchard was black as a chimney when I finally found it, the wall smashed and crumbled. The trees were stark skeletons against a gray and brooding sky—nothing grew; there was no fruit, only a mash of dead sweetness that had once boiled glazing the earth. It was all gone, all gone. I flew over the wreckage and I could hardly keep myself in the sky, so great was my guilt, hanging around my neck like an anchor.

Except that it was not quite all gone. In the center of the garden, where that beautiful tree that had filled me with secret hope had stood, there was a slender green sapling, almost too pale to see when the sun was behind it.

Beside it sat a little girl playing in the scorched soil.

"Oh!" she cried out when she saw me. "Aren't you a pretty bird!"

I landed next to her, my blazing tail dragging in the ash of the old tree. "Ravhija?" I asked, nosing her uncertainly.

"Oh, no, I'm Ravhi!" she cried, bouncing up to stroke my feathers like any other delighted child. She beamed up at me through green lashes; her hair was short, but already twisted into little ropes of pulpy orange.

Of course I understood. No child of an Ixora could miss it—the tree had dropped its seeds in the earth, and no soil is richer than that of a forest after a fire. A new tree had been born, and a new mistress.

I gave her the seeds. It was all I could do.

She thought they were very pretty.

THE GOSLING'S TALE, CONTINUED

"BUT YOUR FEATHER," I WHISPERED, AS A COLD AND snowy lake country fluttered below us like a huge white flock.

Lantern shook his glittering head. "Ravhi didn't have it, and it was no use asking her where it went—she remembered nothing of the old tree, or the old gardener. I think the Wizard must have taken it when he played Death. I feel it still, like an eye or an ear I have misplaced. It was not burned, but it is not near, and no one has called me with it."

I flew a little closer to the warm bird, basking in his

heat. Snow melted from my beak. "I'm sorry she couldn't nest with you, like you wanted," I said bashfully.

He smiled and squinted in the flying flakes. "Drakes aren't meant to nest. It was a silly hope. And if she had, we should never have met, little web-foot, and that would have been very sad."

He flew with me all winter and into the spring, fed me grasses and mice and dandelion heads, until I grew, and my neck was long. When the geese came back, I did not want to go with them, and he did not make me go. I flew under his wings, which were wide as sunset clouds, as chapel doors or cedar shades, and I was safe from Falcons. Together we crossed the wide purple sea and back again, and rested in the fronds of palm trees. He taught me many songs and the language of the Starlings, and the Storks, and the Seagulls. And he did teach me to steal as well as any burglar. I never wanted for cherries.

For us there was no time, only the flying, and the clouds in our mouths. I was happy. I was his. We needed no others. I did not cry. But after two summers I saw that the trees were familiar, and the shadows of the birth-nest were again on the horizon. I shivered in fear.

"I have brought you back home, little one," Lantern said, "for there is a new flock, and they are calling on the moon and sun to find you."

"I want to stay with you." I wept, and he held me in his wings, which were as the evening sky closing over me.

He shifted wretchedly from foot to foot. "We are not the same, gray-heart. Only those who share feather and beak can remain together always. Maybe I shouldn't have taken care of you at all, but you were so poor, and so dear, and I have never had a chick to love. You will be all right now, I know it. You should have a flock, and a nest. I could give you only a burning tree and cold fruit. And . . . there is something pulling at me, here, like a finger hooked into my breastbone. My feather wants me, and I cannot refuse."

"But I don't want a new flock! And you can refuse; you can turn around and fly the other way as fast as you can."

He sighed, and even his brilliant colors, his oranges and golds that lit my world, seemed muted and dull. "It isn't like that, my love. When my feather calls, I have to go. I can no more fly in the other direction than I can fly underwater."

I still did not cry, but it was very hard. We perched on a crooked oak stump outside a great courtyard, and something was there, on the cobblestones, something that smelled like memory. A curl of smoke was rising from it, smoke, and then bright fire, sparking in the morning fog.

"We are not the same," Lantern repeated, "but there is fire, and you can go towards it without dread, and be born again with your own birds, born in fire just like me. There will be a little of what made me, in you."

The smell pulled at me—I knew it, I knew it, and the air above the pyre was now filled with birds, birds with the maddening, wonderful smell on their wings. It was like horses, horses and milk and damp, dark rooms.

It was my mother's smell, and Lantern put his hearth-warm head to my back and pushed me towards it. I flapped my wings slowly and glided into the mist. I did not look behind me; I knew he did not want me to, and there was Mother before me, Mother, whom I had given up all hope of finding. But it was as though my own feathers were ripped from me, each dripping with dark blood.

When my mother burned, I was not afraid. I cut her bonds with my mouth and kissed her flaming lips. All around me were birds that looked just like me, with long necks and gray feathers and webbed feet. They were my flock, they knew me for their own, and she was my flock, and I loved her. I felt no fire, only the path to her, and I helped her rise up from the ash, just as Lantern must have risen when he was a little black chick; I helped her rise up and steal away into the night.

"I WAS THEIRS. I AM NOT YOURS. ONLY FLOCK CARES for flock." Aerie looked at him with her large black eyes, full of mourning and distrust.

"But we are family; we are the same . . . clutch," Leander protested quietly.

"We are not the same. Your father you will put under the claw. He is not *my* father."

Leander's cheeks darkened. His father's face floated in his vision, and he felt no love for it. "He harmed our mother. And all her people. He destroys everything."

"Why should I care what is done on the earth? This is not my place. I belong to the air. I belong to all these ghosts."

"Aerie, you are a woman now; you are on the earth, both feet. You cannot ignore it because you remember when they were wings."

"He is not my father, not my duty," she insisted, staring at the moon-speckled grass.

"No. But it is our mother, and she gave you the wind and the clouds so you could live. I have done so much wrong, Aerie. All I wanted was a Quest—and this one has led only back to the Castle I wished to escape. But if that is what is written, that is what is written. And it is written that because we left the Castle separately, we must return together. There is the Wizard to think of, who killed our grandmother and ravaged her bones. All this is ours, the nest that made us. I am yours. You are *my* duty. Come with me."

Leander put his hand out to her, glimmering in the dark, and slowly, she clasped it with her own, still streaked in blood. "Grandmother," she whispered, "and the flock that once had no wings."

Journeying back towards the Castle, Leander marveled that Aerie could move entirely without sound. Her feet made no impact on the earth as they ran from the Witch's Glen, back and back and back towards the place of their birth.

Of course the guards let Leander through—though he had been missing he was certainly not banished, and they took Aerie for a plaything he had brought home. It was simple as a child's wooden blocks. They crept through the upper rooms, past door after door bolted with great brass locks. Suddenly, the Prince stopped.

"Wait," he whispered, and disappeared behind one of the heavy doors. It was his own bedroom, and Leander stood within it as though he had never seen it before. He was not the man who had slept here; what he knew could not live in these velvet walls. He shook his head, trying to hold to his purpose.

"It is the function," he told himself silently, "of a Prince to kill monsters. If the derivative of a Prince is set to zero, the kingdom survives."

He straightened his spine and opened the carved teak table beside his brocade bed. He had what he had come for. From the drawer he drew a long silver knife with a curving handle of bone. It shone now with a pure light; it glimmered in his mind, heavy with meaning. He had taken it as a child for a toy, from the heaps of knives and daggers and stilettos in the vaults. It had called to him, and in the blade he felt uneasily that he had no choice in the story of this night, that he had strained towards it all his life, and never of his own will.

"Come on," he said to his sister, whose eyes were beginning to take on the panting sheen of the hunt, "we will go to the Wizard first."

They slipped through the door that led into the Wizard's quarters—easily picked, easily entered. It should not be so easy, he thought. Killing should be hard and horrible work, not like this, less effort than drawing water from a well. It had no right being anything but thudding and blood and cries. But there was no sound save the heavy breathing of Aerie behind her brother. She saw the knife glinting at his belt and had already resolved to steal it. She could wait.

The Wizard Omir lay peacefully, prone as a baby, sleeping among white furs, his lips still full and firm. But the rest of him had long ago slid into old age swiftly as a knife slides through ribs. Leander had seen this man nearly every day of his life, but now he saw how deep the lines and wrinkles ran, how terrible the sores were that strange, hidden experiments had inflicted on his flesh. He remembered those sallow, piscine eyes always watching him, and he remembered the tale his mother told him, how Omir had killed Grandmother Bent-Bow with as little thought as baiting a hook. He reached for the knife, certain that he could do the deed.

But the blade was gone.

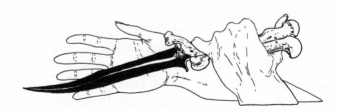

Aerie sat perched on one of the high tables with its gnarled wood. She breathed in long, sighing gasps, and in her pale fist was the bone-handled knife. She must have known it from the moment she saw it—known it for her own, for her grandmother's blade. It must have called to her like a feather, and now they were together, knife and woman, and Leander could not stand before them.

With a soft cry, no more than a gosling gives upon seeing its flock in the distance, she fell on the sleeping form of the Wizard, plunging the knife into him. The old man opened his rheumy eyes in time to behold her, hair streaming, skin flushed with fury and triumph. She leaned down close to him, as though she were going to kiss his rasping lips, and whispered sinuously in his withered ear:

"Death has found you."

Omir saw her, the bird-maiden, crouching over him like a nightmarish falcon, her eyes burning in her skull.

"I knew!" he breathed, choking as she twisted the knife in him. "I knew she could do it! The Witch, she lied, but I knew!"

Slowly, Aerie touched his face, gently, like a child. Her nails parted his flesh easily, as though it were water. She put her fingers to her mouth and sucked greedily at his blood.

"Slave," she hissed, "always a slave, whispering in the dark, stealing what isn't yours."

"Perhaps . . . perhaps he should not be blamed," Leander murmured. "My father, after all, was the one who commanded him."

Aerie did not hear him. Omir chuckled, and blood spattered his chin. "Your father is a fool among fools. And the girl knows, she knows, she knows. Her mother told her about the tower, she knows I did much that was not commanded. But she won't kill me. She knows that I hear tales, too, and I know about her Firebird and how he left her; she knows I had his feather. I kept him in this very room, in an ivory cage."

Aerie's eyes narrowed to silver slivers. Omir tried to sit up, but was pinned by the blade, and simply collapsed again in another fit of coughing. "Oh, yes, girl, just over there, in the corner."

She leaned on the bone hilt, and for the first time, Omir cried out, with real anguish, his white eyebrows arching, his lips peeling back from his teeth. "Where is he?" she growled.

"I don't . . . I don't have him. I swear it. I sold him, him and his feather and his cage, to a man in the city of Ajanabh, I sold him, I sold him, I swear. Please." The Wizard's hands flapped uselessly at the knife. "But listen to me, listen! After all these years I have the secret: I can make you a Firebird; I can make any willow into an Ixora for you, light your wings, and send you to him. I can even change you so that he can quicken your nest, and you will never need the trees. But if you kill me, you will remain this wretched girl, and never fly again, and you'll never find him without me. You will stay in this awful body, with only your little brother to keep you company—and I assure you, he is dreadful company."

Aerie was weeping, her tears falling on the Wizard's weak hands. Her shoulders shook like bare branches, and she looked at him with a terrible hope flaming in her dark eyes. She leaned in, very close, and put her arms around the old man. Through his rattling cough and the dark stain spreading across his belly, he tried to pat her back paternally. He could only manage to lift his arm once and let it flop back to the bed. But he could still speak, and his voice was like leeches suckling.

"There, there, your uncle will make all things well, you'll see. No need to speak; I already know what you want, love. All manner of things will be well."

Aerie raised her silvery head and whispered in his ear. "*Mother.*"

Then Aerie, who had never had hands since her first breath, seized him by the scalp in an expert fist, snatched the knife from his belly, and cut his throat.

The blood was hot and thick, and though it flowed over her hands like mud, Aerie would not let go of the knife. Leander could not pry it from her fingers. He pulled her from the corpse and into the hall—her eyes glittered brightly, ecstatic, wild.

They would never be admitted to the King's quarters at night, so they inched across the stone wall windowsill by windowsill, ivy-covered stair, and finally mere toe-holds in the granite. Finally, they crouched below the King's window, and Leander looked at his sister meaningfully before he swung up and into the chamber. She was not to follow.

So, of course, she slid in behind him as noiselessly as the space between breaths.

The King lay on his bed, alone, still robust and strong, perfectly awake. He turned to his son.

"Certainly I have taught you better than to eschew the use of doors."

Leander expected nothing less at this point, but covered his fear with a blank face. "It seemed the best plan."

"Did it now? And I see you have brought the poor little bird with you. All the masks off, then?" His eyes did not blink, nor shift to Aerie even for a moment. She was nothing to him; she didn't matter.

"If the derivative of a Prince is set to zero, the kingdom survives," Leander whispered.

"What nonsense are you spouting, boy? Did that foul Witch find you at last? She was never worth the price of her bedding. A pity the fire could not be extended indefinitely. Executions must always be handled personally; remember that, when you are King, my son."

"I will not be King. I will kill you here where you lie for what you have done to my mother's people, for what you have made me do to countless others like her when the men rode out under white flags."

The King laughed, low and hooting. "Oh, my son, my son. How do you think *I* became King? I, too, cut out my father's heart while he slept . . ."

The King's Tale

HIS FACE WAS SO FAT ON THE PILLOW. LIKE A SLAB of meat on a white tablecloth, all spidery red blood vessels and swollen nose. He hadn't slept in the same bed with my mother for years—but then, no one did. I think I would have actually preferred it if she had had a lover. It would have meant she was human. But she never let anyone between her legs; she spent every night in a shabby old bed in a shabby old tower, and my father slept in the great ebony four-poster bed that was meant for the lord and his lady.

Didn't you know? My father was never King.

A country Baron at best—some winters, the pigs and cows slept in the great hall to keep them from keeling over in the frost. The stink of it reached the rafters and hung there like a dung-spattered chandelier. My mother was better than that. I was better than that. I used to watch her, her profile against her window, and wonder how she ever married the sack of onions and pig snouts I called a father. I heard from servants that he wasn't always so useless. Before my mother shut up her mouth with grief, this was a rich place, and the cows slept in the grass where they belonged.

But things were as they lay. She never said anything. She never said a word. My mother had kept silent as a nun since the day my sister was taken from her.

I was an infant when she vanished from us; I never knew that sister. But her absence stalked the house like a hungry dog. The hole where she had been took up space at our dinner table, it sagged and slumped in the musty air, it ate and drank and breathed down all of our necks.

My other sisters were married off before I could manage arithmetic. I grew up alone in that silent house with nothing but the stinking cows and my mute mother and the hole. Even my father didn't want to spend his days there; he stayed in the fields directing hay-rolling and goat-breeding until it was dark enough to slip back inside without anyone bothering him. But still, the hole answered the bell when he rang, and he had to scurry to bed with his head down to avoid looking it in the eye.

I didn't think anyone would miss him. He was a fool now, feeble as a sheep after shearing, and I was well into manhood, ready to be Baron, hungry for it, tired of the ramshackle place falling down around us, propped up only by a hole in the air, by empty space. Dirt-farming squalor like my father always has a kind of rude health, and I knew if I wanted a Barony, I would have to take it.

I wasn't even very quiet going up the stairs to his room. I stomped like anything—in that dead house, who would care if one more dead thing turned belly-up by morning? But the hole was there. I could feel it, tugging at my sleeves with sisterly disapproval. If she had been there, the hole sighed sadly, there would have been no silence, and I wouldn't need to hear my own father's screaming just to know I was alive. The hole was sorry for me, and I hated it.

But he didn't scream. It was as easy as cutting meat for a roast. I didn't even think when I slid the knife into his ox-huge heart. I just did it, and it seemed like the most natural thing in the world. Killing, I thought, should be harder than this. His eyes flapped open, and he gurgled a little, no more than a calf will when you cave in its skull for the summer banquets. He didn't scream; I wasn't alive.

But I was Baron.

Mother watched me coming down the stairs, wiping blood on my trousers. She stared, and her mouth was thin and colorless, but she said nothing. She never did.

The Barony was better for my hand, as I knew it would be. The fields gave grain, the trees gave cider, the pigs slept in the penned muck and grew sweet with fat. The dust was swept from every corner of the great hall, and long white banners were hung from the well-scrubbed rafters. Folk came to the Castle again, and there was music and dancing when the summer broke the spring.

The hole never came back.

Finally, it came time to choose a wife. I didn't really care, but I was told it was the lordly thing to do, and already I was considering how to move myself into a crown the way some men consider how to move themselves into a larger house by the sea. A King has to have a Queen. A Baron has to have a Baroness. So it was that I consulted the family books, oily and filthstained as they were, and discovered how my mother managed to marry a sack of onions and pig snouts.

In our backward, beer-addled family, a wife is gotten by contest, not courting. There is a belt of gold and jasper, handed down grandmother to granddaughter, and the next lady of the house must fit the belt, or else she cannot sleep in a tower and ignore her husband for twenty years. Yellow-eyed superstition and idiocy will always outlive the family that perpetrates it.

I took the belt from my mother's waist. She said nothing. She never did.

But when I sent out my summons for likely young women to come and try the belt to their hips, my mother closed herself up in her tower and would not come out, no matter how many sweet-cheeked maids begged her to unbolt the door. From within, she said nothing.

The whole procedure took weeks. They came waltzing up to my door in every conceivable color and manner of dress: rags and bustles, blond and black, velvet and muslin and plain cotton sashed with rope. I slung the gold and jasper around dozens of waists; I fastened it under dozens of blushing cheeks. It slipped off their hips and cinched them till they could not breathe—no one fit the belt; no licit woman lived in all my countryside.

I did what logic dictated. I went up the long, winding stair to my mother's tower, fingering the belt in my hand, watching the dim light glitter on its dull gems. Faced with the thick oak door and its bronze fittings, I knocked as politely as a suitor.

"Mother," I said. "The belt fits no one."

There was no sound from the room.

"Mother," I said, "I must marry."

There was no sound from the room.

"Mother," I said, "the belt fits *you*."

Oh, don't be so shocked. Morality makes way for Kings, and the dirt-virtue of cattle farmers is of no interest to me.

There was a shuffling and rustling behind the door. Finally I was finished with her nonsense, her childish tantrums, her hiding like a crab in its scarlet shell. I put my shoulder to the hinges—I was never a weak man, and the bronze bent after only two blows. They bent, creaked, and gave, and my mother was sitting on a bed in the middle of a room filthy with dust, sheets tangled around her, her violet-black dress torn and too small, her red hair matted and tangled, spilling onto the sagging mattress.

On her lap was the hole.

The edges of it crackled and warped in a way I had never seen, a strange silver light that actually rimmed the outline of a long-haired girl, slumped into my mother's lap. There was nothing there, as though the girl had been ripped out of the air and left but a suggestion of what she might have looked like, what her posture might have been. All I had seen of the hole until that morning was its absence; this thing had weight and heft, weight and heft and light. There was nothing there, but the nothing glinted dully while my mother stroked its shape.

"I made it," she said, and her voice creaked and groaned, a stuck door pried open. "When he took her, I made it. It was the last magic I ever did."

"Magic," I snorted.

"I set it to walk the house as she would have done, to eat and sleep and laugh as she would have done. But as she might have done, it kept coming here, and only came down the staircase to see you grow, and watch you play and frown and sleep."

"It's nothing, Mother. It's less than air."

She shrugged miserably. "It's not her, I know that, I'm not mad, but when I sleep, it puts its airy arms around me, and I can almost smell her skin. I miss her. I just miss her. But after you killed your father, I let it stay here."

I shrugged. "I wanted to be Baron. I won't apologize for it. Father had let this house go to ruin, and you with it. You only married him for the sake of a gold belt, anyway."

She glared at me through her ruined curls. "You'll believe what you want to believe, Ismail. Belts, collars—they only give you a reason to take the woman you wanted all along, without giving her space to speak."

I looked at the damp-warped floor. Not out of shame, mind you, but because I thought that was what a good son in this situation might do. "The belt fits no one else."

My mother rested her hand on the hip of the hole, and her face seemed to sag, as if some final thing slid out of it, leaving nothing but a dry shell, a sea snail rolling in the sand. "If you cannot think of a reason not to come breaking down my door proposing a thing which not even a King would dare—"

"Would it be better if I was King, Mother?" I exploded, pushing through the hole onto the bed and grabbing her violet-wrapped shoulders—she was so thin! "If I were King, would you curtsey and put on your ermine and dance at our wedding? You know the family law. Better wedded to me than to this disgusting display of magic tricks, cloistered with it day in and day out! I won't apologize for my father and I won't apologize for you. Nothing is gotten in this world except by force—a lifetime in this dead place, where *nothing* ever happens because the only people who live here are *dead*, has taught me that!"

She started laughing, hysterical, unhinged as the door to her room. "Yes, yes, if you were King it would be licit; Kings do whatever they please, Kings and their Wizards—no laws for them! They take and take and what does it matter? No one asks the taken; they just forget, they just forget, they disappear and everyone forgets." She looked up at me, her eyes suddenly canny as a fox in sight of a mouse. "I'll play this game if you want to play it, Ismail mine, but you have to perform a deed of honor. That's what young men do when they're courting, if I remember."

I let her go gently. Was that all? Bring her roses or a dragon scale from furthest isles and she'd put up no fight? "What would you have me do? Let us get this over with as quickly as possible."

"Bring me the head and the collar, and whatever other pieces you want to keep, of the Wizard who took your sister."

Well, killing is easy work. I rose from the bed, and the hole coalesced again where I had been. I bowed to her in as courtly a manner as I have ever managed.

"Lady Iolanthe, I am at your service."

I did not particularly want to marry my mother, you understand. If another girl had fit the belt I would have had her just as easily. But protocol must be observed when one is of a certain station, and it wouldn't be so awful, after all, for her to stand at ceremonies and dance at balls. It's not as if she had ever shared a bed with her last husband, beyond what was necessary for inheritance. I was not happy to go off and kill a Wizard who had done no harm to me, besides being part of an unsavory profession, just so I could make Iolanthe a Baroness twice over, but then, what is happiness? I'm sure I've never met the beast.

It is not that we didn't know where the Wizard who took my sister from us lived—there was not a farm-haggarded soul in the countryside who did not know where Omir rested his staff and vial. But one does not go demanding one's daughter back from such a man, especially when he is bound to such a King as we were ruled by in those days.

That King's Palace was surrounded by deep woods whose trunks were bunched and cracked as old women's spines. The thing itself was close-bordered by two strange-watered rivers, one black and one white. As I crossed the bridges I looked into the current—the black one reflected my face like the side of a dead volcano, glittering in flat shapes between ripples, showing a reasonably handsome young man who was not a Prince, but might be mistaken for one on a particularly sunny day.

The white river showed nothing, sheer and dull as milk.

Not knowing much about how to assassinate when it is not a simple matter of a bedroom and a knife, I applied for an audience and, predictably, was told to wait. I busied myself as best I could, and enjoyed a new kind of life: sleeping in proper rooms for once, eating at proper tables, dressing in proper clothes.

I walked out to look at the rivers every day.

Finally, I was called into the high-ceilinged audience chamber, heralded as Ismail of Barony Baqarah—how strange it was to hear my name intoned by a bored scribe!—and stood before the King and his favorite slave. The King was at his midday meal, slavering at hay in a golden trough, shoving his face full of grass with both hands.

Monstrous. Unnatural. For men to be ruled by an animal. I suppressed the urge to vomit onto the silver-tiled floor.

Sorrel, the Centaur-King of the Eight Kingdoms, looked up at me, his forelegs buckled and kneeling so that he could eat his fill. His chestnut tail flicked at the air. Hay still stuck to his brown beard. "Oh," he grunted, "it's you." Behind him, the Wizard, in ill-fitting blue-brown robes and a heavy iron collar that weighed on him like a penance, looked from the horseman to me with an uncertain gaze.

"It is him, isn't it, Omir?" the Centaur said, lifting his huge equine form with some difficulty from the trough and clacking his hooves on the tile, keeping his right side always to me, his left in shadow. His brown pelt flowed into pale skin that seemed to rarely see sun and he wore, as you might expect, nothing. There was no throne—how could there be?—but he rested on a pile of rose-colored cushions on a dais, and I suppose for a horse that is as good as a throne.

"Yes, my lord, I believe it is."

"I'm sorry; who am I meant to be?" I asked, nonplussed. Killing is meant to be in the dark, in the quiet, and there I was in a room that could not be brighter if its foundation had been sunk in the sun itself, and what's worse, expected.

Sorrel scratched himself at the forelock with an expression of boredom on his moon-broad face. "Omir told me you were coming, the man who would replace me . . ."

THE TALE
OF THE
EIGHT-CHAMBERED
HEART

BEFORE MY GRANDFATHER WENT OUT TO PASTURE, it was decided by those much wiser than I that the Eight Kingdoms, as varied in their folk as a field of ten thousand blades of grass, could not be governed by men and women. They were fit for country gentry, certainly, counting things up and doling things out, but how could they be trusted to speak and act for us, the second nation, the nation of monsters?

Obviously, they could not.

Centaurs seemed a likely choice, standing as we do between the bed and the stable, between men and beasts, between the wild and the world. It was thought providential that our massive hearts, necessary to serve such massive bodies, had eight chambers, one for each Kingdom. And so it was that for many lifetimes, Centaurs ruled—some badly as untrained stallions, some well as sweet-natured geldings. That is the way with rulers; we were never immune. But watching the Kings of men before us, we learned that passing the crown to sons and daughters was as foolish as feeding seaweed to a wolf. We decided our rulers in a way more suited to our strengths: with a race.

The morning was crisp and apple-strewn the autumn that I took my place at the starting line. My rival was Dapple, a tall, handsome gray whose chest was so broad I could not have put my arms around it if they could stretch to twice their usual length. I was a little worried—fast as I was, I was not the strongest of my herd, and my chest looked sickly next to this muscled block of breath and bone.

"It is a perfect day for a race," Dapple boomed approvingly, pawing the earth with pearl-bright hooves. "I hope you mean to make a real contest of it; I should not like to be Queen just because you had caught a sniffle." She beamed at me, a winning smile framed by heaps of silver hair. Despite our position, I liked her. She smelled good, like birch leaves and alfalfa and quick-running streams.

The rules were these: Those who had the wish to rule would present themselves at the starting line—and few enough did this, as Centaurs are a reticent folk who generally keep to themselves and scoff at the trappings of power, another reason we were deemed suitable for it—and each of them fastened to a plow. Another plow would be set beside them, and whatever local magician or soothsayer had been chosen for it would enchant the blade to draw itself. The horse who could beat the undrawn plow and the competing beasts would take the crown: Those who could best furrow the earth and make it flourish were those who should help its people to flourish as well.

There were only two of us the autumn morning when I stood beside Dapple and tried my legs at a reign. Each time a race was held, fewer of us turned up at the starting line. In the end, Centaurs prefer the pasture and play and mounting and rolling in grass. But I was not reticent, nor did I scoff at power. I was not the wisest horse ever to whistle through the wind, but I was hungry—in those days, I was so hungry. The crown seemed to sing and whisper and wheedle from its height, slung onto the branch of a tree at the far end of the field. It shone, and sparkled, and sighed that it wished only to rest on my head. I liked it, too; it smelled only of itself, and that was good enough for me.

My thoughts were interrupted as the crowd began to murmur and stamp its hooves in confusion. The trial's Wizard had come into the field with his plow sparkling like a young colt's eyes in the sun, long red robes flashing and flapping in the brisk morning.

He had no collar.

He was ageless and high-nosed, clearly schooled with chairs and pencils, well clothed and well shod—but there was no collar. We did not know how to look at him, how to address him, how he fit with us.

He took all of our glances in his stride and set to rubbing his gleaming plow with powders and oils, murmuring to it like a favorite dog, brushing it with his long, thick-knuckled fingers. When he was finished it did not gleam, but dripped and clouded with baleful colors, ochre and oxblood and onyx. He invited me from my starting position to check his work, as if it were a particularly complex arithmetic problem. I trotted over, meaning to sniff as quickly as I could at the noxious fluids and declare it well done. I was still a simple horse—what did I know about magic, besides how bad it smelled?

But once I was bent over the plow, swishing my tail at flies and scratching the back of my head in what I imagined was a very knowledgeable manner, he turned his pinched face and dark eyes up to me through the share and the shin and whispered, so quietly I thought it was a bee buzzing in my ear, so quietly that he could be sure no one heard him but me.

"I can give you what you want."

"What?" I said, too loudly. Dapple looked over at me through a crowd of impertinent young colts who were trying to measure her height and breadth. Her bared chest was smooth and puffed as she pranced, her proud breasts sheened in gray. She snorted and raised a silvery eyebrow. I coughed theatrically and grinned at her through my sniffle—she laughed, and her laugh was as big and broad as her chest, a laugh fit to burst barrels.

"I can give you what you want: this race, the crown," came the voice again, softer than flies in a yearling's tail. "You're fast enough to beat the plow—that's certain as rain in winter. But you'll never beat her. Look at those shoulders, like spotted boulders they are! She's a better horse than you, a better runner; she'd probably make a better monarch. But she won't give me what I want; I can see that in her withers, her hooves, the fall of her hair, the set of her jaw. She's one of the ones who think virtue can sit easily on a throne. But you, you know how the world really rides, I can tell."

"What is it you want?" This time I was soft as mice in the brush, staring studiously at the workmanship of the plow.

"Why, you, my dear Sorrel! You are precious among creatures, you must know that." He pretended to tighten the joints and brushed a sweaty lock of hair from his face.

"I wasn't particularly aware, no," I answered.

"You are halfway between man and animal—that makes you ideally suited to my interests. Let me pursue my art in peace and without interference. Assist me in the smallest ways from time to time and I will win this race for you."

I thought as quickly as a rabbit with a fox after him. "You have no collar."

He clenched his jaw. "No. I was freed from it by good fortune; I have reveled in its lack. Slavery is a sin."

I thought as quickly as I am able. It was a good bargain, but if I knew anything I knew that it would end up being more than he claimed. I wiped the sweat from my hands on my coat. "If I am King, and I have a Wizard in my employ, it would only be correct that he be bound to me, that he be my doulios. Otherwise, how am I to trust him? What is to keep him from cutting me to pieces on the smallest whim? Virtue does not sit easily on the throne, you say? Well, then, sin may have a comfortable rest there."

The Wizard grimaced, and I could see his teeth grind beneath leather-thick skin. He looked up to the sky imploringly, and down at his hands, which opened and closed as though his palms were pricked by the tip of a brand. For a moment, I thought the man would actually weep. But he did not. His shoulders shuddered under his crimson robes, which seemed suddenly less bright and cheerful. He put his fingers, almost absentmindedly, to his neck, stroking the pale, clammy skin.

"Yes," he rasped, "fine. Yes. I will put the collar on again if you will give yourself to me. It will be worth it, to have you. We will give ourselves to each other."

I tapped the dirt with my hoof. "What . . . what will you do to her? It will not be too terrible, will it?"

In less time than a mayfly takes to flap its wings, the sorrow was gone from his eyes, replaced by an uncut stallion's ravenous glee. "Not too terrible, no. I will burst her heart in her chest, one chamber at a time."

I looked at Dapple, how beautiful she was in the autumn light, savoring a lump of sugar in her ruddy mouth. Her long hair sparkled like a fall of spring rain, and her belly was furred in the softest white. I did like her, I did like her so. But the crown shone ahead of her, and it sang, how it sang!

"No." I swallowed dryly. I could hardly speak. "Not too terrible."

Dapple nosed me playfully when I returned to the garlanded starting position.

"I promise," she said teasingly, her smooth, race-naked skin shining like armor, "I'll let you stay on as my consort. I'm sweeter than apples and sugar and acorns after rain, I'll promise that, too."

I managed a good impression of the grin that such bravado requires, and slapped her rump as comrades will. My fingers were smeared with foul-smelling gray unguent that the Wizard had given me. It would not show against her skin, he said, and no one would be wiser. She blushed with pleasure—and a blush beneath silver skin is something to see.

The bone-horns blared and we were off, running, faster than any rider and horse, and the driverless plow bouncing along beside us, drawing a long, even furrow in the rich soil, its dusts and oils falling off in orange clumps as it went.

For a few seconds, I thought I might win on my own—I am very fast, fastest of all my chestnut-hided family, and sometimes the slender horse will beat the behemoth. My legs clattered quick on the pebbles, but Dapple was only holding back. She spurred ahead with a laugh that shook the elms and firs alike, and slapped my rump with friendly delight as she passed me by completely.

My own heart surged in my chest, as if sympathetic to hers—would he keep his word? She was so far ahead now I could only keep her gray-white tail in view. And then she stumbled.

I felt it in my own chest, a tiny echo of what must have been a cloud-clapping clamor in hers. One by one I felt them go, each chamber collapsing like a hand suddenly clenched into a fist. One, two, three, four. Five, six. Seven. Eight. Dapple tumbled onto the raceway with a terrible dull sound, and pebbles sprayed up all around her like a wave.

I sped ahead. The plow was a full horse-length behind me. I did not look at her as I passed her body, already surrounded by the concerned, soon to be mourners. I crossed the line. The crown sang so loudly, so loudly, and with both hands I seized it, and its voice was pure as sugar, and apples, and acorns after rain.

When we burned her, as Centaurs do their dead, I gave a long and heartfelt eulogy—I was the King, it was my duty to mourn the fallen. The air was filled with the smell of her meat, and I tried not to gag. The Wizard, Omir, came to me after her ashes were combed and looked over the charred bones.

"You will be the last Centaur-King. I thought I should mention it. Perhaps if you were not the kind of beast to whom a crown sings there would be more after you—it never sang to Dapple, after all. But then, if it had, I would not have chosen you, and your sad place as last in a long line is why it had to be you—you will help me, and you will conquer peoples who will help me. After you, the Kings will be men again, and I know already what they are made of. When you are not past middle age, a young and hungry man will come to you on an unspeakable errand, and he will put a knife into the eight chambers of your heart, and he will be King after you."

Slowly, fat drops of rain began to fall from the sky, extinguishing the last of Dapple's embers.

"Shall we go in?" said the Wizard, a wide smile on his face.

THE KING'S TALE, CONTINUED

THE CENTAUR-KING WAS LOST IN HIMSELF. "I MEANT to be a good King," he mused, "I did mean to. But there were revolts to put down and taxes to collect and threats to quell on the borders, and it just becomes too much to carry all that on your back along with virtue. Virtue rides heavy in the saddle, you know."

He rose from his pile of cushions and for the first time I saw him whole, saw his left flank, which had been swallowed up in shadow and rose-colored silk. It was a map of scars, of scars and missing flesh, the cuts, old and new and every age between, crisscrossing his haunches until there was no hide left, only knotted flesh, and long pieces of him were missing, just gone, scooped from him as cleanly as cream from a bowl. Not one of his ribs had been left unbroken. One hoof was as fragile and as filled with holes as a honeycomb, the ankle a mass of scabbed-over wounds. He favored it, and his gait had a terrible lope. He hobbled to me and bent his face to mine, lanky brown hair smoothed back from a haggard brow.

"Tell me—Ismail, is it?—how does virtue ride with your errand in his bags?"

"Lighter," I whispered, "than with an unnatural creature who lets a slave cut into him until he cannot walk."

He looked down as if he had not noticed his ruined side until now. "Oh, yes. This is my use. I don't suppose you have this sort of use—you notice he takes flesh only from the horse half of me, or if I am lucky, the place where horse and man meet. I am happy you came, now that it's happened. Heirs are heirs, after all. I'm sure you two will find some use for each other, and frankly, I am tired of being useful."

I glanced at Omir. He met my stare, stone to steel, unabashed and unashamed. In that moment, we understood each other, and all thought of my mother evaporated from my mind like steam rising from a snow-rimmed lake. She could rot in her tower with her thrice-damned hole. I did not need her; I needed him.

Omir reached into his dark robes and pulled out a long knife. The three of us watched it glint in the light that streamed through fine-cut windows. He handed it to me. I did not know killing could be like this—in the open, in the light, acquiesced to by all. It was almost like being at a church service, and I was as excited as a child at his first altar.

The thrill of it sang to me like a crown.

I took the knife from him and walked to the Centaur-King, patting his shoulders like a rider approaching a nervous mount. He did not shy away, but met my stare, heartwood to iron.

"Monster," I hissed, and slid the knife into his heart, up to the hilt, drew it back and thrust it in again. One, two, three, four. Five, six. Seven. Eight.

Sorrel smiled, and fell onto the dais with the empty thud of heavy bones against marble.

THE TALE OF THE PRINCE AND THE GOOSE, CONCLUDED

LEANDER STARED AT HIS FATHER IN HIS HUGE, empty bed, the gray at his temples, the lines in his face that were certainly not born from laughter. His eyes flickered in the low light. "Omir and I did find some use for each other. He did not take off his collar, and I did not have him burnt. He wanted the horse-people and their Witch; I wanted a Wizard to make the rain fall when I pleased, to make the drought come when I pleased, to poison whom I pleased and destroy what I pleased. We did great things; we conquered his horse-people together, who were certainly as unnatural as Centaurs. I have never liked magic, but I tolerated his, and that bought him for me. That is a fair bargain, since neither of us was interested in his cutting into me like a side of beef—as fair as the one I struck with this country, which has bent to my order as well as any country may. I did not set out to be beloved and just, only strong."

"A King can be better than that," the Prince insisted.

"And so we all begin, determined to better our fathers' performances, knowing we can change the very nature of humanity, make it better, cleaner. But then daggers strike in the night, and peasants revolt, and all manner of atrocities become as necessary as breakfast. Only Princes believe in the greater good. Kings know there is only the Reign, and all things may be committed in its holy name. Now, are you going to cut my throat, or would you prefer the more intimate method—strangulation? I may have a garrote in the drawer."

"No," Leander answered him. "I won't kill you like a thief in the night."

Again the King laughed, low and friendly, as though he were reading his boy a story by firelight. "No, Leander. Thieves are not so bad, and killing wears all possible costumes. There is no death, no murder that is better than any other. If you can kill me, the manner hardly bears consideration. You want to kill your own father, and you think it will make your sleep easier for the next seventy years if you can say you did it honorably. But your honor is blackened by patricide, and no amount of high-sounding formalities will make it white again. Are you waiting for a confession, so that your soul will be clean? Very well. Everything she told you is true, and probably a great deal else besides. I have more blood on my hands than you could spill in a lifetime. I wear it proudly. It is my crown and my scepter. Would that you had such purpose, such drive. But you will learn, as we all do." With this he folded back the rose-colored bedsheets with a genteel hand. Beneath them, he was fully clothed in a beaten leather corselet and breeches, brown from top to bottom, like a chestnut horse.

"Do you need a weapon? Did you really come so unprepared? A father's work is never done. At least there is no shortage here." He pulled a dagger from under the mattress—firelight leapt along the blade like a flashing salmon. Leander took it numbly, hardly seeing the hilt slide into his hand. Nothing, he thought, nothing since he had left the Palace that night so long ago, had happened the way it was supposed to.

He sat close to his father, so close he could smell his dry skin, like burned sand. "I'm . . . I'm sorry."

Ismail of the Eight Kingdoms rolled his eyes and pulled his own dagger from his corselet, holding it to the Prince's skin. "If you can't manage one paltry death, how can you be King? This is how it's *done,* my son."

Before he could plunge the blade into Leander's throat, Aerie, forgotten by the close-caught pair, threw her head back, black hair tumbling to the floor. She screamed again, louder than when she had first emerged, shattering every window and glass bauble, causing the birds to begin to fall from the sky. Crow, sparrow, finch—one by one they fell by the window, like many-colored rain. The cry was filled with rage that swelled like a flooded river as she watched this father-who-was-not-father coming, at last, near to killing the Prince. As his dagger touched the boy's neck, her voice shattered its blade, and one of the shards penetrated deep into the King's royal eye.

Leander hesitated only a second, and then plunged his knife into the King's chest with all his strength, collapsing onto the hilt as it struck true and deep.

But the laughter of the King did not stop, even as blood bubbled from his mouth.

"Remember, my son," he gasped as he perished, "with my death I instruct you. This is what it means to wield power. In the end, the blade is always in your own hands."

Aerie stood in a shimmering white gown on the Castle balcony. She stared out into the highlands, and the mountains beyond.

"All I ever wanted was to leave this place," Leander said, walking up behind her and placing a hand on her shoulder. "To be free. And he caught the last of us after all, locked me into this place forever. I have been set to zero, for all time."

"But the nest survives, little brother," she replied, her voice growing more musical every day. He held her close.

"At least you are here with me, Aerie. At least there is that."

But she untangled herself from him, and looked sadly into his tired eyes.

"No." She sighed. "I am leaving. I must go. There is a duty on me, just as on you. You have saved your father's kingdom. I must tend to our mother's." Her gaze stole again to the far hills like a line of shadows hunting her. "When I flew, I knew what I was; I knew the wings were . . . borrowed, but it was far away. I do not know why I kept my mind in the bird's body—it is not what the spell was meant to do. But the wind and the moon were all I loved, and then my mother. There was no reason behind it; I simply loved her. Now there is a glut of reasons, and the endpoint of them all is that there is a cave somewhere in those hills, and I am the only one left to enter it. You were born for power—they'll call you the Maimed King, who lost his blessing fingers. There will be stories, and eventually legends. You cannot escape it, any more than I can escape the memory of the currents of air under my belly. Perhaps you can learn to use it differently; perhaps you can remain a Prince, though you are called King by all who have voices to utter it. Perhaps not. But I cannot stay to be your teacher. I have lost all that I was. I must find it again, with the poor, lost Stars. We must each find our ways to power, and how to hold it in our hands. Your nest cannot be mine."

Leander struggled with tears he would not let fall on his sister's slender shoulder. "But you will not go for a while, will you?" he said, choking. "I could not bear it. This is such a lonely place. Given time I could learn to hold power like a coal, and not be burned. But you must stay awhile yet, for me. We must be a family, for a while. Just a little while."

Aerie turned to him and smiled dazzlingly, like a dozen noontime suns. "Of course I will stay with you, my only brother, my own."

In the morning, she had disappeared as though she had never been, and the King stood alone in his great ivory hall.

Into the Dawn

THE DAWN HAD BEGUN TO DRESS HERSELF IN BLUE AND GOLD, ADORN-ing her hair with red jewels. She stretched out her hands to the two children, now almost asleep in the window of the tower. The girl cradled the boy in her lap, her hands stroking his hair, as she spoke the last words of her tale. A wind stirred in the Garden, and a whirl of white blossoms leapt into the air, swept along in the cool currents and eddies. Wild birds pinwheeled above their heads, singing with such passion they nearly died of the song.

The boy looked up at the girl, her face crowned in the new sun, which blazed around her like a corona of liquid gold. Her darkened eyes shone warmly, like polished river stones.

"That was a wonderful story!" he cried, embracing the girl in his excitement.

As she slipped down the ivy and crumbling stones, she smiled secretively up into his beaming face, which was washed by the sun's tender hands.

"And I shall tell you another even more strange and wonderful tomorrow, if you will return to the Garden in the night, and to me ..."

Laughing, the girl jumped onto the grass and ran from the tower. She disappeared into the trees, her hair streaming behind her like a promise.

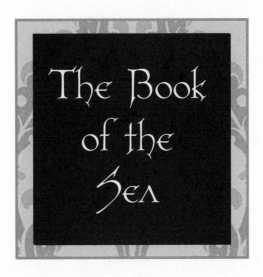

The Book
of the
Sea

In the Palace

"But *Father!*" Dinarzad cried, her voice breaking like a green branch. Her violet eyes flashed indignantly, and there was a high flush in her fair cheeks. "He was with the demon! I saw them!"

"And I believe you, daughter." The Sultan chuckled, shaking the beard that curled down to his chest like a fall of blackberry brambles. "You really mustn't get so worked up about the children under your care. Children, especially young boys of your brother's station, must be allowed some small indiscretions. It is good for my digestion to see them rebel a little. It keeps them from rebelling a lot."

Dinarzad frowned, planting her hands on her hips in a fashion he imagined she had often seen on her own nursemaids. "Father. I *hardly* think this is a small thing. He might have brought that awful child's curse upon all of us! I don't understand why you have not banished her once and for all. Couldn't you leave her to rot on some distant hillside?"

"I perceive that you have a cruel heart, my child. It lies within your breast like a smoldering blade, hissing steam at me. So long as she does not enter the Palace, we do not risk her devilment! When you have lived as long as I, you will learn a little more about dealing diplomatically with demons. To banish her to the wilds would bring down the vengeance of whatever creatures gave her birth. Why should she concern us? She does not even approach the silver gates or the corners of the house. And the boy has promised not to see her again. At the snowy summit of all these things, however, is the fact that you simply cannot go about locking your siblings in towers when they misbehave. It is unseemly and betrays a sad lack of creativity. Find another way, Dinarzad. That is all."

The Sultan dismissed his daughter with a wave of a gold-ringed hand. She blushed deeply red, the shade of harem silk, and walked out of the throne room with a stiff spine, holding her dark head high.

"That girl is a little autocrat. It is a pity she was not a son. She would have made a fine Sultan," the monarch mused, turning to his supper.

Of course Dinarzad was bound to obey her father's word. But as she wove through the halls like a swift loom, she rubbed her shoulders where one of her mothers had beaten her for allowing such treason in their house. She was cruel because it was *necessary*—the Sultan did not take the time to know that the indiscretions of the children were visited on her by the harem. The bruises flared blue and yellow on her skin like wings, and her eyes watered painfully. In her mind, she was already devising a new punishment as she ascended the thin spiral of the tower, and it grew in her like a slim stalk of wheat.

Turning the heavy key in the lock, she entered the high room where she had left her brother. She was entirely prepared to find him gone, the room empty as a dried well. She steeled her stomach for it, hardening her flesh against blows to come.

Instead, the boy lay sleeping in the windowsill, his tousled head resting against the wind-washed stone, eyes darting beneath his lids as though he was deep in dreams as thick as mulled wine. The sun shone through his hair, turning it to embers in an iron grate, to black-rimmed flames. Dinarzad allowed herself a soft smile, pleased at his reluctant obedience. Nevertheless, when she shook him awake, her voice was rough as crocodile hide.

"Get up, you little urchin. You have slept far too long. Today you will work in the kitchen. If you like to roll around in the Garden like a dog, you might as well go beg for scraps. And the Royal Guard is dining at the Palace tonight, so there is plenty for you to do. By the end of this day you will be so exhausted you will not even dream of your little demon friend."

———

The boy woke quickly—he knew better than to show her grogginess or the sand of his night eyes. He followed her in a sullen humor down from the tower and into the bowels of the Palace. The kitchens were as noisy as a stampede of oxen, oven fires leaping and steam bubbling from copper pots as though some magic brew steeped within them. Cooks and maids moved with great gestures, bellowing at each other with equal fury, their smocks stained with all manner of colored sauces, syrups, and spices. Dinarzad gave him a harsh shove into the room.

"Cook will look after you. You obey her, now. I don't fancy returning to this inferno today. One prefers to see food only when it is pleasantly on the plate. Have a *lovely* day, little brother." With this she disappeared in a flurry of white skirts and dark, flowing hair.

Cook towered over him, a great, hulking cow with cheeks fat as a hound's jowls and a belly that tumbled over the waistline of her apron in a massive heave of flesh. Her eyes were a pale, fishy shade of blue, and her right one had gone a bit rheumy, so that when she looked him over her gaze seemed to slither on his skin like a snail. She appraised him like a general sizing up a soldier.

"Eh," she grunted, her belly shaking with the sound, "soft thing like you isn't fit to cook a scrap of toast, so you'd better get to washing the flagstones. Stay out of the way of my feet and no stealing, hear?" She gestured at a wooden bucket of gray water that stank of lye and hurtled towards a clutch of chefs faster than he would have thought possible, like a hippopotamus after hapless river boats, squalling at one of the helpless maids.

The boy scrubbed until his fingers were raw and wrinkled as paper pulp, but he was secretly filled with delight, hiding it within him like thieves' gold. He would be able to bring the girl such a feast tonight, anything she could possibly want from the vast kitchens. They were preparing a huge banquet for the Royal Guard, who were so rarely barracked within the Palace gates that their entrance caused lavish holidays to spring up like dandelions in the courtly soil. A gargantuan boar had been killed earlier in the day, and it sat on the central table like a mighty lord, glistening with fat. All he had to do was wait until the maids left, scurrying like muskrats, to serve at the banquet hall, and the cooks went to report the menu to the stewards. Then the great boar would be unguarded.

And indeed, as night drew on the sky like a bodice, lacing it with the last beams of sunlight, the kitchen cleared of all its citizens and he was alone. Cook, by this time, had probably forgotten his existence entirely.

Slicing off a few fat pink hunks of boar flesh with his little dagger, he rearranged the slick green garnish to cover the missing meat, and cast about for further treasures. He smuggled sugared loaves and a rind of cheese into his vest, packing them in with smoked fish and a few of the little dormice soaked in pepper and honey that the Sultan favored. As he made his escape, the boy looked back over the sorry prison his sister had devised, and with a grin, snatched the shining red apple from the boar's mouth. He crept out the door on his quietest feet, stealing past the glittering silver Gate and into the Garden, clutching his prizes to his chest, where his heart beat like a hammer striking an ivory bell.

In the Garden

BUT THE BOY DID NOT FIND HER THAT NIGHT.

He sat on the lip of one of the great marble statues, his feet resting on the stone tail of a dancing mermaid, and ate his cold pork and apple alone. He could not understand why she would break her promise, why she would not appear as she always had, as if by magic, to deliver her stories to him all dressed in silk and silver. As he chewed the honeyed meat in the dark, he looked into the spray of stars and pictured her face to himself, the private face that was revealed when she was deep in her tales, her smoky eyes shut and moving beneath black eyelids. A terrible fear was born in him suddenly—perhaps she did not like him at all, and only wanted to tell her tales so that her curse would be broken, so that whatever strange miracle dwelt in her stained eyes would release her from the Garden. Perhaps he was nothing to her but an ear. He trembled with it, the crawling cold that chewed his bones. She had abandoned him, and what was left was the roiling weight of sorrow and silence, her absence like a statue in the glowering moon.

That night of all nights, he accomplished his deception easily, and drew the bedsheets over his knees as the sky was beginning to flush an icy gold.

On the last night of the full moon, he wandered out into the western wing of the Garden, where a small lake lay glittering in the cool light, filled with gilt-eyed fish. He had not brought food, having not much hope of finding her. He had returned to eating meals with his brothers after the term of his punishment was complete, and food was difficult to smuggle. Dinarzad redoubled this by eating solemnly at his side each night, ignoring the stares of the other sons. He hated her, her thin fingers peeling back the skin from roasted quail, holding her knife at the angle they had all been taught as though it were an effortless habit, not the result of years of slapped knuckles.

He crouched at the grassy edge of the clear water, scowling into the sparse mist and picking at pebbles underfoot. The boy's mouth had taken on a permanent sicklelike frown, a little moon whose horns were drawn ever downwards to the black earth. He began to skip stones on the placid water, listening to their satisfying *plink-plink-plunks,* when suddenly a gleam of star and shadow on skin caught his eye, and his heart leapt into his throat like a starving fish after a dragonfly.

The girl stood waist-deep in the water, her long charcoal hair clasped into a wet nest at her neck with willow whips, the lake beading on her stomach, her small breasts, her arms, outstretched as though she were trying to catch the moon in her arms like a child. Her eyes were shut; she did not yet see him. And so he watched her unabashedly, unable to move or to call to her, rooted to the mossy soil by the vision of her rising out of the night, pale as the gasp of a star's breath—and the closed eyes, floating black and secretive in her ghostly face. His own breath would not come at all.

The girl opened her eyes slowly—though truly it was as though she closed them, hiding the dark stains of her eyelids with the cold light of her eyes. She looked directly at him, and he flushed deeply, expecting her to be angry, to retreat from him in shame. Instead, she simply stared at him calmly, the moon and the water still pooling on her body, and made no move to cover herself. They stood this way without motion for some time, as the wide-leaved trees whispered to each other overhead. Finally, the girl waded to shore and pulled her ragged shift over her head. He rushed to the mound of thick grass where she sat and, without meaning to, reached out and gripped her by the shoulders.

"Where have you been?" he choked. "I have looked for you for seven nights!"

The girl cocked her head to one side, like a sparrow considering a hand full of seeds.

"You . . . you said that you would tell me another story . . . more strange and wonderful than the last . . . I thought . . ." He stared down at his hands helplessly. "I thought you wanted to tell me your stories. I thought you would tell me all of them," he finished lamely.

"I will tell you another, if you like," she answered, her voice still and cool.

"What's wrong? Why have you hidden from me?" the boy cried.

The girl brushed a fluttering strand of hair behind her ear. "I have not hidden, or at least, I have not meant to hide. It is only that you have not found me. The Garden is wide, and I am sorry. Folk have come and gone since last you heard my voice, and I could not be seen." She looked at him in that strange, birdlike way again, a light sparking deep in her eyes. "Would you like to hear another tale from the folds of my eyes, a tale of ships and saints, of maidens and beasts and a dreaming city?"

The boy bit his lip. He felt that the polite thing to do was to ask how she had fared, if it had been very hard to escape the notice of one or another noble lord, if she had eaten well without him—but he had not heard the promises of her fantastic creatures in so long that they sounded in his belly like the tolling of church bells, like anchors dropping in a soundless sea, and he felt such a desire for them that he could not be polite.

"Tell me the tale, please!" he whispered.

The girl settled herself on the grass, under the perfume of cinnamon trees and stars like hanging gardens, and spoke, her voice once again as wide and soft as the hide of a jungle cat.

"Once, there was a girl named Snow, and she had no one in all the world to love her."

THE PALE GIRL'S TALE

NOW, SHE HAD NOT ALWAYS BEEN CALLED THIS. THE girl had once lived in the city of Ajanabh, a warm and well-built place which sat fat and rich on the golden silt of a wide river delta, scarlet flags flapping proudly, the streets winding marvelously through its jeweled heart. She was loved and safe in her mother's house, and expected that her life would continue that way forever, with the cinnamon-scented wind on her skin as she slept.

But Ajanabh faltered, as cities will, and the day came when her fisheries were no longer so full, and her merchants no longer so eager to pole the sludge of the river to reach her glittering harbor. Slowly, the people left their whitewashed houses. Slowly, they abandoned their thick-soiled fields, which had once been so lovingly and reliably inundated by the clear green waters.

Snow, unremarkable among so many others who would never again call the warm-winded southlands home, stood with her parents on the deck of a ship as the pearl-domed city retreated in the distance, until it was nothing more than a glowing line against the sea. She stared over the rail of the ship for days, her hair becoming tangled and salted with the wind, though her parents begged her to come below. They were bound for the glacial North, other harbors great and small, where whale meat and seal fat were to make new fortunes for all the lost children of Ajanabh. Bound for the city of Muireann, which lay on the gray waters of its stormy bay like a child against its mother's breast, host to every ship that crossed the diamond-tipped waves.

But the passing had been difficult for her parents, who could not bear the savage cold. Even less were they prepared for life in Muireann, whose winter seemed never to end, and whose people were as frozen and implacable as snow on a flat roof. The endless chill set into their bones, and before her family had passed a year in the salt-wind and the sea, Snow's parents died.

She grew, surely as an ash tree, and lived as near to a beggar as was possible without starving, mending nets with the fishwives when they would let her take some of their work, scurrying through the docks on odd errands, simply to get a beaten coin to buy bread and seal fat to moisten it.

Though she was resourceful, Snow was not a beautiful girl. Her face was plain, unmarked and unremarkable. Her eyes were a watery shade of green, like sickly lakes caught in a lightless winter. Her lips were small and perpetually chapped; her skin was neither the milk-smooth of girls who ate breakfasts of oranges and strawberries on silver plates, nor the hardened brown of dockworkers' daughters. She chewed her nails and picked at the skin on the back of her hands. Though she was as old as any of those girls, the ones who spent their days entertaining suitors in parlors of brocade and soft laughter, folk that passed her on the streets of the village thought her a child. She never grew as tall of leg or as fair of hip as those charmed ones—in fact, no one would have noticed Snow at all, were it not for her hair.

Since the day she buried her mother and father, her hair had gone pale as an old woman's. It flowed down her thin body in all the colors of a storm-whipped wave: slate and silver, ice and cloud, smoke and fog, ash and iron. The process had not hurt—she simply woke up, grave dirt still under her fingernails, and saw in the mirror that the colors of her home, which once glinted like lamplights in her thick curls, had fled. She was as colorless as ocean foam against the shivered planks of wrecked ships.

And so it came to pass that the girl became a fixture among the fish-wives who crowded the dock, tying their nets and mending sails, and for her hair they called her Snow. If they did not love her, the Muireanners accepted her presence and found bits of work that would keep her belly quiet, if not satisfied, looking the other way when she slept in the ship-wrights' cavernous warehouses, curled into the skeletons of half-built clippers. She sought the solace of shadows, keeping her head low and moving through her life with no more sorrow than she had already collected to her thin breast.

One evening, as she sat with a round-faced woman, knotting the last of the day's great silver nets with practiced fingers, she looked up from her work to find that the woman had tucked an orange into the yellow folds of her skirts. Snow glanced at her benefactor, whose loose brown hair curled tightly around a face that might have belonged to a well-fed gnome, merrily lumpy and red-cheeked. Her body was solid as a bull walrus, muscles bulging silkily beneath layers of fat. The woman winked at Snow without stopping her quick stitching, fleshy fingers flashing in and out of the flaxen ropes.

"Can't have those pretty teeth falling out, love. Oranges are like rubies up here, loved as gold and twice as rare. But an old friend of mine from the South sends me a crate every winter. And someone like you deserves a ruby or two from time to time."

Snow turned the blazing fruit over in her hands. When she spoke, her voice was soft and hoarse, for she rarely talked at all, and it had grown as creaky as a brass gate from disuse.

"Where I was born, they grew from trees, hundreds of them, like drops of fire. My mother spiced cakes with the peels."

"So you did come from somewhere!" The woman laughed, her thick body rippling like a bear in mid-roar. "You didn't rise up from the waves, fully formed, on an abalone shell? Well, that's a relief. Wouldn't want to think I spent half my shift sitting thigh to thigh with a naiad."

Snow blinked, brushing her high cheeks with lashes pale as snow-crusted sails. "Is that what they say about me, truly?"

"Some, to be sure, love to tell tales. But no one says much about you—you've no prospects at all, and that means you'll be on these docks till you freeze to the boards. Not the sort of life to inspire the gossips to gnash their own pretty teeth."

Snow did not scowl, as another girl might, but simply pulled back the small tendrils of herself which had ever so briefly been extended to a bright-voiced stranger. The woman extended her fat hand, studded with rough iron rings, to the girl's shoulder. "Of course, I don't mean to be cruel, love—I'm not likely to be crowned Queen of Whalesongs any summer soon, either. There, there. Sigrid's tongue does tend to flap away without asking permission first."

"Don't worry," Snow said abruptly, shrugging off the hand. "I won't cry. What you said is true enough, I know that."

Sigrid gave the gray-haired child a long look, slow and appraising, a jeweler examining a use-blackened sapphire. "We shall see, I suppose. I thought I knew what was true, when I was young and beautiful. I thought I would always be able to run as fast as I pleased, and take such pleasure in simple meals of seal flanks and pelican eggs. Then the world changed, and I was no longer a maid, and I never knew again." Sigrid straightened, plunging her stubby hands back into her nets. "I'll tell you a tale of my youth, if you like. It will pass the time."

Snow nodded, willing to hear anything that would take her mind from the cold stiffening her fingers to stalactites, and the frozen night which would find her huddled and frozen in the belly of a hollow ship.

THE
ΠET-ᗯEAVER'Ƨ
TAℓE

WHEN I FIRST BECAME A WOMAN AND THE BLOOD was still high in my cheeks, red and quick, I longed to leave the frozen waste of my family's lands. There was nothing for me there any longer. My brothers and sisters were all grown, gone to Temple or farm, and my mother did not want to look at me, hoping that I, too, would find my way out of her house. But I lingered—there were still things I loved in the snow, and I was a little afraid to go into the world.

One spring, when the lichen was green-fringed and springy, a group of monks came to our village. All strangers are sacred to us, so they were taken in without question. My mother drew the lot to house them, and that was how it came to pass that three brothers ate, and spoke, and slept, under our snow-thatched roof.

At first they kept their deep scarlet hoods over their heads, mumbling thanks and bowing stiffly over their suppers of near-raw fox and leafy lichen. I was intensely curious, as all maids of that age are, and I peered beneath their cowls throughout supper, trying to catch a glimpse of their faces. Finally, the middle brother straightened, threw back his crimson cloak, and fastened his milky yellow eyes onto mine.

"Is this what you wanted to see, little one?" he growled, and indeed he did growl it, for though these monks had the bodies of strong-calved men, their heads were those of great dogs, tongues hanging from their jaws like the clappers of bells. Their fur was thick and deep, falling to their shoulders, rough-cut as the beards of mountain sages. One brother had a bluish-white pelt, another was black and brown in patches, and the last was a deep red-gold, like the hair of a girl. But the eyes of each were chill and hard, the color of old mosses, gray and gold all at once. I could not help but gasp, but my wonder only made the middle one laugh, a sound like the grinding of boulders.

"We're not werewolves, love, if that's what you're thinking," the red dog chuckled. "*Cynocephaloi*, dog-heads. Entirely different."

"Vegetarian, for one thing," said the white one, gesturing at his plate, where the pink fox meat lay untouched. My mother apologized profusely, deathly afraid that she had polluted them—some number of my sisters had entered the priesthood, and Mother was ever sensitive to religious niceties. The middle one, clearly a pack leader of sorts, looked up with his liquid eyes and reassured her.

"No, no, meat does not offend us; we simply choose to eschew it. It appeals to the higher nature of the self to put aside food which once lived—I do not consider myself food, why should I ask all other creatures to consider themselves so? Our Order is, however, rather strict. We certainly do not ask our hosts to know our Scripture—certainly not when we have been so rude as to eat without sharing ourselves. But we, too, are wary of violating spiritual . . . etiquette. This is a land of many faiths. Some do not permit the Sacred Guest to speak of himself, or at all. Others do not allow names to be uttered before the meal is finished. As we have quite finished all that we are permitted to eat, I will begin. I am Bartholomew, and these are my brothers. Balthazar," he said, indicating the blue-white Cynocephalus, "and Bagdemagus," indicating the red. Turning to me, he added in a mischievous tone: "But you may call him 'Bags.' We all do. We belong to the Order of the Scarlet Hood—for beneath the Hood we are one." At this all three made a delicate motion with their hands and whispered some sort of prayer.

Balthazar took up the thread of their introduction then, rasping through his long teeth. "We are traveling home, to Al-a-Nur, City of Light, and the Chrysanthemum Tower. We were a delegation, sent to mediate a great quarrel in our faith, and now that our part is done, we are permitted to return to the Tower which gave us birth."

I must have seemed such a child to them, sitting plate-eyed and loose-mouthed at their feet, savoring the foreign tang of the word on my tongue like a spiced cake: *Al-a-Nur*. My mother eyed me with suspicion, but I ignored her. I begged to be told of this city, which in my heart I already knew must be the holiest city ever to sit on the earth.

"Truly, girl, you have never heard of the City of Twelve Towers?" Bartholomew stroked his fur as though it were a beard and peered at me. "Seat of the Papess, She Who Was Born in the Purple, the Anointed City which shines like a summer star?"

"Never!" I cried breathlessly.

"Very well," he chuckled, straightening his back like a teacher about to give lessons, "your kind mother permitting, I shall tell you of the Dreaming City, enclosed in her seraphic spheres . . ."

The
City's Tale

LISTEN, CHILD, AND I WILL TELL YOU OF AL-A-NUR,
seat of the Twelve Towers, the Anointed City. She was
founded a thousand years ago, in the year Seven Hundred
and Fifty-three of the Second Caliphate. The foundations
of the Towers were poured in agate and porphyry, the tapered windows were chiseled into graceful arches. Clear
green ponds were dug from the loamy soil, tamarinds and
palms were planted, willows and pale-barked birch.
Aqueducts ran with sweet water, gurgling up through
fountains of silver and glass. Roads were arranged in concentric circles, according to the *Lo Shen* board, our sacred
Game, named for the river goddess who laid her waters

around the blessed City. The roads were paved in lapis and turquoise, stones which were plentiful in the surrounding mountains—even today the cobbled walkways keep their deep blue sheen.

Markets sprang to life like mushrooms after a rain, filling the closes and keeps with the scent of saffron and broiling meat; traders came to sell dolls and cabinets, sleek red horses and love charms—but they stayed to contemplate the divinity that resides in the exchange of gold in the marvelous Towers which comprised the many hearts of the City.

The Towers were themselves arrayed in the pattern of the *Chang-O* configuration—the ideal defensive deployment of the *Lo Shen* pieces. On the outer rim rose up the Tower of Sun-and-Moon, whose roof was tipped with a great diamond and a great topaz, melted into one another in an unimaginable furnace. Now one stone, it refracts the light of the heavens onto the City in a shower of prisms. There is the Tower of Patricides, bright with blood trickling between its polished stones, a thin, steady flow which pools in a glowering crimson moat at its base; and the Tower of Ice and Iron, its twisted metallic spire bruising the clouds. On the second ring lay the Coral Tower, its deep rose pocked and rippled with anemones kept moist by loving novices; the Tower of Hermaphrodites, hung with veils and inscribed with sacred ideographs, silver ink on a golden wall; the Chrysanthemum Tower, the living stone ablaze with sixteen-pointed flowers flashing gold and scarlet at the noonday sun; and the Tower of St. Sigrid, bristling with ships' prows and wheels and masts. In the innermost circle were built the Nightingale Tower, through whose walls the wind whistled, singing as sweetly as that tiny brown bird; and the Tower of the Nine Yarrow Stalks, whose very surface was a divinatory device, painted in a thousand shades; the pattern of sun and shadow on the colors is still interpreted daily within those walls. There also were the Towers of the Living and the Dead, which once stood straight and tall, the one walled in hawk and falcon feathers with tufts of fur thatching the roof and doors of serpent-skin, the other riddled black with catacombs and crannies—but over the centuries, they have leaned further and further from their bases, until they almost touch. Now there is a small bridge of silk and ebony between the upper rooms of the Towers, and the initiates move freely between them.

Finally, in the center of Al-a-Nur a slender, simple tower was erected, fashioned from camphor wood and the roots of rose trees, knobbed with silver nail heads glittering like constellations set into the polished walls. Its roof was thatched from willow whips, its windows shaded in soft deer-skin—and this is the Tower of the Papess, the holiest site of this holy City.

For Al-a-Nur is the seat of a dozen faiths, all presided over by the Papess, whose wisdom has guided us from our earliest days. Each Tower is a self-contained spiritual sphere, each with its liturgies and fasts and scriptures. They recognize the divine in myriad ways, but recognition of the Papess ensures peace. The Caliphate, which rules the surrounding countryside, allows Al-a-Nur complete sovereignty; and thus it has gone in prosperous and tranquil fashion across the long years. From every direction come young men and women, seeking to spend their lives in contemplation, and there, under the light of Sun-and-Moon, they find a path that suits them. Al-a-Nur is a carved box which holds the wisdom of the world, knowledge lost to all but our spindled Towers. It is the paradise of the wishful and the wise.

There have, of course, been interruptions in our peace. When Ghyfran the Forgiving died, the Caliphate elevated an outsider, Ragnhild, First of Her Name, to the Papacy and installed her in Shadukiam, a city to the east, in an attempt to draw the wealth of Al-a-Nur to itself, and transfer the religious authority which has always resided in the Twelve Towers to that apostate city, where, by no great coincidence, the treasury of the Caliph was kept. This false Papess, called the Black, was a great crisis for the Towers, for the process by which a new Papess is chosen is a complex one, requiring the consent of all the sects of the City as well as the Papal Household. Ghyfran had died suddenly, and a successor had not been confirmed.

From the Tower of Hermaphrodites a candidate arose, and while the Black Papess became more and more entrenched in Shadukiam and the minds of the people, Al-a-Nur was as filled with chaos as a winter storm with lightning. All agreed that Presbyter Cveti was highly qualified and beloved, purity of soul echoing in every spoken word and graceful movement. Nevertheless, the appointment could not be agreed upon.

As must be obvious even to you, my child, the adherents within the Tower of the Hermaphrodites reveal themselves to be neither male nor female. There is no shame in this for them; it is simply their nature, and the nature of the cosmos as they conceive it. Though each was born a daughter or a son, they clothe themselves plainly, bind up their hair, and uncover the secret of their sex to no one. For them, the most divine of all things is the merging of opposites—of light and dark, of sacred and profane, of male and female. They believe that they are blessed so long as they maintain a balance, hanging like a human pendulum between two states, uniquely able to experience the world as both man and woman, and as neither. But the Papacy is a matriarchy, has always been thus, and to some,

Cveti seemed to be a sacrilege, polluting the Holy Seat. If the Presbyter was male, it was unthinkable that he could claim the seat. If female, she must declare it before all, and preserve the law of the City. The conflagration of this debate engulfed the City in red flames.

Of course Cveti's Tower had never held that highest of offices, and felt that any refusal to accept so illustrious a candidate was a boldfaced insult to their order. Many, such as the Tower of the Patricides, themselves an all-male sect, and the *Draghi Celesti* of the Tower of Ice and Iron, warrior-priests utterly loyal to the traditions of the City who hide their faces behind identical ivory serpent-masks, would not support any alteration to the laws of succession, partly out of fear that their own internal customs could then be altered. No one would dare set the precedent.

Cveti, who loved Al-a-Nur above all things, feared that in the roiling furor the Papacy would be destroyed in the hands of Ragnhild and the Caliphate before a decision could be made, and withdrew from consideration. Yet no other candidate was so worthy, so capable of battle or meditation with equal ease, or so well beloved among the Towers, as Cveti of the bell-deep voice. All agreed that in that time of crisis, only Cveti could lead them against Shadukiam. It was only the shape of hip and curve of lash which was in question, never the holiness of the Presbyter, nor sincerity of faith. The whole City was at a stalemate, and Ragnhild all the while consolidated her authority, growing fat as an engorged spider in the East.

And so it came to pass that Cveti appeared one morning in the Jade Pavilion, which spread out from the Papal Tower, shimmering green and white under the thin winter clouds. She had removed the ritual clothing of her Tower and donned a dress which closed her waist into a curve and flowed over her legs to trail its dark velvet over the jade floor of the courtyard. Her breasts, which had never seen the sun, rose smooth as new paper from the embroidered bodice. She had loosed the traditional seven knots from her hair and let it fall to her shoulders, straight as virtue. She had pulled rings onto her fingers and scented her skin, painted her lips and pulled silk slippers onto her feet. She needn't have done it—her word as to her sex would have been enough—but all that finery was the extent of her humility, showing us all how far she would go to be what the City asked her to be.

She stood before the Tower as though before the hangman's noose, tears streaming down her proud cheeks—yet her mouth never quivered as she knelt at the feet of the Papal Household and forswore the tenets of her faith, vowing thenceforward to serve only the Papal Tower, and never again to hide her nature; in all things she would serve the greater need of the City, emulating the line of Papesses which had come before her. With stunned tears springing to their own eyes the Household accepted her pledge, and the Towers, awed and humbled, confirmed Presbyter Cveti as the seventeenth Papess of Al-a-Nur. On the day of her ascension, Cveti went into the cavernous mausoleum beneath the Tower and kissed the coffin of her predecessor with great tenderness. She announced to all in those shadowy rooms that she would take the name of Ghyfran, the dead Papess, for her own.

Ghyfran II led a great army of *Draghi Celesti* in their thousand identical masks against Shadukiam, and sent the tongue and breasts of the Black Papess to the Caliphate in a silver box. While on campaign, it was noted by her generals that Ghyfran always bound her hair in seven knots before riding into battle. The rest of Ragnhild she yielded to the judgment of the Draghi, who left the apostate's body fastened to the earth with golden chains at the precise center-point between Al-a-Nur and Shadukiam.

And for five hundred years, the Caliphate quelled its desire to interfere with the succession of the Holy Seat.

THE
NET-WEAVER'S
TALE,
CONTINUED

I WAS SLEEPY THEN, RESTING MY HEAD ON THE rough-hewn table and letting Bartholomew's voice roll over me like gentle water over stones. But Al-a-Nur had risen up in me in all its colors, and I could feel a yearning for it turning and warming itself in my belly. All my siblings had gone, I was ready—why should I not leave this wretched hut, where my mother's eyes scalded my back wherever I walked?

"Take me with you," I whispered, sitting up, my eyes suddenly bright and calculating as a hungry little cat in the snow. "Take me to Al-a-Nur, to the Chrysanthemum Tower and the green pools under the willow. I will become wise there, just like you, you'll see!" I clutched his hand tightly, but seeing his startled expression, let the callused fingers fall back to our table.

Bags—for so I already called him in my heart—peered closely at me, his eyes narrowing to tiny moon-slivers in the red bleed of his fur. He looked to Bartholomew and whispered, *"And the wolf shall lead her astray . . ."*

"What?" I asked, straining to hear their suddenly hushed voices. But Bartholomew grinned hugely, his ponderous tongue hanging out of his mouth in a most friendly fashion.

"Nothing, my dear," interrupted Balthazar, shaking his ice-colored fur, "just a bit of Scripture. *The Book of Carrion,* chapter twenty-eight, verse ten. If you are to come with us you will learn that and much more. Certainly we will have you—we cannot turn a seeker away by the laws of our Tower. But perhaps it is not solely our decision . . . ?"

My mother's ponderous back was turned to us, and it shook slightly with tears—sorrow or relief I could not tell—smothered as quickly as snow sliding from a pine bough to the frozen earth. I went to her, and put my hands on her shoulders, leaning my head against her warm skin.

"Go," she spat hoarsely. "Just go. If the Stars wish us to meet again, they will fashion the path before your feet." She shrugged me off and disappeared from the great-room with her heavy, lumbering gait. I began to pack food for myself and my new brothers—we would need bread for the journey south.

THE PALE GIRL'S TALE, CONTINUED

"YOU'RE NOT BORED, ARE YOU, LOVE?" SIGRID shifted on her bench, nets knotted over her hands like silver rings. The sun was well past noon, and the sickly light of the northern summer spilled over the windless water below the quay, thin as milk.

"Oh, no," breathed Snow, her colorless lips spreading into something like a smile. "Don't stop! Did you ever see the Twelve Towers? Did you meet the Papess? Was she very beautiful?"

"I don't believe I've ever heard you put so many words together in the same place, girl. If you're not careful, they'll get together and have babies, and then we'll never shut you up."

Snow was stricken for a moment, then tore her eyes from Sigrid as though she had been caught staring through a shop window full of cakes, furiously tying her net with shivering fingers. Sigrid's face became soft in all the places it had been hard. Her cheeks melted into a rough affection.

"Love, I've never been anyone's mother; I don't know how to talk to young or old. But don't stop smiling just because I flap my mouth and say something that's not dressed around the edges like a lace tablecloth. Thicken up and we'll get along fine."

They were quiet together for a while, listening to the creak and rock of the ships in port, the tightening of the wet ropes that tied them to the pier. Gulls cackled in their witch-reedy voices, swooping into the shallows for fat pink fish. Snow's silvery hair was dark with damp, curling against her dress. At last, Sigrid began to speak again, neither pausing nor slowing in her work as she talked.

"As to the great City, I did go, far to the south, out of the white waste-lands, across a scrub desert where there was no water, and through valleys where wine grapes grew big as plums. The dog-men never seemed to tire, and their red hoods kept out all manner of storm and sun-blisters, where I had only my little shift and a ragged old fur cloak . . ."

The
Net-Weaver's
Tale,
Continued

I WAS SOON QUITE FRIENDLY WITH THE BROTHERS—
who, as it turned out, were literally brothers as well as fellow monks. They talked often of home, and of the other
members of their litter who farmed their fields in peace
and thought nothing of theology. Balthazar had the
quickest tongue, often completing our sentences, as
though he was impatient to hear the ends of them.
Bartholomew was the most devout and kind; he shep-
herded me like a favorite lamb, teaching me from *The
Book of the Bough* and *The Book of Carrion* (though never
the meaning of the strange proverb uttered at the old
home-table), though he welcomed me to choose from

any of the Towers once we arrived—the variety of religion laid out before me would be as a table groaning with feast foods, he promised. Bags was our jester—he tickled me and taught me to wrestle, nipping me playfully if I let down my guard. It was not long before they were the only stars in my little sky.

The four of us kept to the roads, wherever they wound, and had food when it was plentiful—grapes and apples and occasionally soft cheese from a passing cart, but never meat, of course. The Cynocephaloi assured me that they were excellent hunters, with strong, lean human legs and jaws that could snap a bird out of the air before the song died in its warbling throat, but they would never do so. It was with terrible sadness that Bags brought me a skinny hare one evening when the desert spread out around us like a fallen dress, embroidered with sagebrush and dusty pebbles. The poor creature had dropped dead of the heat; Bags did not want to waste the meat, and I was famished. I had grown up devouring fox haunch and seal fat; the desert was unkind to my young limbs. With tears pooling in his yellow eyes, he laid the rabbit in my lap and closed its eyes as though the beast had been his brother.

"Death," he whispered, his throat squeezing out words like blood from a deep wound. "We have seen so much death on this pilgrimage, death common as coats hung up in a hall. Four of us went out from the Chrysanthemum Tower, and four of us return—but not the same four! Do the gods mock us with numbers, tossing them at our hearts like jester's balls? Do you know where we went, where we had gone before we came to your village? What our mission was? Al-a-Nur is the City of Light, yes, oh, yes, and the moon on her dozen towers is like water on my tongue after years of thirst! But she asks so much of us, so much is required to keep that light burning gold and blue!" He put his shaggy head in his hands, his sobs warped by the shape of his snout; the sound of his snorting, snarling grief was terrible to hear. "I can still smell his blood, his blood on my hands!"

I put aside the hare and tried to comfort him—Bags, who was always cheerful and full of jokes my mother would have whipped me for repeating, Bags, who had become my favorite of all the brothers, wept in my arms like an orphaned child. I could see the sullen fireflies of his brothers' eyes gleaming some feet away, but I did not think they would come near. *The Book of the Bough* said: *Grief is a private sacrament. Give it not to others as though it were a gift.* He should not have wept in my lap at all—his brothers would not shame him by witnessing his lapse.

Bags looked up into my eyes and bit his tears into pieces. "Everything that was done was necessary, little sister, so that the City might live. But I have tasted a yielding throat in my jaws, and I cannot tell, I cannot tell: If one sins in order to preserve virtue—is this still sin? I am sorry, girl, you are not one of us, you will not be stained by my sorrow, you cannot be polluted by it. Let me give my grief to you, who are innocent of all these necessities, clean of all darkness. Let me tell you what my brothers and I did in the name of Al-a-Nur, the Anointed City. Let me tell you of the fourth whose place you hold . . ."

THE
ASSASSIN'S
TALE

WHAT BARTHOLOMEW TOLD YOU WAS TRUE, ABOUT Ragnhild the Black, who called herself Papess five centuries ago and was slain by Ghyfran the Selfless. We know the tale better than any, for its continuation lay with us, when we set out from the Salmon Gate—the Gate that calls us home from our first steps into the wild, which reminds us of the river that gave us life, and to which we must return when our muzzles have grown bare.

The Caliphate, now the Fourth Caliphate, has always envied our autonomy, and hated the scrap of parchment with the hoofprint of the First Caliph stamped firmly on its cracked surface, assuring our freedom unto the end of days. Our City is rich beyond the dreams of royal bursars, and we are not tithed, we are not conscripted, we are beholden to no earthly law. After the death of Ragnhild, we had hoped that the time of their interference was finished, that their lesson had been etched deeply enough in blood that no children of our children would ever fear another apostasy.

It was etched to the depth, it would seem, of five hundred years, and no more.

After the death of Ghyfran XII—Ghyfran has become a favorite name of the Papess line, though the wolf of my heart mourns the loss, stillborn, of a long line of clear-eyed priestesses called Cveti—our current Blessed Papess, Yashna the Wise, was confirmed with no great controversy and all due ceremony. The Papal Tower gleamed in its deep hues as always, and its silver glittered as it had the day the nails first tasted the wood. There was no issue of succession. She was of the Tower of the Dead, which has given us many solemn and temperate Papesses. They are suited to it; the dead give nothing so much and so well as perspective. Yet the Caliphate chose this barely noticeable interregnum to interfere a second time, and under the Rose Dome of Shadukiam, the Apostate was born again like a black-mouthed calf.

And worse, she took the name of her predecessor—once more there was a Ragnhild with a diadem on her brow. She had sent men to retrieve the golden manacles that held the first false Papess to the earth between cities, left there as a monument to remind the Caliphate that Al-a-Nur was never again to be superseded by a filthy banking metropolis. It was said that the new Ragnhild wore them day and night, the broken chains hanging delicately from her slender wrists, that ancient gold glowering against her skin. It was said that her hair was precisely that shade of gold, that her eyes were so black that they seemed to have no pupils. It was said that she would not even call herself Ragnhild II, but believed herself to be that murdered Papess reborn, and ever wore the deep violet gown in which those unfortunate bones had finally been interred. Its grave-tatters showed her ghost-pale skin in many places, an indecency no true Papess of the Tower would have allowed.

One late evening last summer, when the blue of the sky was deeper than any sea, my brothers and I were called from the singing blossoms of the Chrysanthemum Tower to an audience with Yashna. We went, I and my three brothers—for Barnabas was the fourth of our number who stood before Yashna and heard her crow-song voice. His fur was perfectly black, without the patches of brown Bartholomew inherited from our strong-hipped mother. He was the strongest of us, and the youngest.

The Papal presence, in simple gray robes and unadorned diadem, soothed the image of the wraith-Papess from our troubled hearts. She is not a young woman, our Mother Yashna; her deep brown skin is folded and creased as a beloved book. When she reached out her hand to touch our bent and reverent heads, her palm was warm and dry as a desert stone after twilight has fallen.

"My sons, listen well to me, for our City is once again besieged. I am not a Ghyfran"—at this she smiled a weary smile that turned up the corners of her mouth like the horns of the moon—"I am not even a Cveti. There is nothing in my body to give to Al-a-Nur. I am a crone; I accept this. I cannot lead an army against Shadukiam, and even if I could ride at its head, we have been so long at peace that I fear the Draghi are not what they were. They train and pray and know nothing of true war. No, this time we cannot simply crush the Black Papess under the weight of our Towers. It is a time for stealth and for cunning—and these things I can give with both hands. I have chosen you because you will not be suspected; the Scarlet Hoods have ever prohibited violence of any kind, and no one would think to question your tranquil spirits. Nevertheless, I must ask you to break your vows, as immaculate Cveti once did, in service of the lifeblood of the Twelve Towers. I am sending you from the river and familiar waters; I am sending you from the sixteen-pointed chrysanthemum. You must go east, and kill the Black Papess."

Oh, sister, I would like to tell you we were shocked, that we agreed only out of duty—but the truth is that words such as "kill" had little meaning for us who had grown up through the cycles of the opening and closing of flowers, who had never eaten animal flesh or struck another creature in anger. We agreed because it was Yashna who asked it, we agreed because it was Yashna who told us we would be forgiven, because we wanted to wear the holy, secret name of Cveti sewn into our chests, because we wanted to be the saviors of our City, which was the deepest heart of our hearts. We thought nothing of Ragnhild, and nothing of the task. We eagerly swore ourselves, and kissed her withered hand, which smelled so sweetly of sandalwood and rustling scrolls. There was no shadow of guilt in us as we departed, as we heard the soprano echo of the Salmon Gate closing behind us.

It was not so far as we had imagined from Al-a-Nur to Shadukiam—it seems, when you rest in the arms of the Dreaming City, that all things outside her walls belong to another universe, impossible to reach by the mere motion of one foot before the other.

The land between the two cities is pleasant.

How we joked and bounded across those well-tilled fields! How we gorged ourselves on wild strawberries and oranges like little flames flashing in the morning fog! Barnabas especially reveled in the open spaces, cavorting ahead of us on his quick, flat feet. "Come on!" he cried. "There is no reason not to enjoy ourselves along the way, even if the task ahead is dreary and dire. *The Bough* says: *Heed not the dark before, behind, and beside; dwell always in the light of the open heart.* And the blueberries are so sweet on the road at first light!" Bartholomew was his usual self, staring fretfully at the night stars. Balthazar allowed Barnabas to cheer him, and the two played and wrestled together beside our nightly fires.

How cordially we were received at the sun-dappled wall of Shadukiam! How brightly her diamond turrets glittered against the great wicker dome that arches over the city, alive with a thick latticework of roses trailing over the slick surface, obscenely red dotted with the most delicate of pinks and whites. The guards let us enter without question, and our appointment with the Papess (it was terribly difficult to bite off all our accustomed prefixes, not to call her Black or False or Apostate—but we wrangled our words into a genial array) was arranged smoothly and with great courtesy. Of course, they beamed. The Papess welcomes all her sons and daughters to her bosom, they assured us. She yearns to bring her family together under the Rose Dome and heal the breaches between them, they said. Her only concern is for their souls. They bowed and scraped.

How easy it was to hate her, little sister.

We needed to smuggle no weapons into her vaulted hall; our daggers were borne in plain view, the sharp teeth of our hunter heritage which had known no flesh but that of apples and peaches. It seemed only a moment cavorting through orchards and we were here, ushered into her private antechamber, kneeling before her strange throne, which seemed to be made of the same roses that covered the city dome—yet they were alive, and writhed against her body with lascivious familiarity.

Her face was obscured by her hair as we knelt—she did not greet us or ask us to rise—the long white-gold length of it falling over her cheeks like a nun's veil. On her wrists were the golden manacles, the chains idly brushing her bared knees; the famous violet gown showed much of her pale body, the low rim of her right breast was bare, patches of her hips and belly gleamed balefully from the ancient fabric.

I wonder, sister, if it was easier because she looked so precisely like the ghoul we had been warned of—if she had appeared without those oft-rumored accoutrements, might we have been moved by that beauty, might we have hesitated? But she was the very image of herself, unmistakable and pure.

"Welcome home, O errant sons," she said, her voice deep and cloying as a many-storied honeycomb. She did not lift her head. "The house is ever strengthened when all its children return to its hearth. It warms me to receive you."

"We are honored, Mother." Barnabas spat the honorific at her, the taste of it surely bitter as lime leaves in his mouth. "Yashna has sent us with missives of peace—"

She raised her eyes suddenly, their black lights flaring like sparks from an ancient anvil. "Yashna has sent you to kill me. To rid your pestilential city of an inconvenient woman. If my attendants are fools leaping to the hope that Al-a-Nur will accept us, do not make the mistake of looking for me to leap with them. I am Ragnhild—I have felt the press of Al-a-Nur's hand before."

We exchanged nervous looks—Bartholomew licked his dark jaw. If she was truly mad enough to believe herself the dead Apostate reborn, perhaps death would be a mercy. I tried to sound the depths of her delusion, murmuring, "I know that your predecessor suffered greatly after the war—"

"No, my son. Not she. *I.* I lay on the rocks and the sun gnawed at my flesh. I pleaded for my life with a useless stump of a tongue. I watched your precious Cveti close up my severed breasts in a silver box. And I listened to the soldiers praise her false name—*Ghyfran! Ghyfran!* The whore who betrayed her god for power. This body is new, but I am Ragnhild, first of my name, and I am the plague which will burn through the marrow of the Anointed City. The crowds will turn east to Shadukiam to look upon the faces of the gods; they will bow to the Rose Dome in wonder and awe. The ruins of your corrupt Towers will become a curiosity, where children are brought to tell the tale of that decadent and wasteful clutch of nearsighted monks, and how my purifying vengeance brought them low. I will not even be slowed by your lumpish, deformed bodies crunching under my feet—Yashna is a senile, drooling serving wench, and her lapdogs are nothing to me."

"You must know," Bartholomew said slowly, "that the purifying vengeance is not yours, but the Caliph's. He is using you to take the wealth of our city for his own. Why do you think he has installed you so near the treasuries, the granaries, the little men counting diamonds in darkened rooms? What has Shadukiam ever been but a bank vault, a plate for the Caliph to feed from? If you are truly Ragnhild, if you have such power, you must know that the blame lies with the Caliphate and their greed—why not loose your hatred upon he who led you like a little calf to the broad-faced butcher? What offense has Al-a-Nur given, save that we have endured in peace and prosperity, that we have worshipped our gods with piety, that we have built beauty into a barren world? Yet the Caliph has used *you* like a painted whore, dressing you up in a corpse's clothes and reaching out with your hand to clutch handfuls of Nurian gold."

"The Caliph is a dog licking himself on a tin chair," she snapped. "The first time, I was a fool, and he whispered in my ear that I could be holy, I could wash my skin in crushed sapphires; he kissed my throat and promised to make me the Queen of Heaven. This time I came to Shadukiam with him crawling before me on a silken leash . . ."

The Tale of the Black Papess

I was the Caliph's lover from the age of sixteen—the first time I was Ragnhild, and the first Caliph I loved. I went happily to him—he was dark of eye and leg, and smelled of spices at whose names I could not begin to guess. He loved that my skin showed bruises so prettily, he loved that my hair was the color of wealth. And one evening, when his war with the Southern Kingdoms had raised a cacophony of metallic death in the desert, he kissed the mole on my calf and asked me if I would like to be a god.

I was a little fool. Anything my Caliph offered me, I took with grateful trembling and adulation. He stroked my lips and said that he required the gold of Al-a-Nur to continue the war, and that their succession was in doubt. He would put a cloak of fur and shining bronze on my shoulders and a diadem on my head. He promised me a city—me, who had spent my childhood learning to breed goats on a wretched patch of scrub-brush! He promised me the diamond turrets of Shadukiam, if I would call myself Papess and take the holiness of the Dreaming City for my own.

I understood nothing of politics, but I cherished every rich meal and soft dress. I was carried on a litter overland to my new home, and my name was sung by a hundred castrati as I entered under the Dome of Roses, the sun filtering pink and flame-red through those petals. What could Al-a-Nur have to compare with the beauty I saw that first day? I was closed into a house grander than a Palace, and took my vows dizzy with sweet, black wine. I made my mark on requisitions to be filled by the Caliph's men at Al-a-Nur, on conscriptions and taxations—my hands ached every night. I knew nothing of the city whose riches I was allocating, or whether the requests were acknowledged; I simply knew the days of rustling paper and the nights when the Caliph would return from the capital and press his face into my neck.

Until the day I was told that there was another Papess, that she had made some great sacrifice for the Twelve Towers—little did I know that she had damned herself for a hat and a sword. She had called me Apostate, they said. She had called me the Black Papess and led even now a grim-greaved army to my beautiful new home. I wept and begged to be allowed to see my lover, desperate to be hidden away from this avenging demon. I knew nothing of the Papacy, I was only a child scribbling on scraps of paper; what would this beast do to me who was born to it, who fought to possess the title I wore as lightly as a sparkling brooch on a festival day?

But the Caliph had gone—his little gambit had failed. He could not beat back the new Ghyfran's army and continue to hold the desert line. He had abandoned me in my filigreed Palace with only the piles of my ignored proclamations to guard me. I do not now believe he was ever serious about obtaining the Papacy—he was not a serious man. I was a bauble, no more than expendable. If I could hold my chair, so be it; if I lost it, the cost to the throne was less than that of a modest feast.

I cowered in my antechamber, ill with terror, rocking back and forth while my hair fell out in my hands. Every creak of the floor seized my heart in its fist and wrenched cries from my lips. I did not eat; I slept clutching a knife. I fancied that I could hear the ivory trumpets of the Nurian horde each day at dawn, and before my eyes at nightfall was the unchangeable image of their slavering faces—everyone knew that strange beasts lived in the Anointed City, and their grotesqueries floated through my dreams, leaving furrows in my flesh.

When I had been told that the army, the Draghi Celesti—words I could barely pronounce—were encamped but a day's march from the city gates, a boy came to me. He found me quivering behind the dais, and stroked my hair as though I was his lost daughter, yet he was no more than a child, ruddy-faced and ruddy-haired.

"What if I told you," he crooned, "that you could survive this?"

I stared like a wounded fawn at his pink cheeks. "Surely you don't mean to be my protector, do you? You're no more than an oversized housecat! The Papess will kill me and bathe in my blood. It's what they do, you know." The boy frowned.

"Well, perhaps 'survive' was hyperbole. But I am not exactly what I appear. Bodies, you see, are as cheap as daffodils in a spring market. This boy died of a fever not more than a week past—and I enjoy being a child. My name is Marsili. I traffic in the dead, in vacant flesh. I cannot technically save you from what the turncoat Papess will commit upon your pretty limbs, but I can keep your spirit safe until the world's wheel turns again and you might have a chance for vengeance. Or to live a nameless life among goats, if that is your preference. Do I hear a yes or a no?"

His green eyes seemed to wriggle into me like twin serpents seeking out their mother's cool skin. "You would do this for me?" I gasped.

"Well, not without payment, of course! This is Shadukiam, the counting house festooned with weeds! What cannot be bought here, what cannot be sold for a handful of copper and silver, a palm piled with blue gems, what cannot be had if the having is worth the cost? Every divinity and perversion is hung up with leather straps in our markets like dead geese in winter, the toes of those myriad desires pointing heavenwards, washed in haggling shouts, desperate cries! This place has always been my home; there is nothing I require that it cannot provide—every day a sweet-faced youth dies for the love of a rich girl, or starves, having gambled his few coins on a footrace! And when they have gone, the beautiful bodies are mine to wear like new-pressed shirts. What I ask of you is so small compared to the magic I can perform. There has never been a greater practitioner of the dead arts than I."

My curiosity wrestled with my fear. "How did you come by this power? Not even the priests of the Dead in Al-a-Nur know such a spell."

He looked at me strangely, stroking with one slim hand a beard he did not have. And then, he began to speak, as the city burned around us.

The Necromancer's Tale

WHEN I WAS BORN, I WAS NO LARGER THAN A farmer's plough-splayed thumb.

My mother was bitterly disappointed—she and my father had waited so long for a son, and yet she had finally given birth to nothing more than a freak. My noble parents sought to sell me to every passing circus—but the elephants stampeded and the lions took sick with palsy whenever they brought my miniature cradle near. Gypsies made the sign of the evil eye and placed small charms on our threshold in the night to ward against devils. Neither Towers nor Temples would take me—what kind of cleric would I make, who could never hope to grip a quill? I could not till land; I could not sell goods.

My father began to believe that I was not only deformed, but a demon.

Every day they went into the market and offered me to anyone who would spare a coin for my wretched little body. My mother would not nurse me. She fed me on scraps of chewed meat and pauper's gruel. She suggested to passersby that I might be used for snake-training, to spy on relations, or as an exotic fish-bait. As for myself, I was shrunken and mis-shapen, but my mind was sharp and fiery as blacksmith's tongs, and I could speak perfectly well by the time I was three days old. Before I reached a full week I also spoke the dialect of the gypsies. Before a month there was hardly a word in that market I did not understand. But I held my tongue against the roof of my mouth and let no word escape—if my mother knew, it would only drive up her price, and I wished her no profit.

Finally, when I was twenty weeks of age and had not grown at all, a buyer appeared. He was very tall, and thin as a length of paper. His skin and cloaks were the color of the moon—not the romantic lover's moon, but the true lunar geography I had heard whispered by Sun-and-Moon Nurians come to buy glass for their strange sky-spying tools: gray and pockmarked, full of secret craters, frigid peaks, and blasted expanses. His eyes had no color in them save for a pinpoint pupil like a spindle's wound—the rest was pure, milky white. He passed three solid gold pieces over my mother's palm, and she shuddered in revulsion at his touch when the money changed hands. She handed me over eagerly, examining the coins like a fat pig snuffling at its supper slop. From then on I belonged to the Man Dressed in the Moon, and my mother, no doubt, got a fine dun cow or pair of oxen out of the bargain.

The Man Dressed in the Moon held me gently in his hand as we navi-gated the market towards his house. His skin was cool and dry; it smelled of leather and gardenias. When we reached his doorstep, I noted that the house was colored exactly as his clothes were: gray and blistered with de-pressions, as if some celestial grapeshot had been fired at the façade. The door was no more than a blasted hole covered in oilcloth, and there were other smells blowing through it as we passed through, a whisper of ice and withered flesh.

The Man Dressed in the Moon set me upon a smooth tabletop in his study and peered at my tiny eyes.

"Well, young man," he said, his voice rolling like boulders down a lunar cliffside, "I know you can speak, so let us dispense with the coy little game where I pretend I do not know your worth, and you pretend that you are not glad to be rid of your family."

I shrugged amiably.

"I do not find it useful to have a homunculus about the house—I manage to keep it clean enough, and I do not have troublesome relations to spy upon, lest they make off with my wealth. But I do find your stature valuable—it is new, I have not seen such a thing before. Bodies are a specialty of mine. How would you like to get out of yours?"

I looked down at my hands, no bigger than acorns, my delicate fairy-feet, my tiny body which would never be able to walk through a street without danger of being gobbled up by a passing sparrow. "Such a thing cannot be, sir, much as I might wish it could."

For the first time the Man Dressed in the Moon smiled, and his face opened up like a pomegranate cracking. "On the contrary, my diminutive friend. And call me Father. I think that's best, considering, don't you?"

He gathered me into his cool, colorless palm again, and together we passed through a thick door and down a long, winding staircase that doubled over and back upon itself, so that it seemed to ascend and descend at the same time. I could not tell where we were, except that the walls became rocky and damp, and I had the sense of being very deep underground. Finally, we emerged into a room filled with people of all shapes, sexes, and descriptions. They were leaned against the walls like rolls of carpet, blond maiden against gray-haired grandfather against sweet-skinned child. In and among the human beauties were strange creatures: Basilisks and Leucrotta and Monopods with their single huge, twisted feet jutting awkwardly into the freezing air—for the room was chill as a witch's heart, and frost spackled the ceiling. Their eyes were serenely shut.

The Man Dressed in the Moon gestured expansively at his collection. "Choose! Every possible combination of features is represented here—will you have breasts or a beard? Will you have the dark skin of an Eastern Prince? Will you have a child's slender arms? All you must do is give up that wretched little form and I will dress you in a new one, sewn up as tightly as a bride's bodice! It is no more effort to me than shifting a lamp from one table to another. We must simply kill you, snuff out your little breath, and all will be well. Let me tell you how it is done . . ."

The Tale of the Man Dressed in the Moon

MY PEOPLE HAVE ALWAYS HAD RIGHTS OVER THE bodies of humans. We were born when the first rays of Mother Moon glided over the surface of the first ocean's face. From the primal water the Yi rose, and we suckled at the rim of the Moon, which in those days touched the sea and churned the salt waves beneath.

Moon taught us how to die. We had to learn it by rote and practice—it is not an easy thing for us. The others, the sun-children, die so naturally and gracefully; for us it is like solving a difficult equation without pen or paper.

Moon taught us that it was our right to take the bodies of the dead—we were hers, and just as the night was her province, the cold and the dead were ours. It was her gift to us, you understand, so that we could taste every kind of life, from the meanest to the most exalted. All the secrets of bloodless flesh she showed to us in the first days of the world. She showed us that it is possible to swim through bodies as a fish through coral; death clears a place for us. But one cannot swim through a living sea; the swimmer and the water must be equally mortified. So, in order to pass from flesh to flesh, we had to learn to die.

The first of us did not succeed—they went under the waves and breathed easily, instinctively. They went into the fire and became incandescent. They dove from high cliffs and their shoulder blades unfolded into wings like origami breaking. They cut open their veins with bone knives and found themselves only lightened and made translucent as diamonds by the lack of blood. We began to despair. The sun-children were prodigies: They died easily all around us, like daisies in winter.

I was the first to discover it. I sat beneath Moon with my mouth on her icy fingers, considering the problem. It seemed to me that we were a race of suicides—it was only our own bodies we flagellated, our own skin we removed like clothing. If we instead helped each other into death, if we made of it a sacrament, then perhaps we could manage the feat.

I went to one of my sisters and knelt before her, begging her to strangle me, to put out my eyes and burn my heart in a clay kiln. My theory babbled out of me like a brook flooding down a mountain, so eager was I to become the first of my people to master the art of death. She, too, was eager and curious, and put her slim, blue-white fingers around my throat, squeezing until I crumpled at her feet like a discarded blanket.

Thus was the first murder committed among the Yi. The celebration lasted for seven days and nights; the silver lanterns swayed and sweet waltzes were played on chalcedony pipes. Our star-spattered world was suddenly a cacophony of death as we leapt from our bodies into the bright limbs of the sun-children. Of course, once we had died the first time, we lost the adamant moon-flesh which was ours by birthright. But we found that the longer we remained in our new bodies, the more they came to resemble our old ones: The color seeped from the eyes and the skin grew pale as shadowless craters. After a few years in the body of a milkmaid, we looked quite ourselves again.

Of course, the sun-children, both human and monster, were terrified by this power. I cannot say why—certainly they had left the bodies, they no longer had any rights to them, and Moon had granted them to us by perfectly legal charter. But they turned from us in horror and forced us to wear gray, pockmarked cloaks so that they could tell us apart from their dead beloveds in the years before we turned the flesh back into our own. Once, they captured a boy not long dead while the Yi in him was weak and did not know his new muscles well enough to resist them. They kept him in a dark well, away from the eye of Mother Moon, and tortured him with boiling oil and thumbscrews and insidious poisons until he revealed some part of our secrets—though never, of course, the technique of traveling into cold flesh. These torturers went to Al-a-Nur and poured mortar into the foundations of the Tower of the Dead, where they practice a mutilated form of our art.

In the midst of our ecstatic dance from corpse to corpse, Moon came down to us while we slept, and spoke into the shell-ear of each Yi. She promised that when one of us—just one—had tasted every kind of life the garden of the sun's world could prepare for us, we could return to her, and dwell in a sea of light, cradled forever in her opaline arms.

And so we leap high, our starlit toes touching briefly on each form, human and monster—and we seek out every shade of claw and eye, so that we may return to the night and Moon's primal pale.

THE
NECROMANCER'S
TALE,
CONTINUED

THE MAN DRESSED IN THE MOON LOOKED DOWN at me with his blanched eyes and smiled, the sparse hairs on his chin quivering.

"I am a great collector, you see. I hold all these bodies in trust for my brothers and sisters, so that they may have a ready supply when they tire of their current ones. Quite a steady stream of Yi come and go from me like a river whistling its water under the moon—come an old crone and leave a young man, come an ice-haired northerner, go a southerner with cinnamon skin. The discards—well, all things must eat, and there is a feast day here every fortnight. But you! We have seen nothing like you! We must add your body to our treasury—in exchange you may have one of your choice."

I suppose I might have been shocked, but all I could think of was long, lithe limbs and a height which would tower over my father's. I agreed as easily as if he had offered to trade me a wooden wheel for a pair of chickens.

He held me up to each row of faces in a most considerate fashion, and I pondered them all in turn. I finally settled upon a youth with skin the color of aged brandy-wine, whose eyebrows arched in a noble, bemused way over his smoke-lashed eyes. He was very tall.

"Ah, excellent choice, my son! That was Marsili—long ago he was a Sultan's son, betrothed to a maiden of unearthly beauty, whose eyes were yellow as a wolf's. But he angered his father in some way or another—gambling or whoring, most likely; young men are so prone to such vices—and the Sultan in his wisdom sold the boy to me and married the girl himself. I'm told there is a whole dynasty of wolf-eyed Sultans some-where in the East. And he is no loss to us. Believe me, we long ago ex-hausted the tawdry experiences of a spoiled Prince." He pushed up his gray sleeves. "Shall we begin?"

I blinked twice, my heart thumping in me like an overworked bellows. "But I . . . I cannot strangle you, Father, I haven't anything like the strength."

His face broadened amiably.

"Oh, I needn't be dead—I am not going to take your body myself. The Yi are communal. It is just as well that any other of my race uses it. A sim-ple process and a cold room keep the bodies intact until they are needed. Only you must die. It will be a very small death, I promise. It will feel like you have swallowed a great portion of bread that has become stuck in your throat, somewhere between your mouth and your belly. Of course, a simple drink of water would push the bread down where it ought to go, but there is a curious feeling of *stretching,* of *bulging.* That is what a small death is like."

This did not sound so very terrible. I straightened myself to my full height—no larger than a grasshopper—and locked my arms as I imagined brave soldiers in war must.

"I am ready, Father. You may kill me now."

"Mustn't damage the body!" he chirped happily, and clamped his great clammy hand over my nose and mouth. He held it there, the smell of gar-denias cloying, while I struggled and sucked at the skin for air. Finally, I slackened and slumped into the curve of his thumb.

He was right, it was very like swallowing too much bread. First the alarm and panic, then the curious *stretching,* then the sliding release of bread into the belly. I did not float above my body as some say one does—I stood beside it, very calmly, as though I had simply been doubled. I watched the Man Dressed in the Moon pass my tiny body through a wash of strange, viscous fluid the color of costly ink. Then, pulling the slack form of Marsili from the ranks, he anointed its forehead with a musky-smelling oil. Finally, he placed an oblong white stone in the corpse's mouth and whispered a few words I could not hear over its bent head.

It was as though I blinked, and when I opened my eyes again, they were Marsili's eyes. When I flexed my hands they were Marsili's hands. When I spoke it was with Marsili's honey-wine voice, cultured by years of tutors. The stone had vanished from my mouth.

"I am . . . I am him!" I cried, looking the Man Dressed in the Moon directly in the eye. It was a silly thing to say, of course, but I could almost have wept for the joy of touching the cool ceiling with my fingers.

From that day I begged to be his apprentice, to learn this magic so that I would never have to die a big death. He saw no point, as the Moon was no mother to me. I could not but stand at the foot of the Yi's long ladder to her. But after some time he relented, being lonely or curious or both, and I began my long education. Any sacrament can be practiced by unbelievers, he always said. It's usually nothing more than eating and drinking, anyway. I could drink all I liked, and nothing I ever drank would become the Moon in my mouth—but drinking is pleasant enough without the promises of religion. And I was always pleasant to him.

I kept the name of my first other-body. It amused me, as it seemed neither male nor female, and there were many more forms to follow, of both sorts. I am not Yi: The bodies do not crumble around me. I simply move to the next fleshly costume when I tire of them. I do not truly understand what it is in the spirit of a Yi which corrupts a body around it, but I was never to suffer that dissolution. I was a good student; eventually, I even helped the Man Dressed in the Moon to pass to his next body. I knelt reverently and cut open his stomach, and prepared the next body for his passing. I placed the white stone on his new tongue; I was the first face he saw with his new eyes—which were wide and violet as a field of lilacs, the eyes of a still-lovely dowager who had died of chill.

It was in that body that the Man Dressed in the Moon became my lover. The Yi are in truth neither male nor female, but follow the desires of their host bodies—and there never was a dowager who did not yearn to have a young Prince as her paramour. We passed many years in this way, and even when the dowager's flesh became gray and cratered, I did not mind. I kissed those peeling, pockmarked limbs, and they were sweet, sweet as dried gardenias. We continued in this way until we exhausted each other—for neither was there ever a dowager who did not eventually grow bored with her beardless playmate—and I went from that house into the world.

All this I learned; all this I performed. When I left his house, no Nurian corpse-wrangler could have approached my knowledge, though her lust for it might burn like winter timber. When my parents died, I took their bodies—ah, the debauch to which I subjected *those* limbs! I punished them in their own skin.

But I am not Yi. I do not take bodies in order to achieve some mystical union with a mythical Moon. What I do, I do for pleasure, and for profit, and it is pleasant enough. I am not bound by their laws, I need wear no barnacled cloak, and so I move among the people of Shadukiam un-known and unmarked—and only once or twice have I been too impatient to wait for a creature to die.

For I am not Yi; I can take them while they still breathe.

I am not Yi; I will go on forever, in whatever body I choose, and the Moon will never take me.

THE TALE OF THE BLACK PAPESS, CONTINUED

"SO PUT YOUR DAINTY LITTLE MARK ON ONE OF those famous parchments. It has always been true that a figurehead's only power lies in her golden seal—no one cares what you say, but we all care what you sign. Give me access to the Caliph's rose-tinted gold, sign open the door to the great vault, and I will keep your spirit safe until the time comes for you to return in a body as ravishing or deformed as you wish, until your name is forgotten by all but the most dotard librarians in the Dreaming City, and no one will drag an army after you again."

"You don't want . . ." I looked down, blushing.

"What? Your firstborn child? Use of those lissome

limbs? I'm not a monster out of some child's tale. I have no need of living bodies, and children are more costly and troublesome than beasts twice their size. Do you think there is a pleasure of the flesh I have not sampled? I do not need the Caliph's trash. I am a magician—it is a vocation like any other, and I require remuneration for my services, as any other tradesman would. Would you try to pay for grain with unborn babes? I think not. Do not insult me; I am no less skilled than a miller grinding his seed."

I nodded humbly, and the necromancer kissed my shuddering lips then, and my brow, my hair, my chin. It was not in lust that his lips brushed my face, but as a strange sort of seal on the bargain as I eagerly scrawled his demand onto a used and crumpled leaf of paper—on the one side it demanded that the merchant-monks of the Coral Tower open their vaults to the Caliph; on the other it demanded that the vault of the Caliph be opened to Marsili.

"What do I do now? How do I know you will keep your promise?" I asked, clutching my elbows to my sides.

"You will know because I have sworn it, and you are the trusting kind. You may want to work on that, the next time you see this city from the inside. This is Shadukiam, after all. Here the trusting are found every morning in one gutter or another. You need do nothing more, sweet Ragnhild, little ragged girl, left all alone." He reached forward and wound a thin length of my hair through his fingers, then, with a sharp flick of his wrist, tore it from my head. "Wait to die." With that, he retreated from the antechamber, bowing gratuitously as he went.

And die I did. The Nurian Papess dragged me from my seat by the ear as though I were no more than a misbehaving child and forced me to my knees before my own altar. With a strange, curving silver knife she cut my tongue from my mouth, and the taste of blood, the meaty, metallic taste of my blood, flooded my mouth. I screamed, I screamed—I thought there would never be an end to the screaming. She moved the knife in the air speculatively; with ridiculous attention I noted its sickle shape, its hilt, the fine engraving. In the midst of pain like stones breaking open the knife filled my vision. I thought then it would be my nose next, or my eyes. I did not understand yet the shape of zealotry.

Ghyfran, the savior of Al-a-Nur, ripped my dress from collar to waist, and cut my breasts from my body as if carving a roasted bird for her supper. But when they had sloughed to the floor with a sickly, wet sigh, she leaned into me, her breath brushing my ear.

"I have saved you, poor, wretched pawn. Now you may go to the dark as a sacred Androgyne, and no door of alabaster or diamond will be closed to you."

That is your heroine-priest, this lying whore who forswore her god in order to kill an innocent—then forswore her oaths of office with her adherence to her mad faith. What is Al-a-Nur but a bedchamber where you may luxuriate in lies and blasphemies, convincing yourselves that they are virtues?

They tied me to that wet, grassy hill, pressing up under my back like the bones of the moon, and the soldiers dangled these chains in my face, mocking me—it was the only gold, they said, I would ever get from Al-a-Nur.

The rest is simple, unutterably common. The sun took my flesh away in its arms, and the moon whitened my bones to dust. I fell away from myself, into some deep well of dreaming—I recall nothing from the last gasp until I awoke, washed in gray light. The necromancer Marsili had bound me bodiless in some strange glass vial, and I watched him as the years flew by like blackbirds—sometimes he was a woman, sometimes a man, sometimes a child as he had been when first he came to me. But I learned to recognize him in each body, the upturn of the eye, the cruel crooked mouth, the gestures of his hands. I learned, and more than that. The necromancer performed many horrible things in his workshop, and I learned from him all the magic he learned from his bodies. After all, he was the only thing I saw for all those years. I had nothing to do but become a student of his every sigh and gesture.

And yet, he waited, he waited for so long. I thought he had forgotten me, that I would be stuck in a bottle like a scrawled note forever. But one midnight, when I had almost lost the memory of what it was to feel my own flesh, he picked up my vial and brought it to a long table, where a golden-haired corpse lay stiff and still.

"You are only a legend now, Ragnhild. It is safe to come out; it is safe to live. The world remembers you only as a ghost in the closet, a wight on the grassy hills." He gestured at the glassy-eyed corpse on his knotted elmwood table. "I keep my word, as any merchant does. She loved a boy her parents could not accept and starved herself to death for the lack of him. Terribly romantic. Are you ready, is she sufficient?"

He sensed my consent in some fashion of his own, and when I woke again, my lids were fringed in lashes pale as raw flax, the weight of a body pulled once more at my bones, and the last vapors of a white stone were still dissolving on my tongue.

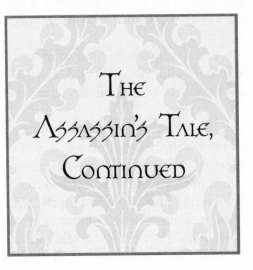

THE ASSASSIN'S TALE, CONTINUED

RAGNHILD LOOKED DOWN AT US, ANGER STREAM-
ing from her as though from a dying star. "This time I
went to no man's bed. I have had time, and time piled high
upon time, to consider how I would spend my new
body—and I chose to be in truth what I was before only in
jest. I will be your Black Papess, and take Al-a-Nur for my
own. I bought the Caliph's blessing on my ascension with
Marsili's gold, and came to Shadukiam, not on a litter like
some pampered babe, but walking on the stony earth, and
I did not lower my eyes when I saw once more the Dome
of Roses."

I swallowed hard. "And Marsili? He gave over his wealth just to bring you back to this little room?"

Her face folded into a satisfied smile, and the Black Papess rose from her flowered chair, the violet gown shifting and trailing obscenely over her skin. She walked past us slowly, without fear, and drew aside a thick cream-colored curtain covering an alcove behind us.

On a deep green cushion edged in silver rested the head of a young, dark-haired beauty, the line of her nose clearly noble, the shape of her lips suggesting an ineffable refinement. The colors of death spoiled her skin into a bluish ravage, and dried blood clotted around her severed neck. Ragnhild turned her head delicately as though appraising the artistry of a statue.

"I watched him for five hundred years, trapped in that glass like an ant in amber. I hated him. The first real hate I had ever known—the first of many. I have begun to keep a catalogue of hatreds, and this was the first in my ledger: the hatred of the trapped thing. He waited so long. I think he would have left me there if he were not bound by love of this city to provide the service he was contracted for. That is the soul of Shadukiam, after all. He was my first act in this flesh—I took his head and his gold in one stroke. You mustn't pity him. What kind of a man seduces a child into centuries of death-which-is-not-death for a few rubies from the Caliph's table? He was a fool and a glutton."

She closed the curtain with a slow hand and turned back to us, bright-faced.

"Will you kill me now or will you wait for a less guarded opportunity? I admit I've been wondering if the inevitable attempt would be daring enough to come while I am ensconced in my antechamber, attendants a mere door's width away—or if the new oath-breakers would wait until I was asleep. For you are oath-breakers, are you not? Your order forbids violence, and yet, here you are. How very Nurian of you—the will of the gods is supreme unless the Papacy needs a puppet."

Bartholomew walked to her very slowly, his head bent in real respect, and when he spoke he made his voice as comforting as our snouts and lolling tongues can manage. We held our breaths, waiting to leap to his aid the moment she moved.

"I am sorry for you. I am sorry that you were once innocent and young, and that the Caliph used you for his ends. I am sorry that you have had to come such a long way, through such suffering and foul magic. I wish that you had been allowed to stay a tender of wiry goats in the sweet-breathed mountains. I wish that we had not heard your story. But you do not know Al-a-Nur simply because you once died at its hand. That you cannot comprehend the selflessness of Cveti-who-became-Ghyfran, or the pity, the love, she must have felt for you, to administer the last sacrament of her faith to a nonbeliever, tells me no more than that you are not fit to be the lowliest novice, let alone the Papess of our spiritual menagerie. You could never understand what we suffer for the sake of that beautiful garden of gods, or why we would incur this stain on our souls so that others may live free of sin. I am sorry, terribly sorry, that you have wagered so much for vengeance when all who harmed you are dead, and that you must fail now, before you could see the spires of the Twelve Towers catching the dawn light and spinning it into a fall of crystal. Before you could even begin what you must have planned all those years in your little vial. But we have sworn, and we are, if nothing else, obedient dogs."

All this while, I and Balthazar had inched towards her, and when our brother stepped back, with tears in my eyes, I leapt and closed my teeth over her throat, but my jaws snapped on empty air. Ragnhild stood suddenly behind Balthazar, and she smiled sweetly, like a little child with a caramel.

It seemed to each of us that her face floated before ours in all its frigid beauty. It seemed to us that she bent her lips to our panting muzzles, and her breath smelled of bundles of violets clutched to the breasts of dead maidens, of gauze stretched over noble profiles and coins pressed into eye sockets. It seemed to us that she kissed our mouths, and our eyes clouded over with red and black, our bellies trembled and boiled in our skin. We were maddened, frenzy licked at our brains, we could not breathe for the blood screaming like blades sharpening inside us.

Ragnhild stood utterly still, a pale column against the wall as we spat and snarled, squaring off against each other. She inclined her head, ever so gently, towards Barnabas.

How can I tell you, little sister? How can I give words to what we did? We, who would not eat the slowest fox or hare! We, who loved each other as limbs of one body! How can I confess? How can I speak of it as though it were no more or less than any other act I have committed, as though it were not the greatest sin of my heart, of my tongue, of my teeth!

At the nod of her head we threw ourselves onto the smallest of us, onto Barnabas, our sweet brother, and devoured him leg by arm by torso, blood swirling rich and smoky in our mouths. We howled up from the ruin of his belly, not in mourning, but in hunger and delight. We snapped at each other, quarreling over the choicest bits. We were no more than dogs, though the hands that held him and the fists that punished his spine were those of men. Our minds fled from us, we exulted in his death.

And Ragnhild swept from the slaughter room without a sound, as though her feet did not touch the crystal floor.

The Net-Weaver's Tale, Continued

BAGS SHOOK HIS HEAD MISERABLY.

"I can still taste him," he whispered, barely giving breath to his words. "Taste his flesh, like ash and lye. We will never be clean of this. She let us leave the city unmolested—what else could she do to us? She had already ensorcelled us into betraying our faith and our brother, she had already made all our vows, our holy will, useless with a kiss. We are lost, and we cannot even say it was for the greater good—she lives, and danger still stalks the City like a cat in the grass."

He held his hands out to me helplessly.

"She is coming, she is coming and she will madden

us all. Poor Barnabas—he sits heavy in my belly and I will never hear him extol the sweetness of blueberries again."

"She is coming, yes. And she does not want to destroy Al-a-Nur, she wants to *best* it. She wants to prove to the world that we are all liars and heretics and faithless grotesques. That she is holy and we are demons. *That* is why she let us go. We are her first victory," Balthazar snapped, his voice bursting from behind me and startling both Bags and me.

Bartholomew sidled up to his brother and added in a thick voice: "However wretched her origins, she chose freely to continue her crimes against us from the moment she woke to this life. It is easy to forgive beautiful women, especially when they lay a sorrowful tale before you like a sugar-dusted meal. It does not mean they deserve forgiveness. We must tell Yashna that we have failed and accept punishment. And we must close the gates against the Apostate, for I do not doubt that she is, as you say, coming."

Bags snuffled away his tears and turned his face from his brother. Shame radiated from his hunched body. When we broke camp in the morning, he leaned over my shoulder and whispered:

"There is a debt between us. If you have a grief that weighs on you, I will take it."

I smiled as brightly as I was able and lied. "I am too young to carry suffering on my back like a pauper's pack."

He nodded distractedly. "Then I will repay my debt when you have grown."

It was only two days later that we saw the gleam of Al-a-Nur flare in the distance like the birth of a dozen stars. My breath caught itself in a net of wonder, and the Salmon Gate rose up finally before me, silver and quartz, carved fish leaping with eyes of onyx, metallic waves brushing their delicate fins. I had come home, to the truest home of my deep bones.

The rings of the City were thronging with monks and priests of all kinds, each wearing costumes that clearly held some meaning for them, but that to me were simply bright splashes of color and patterns wriggling like merry snakes over the fine fabrics. Many sat in small groups, bent over a circular game board and loudly cheering each player's move.

"That is Lo Shen, little love," Bartholomew said, "our sacred Game. It is prayer as well as a Game—the object is to defeat the opposite player's God, surrounding that chief piece with involved patterns of the lesser pieces. The entire City plays at one level or another. It is very complex, but you will learn."

The brothers, though their errand was urgent, seemed to drag themselves through the sparkling city, reluctant to reach its center. Instead, they guided me through its streets, inching closer to the innermost Tower with each step. As ever, they buried their sorrow in the cairns of their wolf hearts, and behaved as happily as the rest of the Anointed City.

The markets were manned by men and women dressed in vivid yellow garments, clasped at the shoulders with a fabulous crest: a golden rooster wrestling a peacock encrusted with bright blue stones. With each sale, which only occurred after extensive and enthusiastic haggling, they bowed deeply and anointed the head of the buyer with water—they were, I learned, the merchant-monks of the Coral Tower. Balthazar explained that the exchange of goods was for them a ritual honoring their chief goddess, Ge-Sai, Star-of-Gold, who in the first days gave birth to all the precious things of the world. Each coin they earn brings the children of Ge-Sai together under the eyes of their mother. The rooster and peacock represent finery for its own sake struggling with finery for the sake of the world—for the peacock's pride is its functionless beauty, while the rooster crows up the sun each day, and his feathers echo the colors of his charge.

Through the streets, whose smells and raucous sounds seemed like an endless carnival, strode the Draghi Celesti, masked in ivory serpent-faces, priests and priestesses of the Tower of Ice and Iron, guardians of the city. Their uniforms were silver and blue, over-tunics emblazoned with a curling winged snake which extended from shoulder to ankle. They were not belligerent, but seemed as merry as any of the Lo Shen players, joking and sparring in the streets. They consulted with the rather plump women of the Tower of the Nine Yarrow Stalks, who were every one of them Oracles of great skill. Bags snickered that they were so fat because they were expert *extispicers,* readers of entrails—a great deal of meat was left over after each ritual, and as they believed waste to be a sin, the women were forced to have a great many feasts.

As we ventured into the interior of the city, I saw the home of my companions, the Chrysanthemum Tower, thrusting up through the earth like a living thing. Indeed, it was entirely hidden in a vast cloak of chrysanthemums, yellow and red and orange, all crowding together like flames licking at a new branch. But at the door, guarded by two impeccably groomed Cynocephaloi brandishing garden shears—for it was necessary to prune the flowers from the door each hour, so eager were the blossoms to engulf the stone—Bartholomew, Bags, and Balthazar stopped and turned solemnly to me. Bags knelt and smiled his toothy smile.

"It is unlawful for those who have not committed their lives to the Tower to enter. If you wish to live in Al-a-Nur, you must choose a Tower—

naturally, we hope you will choose ours, but we cannot guide your decision."

"On the bright side," Bartholomew added cheerfully, "you are somewhat limited. You have not the training to be an Oracle, nor a Draghi. They require entrance in early childhood—you would not pass the first of their tests. You cannot join the Tower of Patricides—"

"Why not?" I protested.

"You are not male. The Patricides are separated into father and son dyads. The father raises his son in the traditions of the Tower, and when the son arrives at the age of Enlightenment, he kills his father—who is normally quite elderly by the time his son is ready to perform the rites. The son then grows to have his own children by women from outside the order, and the cycle continues."

"That's barbaric!" I cried, disgusted. My own father had died when I was an infant, and my fury leapt up as quickly as a pheasant bursting from the grass.

"It is done with great care and love," Balthazar explained gently, "and the solemnity of the ritual is touching—for them, to kill the father is to release the son from the shadow of that great man, and to place your death in the hands of a beloved son is the most noble way to perish. We do not judge. We never judge. Nevertheless, you are equipped with neither male aspect nor a father, and so could not enter the Tower. And since it is rather clear to us that you are female, the Tower of Hermaphrodites is also barred to you—the secret must be kept from all, and we are already aware of your sex."

"You are left with the Tower of Sun-and-Moon," Bartholomew went on, "who have their eyes turned ever upwards, charting the courses of the heavens, and ever earthwards, watching for glimpses of dustbound Stars. They collect ways of worshipping—some say the Stars were chewed out of a black horse, some out of a woman whose skin was the sky, some say they were awled in the belt of heaven, or worried out of the keel of an infinite ship by celestial mice. The Tower has all their gospels catalogued. But the Stars are not gods, they say; they are just lost children, as we all are. They are the most ancient order among us, and also the poorest, for the educated and wealthy have palates refined towards more complex and colorful faiths.

"The Nightingale Tower, too, would take you: Their method of worship lies in music, and the filling of the heavens with their songs, for they serve the sibling-Stars Chandra and Anshu, who made the first music of the world between them with their illuminate voices. There are also Towers of the Living and the Dead. With the Living you would be bonded to a creature: a falcon, or a wildcat, or a serpent, even a little green mantis—for they believe that divinity resides in even the smallest of beasts, and that they are the voices of heaven. Your union with the creature would be absolute; you would hunt and live and die as one being.

"In the Tower of the Dead, you would study the bodies of all those who die in the City—blood-magic and lymph-magic and the arcana of rigor mortis. They believe that this life is only an initiation, that death is the beginning of enlightenment. The corpse is the vessel of knowledge; the soul goes on to other spheres, leaving the body saturated with the secrets of this world. They worship the Manikarnika, who are long dead, their bodies long lost, and raise altars to their ghosts."

"But which one is right? The real gods? The truth?" I asked.

Balthazar smiled gently, as if speaking to a very slow child. "That is not for us to judge. Each of us believes what seems true enough to him, and allows others the same luxury. Who can know what happened in the dim dawn of the world? We can barely decide what to have for breakfast without a theological debate—the Nurian law is polite disagreement. We do our best with how the world appears to our own eyes."

Bags snorted and scratched behind his furry ear. "I think you're forgetting one, brother."

"Oh, yes," said Bartholomew, dismissively, "the Tower of St. Sigrid, which, while we certainly do not judge, is hardly a religion at all. They follow in all things the example of the philosopher-mariner, Saint Sigrid of the Boiling Sea, who was neither a Star nor any other sort of god, and whose feats change each time you ask a Sigrid about their Lady. She was a great navigator, they say. She was a sea-goddess in the lands of old. She was a humble oarswoman. She had three breasts and grew a beard. Who can tell? They are secretive, and they ply the river's current on ships of cypress-wood and tell no one of their rites."

"And there is our own Tower," said Bags fondly, "the Chrysanthemum. And of us you know already—*The Book of the Bough* and *The Book of Carrion*, the sanctity of plants, of all growing things, which give us of their own lives so that we may live." He tousled my hair as if I were a child. "Of course, all the Towers are specialized and rarefied faiths—some have to do with the countryside faith of the Stars, some do not. Religion is a starchy dish, and we spice it more exotically here."

I breathed deeply, intoxicated by the variety of Towers and people—my village had contained no more than a few hundred souls, and only one Temple, little more than a cave of ice in the mountainside. But I did not have any particular predilection for birds or cats, beyond the eating of them; I could neither sing nor play any instrument at all. In the end, I decided that I had spent half my life already in the worship of the sky—I had given enough to them, more than enough. And, much as it shamed me to think it, I did not wish to bow down to flowers and never again eat venison rich with spices. I saw no sin in it; it was not in my nature. And this left but one Tower.

"I will not say I have decided—I know so little! But take me to the Tower of St. Sigrid . . ."

In the Garden

THE GIRL'S EYES SEEMED TO REFLECT THE MOONLIGHT, SILVER TRACKS appearing in the solid black of her skin. Her voice had suddenly ceased, cutting off her tale like a fisherman tying off his line. She looked into the distance at the waving plum trees, their leaves glinting dark and light as the wind shuffled them lazily. The pond rippled silkily beside them, lapping against the cattails and arching roots of bowing willows. The boy shifted, feeling that he was hardly noticed anymore, that the girl was telling her tale to the night itself, and did not even see him sitting before her. Would she now brave his tower window to sit beside him? He feared to leave her, that he might never find her again in the vast Garden, with its labyrinth of hibiscus and jasmine, its flocks of tame birds, their tails glittering like a treasure house, its tall cypresses pointing upwards like hands of pilgrims.

His breath was as short as it ever was when her voice slid into him. Despite his confusion, the city of Al-a-Nur had laid itself out somewhere in his belly, spreading its Towers through his little body, and he had fallen into the trance that the girl could induce in him so easily, roaming those profoundly blue streets and smoke-filled alleys in his own dreaming gait, nibbling a sugared apple bought from a yellow-robed monk, and yearning to vanish into a Tower of his own.

Suddenly the girl focused her attention on him, and his heart leapt like a frog after the moon at its sound.

"I am sorry . . . sorry that I left you for so long. I didn't mean for you to be hurt by it." She hid her face in the shadows, and the boy trembled a little, but did not let it show.

The girl smiled, tentative as a hare in a field, and began again.

THE
PALE GIRL'S TALE,
CONTINUED

SNOW'S FINGERS WERE WET AND THICK; SHE COULD hardly feel the coarse net ropes between them. She turned her head away from Sigrid, shamed. She felt suddenly as if she were a ghost in her own life—this woman had been young and alone like her, and had found her way to a city of gods and wolf-headed friends, whereas Snow had found nothing at all but a cold waterfront and a teasing nickname spoken so often she had forgotten what her real name might ever have been. All she had done was slowly turn the color of this freezing, heartless town, and the color of the sea that battered it with salt. She wondered if she had any blood left in her, or if her body had just filled up with water and cold.

"I wish," she whispered, "that I were as brave and bright as you, that I could go to such a place, and meet such folk, and know about such things."

Sigrid frowned, her curly hair flattened against her broad forehead by the damp, like a monk's tonsure. "That's funny, you know. I spent most of my time in Al-a-Nur wishing I were as brave and bright as Saint Sigrid. We all have someone we think shines so much more than we do that we are not even a moon to their sun, but a dead little rock floating in space next to their gold and their blaze."

Snow breathed on her fingers. Their tips did not warm, even the littlest bit. She looked up sidelong at Sigrid, whose cheeks were whipped to scarlet in the wind.

"I certainly thought everything in the world outshone me then, and Bags the brightest of all, until I met the next brightest of all, and the next . . ."

The Net-Weaver's Tale, Continued

BAGS AGREED TO TAKE ME TO THE TOWER OF ST.
Sigrid before the trio reported to the Papal Tower to finish
their unsavory quest. All agreed that it was not appropriate for me to go with them—and no uncommitted youth
could be given audience with the Papess. My farewells
were made with Balthazar and Bartholomew. Secretly I
was not so grieved to leave them as long as Bags was with
me—they were both so fierce and serious. Bags was dear
to me as a pup to her litter-mate, but his brothers frightened me sometimes, with their solemn yellow eyes and
muzzles that seemed to cease their smiles when I turned
away.

His rust-colored fur caught the late afternoon sun and turned it into a sweet, merry fire. The darkness of the Black Papess seemed to have slid from him like old clothes once he had crossed the threshold into Al-a-Nur, and his wolfish face wore a wide smile; he seemed to be breathing in the city as we walked.

"It's all right that you're not coming with us, you know. You might be . . . uncomfortable. Most of the Chrysanthemums are like me—if not Cynocephaloi, other half-breeds of various kinds. The Sigrids are lovely, despite what Bartholomew says. We don't strictly have a deity like most of the Towers. We don't really pay much attention to Stars, either way. The divine is present in the *earth*, in all growing things, all life and all death, and the *Bough* guides us through life, *Carrion* through death. That's enough for me. Bartholomew looks down on some because they don't have any sort of worship at all, like the Patricides, or because they idolize a person who couldn't possibly be better than any other person—but I never met a Sigrid who wouldn't steer her boat to your aid if you called her, and that's the truth." He giggled behind his brown, splay-fingered hand.

"Of course, they're *terrible* at Lo Shen. They can't help it—they lead with their Triremes every time." Suddenly he stopped, and a shadow passed over his face like a cormorant's wing. "I wonder if we'll be allowed to enter our Tower again. I don't think there is divinity to be found in the death we gave." He snapped back to me as quickly as he had gone into himself. "Ah, here we are."

The Tower of St. Sigrid was a mammoth spire made entirely of broken ships. Prows jutted out at all angles, long keels and tall masts wrapped the walls, rigging and sails like vines and veils hanging haphazard from every window. At the entrance stood a gargantuan ship's wheel, warped and splintered with age, casting its long shadow towards the bolted door. The sentry was a muscular woman whose head had been roughly shaved. Her wide, flat teeth shone brightly. At the sight of her, Bags's eyes lit like lamps on a midwinter night. She greeted my canine friend with an enormous embrace that would have cracked the bones of a musk ox.

"Bags, old mate! You whelp! You never come to see me anymore! Afraid I'll take your God down a peg or two?"

"Not as long as you keep throwing your 'Remes around like they're ten for a penny!" He clapped her prodigious back and rubbed her bald head happily. "I've got a recruit for you, Sigrid—we picked her up on the lichen flats up north. She's a dear, eager little thing, but she hasn't quite made up her mind as to a Tower yet. Likes her morning bacon a bit too much to come in with us." He winked at me and I blushed deeply, ashamed at his guess.

The woman looked at me, her gaze roughly measuring me as if for some bizarre suit of armor. "She's skinny and the hair will have to come off" came the judgment.

Bags rolled his eyes. "She needs to know about your thrice-damned Saint Sigrid so that she can decide, you salty old dog. And I can't stay. We cannot keep the Papess waiting."

At this the woman's brusque expression softened and she dropped an elephantine arm around my shoulders.

"No, no, of course. You go—I trust it went well, or you wouldn't be back. We all . . . appreciate what you've done, you know, Bagsy. I'll tell skin-and-bones what she needs to know."

Bags's eyes filled with tears—but he hid it well, like a thief slipping a ring into his pocket. He hugged me as tightly as a bear shaking a tree for fruit, his furry face buried in my neck. He whispered a tight *thank you* and turned to go. I reached out to stop him.

"Wait, Bags! When I asked to come, back in my village, you said something strange to the others, something from *The Book of Carrion*. What was it? Tell me!"

Bags grinned, looking impossibly like a cat, and laid his finger aside his nose.

"*And the wolf shall lead her astray, unto the edge of the sea, and there she will find the City of the Lost, where her skin will fall away, and the Beast will swallow her whole.* Prophecy, love. Best hope it's not you."

When he had gone, the bald woman sat heavily on the snowy ground and gestured with a tattooed hand that I ought to sit beside her.

"He's only teasing. That *Book of Carrion* is full of gibberish and dog-speak. Pay no attention—it means less than a flapping sail in a strong wind. I'll tell you the way of things. I'm called Sigrid—we've all taken the name of the great Lady, in her honor. I don't care in the least what your name is; it'll be Sigrid if you want to sail with us, anyhow. Listen to this old deckhand, and I'll tell you the tale of the Great Navigator . . ."

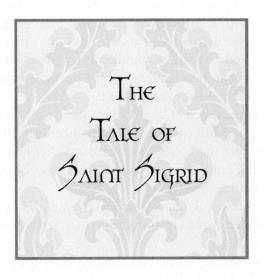

The Tale of Saint Sigrid

IN THE NAME OF THE MOTHER, AND THE MONster, and the Mast, Amen.

In the fifteenth year of the Second Caliphate, a child was born in the Blessed City of Ajanabh to a family of traveling spicers whose fingers smelled forever of cinnamon and coriander. Their barge stayed in the port of Ajanabh for many years, but they were not native to the city that witnessed the birth of the Saint. Where they came from in truth is lost to us now. Indeed, Ajanabh seemed not to recognize the Blessing of Heaven, and tried many times to expel the merchant barges, which were as great in number as flocks of sparrows in the autumn sky, from their Great Harbor, claiming that the families brought disease and sloth with them from notorious lands.

The child was christened Sigrid, and she was a great beauty even as a girl, with rich brown skin and thick hair the color of all her family's spice stores milled into a shade of dark brown shot through with gold and red, and eyes the color of a lion's paw. But she had been born with a strange deformity which brought a secret shame onto the backs of her parents. Her father wept and accused her mother of coupling with a demon; her mother suspected that their family gods had turned against them and delivered them a daughter with harpy blood.

For Sigrid was possessed of three breasts, and as she grew, this strangeness became impossible to hide. So each morning before taking her daughter to the spice market, her mother bound her breasts with lengths of rough cloth. Each morning, she patted Sigrid's cheek and stifled tears as she wound the fabric.

When she became a woman, Sigrid performed this penance herself, crushing her small but plainly monstrous chest beneath straps of leather and buckles of lead.

After a long while, she stopped weeping while she did it.

When Sigrid had reached the age of sixteen—as all men know, this is the age at which such catastrophes of serendipity occur—a troupe of pirates attacked the floating city of harbor barges. This was not uncommon in Ajanabh, which was in those days altogether a raucous network of villain-strewn streets; an Ajan never touched a gold piece which had not been stolen at least thrice in its lifetime. But the barges were sacrosanct, bargers being themselves distant cousins to pirates. So when the *Maidenhead* sailed into the Great Harbor, her red sails billowing like dead moons in the night, the merchants simply rolled over in their sleep, thinking it would pass them by and ransack the city as such masted beasts had always done.

Instead, the pirates set fire to the skiffs and scows of the spicers and the tinkers, the cobblers and the armorers and the potters.

Sigrid, like her brothers and her parents, slept in her cot, breasts unbound, curled around herself like a snail's shell. She awoke to a hand clamped over her mouth and a toothy hiss in her ear:

"Hush now, precious. Wouldn't want to wake Mama." The voice's owner scooped her up into its arms like a cat snatching the scruff of her kitten's neck. In a whirl of smoke and flame, Sigrid found herself dragged across the barge of her birth and away—and thus did she exit a tale which surely would have comprised a life of derision and exclusion, ending in a cinnamon-and-coriander-scented corpse shoved overboard into the Bay of Ajan.

Instead, Sigrid was deposited by her abductor onto the deck of a shadowed ship, and entered another tale entirely.

In truth, her family was not sorry to see her go. They would never have been able to induce a man to marry her, even with sacks of musky saffron to barter. It seemed to them best to cherish their other, beautifully shaped children, and let their misshapen daughter go to whatever fate the Stars had ordained for her.

Whatever owned the strange voice had brought Sigrid to the *Maidenhead,* and once the crew had plundered, stolen, and kidnapped as they pleased, the ship relinquished the harbor as gracefully as a lord sheathing his sword, and unfurled her scarlet sails to catch the salt breath of the open sea.

There is nothing quite like the moment a sail clutches the wind and opens under it like the legs of a merry fishwife. The sound of it, the echoing billow as the air blows out the fabric, the surge forward and the spray in the teeth—it is the sound that heralds the beginning of new worlds, the birth of litters of wish-granting seals in a hundred secret grottos, the grinding of new rivers through mountains which witnessed the first flood and chuckled at their wet toes.

It filled Sigrid's heart like wine into an oak barrel. She leaned over the rail and grinned into the sound, marveling at the ship that now carried her—the cannons were worked into the shapes of animal heads, mouths agape. Along one side screamed silent manticores, on the other, crocodiles gaped wide. The ship itself shone a rich red color—some strange wood she had never seen before. The mast was massive and tall, seeming to bruise the stars, and from its polished surface sprouted glossy green leaves and branches the size of children's arms. It was a tree, a living tree drinking from the sea and sky, bearing the sails and lines with good nature. It did not seem to mind the salt or the rough wind, but opened its leaves like glad hands. Where the crow's nest ought to have been was an explosion of branches heavy with leaf and orange fruit, thick enough to bear a lookout. The sails were deep red, and Sigrid wondered if this was not a very disreputable pirate ship to flout the sage tradition of black sails. The rails were curled and carved with arcane designs—it was unlike any ship she had ever seen in Ajanabh, and unlike, she suspected, any ship on the dark-waved sea.

The usual bustle of a ship under way streamed around her, for the most part ignoring the new passenger, as sailors are wont to do. But they were an unusual crew. Besides the standard complement of inhuman creatures galloping—yes, she certainly saw a Satyr and possibly a small-shouldered Centaur—or slithering—that woman struggling with a bag puffing yellow spices was surely a Lamia—across the decks, the ship appeared not to possess a single male occupant.

"How do you like her, my Ajan waif?" The strange voice sounded again from behind her, soft and hard altogether, like a golden hammer sheathed in fur. Sigrid turned and beheld a large part of her destiny: Long-Eared Tomomo, captain of the good ship *Maidenhead*. Tomomo was strange-looking for that part of the world, but not un-handsome—her eyes were dark and desultory, her hair long and black, straighter than a crow's leg, her skin like oft-touched ivory, its shade having long since lost its white to the strokes of many fingers. Her dress was not garish, as the coats of pirates so often are, but simple stag-skin vests and trousers, and her hair bound in a long braid that brushed her thighs. Later, Sigrid would often hear her refuse the captain's hat, with its bouncing peacock feathers and golden buckles, remarking that if she were to die—as she would surely draw attention of the murderous kind in that hat—they might never get the hideous thing off of her, and her gods would laugh at her when she met them in hell.

"The ship, ma'am?" Sigrid paused, unsure. "Sir?"

"Tommy is good enough for my girls and it's good enough for you. Yes, the ship." Tommy slapped the rail and rubbed it affectionately. "She's my prize—a gift from a bird, a tree, and a Witch. Not a nail in her; the whole thing held together with breath and blood and starlight."

Sigrid swallowed hard. "And you'll be needing my blood to pay the Witch, I suppose?"

Tommy's eyebrows arched like bows springing to fire. "I think not. The mess would be more trouble than it's worth."

"Then why did you take me, if not to kill me? I'm told that's what pirates do. And besides, you must be the worst kind of pirate if you attacked the Ajan barges."

The captain smiled and leaned into Sigrid's face, her expression almost, but not quite, motherly. "We don't really hold with tradition. We heard there was a monster-girl living on the barges. You'll learn to trust one kind of rumor and laugh at the other when you live at sea—this was the kind you listen to. When the Stars speak, you listen. Look around; we like monsters here. It's not easy to crew a ship with only women—girls don't exactly study to be sailors these days. When we hear of some ghastly beast, we snap her up as soon as we can."

"So, all of that, the fire and the raid, was for me?"

"Certainly not! We stole plenty of other things—just no other girls. You're part of our crew now—you've been pressed into naval service, my little powdermonkey."

Sigrid leaned over the rail and stared at the water running past the red hull swift as otters fleeing a hungry shark. She contemplated the loss of her family—which she did not feel greatly—and her new place as a monster among monsters. Though some of the sailors had appeared human, she began now to suspect that none of them truly were. And at that moment, Tommy leaned over the bar alongside her.

Tomomo's reflection in the water was that of a woman's body, but it was crowned, not with Tomomo's smirking face, but with that of a bright-eyed fox, its fire-shaded fur buffeted by the wind.

The
Pale Girl's Tale,
Continued

SNOW LOOKED UP AT SIGRID'S WIDE FACE CARE-
fully as a deer nosing a blackberry bramble.

"I was born in Ajanabh, you know," she said softly.

Sigrid nodded, but it was not precisely a confirmation
that she had known. "Then you are blessed as a spring
babe—though I'm told it's no more than a shadow of the
city it was. All cities are shades of what they were these
days; even Muireann was once a metropolis, with towers of
ice and silver and queens who sat on tuffets of whale fur
drinking Ajan orchid-wine from cups of seal bone. It was
the capital of the North, a thousand years past. Now it is a
village, an outpost on the hostile sea. Only the Stars recall."

The afternoon had grown fat and red-faced and the first thin wisps of twilight were waiting behind its jowls. Sigrid and Snow worked in unison now, like fiddlers plying their bows.

"Clearly you joined the Sigrids," Snow remarked, keeping her eyes fixed on her friend's prodigious elbows, "or it would be a great coincidence indeed that you are named Sigrid yourself."

"Clearly."

"Yet"—and here Snow blushed, flushing her colorless face with pink—"you don't swear by Saint Sigrid, you swear by the Stars. I think it must have been a very strange road for you, from there to here."

Sigrid's smile crept away from her face like a cat through a door left ajar. She shut her eyes and for a moment Snow thought the hulking creature would cry. "I am not worthy to swear by her name," she croaked, her voice like a hundred frogs lost in mourning. "I've failed too often, and too profoundly. I was supposed to accomplish a thing—the only thing, I once thought, I was ever meant to accomplish. I abandoned that when the wolves led me astray and into the City of Light. And there I dropped a second destiny from my hands as though it burned me. And now I've no destiny left at all, only these nets to tie off like umbilical cords." Sigrid wiped her nose and shook her head like a horse discouraging flies. "So I lapse. I lapse into the faith I happily held when I was young and I swear by the Stars, for I have yet to do much to offend them. Surely there is some Ajan god you whisper to in the dark?"

"I don't really remember—my parents died before they could give me a god of my own. I have heard that the Ajans worship the Stars now, since the city died and all the monks left with their complicated new religions. But they also say that the Ajans eat caterpillar pies and fly on wings of horsehair and rose petals. I've stopped believing what everyone else says of my home. Anyway, I never heard of a saint being born on the barges."

"That's because she wasn't a saint when she left Ajanabh. It was much later that heaven touched her head. It is rarely the places that birth us that see our true worth. Nor even," Sigrid added with half a smile, "the places that adopt us. But you may whisper to Saint Sigrid if you like, when you are alone and the Stars are not speaking. She will not mind."

She cupped the girl's white head in her large, callused hand. "I had just gotten to Tomomo, had I not?"

"Yes," Snow breathed. "Go on."

The Tale of Saint Sigrid, Continued

SIGRID WAS CERTAINLY SURPRISED TO SEE TOMOMO with a snout and ears sporting tufts of cream-yellow fur. Yet she seemed to be a pleasant enough beast, and her graceful hands rested on the rail like carefully arranged flowers. In fact, when Sigrid looked up from the water, the captain appeared just the same as she had—her hair was bound as neatly and her lips, grinning merrily, were just as thin and chapped as before, as any seafarer's lips would be. Only the water showed the fox head.

"So I, too, am a monster. Of course, I am almost never discovered, prettiest of all possible barge girls—only the sea's reflection shows this face. I have a natural disguise. Whereas you"—and here Tomomo eyed young Sigrid's chest meaningfully—"must make your own. Yet, like yours, my mother could never bear to look at me. She would not let her eyes meet mine, even when I was a baby; she said she could see an unholy thing moving behind the iris, something watching her which was not her daughter. They like to tell us we are unholy, Sigrid. It makes them feel as though we cannot harm them, for surely they are as holy as we are dirty and foul. But, of course, we can. Let me tell you how I first came to know that I was a monster . . ."

The Tale of the Good Trick

My mother was particularly dutiful when it came to the binding of my feet, though by the time of my birth, the custom was as antique and unfashionable as stone tools in our country. I believe she thought that if she could confine me to a litter for the remainder of my flower-strewn days, I would not be able to cause much mischief.

Every night I loosened the wrappings and crept from my bed to splash naked in the garden mud. I am sure she knew—after all, my hair was always damp and grass-scented in the morning—but she said nothing, swaddling my toes in raw silk with reproachful glances at my dirt-caked heels.

One year, when I was no more than ten or so, the fortune-teller Majo returned to the capital. This was a great event; though she would not have been received in polite society, her wares were greatly desired by all the ladies of rank. Love potions, spells for a safe childbirth or charms for a male child, talismans for luck and wealth, even incantations to change the weather from drought to rains. Her cart was a thing of wonder, shaped like a tiny, moveable house draped with purple and red cloths, green under-curtains and clanking silver chains, leather charms hanging like fringe from the miniature eaves, crane feathers and cat fur and unguents in clay pots issuing from its dark door. All this Majo carried on her back from town to town—though the shriveled, bony frame of the old Witch seemed hardly equal to the task. When she stopped, stilts unfolded from the bottom of the contraption, and Majo would release the straps that bound it to her to ply her trade.

After dusk, my mother and many other ladies with perfumed wigs and lacquered lips gathered in the pavilion like birds alighting on a fountain, squeaking in delight and waiting breathlessly for the telltale rattle of Majo's cart. I was brought in my litter, resting on rose-colored pillows with my strangled feet propped up so that the blood would drain away from them.

Soon enough it came, singing its dilapidated song of pebbles underfoot and magic practical as cooking. The women pressed around, pushing their coins into Majo's hazel-twig hands and pocketing their charms, their wishes, their scraps of paper to be placed beneath the pillow, their drafts to be swallowed at the next new moon.

Somehow, through the crush of rustling robes and greedy hands, Majo caught my eye with her beady black one. She had only one—the other had been lost somewhere along her travels, some said by a fight with a tiger, some said by a battle with a sorcerer; some even claimed to have scratched it out themselves when a spell had gone awry. The remaining eye clamped on me like a hand, and Majo's spittle-strung lips parted into a smug little grin.

"What is your daughter's name?" she croaked to my mother, without needing to ask which of the powdered ladies she was.

"My child is called Tomomo," Mother answered, her voice quavering.

Majo clicked her tongue twice and produced a yellow pouch from her skirt, tossing it lightly in her hand. "Give her to me and I will give you this—keep it always next to your skin and it will produce one gold piece every time the cock crows."

The women all caught their breath like fishermen snagging fat salmon and murmured among themselves enviously—after all, who cared about a useless girl-child in the face of all that gold?

My mother's eyes flickered furtively from me to the old Witch. Finally, she agreed and snatched the yellow charm, scurrying back to the inner rooms with the rest of the women, full of this new wonder. She kissed me on the cheek and almost as an afterthought warned me to be careful. In a moment, Majo and I stood in the courtyard, alone, save for the marvelous cart.

She said nothing to me, but pulled a great copper pot from her cart and filled it with water from a pitcher so large I could scarcely believe she had concealed it in the folds of her skirt. When the ripples died down to nothing and the moon shone in the pot like a potato floating in soup, she indicated that I should look into it.

Of course, I saw there my true face, my snout thin and sharp, my moist black nose, my ears flicking curiously in the night wind. I suppose I should have been frightened; my fur was so red and my teeth were so bright. But truly, I was relieved—*this* was the thing my mother saw pacing behind my eyes. I was not wicked, simply a monster.

"There you have it, Tomomo, my girl." Majo patted my back in a strangely congratulatory way.

"How did you know?" I asked.

"We know our own; we can smell it, the scent of fur under skin like sugar dissolved in tea."

She leaned over my shoulder and her face floated beside mine in the water, a mangy wrinkled face with her one eye slashed out, her lower lip scarred and her jowls heavy as saddlebags. We grinned together, and our reflections bared their teeth, hers yellow and blunt, mine white and sharp.

"You belong to me now, little fox-girl. If I had known sooner, I might have spirited you away at birth and found a den for you in the mountains. Now, it is more complicated. You are much too old to join your cousins there. But it does not really matter so much—if you learn well, you may be able to find a place in the world, as I have. But be always wary of water—it reveals us."

She poured out the pot onto the pebbles and packed it away into her cart, pulling wide leather straps over her shoulders and hoisting the miniature house onto her back. The wooden legs snapped up under its floor and Majo sniffed the wind.

"A fox must be always alert and wakeful," she said sternly. "Now that you know that you are one, you have no excuse for this laziness. I have enough to carry without your thrice-damned sedan chair. Get those ridiculous things off your feet."

Happily I ripped them off, chewing at the thick knots with my teeth. I nimbly walked alongside Majo with a heart so full and bright it threatened to burn through my robes.

"Where are we going?" I asked.

"I am taking you to a place where you can learn things. You have been sleeping on bedrolls soft as clouds lined in silk and feasting on fatted deer. But outside Palace grounds, deer are clever and hard to catch, and bedrolls are too heavy to carry. There are other ways of living, and on the whole, they make for better women. A pity your mother never slept on a cave floor with leaves for blankets—I hope she enjoys her prize. By morning, all the cocks in the capital will have dropped dead, dead as gold and daughters unwanted."

I gawked, unable to imagine so many dead roosters, or how the bent old hag could have managed to leave a wake of strangled chickens behind her. But before I could ask, she was trundling away.

I kept pace, though not easily. She was surprisingly fleet for her age, and I began to understand how she could travel from city to city with such ease. Before long, we were deep into the forest, where bamboo was as thick around as a woman's waist. Before much longer, I could smell the sea, faintly, and damp began to weight my hair. When the night had become cold and clear as pond ice, and we had reached a long beach which was softer underfoot than sweet cakes, Majo spoke again. Her voice was no longer rough and scabbed, but high and sharp, unsurprisingly like the bark of a fox calling to her kits.

"Well, here we are."

"Where is it we're meant to be?" I saw nothing but the long sea, and the breakers foaming white, and a slender pier stretching into the water like a skeletal finger.

Majo rolled her eyes. "A fox must be clever and self-sufficient. Put your educated mind to use and figure it out yourself. I brought you here; my part is finished. I am not a book; you cannot look up the answer in my index." Majo shifted under the weight of her house. I stood there on the sand, nonplussed, trying not to look like a simpleton. She rolled her eyes. "You see the pier? It's the only damned thing around, so why don't you go see if anyone is living under it, hmm? Or shall I just do everything for you like your addle-brained mother?"

Majo released the cart straps from her shoulders and let the wooden

legs unfold. She rummaged inside the hutch for a moment and drew out a thick cushion. Settling on it, she pulled a rice ball from her skirts and munched happily on it, gesturing towards the pier and urging me to get on with it. My cheeks stung as if switch-whipped. I would certainly not be shown as a spoiled brat in Majo's presence. I ran off after the rickety pier, tiny shards of seashell spraying up behind my pounding heels.

It stunk under the rotting slats. Algae and mussels and barnacles stuck to everything in wet clutches; old crab nets tangled in rusted-out clam buckets. I held my hand over my face and nearly gagged—few of those nets and buckets were empty of their last unfortunate victims. I saw nothing here which could be an errand worthy of Majo's attention, and much that would not be worth the attention of even a starving seagull. But she was not wrong, I was sure; she could not be—and indeed, behind a well-chewed pillar, a dark shape scuttled by. I trudged towards it, my bare feet squelching in the tidepools and soggy sand, and soon I was knee-deep in the brine sea, splashing forward in the moonlight after a quick black shape.

"Wait!" I cried, and to my amazement the shape did stop, turning its sleek head back over its shoulder.

It was a large and well-fed otter. It rolled over in the waist-deep water and floated casually on its back, showing a wet golden belly against the rest of its slick, dark brown fur. Its face seemed friendly enough, if not exactly welcoming. Its whiskers were almost as thick as a mustache. In its paws was a large abalone with several bits of shell chipped off—the otter struggled with it, glancing up at me from behind its stubborn prize.

"What?" it said, and its voice rasped like dry kelp dragging over sand.

I didn't at all know what to say. I was sopping wet and cold, and slime wriggled between my toes. I almost missed the swaddling bandages in all that muck. The pier water rippled around my thin robe as I stood like a child attempting to recite a poem she has not even tried to memorize.

"Majo sent me." I shrugged, trying to look as though I conversed with otters every day. "I guess. I mean, I guess she sent me. She said to come to the pier, though it's very dirty and I think a great many things have died down here."

"No doubt," said the otter, finally popping the shell open and ripping a thick piece of abalone flesh from the shimmering shell. "And each more delicious than the last." It chewed hard for a good while on the tough meat before speaking again. "Well, if Majo sent you, I suppose we'll have to make ends meet with a scraggly, skinny little fox, won't we? No worse than most. I am Rakko, King of the Otters. If you haven't brought me any shrimp or clams or such as tribute, I'll just notch it down as owed."

"Oh," I said, trying to bow in the brackish water, "I didn't know you were a King. I certainly would have brought something."

"Well," he said, paddling past me to one of the rusted buckets and fishing something foul and greenish from its depths, nearly tipping the bobbing pail over in his enthusiasm, "mainly I'm King because I said I was, and nobody said any different. But this pier is as good as any throne room, and there are riches in every cage and pot. That's how kings are made, my brush-tailed girl—they pick a place, shove a stick in it, call themselves King and wait to see if someone gets angry about it. No one has gotten angry so far, so that makes the otters mine."

"I see." I nodded, and wondered if this was entirely how the King of my own country began. "Well, I'm not sure what Majo means for me to do—"

"What are foxes good for? She means for you to steal something for me. It's not an easy thing. I hope you're up to the task—she sends me girls from time to time, but they are usually far too frail for thieving."

I blushed a little, thinking of my tiny feet, hidden by the sea.

"What is it you want me to get for you?"

Rakko looked up out of the buckets, his furry face suddenly quiet and sad, water dripping off his long whiskers like rain from stalks of wheat. He rubbed at his round brown eyes as if he had not slept since the sea was a puddle, and the moon pulled at dry land. "It's not for me"—he sighed— "not for me at all, but I need you to steal a Star . . ."

The
Tale of the Loon,
the Otter,
and the Star

I REMEMBER THE SPLASH MOST OF ALL.

Sekka and I were diving—Sekka is the Queen of the Loons. She taught me the trick of saying you were Queen. But where I'm King-Under-the-Pier and even bratty girls don't bring me so much as an urchin as tribute, once Sekka said she was Queen, the other loons saw just how black her head was, how vast her wingspan—for poor Sekka was born larger than any other loon, and suffered a great deal for it when she was a chick—how white her belly, and how haunting was her wail and cry, and immediately agreed that she should certainly be Queen, and right away. Unfortunately, she found out that this is a pretty inferior way of becoming a ruler, because it usually means you have to add responsibilities into the bargain, and not simply many, many buckets of delicious rotted fish. Her nest is the thickest and best-thatched of all the seabirds, but she has to visit all the hens during mating season, and she tries very hard, but loons are heavy fliers at best, and she rarely makes the full rounds.

It was not mating season when the splash came. Loons and otters are alike in love of diving—we puff out all our air and make our stomachs quite flat, and swoop to the deep, cold currents where the fat fish fly. Sekka and I are the best divers you could imagine, should you spend your time imagining how gifted divers can be. We raced; we played; we fished. It was night, and thin blue light shafted through the water like anglers' hooks. The shadow of a passing ship flittered through the water overhead.

Just as I shot past her to pry up a clam from a deep rock, the whole sea lit up as though the moon had been dropped whole into the water. The currents flashed suddenly bone white, and I saw Sekka's shape flare purple against them, and my own tail was washed in it, and my eyes were burned. I rubbed at them furiously, and when I pulled my paws away the light was dimmed, and there was a small boy floating down from the surface, sinking terribly fast into the blue-black deeps.

We dove after him like one animal, our chests burning with air-need, dropping like two stones after the spiraling body. I do not know now, when I think back, why we thought it was so important to catch that near-dead thing before it slushed into the ocean floor, but without thinking, we would have drowned in the dive if it meant we could have stopped his fall. In the end, it was Sekka who caught him, snatching a lock of his hair in her dark beak. I stroked through the last inches of water to grip him around the waist, and we drew him up to the surface hanging between us like a net of salmon—and you know, he was so heavy, so heavy, I thought then he must have been filled with silver weights.

When our three heads broke through the waves, I pulled him up onto my belly like a scallop shell, and he lay there, limp, holding his head in his hands, as the night threw shadows on his skin. Finally, after a long silence which left Sekka and me fretting like new parents over him, he coughed, and spat water onto my fur. Moaning, he lifted his head, still clutched in his hands. I noticed two things right away: the first was that there was a thin line running all the way through his scalp and head, which oozed with a kind of wet darkness.

The second was that he had two faces where his ears should be, and nothing but smooth skin where I expected to look him in the eye. It was this skin which was split by the black line.

He held his head on either side, his hands covering his noses and foreheads, leaving his wet lips open, and stringy hair covered his hands. When he spoke, he used both mouths, in chorus with himself, one high, reedy voice, a child's, and one low and grave, a man's.

"I'm alive," he croaked.

"Matter of opinion, little drowned dear," clucked Sekka, who had already pecked at the black stuff on his faceless face and declared it horrid. It was not exactly blood, but it was not exactly not-blood.

"Sekka," I said softly, "what do we do? Float him back to shore?"

She stretched out her long black wings to cover him, and the white spots on her feathers glittered like stars. "Little lost thing. Can you swim? Perhaps if you let go of your poor head—"

"No!" the boy cried, awkwardly shrinking from her and almost toppling into the water. Both his faces looked sheepish as he clung to me with his elbows. "No, I'm sorry, I can't. I can't let go, I mean."

"What happened to you?" Sekka prodded, nuzzling his ribs as she would a chick with a broken wing.

"I fell." He sighed.

The Tale of the Ship, the Canoe, and the Raft

I AM NOT LIKE THE OTHERS.

I wanted the world. Even after, even after, when they all went into the hills, into the ground, into the dark, when people opened up deep stone wells of forgetting in their bellies and all the Stars dove in, I stayed. No different from when I first took that step, that long step down from the black, I wanted the grass and the salt and the hard, round cheeses and the houses with tiled roofs and the beach with countless, countless sands. I was happy here; I didn't want to pull brambles over my head and pretend I heard nothing of the world going by.

So I touched everything, everything I could reach, to

leech the light out of me, to bleed out enough that I could pass for a thing that had never been a hole in nothing. I touched men and women and children sleeping in tamarack cribs, I touched cups and plates and bushels of roses, I touched haywains and haystacks and the thick doors of prisons, I touched the grass and the salt and the hard, round cheeses, I touched houses with tiled roofs, and I let the countless sands run through my hands until my skin no longer glowed.

But my faces, you will say. Surely no one would mistake me for a man.

And I say that we all chose that which was most like us, and I could not decide. I looked at the grass and the salt and they were nothing like me. I looked at the hard, round cheeses. I looked at the tile-roofed houses and I looked at the countless sands of the beach. Nothing matched me like one shoe to another.

And then I saw children who had faces just alike, walking two by two, and these were twins; I knew that I also walked two by two, even though I had only one body. I split my face and became the Twinned Star, and though I would puddle out my light on the dry ground to fit in the cities of men, I would not change my nature. And why should I? The cities were always filled with monsters, and I could easily be mistaken for one of their number. I called myself Itto, and vanished into a noisy tangle of streets.

I lived, I ate, I worked, I walked two by two.

I watched the world forget what we looked like, and then pile up flowers on altars in our names. I shook my head.

I lived, I ate, I worked. I passed well for a monster, and men did not love me.

After a long while I took it into my head to try the ocean on my skin. I set out to build myself a ship, and bought a great quantity of wood in a seaside town—beautiful wood, like none I had ever seen, with a grain like veins filled with blood, deep red and glossy. I made a place for myself out of the way of the other shipwrights, who laughed when the freakish child came striding by, his arms full of their tools, and set to the keel with a hammer and his own callused hands.

It was not long before the shipwrights came to me and said: "Itto, that wood is too fine for your kind. By rights we should have it for our ships, for surely your stunted ship will be as misshapen and deformed as you, and spoil the wood."

I did not want them to take it, of course I didn't. But they held me back and gathered whatever of the red wood they liked. What could I do? We are not marvels; we do not have the strength of ten. When our light is spent, we are less, even, than a knot-faced, salt-shouldered shipwright.

When they had gone, I looked at what was left and said, "Very well, I cannot build a ship. I will build a canoe."

It was not long before the shipwrights came again and said: "Itto, that wood is too fine for your kind. By rights we should have it for our ships, for surely your crook-beamed canoe will be as misshapen and deformed as you, and spoil the wood."

I did not want them to take it, of course I didn't. But they held me back and gathered whatever of the red wood they liked. What could I do? I had spent myself on the grass and the salt—I could not blight a man with a glance.

When they had gone, I looked at what was left and said, "Very well, I cannot build a canoe. I will build a raft."

There was hardly enough wood left even to make a raft, but I lashed plank to plank, pole to pole, splinter to splinter. Before long I had a red raft, and it was sturdy and small, and I loved it. It was my own thing, a thing I made as the sky made me, and no less dear to me than if it had been a child.

It bore me on the purple waves as surely as a hermit bears his pack. I fished well from its edge, and my shirt was a poor man's sail. It filled; my nets filled. I lay on the rough surface of the red wood and smelled its fibers, like blood and cinnamon prickling my nose. I spoke to it, and I thought, lonely as I was, that it answered, and its voice was smooth and dark as the sky. It pressed up under my back at night, and the dark washed both my faces with gentle hands.

When I returned to the city, I kept it folded away in long, oiled cloths, stained with fish skins, certainly, but as soft as I could afford. It leaned up against the meanest wall in the smallest boathouse on the docks. And one day, when I came to unwrap my raft and put out into the shallows, there was nothing leaning against the mean wall but filthy, stained cloths and a single broken plank of scarlet wood.

As I stood trying not to weep, a voice came from behind me. I turned— it was the scraggly, lanky son of one of the other shipwrights. He shoved greasy hair out of his eyes, which darted like a guilty dog's between me and what was once a raft. "Itto," he whispered, licking his lips, "that wood was too fine for you."

He ran from the boathouse, leaving me to the remains.

I carried the broken plank away from the countless sands of the beach, away from any house with a tiled roof, away from the makers of round, hard cheeses, over the grass and past any place which salted its meat. Finally, I reached a forest wide of branch and root, and in the center of the forest I found a patch of deep earth, where I buried the shard of glossy red wood just as I would a child of my body. I wept into the grave, as bitterly as I have done any thing since I took my step down out of the sky.

I did not know what else to do; I returned to the city, to my wretched, shingle-shack home. The lanky boy was waiting for me. As if in apology, shuffling his feet and picking at his pimples, he offered me a place on his father's ship. "If you want to sail, it is easier to serve on another man's ship than to build your own, you know," he said, as if he knew everything that could be known about the matter.

My raft was gone. One set of planks was like another. I went aboard the ship, and for weeks washed the sickly brown boards as they told me, stitched the thick sails as they told me, slopped tar in broad barrels as they told me.

And then one night, the shipwright's son sunk an oar in my head.

The Tale of the Loon, the Otter, and the Star, Continued

"I SUPPOSE HE WANTED TO MAKE HIS FATHER proud," the boy groaned, leaning heavily on my taut stomach. Truthfully, my back was beginning to ache from balancing him above the waterline, but it behooves a King to be patient. "I did the natural thing—my hands flew up to my head, while pain thrashed in me like a raft in a storm, and when he drew out the oar, I held myself together, somehow. The boy saw it, he saw that I still spoke, and staggered, and that what came out of me was not exactly like blood, and with his stringy arms he threw me over the side, my hands still clutching my head together like two halves of a cut peach and what light was left in me blanched the sea." Itto turned up awkwardly, to look at Sekka with his left eyes. "But you see, if I let go I am sure I will perish, and I am afraid. So few of us have ever died. I am afraid."

I didn't know what to say. We floated there like pieces of a shipwreck, and the moon moved on his frail back.

"Where do you want us to take you? I'm afraid you wouldn't like my pier very much."

Sekka was very quiet. Her huge black eyes were fixed on the bedraggled boy. "You want to go back. Up there."

"I don't know," he answered, but his voice hitched itself into a half-sob. "I couldn't get back, even if I did. I let all my light out, or most of it, and I'm so weak, I can hardly heave myself off an otter's belly. But I'm afraid. I don't know what's up there, if that's where the dead go, if I can go back without dying. I don't know anything. But it doesn't matter; I can't get there any more than a mouse can get up a mountain."

Sekka fluffed her feathers lightly, making her look even bigger than usual. "Would a mountain do?" She turned her head to one side, like a rooster in the morning.

Itto took a long time answering. I felt his breath on me, light and fast, a little wing fluttering against my fur.

"Maybe," he said. "Maybe it would."

The Tale of the Good Trick, Continued

RAKKO RAN HIS THICK PAWS OVER HIS BELLY AS IF in memory.

"Well, what happened?" I cried eagerly.

"Sekka took him up to the mountain, long years ago, and she can't bring him back. He won't come down. Poor Sekka circles the mountain and cries her long cries, but he doesn't hear. I want you to bring him back for me, and for her, like a good little fox. Steal him from himself. Drag him. Throw him over your shoulder." The King of the Otters frowned. "He shouldn't be there all alone. I'll share my buckets and my nets. Sekka would cover him with her wings for the rest of her days and let the nesting be damned. He doesn't have to be up there alone."

"And how am I supposed to get to the top of a mountain? I'm a fox, and I've only just discovered that much. I'm not an eagle."

From behind one of the paint-stripped pillars, a huge bird emerged, with clear black eyes and white spots on her wings. She was just big enough, I supposed, to carry a child on her back.

"He told Sekka where he buried his raft, you know. If you bring him down, she'll tell you."

"Why would I care where he stuck an old piece of wood?"

The loon Queen glided up to me. "You ask too many questions," she said with a sigh. Her voice was low and sad, softer than the loon wails I had heard when the black-and-white birds gathered in my mother's pond. I looked back over my shoulder at the long pale strand of beach, and the dark shape of Majo and her house-hunch surrounded by tall grass. She looked quite asleep.

Without another question, I climbed onto Sekka's broad back, and put my arms around her slim neck. Her feathers smelled like scallop shells, and seaweed, and eggshells. She lifted us both up into the night.

THE
NET-WEAVER'S
TALE, CONTINUED

"DO YOU NEED FOOD?" SIGRID SUDDENLY SAID, AS though it had only just occurred to her that folk occasionally eat.

"I am a little hungry."

The woman heaved her bulk onto her feet and disappeared inside the ship-tower. I was left in the last glow of the sun, the scent of the not-too-distant market in my nose: saffron and roasting meat and sour silk-dyes, sweat and barrels of still oil and molten metal poured into molds. Al-a-Nur was warm, and alive, and there was no snow or lichen or ice anywhere.

Sigrid reemerged with a wooden tray and dropped it

unceremoniously at my feet. On it were a few brown squares, a single strip of desiccated meat, an iron flask, and an orange. "Hard tack, jerked vole, rum, and a bit of fruit to keep your teeth in your head. If you enter the Sainthood, it's all you'll have to eat for your first year, so learn to like it." A lopsided smile crossed her creased brown face like a pale page turning in a beaten book. "For me, it still tastes as good as wine in crystal and doves stuffed with blackberries. The best stuff there is."

I ate politely. It was hard and crumbly and tasteless as a shingle. The meat was like a solid strip of salt, and the rum bitter as fox bile. The orange alone was sweet and golden.

"So you believe in the Stars?" I asked tentatively.

She shrugged, like a mountain settling its boulders. "The Stars are here and there, whether we believe in them or not. I could believe in you or declare to all passersby that you are a lie and a silly story, but it wouldn't change the fact that you're sitting here, you mark the grass, you ate my food, you take up space. But the Stars don't act. They give us no model for living. They teach us nothing. The first Sigrids looked for more than that. But that's putting the stern before the bow. We're hardly at the beginning of Saint Sigrid, but nearing the end of Tomomo . . ."

THE TALE OF THE GOOD TRICK, CONTINUED

BENEATH ME, THE QUEEN OF THE LOONS WAS WARM. Above me, the night was cold as dead hands, and those hands pulled at me, at my thin nightrobe and my bare, unbound feet. I buried my face in her feathers.

"He doesn't even speak anymore," she crooned, and clouds whisked across her beak. "He just sits up there in the frost and stares. I don't think you can do much, but I have hope. He's heavy, so if you have to carry him, it'll be tough going."

"Did he speak much in the beginning?"

Sekka lowered her dark head. Her webbed feet opened and closed beneath her. "We talked all the way to the top of the mountain. Sweet things and soft things and sighing and whispering, and stories of the dark at the beginning of the world, stories of the eggs at the beginning of the season. Rakko doesn't listen too well—except when I told him how to be King—but Itto listened, and I didn't have to tell him any tricks just to get him to stop interrupting me like a fur-brained fool. And after I left him in the cold at the roof of the world, I used to fly back up when the drakes stopped squalling for mates, and then we'd sigh sweetly and whisper softly again, and tell stories about the dark and the eggs. But after a few seasons, I was the only one talking, and nothing about him was sweet or soft anymore. Now he sits on the rocks and there's nothing but him holding his head together and looking at the black. I haven't been back since the last girl Majo brought, who gave up after only an hour."

"I won't give up," I whispered, soft and sweet.

I cannot say how long it took to reach the top of the mountain, though it seemed that some number of suns rose and set on my wind-whipped skin. At the peak, though, it was always night, as dark as the belly of a blackbird. And Sekka set me down in that endless murk, on the craggy summit. The summit of a mountain is smaller than you think, and there was hardly enough room for me and Itto—for there he was, knees drawn up to his chest, hands pressing two faces towards each other—to sit side by side. Sekka roosted on a lower rock and waited for me to fail.

"Hello," I said, for lack of a better word.

The Star said nothing.

"I've come to get you down from here, away from here. It's cold as still blood, and your Sekka wants you."

The Star said nothing.

Well, she had said he wouldn't. So I pulled at his limbs and tried to put him over my shoulder—I was skinny, but so was he, and not much larger than I was. I was sure I'd be able to do it. A fox carries a kit in her mouth, doesn't she? But he was much heavier than he seemed, like a sack of iron slugs, and I could not budge him, no matter how I pushed and pulled.

The Star said nothing.

So I said nothing. I sat and looked where he was looking. It was a long expanse of black, marked with seven stars all in a tight cluster, leaning one against the other. It was very boring.

"I can do a trick; would you like to see?"

The Star said nothing, but his right eyes flickered a little. I gathered a lump of snow from the gray rock of the summit and warmed it in my hands till it became water. I held it out between us, and, leaning over the little pool in my palms, I showed him my fox face with its creamy tufts of fur at the ears, and smart black nose.

He laughed a little, a sound like water trickling off of high stones. "That's a good trick," he said, his throats hoarse from cold and silence, and he did speak, just as the otter said, in unison with himself, one voice high and one low.

"I've only just learned it," I confessed, "and now that you're speaking, won't you please come off the mountain?"

"There isn't a good enough trick played by the best of all tricksters to make me do that." He sighed. "I'm holding vigil, and a vigil doesn't vanish because one's toes are frozen blue."

"Why are you holding vigil?"

"Do you see those seven stars there?" he asked. I did, of course—there was little enough to look at but those glittering specks. "You might say those are my cousins. Of course, you might not." He coughed and rubbed at his four temples with his fingers. "I came up here because I was afraid. I was afraid to let go of my head, afraid to die, even though I should be dead. I came up here to see if the seven stars in the sky were my cousins, who died so long ago I hardly remember what they looked like, safe home and no worse for death. If they were, if they were safe as rabbits in a hutch, then I wouldn't be afraid, then I could let go of my head and drift up. This is the roof of the world, and you can almost touch the tiles. I wouldn't have so far to go."

He looked at my still-wet hands, just beginning to frost over, and I think if he could have he would have taken them in his. I reached up, as I imagined he wanted me to, I reached up on my toes to touch the sky—and I did touch it, I did; my fingers pressed into the black and oh, it felt like flesh! It felt like skin and a soft, glistening leg or belly behind the skin, and a diamond bone behind that. I could not guess whose skin it might be, but it was warm under my chilled fingertips, so warm. And when I touched it I saw the seven stars as he must have, and they were nothing like stars at all, but just seven troughs dug in the sky, pale as sea-bleached bones.

"They're graves," he whispered, "nothing but graves, and their light is nothing but a headstone, and they are not there, not there at all, the sky is a tomb and I cannot die, because I am still so afraid. Where do we go if not here? I am so afraid, and so alone, and all I have ever loved is a pathetic broken raft, and it is all that has ever loved me."

Itto was weeping then, great hot tears from each of his four eyes, and they froze on his cheeks as they fell.

I crouched on my knees before the Star and took his huge, misshapen head into my hands. I stroked his brittle, snow-crusted hair and pressed my face to his. I said nothing; I crooned like a bird, or how I thought a bird would sound, and I held him for a very long while. I did not know how to get him down, but I supposed that I did, in the end, know how to steal him from himself.

I wrapped my numbed fingers around his wrists and began to pry his hands from his faces. He stiffened and shrunk away. "No!" he gasped. "I can't!"

"It's all right," I said, and I said it over and over. "It's all right. You're hurting your Sekka, who loves you like a raft, and would rather see you snug under the forest loam, safe and no worse for death, than alone on a crag feeling sorry for yourself. It's all right, I'm here, and I know you're too afraid to do it, but I'll help you."

His lips were dry against my arms as I pulled at his hands. "But couldn't I stay like this, forever, in the freeze?" His doubled voice was plaintive as a child asking for a sweet and a man asking for a sweetheart—but he answered himself. "No, I am tired, so tired, and my arms ache from holding myself to myself."

"I know a good trick, Itto," I whispered, "a very good trick."

He turned his head so that one of his faces could see me, his great dark eyes sweet and soft. I kissed him, very lightly, on each face and his lips under mine were cracked and torn as old paper. It was my first kiss, and my second, and they tasted of snow.

He went slack, and let me pull his hands from his head. I folded them in his lap. He stayed whole for a moment, and then his head opened into two halves, like an iris opening in the sunlight. Black fluid poured out of him, cold and ugly, over my hands and my robe, lumpish, dead stuff which had no scent at all. His body slumped forward onto me, and finally, after I had been soaked in his blood which was not exactly blood, two tiny silver drops of light squeezed out from the center of him, falling onto my hand like tears. I closed my fingers over them.

Sekka turned her head away when she saw my dress spattered black. She sent up a long, low cry, that strange loon-cry that makes the moon weep. She took me again on her back, and though she sang her funeral dirge to every passing cloud for all the days and nights it took to descend from the tiled roof of the world, there was a kind of happiness in it, a relief, sweet and soft in the lowest notes of her song.

And I must have done well, for she told me where the raft was buried just before we landed softly by Majo's snoring form, her house-pack creaking in time to her grunts and snorts. She woke with a start and saw my fluid-stained dress clinging to my thighs, and nodded as if it was all no more than she expected. And Sekka left us, tottering down the beachhead to the long and lonely pier.

But I did not go to the forest that morning, or the next. I stayed with Majo, and nearly forgot about the plank of wood planted in the earth. I aged slowly, but when I asked, she only shrugged, grunting that each creature lives out its natural term. I learned much—though I was always hopeless with magic. I could no more fashion a charm than a horse could knit its own saddle blanket. My talent was in the hunt and the chase, and in the kill. These things Majo taught me with pleasure, and my skill grew great. I had too much fox in me, she would say sadly over countless night fires. I could perform only fox magic, which was ever the magic of stalking, invisible in the shadows, and the snatching of prey from the air. The truth is that there are many kinds of magic, and her kind, the magic of precisely ground herbs and charms bound at the right phase of the moon, lay in the human half, not the animal. What use a fox's paws in the lashing of seven-knotted spells? It knows only the magic of hot blood and swift fur—and these are powerful, so powerful they need no little satchel of leaves to help them along. But the fox is not overfond of tools.

"We can be certain," she would cackle, "that you would have been a most dull and tedious woman. It is the fox that saves you from total idiocy."

But it was clear that Majo was not the guardian of my destiny. I wanted her to be; I wanted to be a good Witch and carry her cart for her over silver fields and slushing marshes in the early morning light. But I could never accomplish more than a simple tincture or poultice for a slashed ear. In her eyes I saw the truth: We would soon part. She would find a better student, and I would find a life that contained no carts or eager women begging for love spells.

The day we parted she showed no more emotion than the day we met; she was bemused, proud of herself, conspiratorial. She took me walking as we often did, and the sun was crisp as apple skin on my back. It was not long before we reached the edge of a forest, the very forest I had told her Sekka said contained the buried plank. I had forgotten, like the summer forgets the snow. Majo grinned. "You were always an absentminded girl. Try to work on that."

She tapped my right hand with her finger and I opened it—lying on my palm were the two drops of silver light, shining like tears, which had long ago seeped into my skin and disappeared. I looked up at her, wonder written as plainly on my face as a tattoo. She gripped my hand in her withered old claws and tipped the palm so that the tears fell onto the earth, and then embraced me, I knew for the last time, as a kit always knows when it is time for her to catch mice by herself and not trouble the vixen any longer.

The two tears wet the rust-red soil beneath me, pooling there like rain in a cottage gutter. But they did not seep into the ground as they had once disappeared into my skin—they began to trickle away from me, faster and faster. I held Majo tightly for a moment, tears clouding my last vision of her face like the trunk of a great tree, and then, eyes dry, I chased after them with a cry of excitement.

I looked over my shoulder only once as I ran—and soon I was running as fast as I could go—to see Majo trundling away with her house on her back like some ridiculous turtle, and it seemed to me that there was a kind of light at her heels, silver as the old woman's hair.

But the twin tracks of salt tears were swiftly disappearing into the distance, and perhaps it was only a trick of the sun. I rushed after them for almost an hour, ducking under bough, leaping over root. It was a marvelous hunt. Finally, they stopped and parted, each streaming around the trunk of an extraordinary tree.

At first, I did not even realize it *was* a tree. The drops of Itto's light had grown as they flowed on, until they surrounded it as a knee-deep moat, rippling in the dim light. A tree rose out of that water which was not water, yet it was not a tree, either, but a menagerie of ship-shards, twisted together into the shape of a trunk, of branches, of roots arching into the moat of tears. Prows jutted angrily from the base, masts and keels winding around each other, chasing rudders and booms of colorful wood, ruddy and golden. An enormous oaken forecastle hung from one side of the tree, while smooth wheels spun lazily in the wind on high and low. There were only a few dusky green leaves hanging from the branches; instead, they were hung with lines and rigging, and sails half tangled in the crows' nests that served as the topmost boughs. Lazy breezes filled them and left them sagging as they liked. The forest was filled with the sound of billowing sails and creaking wood. In the center of the trunk was a figurehead whose paint had been faded by sun and salt: a sea-goat with a curling tail and furry breasts, a wisp of a beard at her chin, her arms braced against the jumble of tree and ship, her large eyes cast heavenward, mouth agape.

The wood of the tree was a deep, glossy red, the grain of it like veins filled with blood.

As I gawked at the spectacle of the Ship-Tree, her eyes rolled slowly down from the sky, like a stone rolling across the mouth of a cave, and her jaw unlocked to speak.

"Is that you?" she said softly, her voice rustling like leaves, or sails.

"No," I said, "I don't think it is."

"Oh." The tree sighed. "It never is. I'm used to it by now. When I was a sapling I was sure he'd come any day. Is that . . . is that *seawater*?" she gasped, her timber-flanked body quivering with surprise. "The real thing? From a port full of drunkards and thieves and shipwrights' sons? Drawn from a pier full of crab fishermen with nets like giants' bracelets? Oh, is it?"

"No," I answered, "it's the last thing the Star left behind him: blood which is not blood, light which is not light, water which is not water."

The masthead's face became as soft as wood can manage, and tears of sap flowed down her face. She spoke to the moat around her.

"Itto? Itto? Do you see how big and tall I've become? I'm a real ship now, not a silly broken raft. Aren't you proud of me?"

I thought, then, that I had done what I came to do, and that no one who knew the Star could have asked more. I turned to leave the Ship-Tree alone with the tears.

"Oh, please, oh, please wait!" The figurehead writhed towards me, and it seemed at any moment she would twist right off the tree and tumble into my arms. But the Ship-Tree moved with her, and the sound of creaking grew even louder, accompanied by the rusted squeaking of the hanging rigging. I climbed up a little onto a keel-root.

"I'm here."

She blushed, her red wood becoming even darker and more crimson. "Thank you for the water," she said.

"I would like to give you something too, even though you never rode me through the dark water—I would have done it for him, but I can still do it for you, I can bear fruit for you, just like all the other trees."

I was immediately unsure. "What sort of fruit do you have, Ship?"

She smiled, her bright cheeks quivering with barely held tears. "It's my present to you: the best dream of a lonely raft, everything I ever wanted to be when I slept wrapped in oilskin."

The Ship-Tree seemed to bulge, and its groans vibrated through the forest. The sails twisted together, the rigging knotted itself into half-hitches and bowlines, the keels and prows clattered together like branches tapping against a window. The figurehead kept laughing, louder and more shrilly until I felt my ears would burst from the sound. The creaking and cracking of wood was like a storm rolling across the wood, and all the while, the moat of tears was spreading and growing deeper, until I was trying desperately to swim as little waves sloshed over my chin. The tree was so large then that I feared it would engulf me entire, if I did not drown first.

But I did neither. From the topmost branches of the Ship-Tree, a thing began to take shape. A prow, a mast, a jib, then a hull, a keel. A bright wheel spun into being like a sunflower opening. A ship, full-grown, descended from the branches like an apple falling, and came to rest comfortably on the now swift-flowing river of tears. The figurehead quieted herself, and drew one of her huge wooden hooves from the side of the trunk, scooping me out of the still-rising water by the scruff of the neck.

"Don't wreck her too quickly," the figurehead said worriedly, and set me down at the new ship's wheel.

When my feet touched the newborn wood of the decks, I felt suddenly at home. It was not a question of which line to pull taut or which sail to trim; the sleek schooner was as familiar to me as my own limbs. The ship was mine, made for my hand as surely as a child of my own womb.

And the river of tears, now deeper than the fruit-ship's keel, moved gently away from the tree which was once a raft, flowing ahead of itself, carrying me along the forest floor in silence, save for soft ripples against the hull, like a child kissing her mother's cheek.

And slowly, ever so slowly, it bore me past the edge of the wood, down through ripe fields of wheat, over grass and salt and the huts of the makers of hard, round cheeses, past houses with tiled roofs and the countless grains of sand on a pale beach, past a long, lonely pier and into the sea.

THE TALE OF SAINT SIGRID, CONTINUED

TOMOMO LICKED HER LIPS, THE FOX REFLECTION flicked its pink tongue over its muzzle.

"And that was how the *Maidenhead* was born. I named her for a thing I had long lost, and sailed her true. Who would have thought a fox could grow sea legs? As soon as I had mastered her I glided into the nearest port and took on sailors. At first it was not that I asked for women, or for monsters, to serve. But the men would not sail under a female captain, and women without our . . . unusual histories were clamped into their houses like fireflies in a glass jar, and had understandably never learned any seacraft. Thus the *Maidenhead*, with all her strangeness, became even stranger, and more wonderful. We are happy, we are free—you can be, too."

Sigrid nodded, her eyes lit with joy like beacons on high hills. She had never imagined her life would be filled with anything but the measuring of cinnamon dust and the keeping of her father's books. At that moment, her heart belonged to the black-haired Tomomo, and there was nothing she would not have done, if her captain had asked it.

Being the captain she was, Tomomo knew this; she knew the light in Sigrid's eyes, she knew the eagerness of her posture. Many a girl before her had been enchanted thus, and not for the first time Tomomo thought that the magic of the hunt was not limited to the chasing of mice across a rain-wet field.

"Since you know nothing of ships yet, barge daughter, you will have to make yourself useful in other ways until you have learned. Go below: find a Satyr with green rings on her fingers—she will introduce you to our passengers, and you will see to their needs for the night."

"Yes, Tomomo—I mean, Tommy!" Sigrid smiled, a smile which had never before touched her face, the deepest smile, which comes from the belly, and gleams with its own flickering light. She turned and instinctively ran towards the door which led into the innards of the scarlet ship, letting the door bang closed behind her with a merry clang.

In the Garden

"I MUST GO," THE BOY WHISPERED, HIS HANDS ALREADY ILLUMINATED BY the blue-gold light weaving its way through the sky as the night died away from them. The girl said nothing. She stared at her hands as though she might read there some arcane method of freezing the sun in its ascent.

"Will you be here when I return?" The boy was sure she would not be, whatever she might answer. She had slipped from him, somehow, like a veil sweeping over his hands. When she had sat on his windowsill and told him of the death of the wicked King, and the flight of the bird-maiden seeking her cave, he had been able to touch her, to rest his head on her lap, to feel her warmth like a sparrow's wing in the sun. Now, she seemed thin, transparent, and he feared that if he reached out his hand to her it would pass through her skin as though through a waterfall. All he could think was that he would steal her any feast, any cloak of feathers or fur, any flask of wine or even the jewels from Dinarzad's fingers if she would only smile at him again, the way she had done that night, like the sun breaking over the first sea of the world.

He frowned at her, picking at a clump of dirt with his civilized hands.

"Meet me on the cypress path, where the stones are painted red. I will be there, I promise."

And then she did smile, soft and wide as a river trickling through a secret wood.

He had not set down his second foot past the arching gate when Dinarzad's voice cut cleanly through him like a hot knife in his stomach.

"Why do you insist on hurting me this way?" Her tone was petulant, sorrowing, but he knew the danger in it.

"Sister," the boy began, "she is not what you think—"

"I do not care what she is! She has not broken the rules of her house—she does not have a house to disobey! It is you who have defied me and the Sultan, who have kept the wives in a constant panic, like birds chasing after seed!"

Of course they had done no such thing. The harem was massive, so huge that the comings and goings of the many children were largely unnoticed. How could he be so special as to be missed by anyone save Dinarzad, who hated him so? The wives were desultory and sage, lounging in their halls like lionesses, occasionally swatting an errant cub. The army of tutors and guards and older sisters on the brink of marriage kept the brood in check, and it must be they who marked the boy's nightly absence.

"What are you doing out there with her? You must know you are of an age where it is more than unseemly to be alone with an unmarried girl all night. Why can you not behave as you ought to, as a noble son ought to? How can it be worth all of this just to sit with another child under the stars?"

The boy saw his chance to make her understand. But when he tried to tell the girl's story and make her see how his heart strained towards the Garden like a horse who senses home is near, it became jumbled in his mouth. No matter how he tried, he could not make it beautiful, he could not tell the same tale that the girl unspooled from her eyes like strange, black thread.

"Dinarzad, let me tell you a story. Once there was a girl that no one loved, and she was called Snow. She lived in a town by the sea, and one day another woman, who I think was very fat, made friends with her by giving her an orange because both of them worked mending nets and Snow came from the South where there were lots of oranges. Or—yes, I think that's right. The woman, who was named Sigrid—that's important, you know—told Snow a story about how three men with the heads of dogs took her away to a holy city and then the dog-men told her a story about a terrible lady called the Black Papess, who could drive men mad just by kissing them. And the Papess kissed the dog-headed men and made them eat their brother—"

"Have you gone mad, child? Has she cast some spell over you and softened your brain like an apple in the rain? I will hear no more of this."

The boy protested, but Dinarzad would not listen. She seized him by the hair and dragged him across the courtyard under the sunshine of the new day, clean and bright as washed linen. He did not cry—at least he told himself that he was not crying, though tears streamed silently down his cheeks. His sister's fingers were very thin, and curled like the claws of a starving hawk. She hauled him behind her and into the stables, which stunk of horse sweat and dung, depositing him at the feet of an old man with greasy hair and enormous hands. All the boy could see of him were the huge hands, knuckled like the roots of an elm, laced together at the level of his eyes into one massive fist.

"Treat him no better than one of the mute slaves, and if he escapes in the night you will both be whipped," announced Dinarzad curtly. She turned on one flawless heel and left the stable in a flurry of violet silk and black braids.

The boy stood and brushed himself clean of the bits of hay that stuck to the floor and now his shirt. He was careful to look as contrite as he could, though of course he was already planning to slip out as soon as the old man was in his cups that evening. He could see the man's face now, which was lumpish and ugly, but not very frightening, more of the gnome than the ogre about him.

"That one's a she-dragon and no doubt about it," the blacksmith grunted, cracking his huge knuckles with a sound like the breaking of stone pots. "Firstborns are always trouble. Ask me, they should expose the first brats out of the Sultan's women just to be safe. If not for what's between her legs, she'd have been Sultan herself—no doubt that's why you trouble her so."

"But I'm not to be Sultan," the boy protested. "There must be dozens of sons ahead of me! If I were the heir, they'd have told me by now! I certainly wouldn't be allowed to run around the Garden—or put to work in the stables!"

"Look who knows so much!" the old man chortled. "The servants always know ten times what the master guesses. Mark me, boy—you shoe the horse today that you'll ride tomorrow."

The boy stared, nonplussed. He might have explained further that it was perfectly impossible for him to be anything but a minor courtier, but the old man had begun to pile equipment into his arms—a curry-comb, hammers of varying sizes, horseshoes, new nails, hooked tools he could not possibly name.

"We'll start with the black one on the end, eh? He's not too out of sorts in the morning—some of the others like their beauty rest." The boy began to follow obediently, struggling to contain the tools in his small arms, but the blacksmith turned back and gazed through his cloudy eyes at the boy.

"When the sun's down, you can find your way out to the Garden through the sorrel's stall. There's a loose board and a little crawling passage. If you just manage to come back before dawn, she might not catch you. Take the girl some of my lunch—I don't eat much these days and she's a growing thing."

The boy, stunned, nodded and ducked into the great black gelding's stall, dropping several nails.

He found, to his surprise, that he liked working with the horses. Most were patient as parishioners, lifting their hooves in a bored manner and nosing his chest for apples. He liked their smell, their big barrel ribs, their sloping heads, the softness of their throats. He liked their blustering noises and their quiet company. He felt, truly, like one of the Witch Knife's tribe, tending his horses on the steppes, preparing for a raid on an offending village. That tale seemed so long past, now, but he immersed himself in it again, and passed the hours in a merry haze.

When the sun's rays had grown long and red as ruby tongues, he bundled up the food the blacksmith had left and started off through the door at the far end of the black-eyed sorrel's stall. He felt a little foolish—of course all the servants would know about the girl. What scandal passed under the many roofs of a Palace that some servant did not know it and tell it to another? They might even feel badly for her and wish to take her in as their own daughter, raise her to bake bread and sew gowns, but could not for fear of the Sultan or the girl's parents, whichever of the diamond-strewn nobles they might be. All the same, he had begun to think of her as his, his secret, his own friend who belonged to no one else. He was almost sorry that she had friends among the cooks and blacksmiths.

Cursing such ungenerous thoughts, he searched out the cypress path, where the thick green trees pointed skyward like minarets reaching up to the first twinkling stars. The path was a complicated mosaic commissioned when he was no more than a baby—the pebbles were arranged in every color imaginable, illustrating a scene from one of the Sultan's great victories. He found the place where it was red for several steps together—the blood of an unfortunate barbarian—and saw that the girl had already arrived, leaning on a cypress as though she had waited for hours.

"I meant to bring you better, but my sister gave me to a blacksmith and I could not get to the kitchens." He held out the horse-keeper's thick crust of bread and yellow cheese, and a fat peach.

"You don't have to bring me anything at all, you know. You don't have to supper for your song." She laughed at her own awkward joke, a high, startled sound like a spooked horse.

The boy shrugged and set out their small supper on a square of linen in the midst of the scarlet pebbles. "Of course, you might be high above me in rank, in which case I'd have to serve you; it would be my duty. I've no idea which of the men at court is your father—no one will admit to it. They talk as if you sprang into being out of the air like a Djinn! You might even be my sister! The Sultan has many wives, after all—"

The girl laughed. It was a hard laugh, like the edge of a plate rolling over a stone floor. "I am not your sister." The boy was a little abashed.

"I just like to bring you things, that's all."

"You like to hear my stories, and supper is their price. A noble boy cannot think of anything but cost."

The boy started as though she had struck him. "Are you so angry that you cut me because your eyes are dark and mine are not, because I sleep in a house and you in a bower?"

Her eyes softened immediately, chagrined, and the dark shadows of her lids seemed to glow silver and black, like the shapes of fish underwater. She put her arms around his slim neck, and for the first time, embraced the boy. His breath caught, and they stood awkwardly for a moment in the sea of red pebbles.

"I'm not angry, I'm not. I am sorry. Let me tell you what Sigrid found below the decks of the pirate ship . . ."

The Tale of Saint Sigrid, Continued

SIGRID DUCKED AND STEPPED GINGERLY ONTO THE first stair leading to the innards of the *Maidenhead*. The interior was dark as a belly, dusty and filled with strange noises—the knocking and creaking of a ship which Sigrid had not yet come to know as her own heartbeat. Suddenly, a face appeared out of the dark swirl of dust motes—wide and open, with a huge flaring nose and great green eyes the color of a deep-thatched forest. All around the grinning face were tight curls of deep brown hair, almost as tightly curled as the fleece of a sheep or the fur of a wild dog. The shaggy mane fell long past the chin, and Sigrid peered closer to see the body attached to the face floating before her like a lantern.

"Hullo!" it cried, and pulled Sigrid down into the ship by her forearm. She saw that the face belonged to the woman she had been sent to find— the curly hair bunched and knotted all the way to her waist, where she ceased to be a woman and became a strange goatlike creature. Her haunches were thickly furred in brown and red, tapering to delicate hooves that had clearly been polished to their current bronze shine. She kicked them against the floorboards for good measure.

"Satyr! Yew copse, to be specific—but then that won't mean a thing to you. Welcome, little one! You've nothing to fear now. Eshkol's got you clamped to her side and Tommy's at the wheel. You're safe as a vault! Now, you must make yourself useful and earn your board and at the moment you're use*less* at anything the least bit nautical—so you and I are going to play nursemaid to our pigheaded passengers!"

Sigrid went along amiably, admiring Eshkol's hooves. Indeed, they were shiny as mirrors, copper-colored and clearly strong as a mule's kick.

"I admit I shine 'em up every morning," Eshkol said with a laugh, "but at sea you tend to cling to little vanities. Besides, I can still kick a hole in solid silver with the blessed things! Now, the thing you must remember about passengers, paying or otherwise, is that they think they own the ship. They fret about this or that and snipe at us about the rigging, or the sail material, or the type of wood in the mast. Best to humor them if they're paying, best to show them the plank if they aren't." The shaggy woman stopped and turned quickly to her charge. "Not that we have a plank, you understand! We just keep a good solid board below and tell folks it's a plank to scare them into giving us some peace! If we wanted to kill them, we'd be proper about it and put a blade in their guts like any civilized crew."

Eshkol led Sigrid through an astonishing labyrinth of rooms and stairs—so intricate that Sigrid could hardly believe they could still be on the *Maidenhead*. Finally, they arrived at a heavy wooden door from which issued the unmistakable sounds of a hearty dinner in progress.

"Part of the fun of it, you know," Eshkol explained. "The *Maid*'s a bit bigger belowdecks than above. I don't ask questions about that—I'm not a shipwright, it's none of mine. Now, these are the ones directing our prow for the season—Arimaspians. They're a bit frightening to look at and Lord knows I told Tommy it's bad luck to have a man aboard, but they pay in gold and they keep to themselves, and that's the best you can hope for from anyone. Now take this beer in and mind their needs and I'll see you in the evening—you'll bunk with me in the stern."

Eshkol disappeared as suddenly as she had arrived, and Sigrid was left face-to-face with the thick door, a clay pitcher of frothing black beer in her hand. She did not quite fancy being a serving wench to whatever monsters lay on the other side, but she hoped that it would only be for the night, that in the morning Tommy would assign her to sew sails or some other thing which befitted a sailor. She slipped into the room and stood dumbly at the threshold, staring at the inhabitants.

At her entrance, six or so of them had scurried behind a seventh, clearly their leader. He was enormous as a bull elephant, shoulders and chest straining with muscle, and black—not the ruddy brown of Sigrid's own people, but true black, the color of midnight and lightless rooms, as though he had been cut from a block of onyx. His hair was braided in complicated patterns and threaded with gold, falling down his back like a woman's. His eye cut into her, no less black than his body—but he had only one true eye. The other was an eye fashioned out of gold and set into his skull like a diamond into a ring. It was a perfect likeness; one almost expected it to blink. She could see that his companions also had but one eye each, though their artificial eyes were not of gold, but of silver and bronze and copper and crystal. Sigrid felt reasonably certain of her guess and curtsied before the mountainous man as she would before a King.

"I am Oluwakim, King of the Arimaspian Oculos. Who is this insect who presents me with drink as if she were fit to serve me?"

"I . . . I am Sigrid, my lord. Of Ajanabh."

The King looked skeptically at her, his eye roving over her slight form like a hawk surveying the geography of a mouse's haunch.

"Are you human? You look like a human, girl. I will not be served by humans."

Sigrid stared determinedly at her feet. "I'm not entirely sure, sire. I see what you see when I look into the mirror, but I have a deformity—"

"Long-Eared Tomomo sends me *mangled* humans to pour my drink?"

"No, no, I am whole, it is only that I was born with three breasts instead of two. My parents were ashamed of me, Tomomo—Tommy—took me from the barges of Ajanabh."

Oluwakim blinked with his one colossal eye—once, twice.

"That is a meager qualification. I suppose your provincial modesty would preclude you from *showing* me this miraculous breast, and so I must take you at your word. Yet who would dare lie in the presence of the

Ocular? Very well, I accept you as a decent enough monster; you may pour the ale."

He settled himself at the head of the table, a gesture that was not unlike a boulder settling onto a valley floor. His companions seemed to come to life and went about their business, ignoring Sigrid completely. She poured for the King and stood silently aside, waiting for him to finish his cup. He had finished three before he spoke again.

"Come, Sigrid. Sit."

Obediently, she sat, a safe space away from the blue-black monarch.

"We have chartered the *Maidenhead* for our Hunt—you know what it is the Arimaspians hunt, do you not?"

"No, sire."

"Ignorant Sigrid, your education does not befit the serving-girl of a King. We hunt the Griffin, the White Beast of the Hidden Isle . . ."

The Tale of the Griffin and the King

THE GRIFFIN AND THE ARIMASPIANS HAVE BEEN enemies since the birth of the World-Eye at the center of the heavens. For them, the World-Eye blinked three times: They received the strength of both Eagle and Lion, and the size of Elephant. For us, the World-Eye blinked four: we received the strength of Bull, the beauty of Wildcat, the skill of Spider, and the secret of forging the Great Ocular, which is the golden eye you see in my skull, the mark of the King and of the Oluwa clan, the magical iris which grants power beyond the dreams of little deformed girls. These other eyes of bronze and silver are merely fashion, imitations of glory. It is only the Ocular which confers power, only the Ocular which is the heart of our people, who come into this world one-eyed, in the image of the World-Eye which is our beloved parent.

The Griffin have always been jealous of the Fourth Blink.

We have learned through the ages to wage a civilized kind of war with them: In the spring, they steal our horses for their suppers; in the winter, we steal their gold to adorn our hair and to fashion the Ocular—for all Griffin love gold as they do their own lion-haunched chicks. Their nests are woven of the stuff, their beaks and talons are solid metal, they bathe in underground pools of liquid light. But though they love the sight of gold, they cannot eat it. Their favorite meal is horse—it is to them as chocolate and peppermint are to children. They snatch the beasts by the bellies and devour them in midair. A Griffin-Raid is truly a sight to see: The sky is alive with wheeling wings of red and violet and slashing paws of tawny yellow, stained with horse blood.

Our horses were the largest of chest and powerful of leg, great behemoths of horse-kind. Each of us possessed what the other desired. And so it went in this way, in the *proper* way, for century upon century. The Griffin were careful to leave enough horses for the next spring's colts to thrive; we took only what gold we needed for our rites, for it is well known that when a Griffin's gold is gone, it perishes of despair.

But the fathers of our fathers became greedy as dogs in a pig's trough. They began to take more and more gold from the nests of the Griffin, and to hunt them down when the season was not right, when the sun blazed in the sky instead of hiding its face under the snow's crossed spears. The Griffin took their revenge—they gobbled up our herds, mare and stallion. They slurped the marrow and lapped up the eyes of our most magnificent animals. When we had no more horses, the Griffin began to take the beautiful maidens of our tribe, whose dark shoulders glinted like the pelts of cats and whose voices were sweet as autumn harvests.

When I was born, there were only a few Griffin left in the world, hidden away in mountains and forgotten mines, in vales concealed by sheets of ice, in the desert where the wind burns. Likewise, there were only a few maidens left in the Ocular—and no horses at all. When the time came for the Ritual of Ob, which would make me a man and allow me to take the place of my father, Oluwatobi the Ever-Watchful, as King of the Arimaspians, there were but two remaining Griffin. One dwelt on the Hidden Isle, in the Boiling Sea, whose water steams with constant bubbles. The other hid itself away in an aerie atop the great Mount Nuru, a mountain made entirely of ruby, whose light blinds all who approach it.

Oluwatobi gave me a choice of these dangers, for the Ocular must be forged of Griffin-gold according to the ancient rites or else it is no more than a lump of slag pressed into a man's face. Of course we bent under the guilt of our fathers' fathers' lust for gold, but we could not defy the traditions of our people. We had to have the gold, whatever the cost to the Griffin—it is our *right,* you understand. The Ocular is all things; without it we are like a leopard without a head. I could no more deny the Ritual of Ob than I could deny my own limbs. And after all, we had no more horses left; the scale would not be balanced until the Griffin had no gold. In the end, I chose the ruby crags, for we are not a seafaring people. With the blessing of my father I clothed myself in the spotted skins of wildcats and the mirror-bright breastplate of the sons of Oluwa, forged from the gold of the first Griffin's hoard. I went out from the Arimaspian veldt, and sought out the Red Mountain of Nuru.

In those days I carried in my head an eye of beryl, which is the mark of the heir, for the Griffin lay eggs of beryl, and the gold of their yolks is the purest of all. I traveled easily in my strength, and ate the meat of young deer at my night fire. The Red Mountain was not far from the boundaries of the Oculos—indeed its scarlet lights could be glimpsed from my father's hut when the sun set low in the winter sky, shining through the peak like arrows dripping with blood. I followed the light of Nuru, but in my heart I quailed, for I did not know how I could protect my precious fleshly eye from the scalding prisms of its faceted stones.

But the World-Eye does not close on its favored children, and on the ninth day of my travels, I sighted another creature hobbling through the smoke-scented brush. As I drew closer, I began to perceive what sort of beast it was, and guess at its shape. It was a Monopod, a race of beings who live further to the East than even my people, and whose lower bodies are twisted into a single huge calf and foot—the foot itself so large that legend tells of a bygone age when fleets of Monopods sailed the ocean on those huge, curving soles. My fellow traveler was just this sort of man, but not being on the waves his gait was somewhat less than graceful. He was hopping and shuffling merrily along, dressed in a beautiful vest of many colors and a strange kind of skirt which accommodated his fleshy leg, kicking up a great cloud of broken leaves and dust.

"Hail, Monopod!" I cried, and held up both hands as a gesture of friendship.

"Hail, Cyclops!" he cried in return, turning towards me with a toothy grin. Indeed, several of his teeth were missing, and his hair was a disaster of curls darkened by the dirt of the road.

"You are mistaken, Stump-Leg," answered I with some indignant pride. "The Cyclops is an island-dweller and a drunkard besides. They are not even cousins, the sheep-herding simpletons, but an embarrassment to all one-eyed folk. I am the heir to the Arimaspian Oculos, Oluwakim by name."

The Monopod looked shrewdly at me, his blue eyes glinting like gems in a vault. "Then you'll be headed for the Red Mountain, yes? For Jin's nest. I did not realize the old Oluwa had grown so ancient."

"He is still hale, but the generations increase in the sight of the Eye, and the time of Ob has come again. I aim for the red peak of Nuru, and the Griffin—I did not know his name."

The Monopod seemed to consider something private, and come to a decision I could not guess. "Well, then! I offer myself as companion and guide to the honorable son of the Oluwa! Chayim is my name, and I am bound for the aerie myself, so it will be no trouble to walk alongside you. With your one eye and my one foot, we almost make a full man! Certainly together we can both get what we want." He clapped me on the back with his splay-fingered hand and rocked back and forth on his great foot. I agreed—I was glad of the company, I will admit.

"Why do you seek the Griffin?" I asked as we walked—rather, as I walked, and he hobbled.

"Well, that's quite a story, my young Prince . . ."

The
Monopod's
Tale

I WAS BORN FAR FROM HERE IN THE SILVER-RICH
city of Shadukiam, in the year that the Rose Dome was
erected and the diamond turrets were completed in their
perfect beauty—all things built with tax money are beautiful: so we must think or go mad. My family was
modest—like all Shaduki Monopods we lived in the
Ghetto of Moss and Root, a great expanse of open land on
the north edge of the Dome. There we were allowed to live
as our ancestors had, without the painful constriction of
human houses—which we wreck with our clumsiness and
which scab our feet with their difficult corners and edges.
In the Root we lived out our days on the open moss under

the moon that shines like the white rim of a toenail. When the night pulls on her dark socks, we lie on our backs, and our curving feet arch over our heads, protecting us from cold and rain. During the days we work side by side, makers of the famous Rose Vintage, the delicate wines of Shadukiam, whose tiny white grapes we are uniquely equipped to crush.

The Shaduki are disturbed by Monopods. Though monsters and angels of all description walk the streets of the city, though indeed it was the Hsien, men whose wings are greater in span than even the Griffin's and who are no more human than we, who raised the Rose Dome over their spires and rooftops, the Monopods seem to trouble them like no other. To them we are ugly and misshapen. To them we are stupid and slow. To them we are scheming and slant-eyed. Though the wine we crush between our many toes brings in great sacks of silver for the city vaults, whenever disaster occurs we are blamed. If the snaking Varil does not flood its banks or floods too severely, our hideousness must have offended some god or another. After all, beauty is, of all the exports of Shadukiam, by far the most prized. Beauty and money, and not those diamond sticks, are the twin pillars that hoist the city into the skies.

We take this as gracefully as we can. We live peaceably in the Ghetto of Moss and Root; we do not ask for more. We sleep beneath our feet knowing that we are virtuous, and that one day we will take our wine barrels and sail south on our heel-ships to the promised kingdom of the Antipodes, where the first Monopod walked, and where legend tells us whole nations of our people still dwell.

Because we are not liked, when the Yi came among our people, no one would help us. There was no outcry. The Shaduki shrugged together and were grateful that the Yi had moved on into less desirable portions of the population. Clean out the rats, they said, and leave the cheese for the rest of us.

It was a year before I set off for the Red Mountain that my Tova died. The tendon in her foot was severed when the horses of a passing Shaduki cart trampled her underfoot. This tendon is to us what an artery is to most creatures—when it is cut there is no hope. She survived long enough on her bed of peonies and crabgrass to whisper to me that she wished we could have been married, as we had planned to do after the next barreling season. It was a horror to see her there, unable to lift her foot, the thick leg hanging at a limp and weeping angle, like a broken hinge. We buried her that night, and asked the Root-Paths which connect us all to guide her spirit to the Antipodes, and to rest.

The next morning, I awoke to find my Tova staring curiously at me, her familiar red braids neatly plaited, her cheeks as fat and well-colored as ever. But in her eyes there was no Tova. There was something strange and cold instead, something with teeth. The Thing-That-Was-Not-Tova laughed harshly, a sound like spoons scraping against stone, and hopped away from my patch of violets and bladderwrack without looking behind her.

Of course it was clear to all of us what had happened. We knew of the Yi, but until now it was a plague that only visited the Shaduki. Only they suffered the gruesome sight of their dead loved ones walking among them; only they were forced to watch their children worn like clothing. We had never guessed it could come among us. But we should have guessed—the Yi could not pass up the *experience* of our strange bodies.

The elders did not want to see the Tova-Thing. They ignored it as though it did not walk through the Root; they would not speak of it, as though not giving it a name would make it leave our home. But the Tova-Thing seemed happy to stay in the Ghetto. We could not force it to wear the moon robes Shadukiam enforced outside our places. It hopped wherever it pleased, curious and silent, except for that awful laugh. I begged the elders for permission to put the body of my Tova to rest and kill the thing that wore her, but they would not give in; they would not soil the Root with a stranger's blood. Finally, I could not bear it any longer—to see my beloved's face laughing at me each morning, as if the Thing inside her knew that she had loved me, and specially enjoyed seeing my face twisted up in pain. I went into the city center, to find a way to give my Tova peace.

It was said that one of the Yi kept a human apprentice, but I could not risk consulting such a corrupted creature. And anyway, what Yi would reveal a secret weakness to a human? He would just as likely strangle me and give my body to his master. No, I had to find a deeper knowledge, a knowledge as old as the Yi itself.

Those who are not accepted with open arms into the bosom of a city often know more about the goings-on of its dark corners than those who sit high on the hill and dine with sapphire forks clinking against golden plates. This is how I came to know of the Anchorite.

In the central square of Shadukiam stands the Basilica of Rose and Silver, whose spires are famed throughout the world for their intricate carvings, whose gargoyles have made women faint at the sight of their grimaces, whose door is carved from a single living cedar whose roots delve deep into the earth beneath the Basilica and whose branches crown its towers. This is what the beautiful and wealthy Shaduki see.

Behind the Basilica, concealed behind a brick wall overgrown with belladonna and other poisonous tendrils which creep and twist, a woman is chained to the church wall. She is clothed in a dress woven from the hair which even still sprouts from her head—as the black strands grow, her gown lengthens. Her eyes are bright and wild, rolling in her head like a baker's pins. She has no mouth; her face is blank and smooth where her mouth should be. It is said that she scrapes letters in the soil when she wishes to speak, and that there is nothing she does not know. It is for this reason she is hidden and chained, so that she will not reveal the secrets of the Shaduki. This is what we who are hated see.

I went to the Anchorite in the early hours of the morning, before the Basilica held its Mass of Coins, before the Tova-Thing roused itself. I ducked behind her wall, careful not to touch the green growth that clutched hungrily at it, and crouched at the side of the mouthless creature. She was huddled against the stone church, knees clutched to her chest, staring at me with her blank, mad eyes. She made no sound—I suppose I could not have expected more.

"Help me, Anchorite. One of the Yi has taken the body of my Tova, and I cannot bear to see her used so, as though the heart of my heart were no more than a fashionable hat. Help me to kill the Yi in her, and lay her body to rest. I beg you, holy Anchorite, to tell me the secret of bringing death to the deathless."

She stretched out her thin legs, truly no more than bones, and touched my leg with her skeletal hands, stroking the ropy muscles as if divining some fortune from their patterns. Finally, she drew back, her chains clinking against each other like dinner glasses. She pulled at her gown of hair, opening the tangled strands covering her stomach and pulling the plaits open as though they had been fastened with buttons.

Underneath her thick black hair was a fleshy expanse of belly, and in the center of the belly was a perfect mouth, lined with teeth.

It was not unlike any other mouth, except that it opened in the middle of her body, and the voice which issued from it was lower than any woman's voice.

"This Anchorite wonders if you want to get it out of her body, or kill it altogether? A very different procedure, depending on which it is you aim for." A dark pink tongue slid out of the mouth and licked its lips.

I looked down in shame at my foot, whose once-thick hair had grown sparse with grief. "I want to kill it. I want to destroy it."

"Well enough. I won't ask you if your love is true or any of that rot—it's not my place to judge. After all, I'm a naked woman chained to a wall; I've no business questioning the lifestyles of wine-makers or anyone else."

"Did you choose this prison, my lady?"

"Don't 'my lady' me, little limp-leg." She chuckled, settling herself against the wall so that her chained arms cupped the speaking belly, almost as an expectant mother would cradle her womb. "Of course I chose it! Do you think the priests of the Basilica could keep me, if I did not wish it?"

The Anchorite slipped her wrists from her chains as easily as a child undresses for her bath. She shook her hands at me teasingly and pushed them back into the manacles.

"I am not here for them. I tell them nothing, I give them nothing. Shadukiam is a necropolis; it is only that the streets do not know they are dying. It is a slow poison, a rot that takes centuries to kill. Love of silver, love of beauty, love of *seeming*. The oligarchs do not care what justice is, only what seems just. They do not care what mercy is, only what appears merciful. Thus justice and mercy will always escape them. I am the canker; I am the sore on the flesh of this dying pig. I am for you, and for the others who dwell on the fringes of Shadukiam, who can be saved from its ruin. What knowledge I can give to those who are treated with what seems like kindness, but is unkind, I give. When a Monopod comes to me, I open my hair and show him my true mouth. When the Hsien come, I let them cover me in their wings and I tell them secrets in a cloud of feathers. When a priest comes, when a banker comes, I roll my eyes and piss on their shoes, and they think I am mad."

I knelt—which is not easy for us—and pressed my lips briefly to that secret mouth, in sacrament and thanks. When I pulled away, I saw tears shine in the Anchorite's eyes.

"Then I have no thanks enough, and whether you like the word or no, I will call you Lady. Tell me how to kill the Yi."

The mouth smiled, and the smile was as full of pity as a spring well is filled with rain. "The only thing that can destroy the spirit of a Yi and force it to the underworld, the only thing that will bind it and keep it from taking the body of another dead wretch, is to pierce the Yi through the eye with the golden talon of a Griffin."

"Then I shall seek out the Griffin."

"Ah, I am sorry, my boy, but there are only two left in the world. The Arimaspian hordes have slaughtered the rest in their lust for gold. The female, called Quri, dwells in the Boiling Sea; the male, called Jin, at the peak of the Red Mountain of Nuru, whose slopes will blind you before you approach its smallest peak. And neither is in the habit of severing his or her talons for grieving lovers."

"Nevertheless, I will seek out the Griffin. I cannot do less for my Tova. I cannot leave her like this, to be used up and discarded when she no longer even bears the face I know so well."

"Then I suggest the male," she said with a sigh. "The female would dine on your liver before you had hopped three steps onto her beach. Go, if you are determined. But go now; the parishioners approach and the Yi is even now turning the flesh of your woman to crags and craters."

The Anchorite closed her gown of hair over her mouth and huddled once more against the wall, keening back and forth in an impressive display of madness. That very day I left the Rose Dome and turned my foot toward Nuru and its red cliffs.

The Tale
of the Griffin
and the King,
Continued

I WALKED ALONGSIDE CHAYIM, WHO HAD GROWN slower in his halting gait as he told his story.

"I am sorry my people have made this more difficult for you. It is true we hunted the Griffin and took more than our share. We are ashamed of this."

"But you still hunt the poor beast. And how can you take your share of something that is not yours?"

"You do not understand; you are not of the Oculos. Our mistake was not in hunting the Griffin, but unbalancing the war between us. The Griffin's gold is ours; we are blessed by the Fourth Blink of the World-Eye. It is ours by right and by strength of arms. But we should have been satisfied with the world as it was, and not sought more gold than we needed. Without the Ocular, we are nothing. It is the golden eye that makes us Arimaspians. How can we be denied that which we are? How dare any Griffin deny it to us, even to the last of their kind?"

Chayim scratched his grimy hair. "What exactly does it do?"

"When forged according to the Ritual of Ob and pressed into the skull of the King, it grants him the strength of ten men, and a lifespan three times his natural length. The Ocular can see far beyond our kingdom, into cities and wild lands on the other side of the world. It allows him to guide his people, to influence them and give his vision to the tribe. He sees far beyond the space of one tribe, and far beyond the life of one man, for his own life sees the death three times over of all he loves. The Ocular draws the Stare of the World-Eye, and ensures the survival of our nation. Without it, the Eye would slide from us, and we would perish from the face of the earth." My voice shook with passion—these are the deepest faiths of my father's fathers.

"And with all that perspective, no King of yours could see that the line of Griffins would end, and there would be no more gold for your Ocular?"

I shrugged. "The Eye will provide. They ate our herds by the hundreds and thought nothing of it—why should we be counted as less than they?"

Chayim shook his head—like most outsiders, he could not accept the superiority of our claim, or the obvious need for the Griffin to submit to us. I was a little disappointed. After all, I understood his need to put his woman to rest perfectly. "I had hoped to simply ask for the gift of a talon, but after such losses surely Jin will not part with one. It will have to be stolen."

I put a comforting arm around my compatriot. "One must always steal from Griffin. They cannot be reasoned with. You would not try to beg a gift from a wild hog—a Griffin is no different."

We walked in silence for some time, and the red silhouette of Nuru grew before us like a living flame. It had begun to prick at my eye, to scratch at my lashes and pull tears from behind my lid. I rubbed at it, trying to clear my sight, and knuckled away the tears as they swelled up. I could see that Chayim was also weeping; only a little at first, but then more and more until tears streamed down his face and mine in salt rivers. We could not look at the jagged peaks, or the sunlight filtering through them in thick red-violet shafts. I fell to my knees; Chayim crumpled and lay on his side, breathing shallowly, unable to raise his head towards the glowering mountain.

"It is like a riddle," he gasped, his hairy toes twitching. "How do a man with one leg and a man with one eye climb a mountain without looking at it?"

My chest was tight as a skin stretched over the barrel of a drum. I loosened the leather straps of my breastplate, trying to catch my breath as my eyes clouded with tears. As I pulled it away from my body, I glimpsed the mountain reflected in its polished surface, and found that I could look at the image in the metal without pain. I turned to the Monopod and smiled.

"The breastplate, Chayim, the breastplate will guide us. I will carry you on my shoulders and your foot—your colossal, beautiful foot—will block the sight of the ruby slopes from us both. Hold the cuirass before you like a mirror and direct my steps. It will be slow, but we will reach the Griffin's aerie."

And in this way, an ungainly beast ascended the heights of Nuru. Chayim's gnarled trunk was not so heavy as it first seemed, and his great knee pressed only a little into my now-bare chest. The scarlet facets rose up around us, but I saw none of it, only the fleshy surface of his foot, covered with hair like moss on the root of an ancient tree. I studied the patterns of his yellow toenails; I counted the pores in his heat-cracked skin. Only the Monopod glimpsed the beauty of those crags; only he saw what no man yet had seen without paying the price of his eyes.

I still envy him that sight.

After a full day and night of climbing, Chayim called out to me that the peaks were no longer blindingly red, but had darkened to violet, and gave off no light to harm us, but rather seemed to pull the light of the sky, the spires below, and the breastplate into itself and extinguish it. We could look at it—so long as we did not look down into the inferno of stones below—and not be hurt.

I set him down and we clambered up the last few boulders, strange and alien stones pocked like purple moons. No plant grew—the mountain at this height was a great dead thing, scarred and pitted—and the sharp rim of the windswept crater loomed up ahead of us.

Perched just below the blasted crater, so precariously it seemed ready to tumble from its niche at any moment, was the nest of the Griffin.

I was surprised—the nest did not shine or sparkle as I would expect gold-thatch to sparkle. It was a dull yellow, mottled and dim, clearly gold, but dusted with feathers, its color dampened by the use of its owner. The Griffin itself was, of course, predictably magnificent. His haunches took all the burden of golden shades his nest had abandoned, his tail whipping back and forth behind him like a snake, tufted with a little flame of orange fur. His plumage was a garish turquoise and green, with flashes of deep

red underfeathers peeking out from beneath the sea-colored wings. His face was broad, his metallic beak half a mouth, drawn back in a snarl. The wind roared around us, his voice vying with it for deafening power.

"Go away, Arimaspian! I have nothing for you! Your ape grandfathers have killed us and stolen from us and cracked our eggs on their knees— you think I will portion out my gold for you like a shopkeeper? I wish rotting diseases on all your children!"

I was prepared for the abuse. Those who are not beloved of the World-Eye always harbor hatred for those who are. But the Monopod looked panicked—it seemed to him, I imagine, that it was impossible to convince such an irrational creature to part with any piece of itself. Of course that is true—I never had his silly intention of asking for what I needed. I drew my curved silver knife and advanced on the Griffin, who reared on his hind legs and beat the savage wind with his blue wings.

"Jin, Jin!" Chayim cried, falling to his knee in desperate terror. "Listen to me and I will not let him hurt you!"

The Griffin and I laughed at the same moment, both amused by the idea of the hapless Monopod staying my hand or protecting such a beast in any way. Chayim looked at me pleadingly, and his chapped lips mouthed the single word: *Tova.* I lowered my knife but did not sheath it.

"Who told you my name, one-leg? Griffins guard their names as their gold!"

"It was told to me by the Anchorite of Shadukiam, noble Jin. I am sure she meant no harm—she knows my need is great."

The Griffin folded his wings swiftly and leaned forward, his face suddenly soft and eager as a chick's.

"Giota? Giota sent you to me?"

I was forgotten. The two creatures were suddenly intent on each other, and on the ghost of this third creature who was not on the mountain. I could have sunk my knife in the Griffin's emerald flank then, and had my choice of his body or his nest to make my eye. But I did not; I was merciful; I was, I admit, curious.

"Yes, yes, she sent me; she said that you would help me. Please—I must have a talon of yours, so that I may kill a thing and save my beloved."

But the Griffin was not listening. He beckoned Chayim to him and allowed the Monopod to awkwardly climb into his nest, so that the excited, reedy voice of the bird-beast, now soft with wonder, could be heard easily above the wind. I strained forward to hear, and Chayim lay like a babe cradled in those iridescent wings.

"Little lumpish man, Giota brought my sister into this world . . ."

The Tale
of the Griffin
and the
Anchorite

SHE WAS THE RUNT OF OUR LITTER—THE SMALL-
est egg, last laid, white beryl with stripes of cobalt and a
cord of quartz streaking through the curve like a splash of
milk. My mother feared that it would not hatch at all, and
she would be left with a dead rock to nurse. But she sat on
it all the same, sharing the warmth of her hindquarters
with three other eggs, all much grander and larger than
the white one. They were her real hope—the violet, the
flame-colored, and the deep blue.

Of course the Arimaspian horde came when the greedy
Oluwas needed another bushel of gold. They were delighted to find my mother had laid her eggs; the yolk

of our agate eggs is the purest ore of all. Though she screamed and slashed at them with her forepaws, the men dashed my siblings against the rocks and scooped up the precious stuff. The indigo Griffin squeaked and died, half-formed, in a puddle of golden yolk, and the flame-bright brother I might have had did not even manage so much—his skull was cracked when the egg burst. Only I survived, who was laid first, for we are not birds: we give eggs one at a time, during each moon of the mating autumn. I was large enough that I tumbled out, a bundle of screeching feathers and fur streaked in ropy gold. But Arimaspians have no use for live Griffin chicks; our beaks are too small to yield much metal. They made their escape, baskets brimming, though a handful met my mother's claws.

My sister's egg was so small that they had not even noticed it.

In her grief, my mother could not accept that all her children but one had perished, and with me clutched to her back and the unhatched egg clasped in her talons, she flew from the heights of Nuru into Shadukiam, where all manner of secret things are known. It is said that in Al-a-Nur all the wisdom of heaven is kept, but if you seek the dank, reeking magic of the underworld, if you want real power, to Shadukiam you must go. My mother was wise; she went directly beneath the Rose Dome and ensconced herself on the roof of the Basilica, among the waving branches of the Door-Tree, where she sent up her mourning cries like bells tolling the hours. So it went for a full fortnight, and the city could not sleep for the noise.

Giota was young then, and she alone was brave enough to answer my mother's cry. She climbed the walls of the Basilica like a little monkey, her short braids swinging. In those days she did not wear her gown of hair, but dressed as any of her kind would, and kept her locks cropped and knotted like a penitent. She crawled over the arched cupola painted with silver stars, and crouched before my mother, panting. Her face, of course, was smooth where her lips should have been, but she pulled open her tidy black vest to show her belly-mouth, and called out:

"Mother Griffin, cease your cries! Giota is here, she will mend your egg."

"How can you know that it is my egg which wounds me?" My mother beat her rose-gold wings impressively, to instill the proper fear in a flightless creature. I chirruped beside her, eager to help.

"Giota knows much. She can hear your wails—and would never mistake a mother's grief for any other kind. Give over the egg; I will quicken it."

My mother was desperate, and she knew no other would come clambering up the cathedral walls. "These are the last, little Giota. My bright blue son and this stunted white egg. The last Griffins in all the world. The one-eyes have slaughtered all the rest, and the next time one of their Princes itches for an eye, they will slaughter me. Save my egg and you will have gold, more than you could wish for."

Giota shook her head ruefully. "That is the other Shadukiam, the one which does nothing if it does not bring them jewels and silver. I will do this because I wish to. If reward comes to me, it will come in its own time, and in its own way. Giota does not bargain for lives. Only pray that the egg contains a hen."

My mother held out her massive paw and relinquished the snowy egg into the hands of the strange-mouthed woman, whose blank face showed nothing. She held it for a moment, as if measuring the heft of the beryl, and then, without warning, she opened the mouth in her belly and swallowed my sister whole.

Mother and I howled together in rage and betrayal, and we lunged at the little woman, blue cub and crimson dam. But Giota held up her hands, her eyes flashing warnings no mouth could utter. Her voice was choked by the egg, and it took all her strength to speak around it.

"Giota has not hurt the egg! How do you expect a woman to quicken an egg if not in her belly? I will carry it until it is ready to hatch—alone of all Griffins it will be born of woman, not of hen, not of lioness. See? Already it has begun to grow! Ah, my jaw! Have no fear, Giota is a good house for your baby."

Indeed, her belly had swelled, and her mouth now stretched over a little paunch, a firm moon-shaped bulge that increased in size even as we watched her, in mixed horror and hope. She patted the bird-swell with satisfaction.

"Giota is hungry. You must feed us until the egg is ready to crack."

And so my mother swept down from the turrets of the Basilica each day to hunt for her surrogate, bringing her strips of nameless meat and branches dripping with fruit. I worked the meat around the corners of the egg, into her throat. I trickled water past the shell into her parched belly. She ate a horrifying amount of food—my mother could not keep her full. From dawn to eventide she ate, and grew, and ate again. After a single day she could no longer speak. After a week she could not walk. But while my mother combed the city for sweetmeats, Giota and I played in the strange nursery of the many-towered, many-branched church roof—she tousled my fur and groomed my feathers, leaning weakly against the spires. I picked flies from her hair with my beak. I was sorry she could not wrestle with me, but her belly made her tired, and I did not want to hurt the chick inside. A baby Griffin is not small—I was already the size of a young horse, and before long, the paunch of Giota's stomach had grown so massive she could not move at all, and her mouth was pulled into a continual grimace by the growing flesh. She never cried out in pain, and she was always ready to stroke my tail. I was sorry she could not play anymore, but I lay down and let her prop herself up against my flank where the feathers meet the fur—a thing which is almost never done between Griffins and humans, even humans as inhuman as Giota. But I did not know about propriety then. I knew only that I loved Giota, and inside her was my sister, and I wanted her to be comfortable.

Finally a day dawned when Giota was so large that her belly dwarfed the rest of her body, as though she had become a snail, and her shell was made of skin. She gave one long sigh, and the mouth crowning her monstrously stretched womb gaped open further than I could have thought possible. I admit that I turned away from the sight—I was a child, and easily disgusted. But I peeked through my feathers and saw an enormous white egg emerge from Giota, perfect and round, its color no longer sallow and opaque but lustrous as a pearl, shot through with delicate blue veins of cobalt and amethyst.

My mother crowed and nuzzled the egg tenderly, rubbing her body over it to give the gem her scent. She clucked and preened in delight, and as she wrapped her long rose-colored wings around her egg, a deep cracking sound filled the windswept towers. The top of the orb split, much as Giota's belly had split, and my sister Quri emerged, pure white, blinking her deep black eyes at the sudden sun.

She pecked her way out of the shell with an almost dainty fastidiousness, and my mother, seeing that she had produced a daughter and that the race of Griffins would survive, began to weep in relief, her golden tears dripping onto the dome of the Basilica and mingling with the painted silver stars. My sister fluttered her pale wings and stumbled from the wreckage of her egg into Mother's wings. I crooned and cleaned the last of the yolk from her feathers with my beak. We were a family, happy and whole.

Into this new nest came Giota, who extended her hand and gingerly stroked her adopted child's fur. We had, of course, forgotten her entirely in our bliss. She was whole, as well, and showed no sign of the strange birth, save that her belly was worn and loose, like any woman who has just given birth. Her weary mouth smiled.

"Giota has done well," she said roughly. "Griffins will live, and keep their gold. For a while, anyway."

My mother turned to the little Witch and enfolded her entirely in her wings, an embrace I never saw her grant again until the night she died, when she held my sister and me thus. When she pulled back, both mothers were weeping.

It was much later that Giota became the Anchorite of Shadukiam, and wove a dress from her hair. My sister was with her the day Giota forged her chain—she helped her fix it to the Basilica wall. Since our mother was killed, as she knew she would be, by an Arimaspian Prince, Giota has been the beloved friend of my sister and me—though she and Quri have always been the closer pair. They share the womb bond, and I cannot touch that, born as all Griffins but one are, from egg and never flesh.

Alone of flightless things, Giota is loved by the Griffin. We miss her, both of us. We miss her so.

The Tale of the Griffin and the King, Continued

I WAS UNIMPRESSED BY THE GRIFFIN'S DISPLAY OF sentiment. But Chayim had tears in his eyes, and the two were clearly tight as a King and his eye over the memory of this village Witch.

"Jin, the Anchorite must have known you would remember her; she must have meant for you to help me. Give me your talon, so that I may kill the Yi that possesses my love and give her peace. I beg you—take it from your hind paw, so that you are still fierce, but give me a talon!"

Jin cocked his head to one side, for a moment ridiculously like a chicken contemplating strewn corn in a yard. "Why should I sever a piece of my own body so that you can borrow it? I do not grow new talons if one is ripped from my footpad. Would it not be simpler for me to carry you on my back to Shadukiam? I will kill your Yi for you myself—a claw through the eye is easy enough. And I will see Giota again—my heart longs to see how long her dress has grown."

The Monopod leapt to his foot and shouted his assent over the howl of the mountain wind. The two were quite prepared to disembark at that very moment, without a thought for me, who had carried the selfish cripple all the way to the summit! I cleared my throat loudly, and both fools turned to stare at me, as though I had suddenly appeared in a puff of magic smoke. For a moment the three of us simply stood, blinking stupidly.

Finally, Jin—for I suppose, since I know the mangy bird's name, I should use it—rose to his full height and shook his feathers clean of gold fibers from his nest. He was larger than I had suspected, dwarfing the elephants I had killed with my hunting mates, and his feathers were so blue they seemed to leech the color from the sky.

"Take it from the nest, Arimaspian dog. Take it from the nest and I will not stop you. But swear to me that you will never return to the Red Mountain, and that your people will never again trouble me for my gold. Swear it on your Ocular, on your rheumy, stinking World-Eye, and you may have my nest."

I smiled, beautifully, and my teeth glistened in the sun.

"I swear it by the Ocular and the World-Eye: Neither I nor any of my race will come near to you again."

Jin nodded curtly and seized Chayim by the grimy collar of his vest and swung the poor man onto his broad turquoise back. Snorting in derision, he leapt from the peak and I was left alone, with Chayim's ecstatic farewells echoing in the fierce wind.

I knelt and began to collect the glittering straws of the Griffin's nest, but my mind was full of the White Beast, Quri, and visions of my sons festooned in her gold.

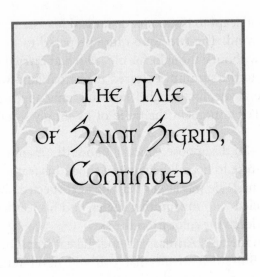

THE TALE OF SAINT SIGRID, CONTINUED

OLUWAKIM GRINNED HUNGRILY AT ME.

"This is where we steer your ship now—to the White Beast in the center of the Boiling Sea, the Searing Sea, the last of all the Griffin, and we will take all the gold we need. I will forge a new Ocular for my heir and we will have victory, finally, over those not blessed by the World-Eye."

Sigrid sat back, stunned. She pulled nervously at the frayed ends of her hair.

"What happened to Chayim? Did he and Jin kill his Yi? I hear the Yi are terrible creatures—they have never come to Ajanabh, thank all the Stars in the sky."

The King of the Arimaspians shrugged impatiently.

"When I forged my Ocular in the fires of Ob, I glanced towards Shadukiam—out of curiosity, no more—and saw the rotting body of his Tova safe in the earth. I suppose they must have done as they planned. It matters nothing to me what a chicken and a cripple accomplish. Jin is dead—this I saw as well, with some satisfaction. Chayim I have not bothered to seek out again. Only the White Beast matters. Only the gold."

Very softly, casting her eyes towards the floor and praying that he would not become angry with her, Sigrid ventured, "Surely you see that if you destroy this last Griffin, there will be no more Ocular for any of your sons? Why not let her live to birth chicks, and ensure the supply of gold for future generations?"

"Ah! She has laid her eggs already, clever Sigrid! This is why we must go now, so that we may catch her before she has hatched them, and harvest the precious yolk! As for the race of Griffin—they robbed us of our horses! No longer are we a clan which can expand our borders, riding swiftly over the steppes with four legs instead of two! We must beg and steal colts from neighbors—and the colts are weak and sickly, they do not thrive! The Griffin deserves extinction. Oh, we will ration the bounty of the White Beast so that the Ocular survives—but I will not let her live!"

"Wait—noble King of the Oluwa, why are *you* questing for the Griffin's gold? If the new Ocular is for your son, why does he not charter the *Maidenhead* and hunt Quri himself?"

At this, the King scowled and blushed at the same moment, his face turning purple with rage or shame—Sigrid could not tell—and within herself she quailed in fear of the giant man. But when he spoke, his voice was small and soft, almost a whisper.

"I have no son, young Sigrid. It is the shame of my house. At first we thought it was a blessing. Since the Griffin took their revenge on our women, we have had few maidens among us. But from the day I swore to let Jin have his wretched aerie, no man of the Oluwa has sired a boy—only girls, acres and acres of daughters, each one more beautiful than the last, and none of them able to take the Ocular. We understand now that it is a curse, and our passion to destroy the Griffin has redoubled. It is against our law, the mandate of the Eye, to allow a female to rule us. We have waited as long as we could, praying and sacrificing oxen, so that the Eye would allow some lesser Oluwa at least to sire on his woman a son. And now there are no Oluwa sons—these men you see are from other families, and though they cower in my presence, if the Oluwa do not bestow the Ocular on an heir, they will seize the Kingship for one of their own. I decreed, to preserve the sacred mandate of heaven which by right belongs only to my blood, that my eldest daughter would receive the golden eye this very winter."

The King straightened his glossy back and spoke loudly then, his rich voice booming in the cabin. "But it is not seemly for a girl-child to Quest, or to kill—the honor of the last Griffin-Hunt *must* belong to a man! Thus I have taken the burden of the hunt in the name of the fair Oluwafunmike, who will be Queen. In her name I will slaughter the White Beast, and forge the golden eye—alone of all Kings I will brave the fires of Ob twice!"

The men around him, with their many-colored eyes, bowed and scraped their allegiance and praised the name of Oluwafunmike. Sigrid hid her disgust and resolved silently to help the poor Griffin if she could when they arrived, even if Tommy and the rest were obligated to allow their passenger to do what he pleased.

"Sigrid, you listen well. In a woman, this is a kind of beauty, even if you have breasts like a cow's udder and your skin is pale and unhealthy. You will have the honor of serving me until we reach the Boiling Sea. If you perform well, I will make you a pretty trinket from the gold we harvest. You may rejoice—few who are not of the Oculos are allowed so near my person."

Sigrid knew not to argue, and though her stomach lurched in rebellion, she bowed low. In her heart, she fashioned a tiny prayer that Oluwafunmike was wiser and kinder than her father, and sent it up to the Stars, for she knew of no other place to aim.

"But you may go and sleep now, girl, so that you will be fresh for tomorrow's work. I am a good master and I do not expect my attendants to display heroics of endurance. Go and find the Satyr-woman; she will bed you well."

Gratefully, she left the audience of the King, still bowing as she closed the heavy door of the cabin behind her.

THE PALE GIRL'S TALE, CONTINUED

SNOW HAD FINISHED HER DAY'S NETTING. A PILE OF damp gray rope had risen up neatly beside her, and the foreman had pressed two coins into her hand—barely enough to fill her belly for the night. The last of Sigrid's much larger net still trailed from her hands like silver umbilici, the knots skillful and small, catching the last light in their tight twists. But at length, Sigrid, too, finished her tasks and collected her pay—many more and larger coins than the albino child had gotten. Snow screwed up her courage and looked up into Sigrid's creased face.

"I cannot bear not to hear the end of your tale!" she

cried. "Let me buy you a husk of bread or a mug of beer and tell me the rest!"

Sigrid laughed, her great body shaking like a walrus caught on a drifting ice floe. "Child, you've barely enough in your hand to feed a sparrow! I'm surely parched from all this talking—how I do go on when I'm not interrupted! But I won't take your meager wages. I shall do the buying, and I shall choose the tavern. Good enough?"

Snow nodded eagerly, and as the two walked along the quay, among glittering torches and warm-windowed inns full of rough laughter, she gently slipped her thin fingers into Sigrid's warm hand. She hoped the older woman, whom she now thought of as quite beautiful, would not mind. In answer, Sigrid squeezed her freezing fingers tenderly.

At length they reached the end of the Muireann pier. The salt-scoured boards smoothed out to a well-maintained dirt road, the noise and bustle of the other seaside folk faded. There Sigrid stopped below a dilapidated sign, which swung like a weathercock above a windowless tavern. The sign was painted oddly, with a rough image of a muscled arm grasping a fat, squirming fish by the tail. Below this strange insignia, it read:

The Arm & Trout

"Here we are, girl! Best in town, I promise."

She pushed open the heavy oak door and they slipped inside a tavern much quieter than any Snow had seen. It was terribly dark and smoky—pipes sent up tendrils everywhere. A few tables were scattered about the floor, which seemed to have far more than four corners, peopled with shadowy figures she could not quite make out, but they shrunk away from the open door. The bar itself was a decrepit slab of what might once have been cherry wood, but had petrified over the years. It was slightly uneven, and patrons clutched their mugs and tankards to keep them from sliding to the floor. Wedged behind the bar was a great hulk of a man who looked as though some giant had simply dropped an armful of limbs into a heap. He brandished a thick rag like a sword, and the rusted iron of his eyes dared anyone to order a drink. His hair was the color of sandy shoals that trapped the hulls of ships; his hands were the size of well-wrought drums, and he smelt of lamp oil and brine.

Sigrid marched directly to the ramshackle bar and slapped her thick coins onto the stained wood. "Evening, Eyvind! Beer for me—spiced wine for the little one."

Eyvind grunted assent and busied himself with the drinks, turning his back to them. Snow saw that Sigrid did not take her eyes from his hulking back while he worked, seeming to linger on his enormous frame as though trying to memorize it. When he turned back, she drew her eyes back like a thief caught with her hands full of pocket watches.

Sigrid collected both drinks and settled herself at a small table that gave a wide view of the rest of the tavern. She pushed the wine towards Snow and smirked with satisfaction as the girl swallowed it down—it warmed her from the roots of her colorless hair to the tips of her shivering toes.

"Specialty of the house. This is the Arm—it's where those of us who are, well, slightly off the map of Muireann come. Look around, love. Here there be monsters."

Snow saw then that the figures huddled at their tables were not so shapeless as they had seemed: Under a woolen hood, one had the beak of a pelican; another's webbed legs were tucked under his chair. Each drink the Arm had served was attached to some fabulous creature—some on all fours against the back wall drinking from a trough. In the dim light of a rusted chandelier Snow thought she could make out the shapes of creatures at least half animal, and some men on all fours, slurping happily beside their bestial brethren. She could not be sure that she did not spy a Djinn sitting on his cushion of smoke near the back door. Some of the faces were human, but their eyes belied their features. Even Eyvind seemed to be different, his movements not quite manlike. Not for the first time, she wondered if her new friend was indeed all she appeared to be.

"It is the only place we feel welcome, the only place we belong. Eyvind keeps the place and he turns no one away—it is a kindness. The Muireanners leave us alone, so long as we hide ourselves away. There are two Shadukiams; there are two Muireanns. Maybe Al-a-Nur is the only city which does not have two of itself. Maybe not even Al-a-Nur. But we were not yet returned to my city, were we? We were on the *Maidenhead*, with Saint Sigrid in her bunk, sharing blankets with a Satyr . . ."

The Tale of Saint Sigrid, Continued

THE SAILORS OF THE *MAIDENHEAD*, DESPITE THE apparently endless amount of room belowdecks, slept two to a bunk. It was drafty in their quarters, and the doubling up kept them warm—besides which, the habit among them was to pair a senior woman to a more inexperienced girl and trust that the one would educate the other in all she needed to know about the running of a ship and the life of piracy.

Eshkol and Sigrid huddled under their blankets in the damp and cold of any bed at sea, though beneath her fur Eshkol seemed not to feel it at all. Sigrid shivered and was restless—a ship rocked and creaked much more than a barge, and she could not find comfort in the constant rocking and lurching.

"You get used to it." Eshkol laughed quietly. "It took me months to be able to sleep without solid ground under me. Some of the other girls take to it like bees to a hive. It's different for everyone."

Sigrid held the gray blanket over her head with tented fingers, studying her companion's face—it was soft and friendly, and the woman seemed to be made entirely of shades of brown, like the trunk of a tree. Her hair and fur were deep as earth, her skin tan and tawny, her eyes nearly black. "How long until we reach the Boiling Sea? I imagine it will be much worse then. Will the *Maidenhead* survive the water?"

"Oh, the *Maid*'s all manner of magic. Comes from being born, not built, you know? That and the Star's tears. Don't you worry—a little hot salt water won't even chip the paint. We should reach the edges of it by morning."

Sigrid sighed and tried to shift to a better position on the wooden bunk. "How did you come to be here, Eshkol? Did they kidnap you, too? Surely the captain can't steal all her crew; it seems like that would take a great deal of time."

Eshkol laughed again, a sound like damp leaves falling into a swift-running creek. "No, no, I came aboard of my own will. I volunteered." She propped herself up on one elbow. "I'm not tired either. I don't mind telling the tale—it'll pass the hours till dawn . . ."

THE TALE
OF THE SATYR
AND THE SELKIE

I WAS THE FAVORITE DAUGHTER OF MY COPSE—NO other of my sisters or my briar-bearded brothers did our parents love more. The Yew was a large and prosperous family; we had enough to eat and plenty of wine to make us merry. We were known far and wide for the amazing number of offspring each Yew managed to produce— daughters and sons dropped from each of us like cones from a pine. We were envied by the Willow and Larch copses, positively worshipped by the poor Firs, who were lucky to have one child in a century.

The Forest held us all in its green shadows, and the race of Satyrs went about life as we always had: we chased the prettier fauns and drank ourselves into fits of giggles under a cornucopia of stars. It was a simple life. If a Satyr died, which did happen now and again, he did not so much die as plant himself, and from the place where he went to root a tree would grow that we could still love and converse with as though our uncle or cousin were still with us. From this had come the names of our copses, in the beginning of the world when the Forest was new—the first of us sent up trees of unrivaled beauty and size, whose branches arched like embracing arms over the meadows and glens. Their descendants took the names of these gods among trees and thus I am called Yew, my friend is called Birch, and her friend is called Pine.

And so it was that I sat under the bristling branches of the great Yew the day the man in the vulture-skin came to the Forest.

I was too young to mate, but only barely—the fauns were beginning to gather around our door like snails after a rainstorm. As all the Yew girls are, I was lovely as a spring sapling. The color was high and bright as a dahlia in my cheeks, and my voice was high and perfect as a grass whistle. My father kept me near to him, for Satyrs are not known for their restraint in the presence of a sweet-faced girl. But that day of all days, I slipped his sight while he prayed over the cut wood for the evening's fire and curled up against the dark, knotted wood of Grandfather Yew.

Good rainfall last winter, he hummed. *Too many squirrels, but what can you do?*

I chased a few of the chittering fellows away with flung cones.

Sunshine this spring was of the highest quality, he harrumphed. *Savory as biscuits.*

I scratched affectionately at the bark behind a sappy burl.

"Would you like to buy a skin?" the voice came from behind the Yew, and for a moment I had the two confused in my ear, wound together like a weed and a rose. But then they separated, and the strangest creature emerged from behind my grandfather.

He had a lion-skin pulled up over his head—a frayed, ratty old thing with mats in its fur and a mane that hung down into his eyes like unkempt hair. The skinny paws hung limply over his shoulders and the sorry tail hung down around his ankles—which were scaly and black, and tipped in claws like a buzzard's, and beneath the lion pelt I saw the tips of wings. In his hands was a fat leather satchel, bulging like a wine-skin.

"How about it, pretty goat-girl?" He smiled, a broad young face with a pointed chin and hairy eyebrows.

"A skin, sir?" I said, curious as all young things are.

"Oh, yes, my dear. I am Ghassan, the Skin-Peddler. All sorts of skins!

Skins for a penny, skins for a meal, skins in trade and skins in debt, skins for all occasions. Besides the noble lion you see displayed on my own humble shoulders, I have on my person many fine articles: Strix-skins and Manticore-skins and Mermaid tails, cloaks of Harpy feathers and capes of Catoblepas, a number of lovely red Leucrotta-skins, very fashionable, shining salamander coats and even a rare ghost-skin, human-skins and Yale-skins and any skin you can think of."

"What in the world would I do with a skin? I've already got a very nice one." But my hand was already reaching for the satchel.

"Why, you wear them, girl! Make a fine dress for those fetching hips or drape it over your comely shoulders when the winter's nip comes a-happening by—skins have a thousand and one uses. Some are magic, some are plain, some will change you, some will change in your hands. A skin is a door—step through it, and see what's on the other side. Me? I like the girl-skins—now don't look shocked. I peddle; I don't procure. It's none of my nevermind how they became detached from their owners."

"How odd, to prefer another person's skin."

"No more odd than court ladies who prefer to wear blue sashes or shoes of jade and glass. Why, I'm wearing six or seven skins at this very moment—it always pays to display the merchandise to effect."

I peered at his legs, his wings, his long, silvery hair, but could spy no seam. "Then . . . what are you beneath your skins?"

He leaned into me, confidant-close. "I'll never tell," said Ghassan. "But enough about me! Wouldn't you like to try one for your own? Better than any blue sash, I assure you."

I blushed, deep as damask. "I haven't any money, sir. My father thinks young folk ought to keep to acorns and leaves until they've a good pair of horns on their head."

"A shame, a shame. But a man must eat, no matter what skin he's in."

The Skin-Peddler turned to leave, to go on to his next customer, who would surely have piles of opals and emeralds in his fireplace grate and buy up the whole lot, while I had to suffer skinless with no coin at all of my own. I was paralyzed with anguish, and I must have let out a little cry, a half-bleat, because he turned halfway back to me.

"I suppose I could let you have this one for very little," he mused, and pulled from his satchel a very strange skin, folded over many times. It was rubbery and gray, dull and mottled, and did not look like it would make a very fine sash at all.

I did not care—I wanted it like a squirrel wants the highest nut in the walnut tree. "What would I have to do for it?" I asked, shuffling my hooves a little.

"Well, I don't suppose you'd trade your own skin—and I've no need of Satyr in my inventory at the moment anyhow. But I would take a strip or two of bark from this lovely tree of yours. Quite a rarity, the grandparent-trees."

I think not, groused the Yew. Of course Ghassan heard nothing—blood speaks to blood, sap to sap, and to the rest the forest is silent.

"Oh, Grandfather, you'll never miss it," I assured him, "and it won't hurt a bit, I promise. And I shall keep the squirrels off you all winter this year." Hurriedly, before he could protest further, I stripped off two long pieces of black bark and handed them over.

I tried not to listen to him whimper as I pulled them from the wood.

Ghassan handed over the rubbery skin with a grin on his sparsely whiskered face. "A pleasure, prettiest of girl-slips. Farewell—I don't imagine we'll meet again." He pocketed the bark and strode back over the damp grass.

I pressed the skin to my heart and hid it beneath my bed when I came home for supper—I breathed its salty, watery scent dozens of times before I reached my own door. How proud I was! When I lay down to sleep I pulled it out again and held it to my chest, feeling its cold weight on my own skin.

It was such a small sound, when I think on it now. Knuckles on glass, a rapping at the window. I was startled as a sparrow to look up and see two huge, gray eyes looking through the pane at me. They belonged to a young man, no older than I, with dark hair and skin so pale it seemed bloodless.

"Please," he said, "let me in."

"Certainly not," I whispered, so as not to wake a father already suspicious of every suitor's knock. But I unlatched the window and opened it, just the smallest of cracks. The youth looked at the skin clutched in my arms.

"Miss, I'm afraid you have something that belongs to me."

"And what's that?"

"The skin. It's mine."

"I see plenty of skin on your bones as it is. This is my skin, I bought it, just as fair as a pair of golden scales."

The youth shook his dark head sadly. "You bought it from a beast and a thief, who stole it from me when I was sunbathing on a craggy rock. I am a Selkie, and that is my skin."

I tightened my grip on the little bundle. "But I cut into my grandfather for this. It will grow back, I know it will, but I oughtn't to have done it and if I lose the skin then I will have done it for nothing. This is the only thing that is mine, and not my father's or my mother's or my sisters' or my brothers.'"

"It is not your father's or your mother's or your sisters' or your brothers'. It is *mine*. Please give it back, lovely Satyr, I want to go home, and I cannot until you give it over."

I did not want to cry, but the tears pricked all the same—but I was a clever girl, and I knew all manner of tales. "Wait a moment—what is your name?"

"I am called Shroud."

"And I am Eshkol. If you are a Selkie, and I have your skin, that means you must stay with me and be my lover until you can get the skin back, doesn't it?"

Shroud's shoulders slumped. "Yes, that is the way of it, but I was never like the other seals . . ."

The Tale of the Skin

I WAS ALWAYS SO CAREFUL WITH MY SKIN. THE others let them lie around just anywhere—it is who we are: Who might take it? Whose house might we enter, whose sardines and black bread might we eat, who might we love? It is the chief activity of Selkies to have their skins stolen.

But I was careful. I loved the sea, I loved the waves and the breakers and the curling white foam. I loved the changing character of the sea, how it could be choppy and gray or smooth as glass, like the brow of a wife. I loved the taste of the water, and I was afraid of what it would be like to be closed up into a house, without the slap of the wind and the cry of the gulls.

I did not mean to fall asleep. I was sunning my silver stomach on a desolate rock in the shallows, basking in the heat reflected off of the violet waves, breathing the kelp-spattered air. I had only closed my eyes for a moment when he slipped up, silent as a spear fisherman, and sliced through the skin of my back just as easily as tearing paper.

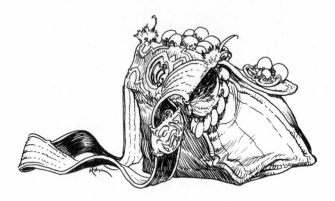

Such a thing had never occurred—he stripped my skin from me, ripping and rending it, pulling my fingers out of my flippers, my feet out of my tail, my face from my muzzle—I cried out, but my sisters saw from afar only that someone was stealing my skin, and high time, too. They did not see the knife. They did not hear my screams. They cheered from a distant outcropping of stone.

When he was finished he paddled easily to shore and began packing the skin into a fat leather satchel. I followed, swimming clumsily in the man's body I had never once lived in. When we clambered onto the sand, I lay gasping, air burning my unused lungs.

"Where are we going?" I gulped.

The man I came to know as Ghassan stopped and turned to regard me. He was, as he often is, dressed in a woman's skin in those days, a crone with long tangled hair. "Whatever do you mean, young unfortunate?" the crone said.

"You have my skin."

"Oh, yes, that I do."

"I am yours, then. What house will you take me to? What fish and breads shall we eat? Who shall I love?"

"I don't care who you eat or who you love, seal. I only want the skin, and I only want the skin for selling. You are incidental, a pit in a peach."

I rose shakily to feet I had never known. "But this is what I am. My skin is stolen; I must belong to someone."

"You do not belong to me, and I do not want you," the old woman who was Ghassan snorted.

"Then give me my skin back, if you will not have me."

"Not after I cut it with such difficulty from you—you have very stubborn bones."

I was stricken. Ghassan would not close me up in a house, or feed me, or love me. Once I was out of my seal's body, I no longer feared those things, but needed them, needed them as violently as once I needed the sea. I became panicked; the slate sky turned frightening, the dark sea horrible. I did not know where to go; this body seemed afraid of everything. It was chilled easily and always hungry. I followed the crone because the crone had my skin. That is what a Selkie does.

Please, I would say. *Love me or give me my skin. You are hurting me.*

I do not want you, would come the answer.

Please, I would say. *I can be useful. I can make stew and tea. You would like me, if you tried me. Or give me back the skin. You are cutting me.*

I do not like you, I do not want you, would come the answer.

Please, I would say. *I will wash house walls and mend fences, I can build cradles and beat the dust from rugs. Let me be a Selkie, or give me back my skin. You are killing me.*

I do not care, would come the answer.

And so it went on, but I could not stop. I learned he was not a crone at all, and what house he had was on a far distant island where he would certainly not lead me. But I could not stop. The skin is knotted in my belly like a sailor's rope, and the harder Ghassan pulls to escape me, the tighter the knot becomes, and the more desperately I chase him.

My skin is gone, but I belong to no one. I am no seal and no man. The skin calls to me, but I cannot answer.

Please, I would say. *You are killing me.*

The Tale of the Satyr and the Selkie, Continued

"He only traded it to you to be rid of me. I have hounded him for three years and he would not let me touch it, but he traded it to you for two pieces of bark. They may have cost you dear, but to him they mean nothing. They are pieces of skin, not a skin. He only wanted to show me how little my skin was worth. I am so tired, Eshkol. Please."

I grinned up at him through my curly hair. My voice was soft as pine needles underfoot. "I am very good at hiding things, Selkie. You could belong to me. I could close you up in a house, and feed you sardines and black bread, and love you under towering trees. And you know, we Satyrs have very well-deserved reputations. My father says I am too young for a lover, but you are very handsome, and I am not tired at all."

I leaned out of the window very suddenly and kissed the Selkie-boy right on his pale lips—I don't know why I did it, but the moonlight was so bright, and he seemed suddenly ever so much more lovely than the skin. Our lips met over the windowsill and his mouth was so cold, cold and salty and sweet as the sea, and my lips warmed him as the sun warms a tidepool. Even through the kiss I was smiling, and he put his silvery hands gently on my face, just the way a faun does. I moved the skin behind my back.

"Oh, Eshkol," he said breathless and bashful, when we parted, "perhaps I could rest here."

Shroud stayed with me for seven years and seven days. My father was in a rage fit to crack oak boughs when he found us in the morning, a sea-eyed boy with arms wrapped around his daughter's downy neck, but it passed. Shroud was gentler and quieter than low tide, and like the tide, no one could resist his slow presence. We could not kiss often enough—the water loves the green earth and the green earth loves the water, and so we were, twined up like vines on a riverbed, and he told me I tasted of red berries and sunlight on long grass, and I told him he tasted of clamshells and kelp and a wet wind. I taught him to plant grapevine, and he taught me to fish with my bare hands. I grew up; I grew less silly, though no less overeager and bright of heart, and in all my barters since, nothing I won was ever so precious to me as that gray and mottled skin.

My only sadness in those gold-specked years was Grandfather Yew, who had not spoken to me since the day I took his bark, who would not speak to me even after it had long grown back.

One evening Shroud sat next to me in our own house and took my hand. "Eshkol, heart of my heart," he said, "please give me back my skin."

I laughed. We had played this game many times. "It is my skin, my love, and I like it very much."

"No," he said, very carefully and slowly. "I am not teasing; I am not playing. Give it back to me, if you love me."

"Shroud, why? Have we not been happy? Do I not still taste of red berries and sunlight on long grass?"

"Warmer sunlight and sweeter berries than I ever thought possible. But I am a Selkie. No amount of wishing will make me a Satyr. This is what I am. Selkies stay until they leave, and the instinct for leaving is so powerful in us, far more powerful than the instinct for the sea. I understand that now. It is not the sea that calls us back. What calls is stronger and more inexorable than any current. I long for the sea, yes, my skin is always dry, and I am always thirsty, and I miss the crash and swell of the black waves, but more, I long for the *leaving*. I am restless, I am ready, and the leaving whispers to me at night. It says that I will breathe easier when the air is full of fog and seagulls, that I will breathe easier when I am at the start of a story, rather than at the end."

Tears trickled to my chin. "No, no, I won't give it to you," I whispered.

"Eshkol, I have not looked for my skin for seven years. I have not rifled the thatch of the roof, or pulled up the floorboards. I have not thought of it; I have not checked the hanging wash for a gray scrap. But the leaving will not let me be, and I must answer it. I don't want to." Shroud clenched his fist and for the first time his pale face colored, red and pained. "I don't. I want to stay with you and eat chestnuts and curl my fingers in your fur. But the seal is stronger than the man, and the leaving is stronger than the seal." He spread his hands helplessly. "This is what I am."

"If you don't want to, then don't! I am a Satyr, yet I am hopeless at playing the pipes—we are more than just our bodies."

"It's no good, dearest of all bodies to me. If you do not give it to me, I will find it, and one day you will wake up and I will be gone. I have looked for it for seven days and found nothing, but you are not so good at hiding things that I will not find it one day or another. Please. You're hurting me."

Slowly, I unbuttoned my vest and my belt, and reached into their folds. I drew out the gray skin, warm from lying next to my own.

"I've always had it just here, sweet seal-boy. I wore your skin every day."

Shroud reached across the table and took it from me—I only resisted a little. He touched it with wonder, as though it was woven light studded with stars. "I am not tired anymore, Eshkol," he said, his voice hushed as river rushes.

"Oh," I said, sighing, "then I am happy for you. But I am as tired as an old aspen bent double."

In the morning he was gone, and I went walking in the dew-and-dim to see Grandfather Yew. I lay next to his roots and stroked them, chased off a few squirrels. I didn't cry; I couldn't bear the touch of water on my skin.

I liked him, hummed the Yew. *And I've thought about it some—it's all right about the bark.*

The Tale of Saint Sigrid, Continued

"I WANDERED FOR A WHILE, OUT OF THE FOREST and away from everything. I didn't mean to find the sea, but eventually the soil turned to sand and the air became full of fog and seagulls, and there it was. A dockside beggar told me of a ship which wanted women for a crew, a magic ship with a red hull and a fox for a captain. I signed on faster than a leopard catching a rabbit in her jaws—Tommy was glad to have me. I never understood what he said about the instinct for leaving till I saw this ship, but once I did, there was no telling me I couldn't have it. The leaving had me, and I went with it, just as my Shroud did. I don't miss him the way I used to—Satyrs aren't made for grieving. But once in a while, when the sea is very calm, I dream of skins, endless skins, like the layers of an onion. But here I am—anything that happens belowdecks on the *Maidenhead* is my territory—and that's not such a bad story to be in the middle of."

The ship suddenly lurched to one side and a strange sizzling sound filled the air. Eshkol leapt from the bunk, her hooves sounding heavily on the floorboards.

"The Boiling Sea!" she cried. "Sigrid, you won't want to miss it! A sight no other crew will ever survive!"

The pair emerged above decks to find a riot of sound and movement. The Arimaspians were leaning over the prow in their eagerness, oblivious to how difficult it was for the sail-riggers to work around them. One of the lesser men leered at a young Djinn, who flicked her fiery fingers at him and ignited his beard. His companions howled in indignation and beat out the flames.

Tomomo herself stood calmly at the wheel, guiding her ship through the Boiling Sea, which no longer buffeted the sleek craft with waves, but with violent bubbles and hissing steam. The ocean was alive and furious, sizzling against the flanks of the ship, sending up rolling columns of scalding water that caught more than one woman across the face with its blistering spray. At first, most had been fascinated by the suddenly raging sea, but one by one they learned to stay well away from the rails and give their attention only to the lines and sails. The sound of it was deafening—it was like a scream of wind tearing through a child's paper house, crumpling the walls and rafters as it blows.

Sigrid hung back near the stern, leaning over the rails and breathing the steam of the sea. She looked into the horizon, wind whipping her dusky hair into her cheeks, and for a moment, just a moment, she could see, on the edge of the water where the calm met the boil, a gray seal's head bobbing up and down in the surf, barking softly, mournfully, unable to follow.

"Sigrid! Attend me!" Oluwakim hollered from his position at the bow. She turned reluctantly and trotted up to him, standing just behind his group and hoping he would not need her for anything. The King held a long brass spyglass in his fierce black fist, brandishing it like a sword.

"Look! The Hidden Isle! Not very well hidden, of course, but no stupid Griffin hen can hide from the Ocular!" He held out the spyglass to Sigrid with an expression that made it clear he felt he was being extremely generous. She put it to her eye and indeed, a slim line of land was glimmering in the distance, looming larger with each moment that passed. The

Maidenhead was cutting through the roiling water with incredible speed, hardly slowed at all. Sigrid hoped in vain that the wind would die, that they would not be able to reach the isle and murder poor Quri. But before she knew it they had moored offshore and filled one of the longboats with eager-faced Arimaspians and Long-Eared Tomomo, and Sigrid herself was reluctantly climbing into the crowded craft.

The Hidden Isle was little more than a scrap of sand in the middle of the angry sea. The surf bubbled up onto the white beach, and the drift-wood scattered along the shore was scalded red as flesh. There might once have been a tower in the center of the patch of earth, but it had crumbled into little more than a jumble of broken rocks. Some of them still stood, one atop the other, so that a piece of a wall could be seen, and the arch of what might have been a window—but no more. The troupe clambered onto solid ground and almost immediately the Arimaspians charged over the dunes with a dreadful cry, having easily sighted the nest of the White Beast on the north end of the strand. Sigrid hung back with her captain.

"You're wondering why I would take these men aboard, when they are only going to render an entire race extinct," Tomomo said gently. "You think it is hard and cruel—but that is what piracy is. We are free women, and so we do not obey the rules everyone bows and scrapes to. If the gold they give us will patch our sails and put wine on our table, we will ferry them. If it turns your stomach, I will leave you on this island and you can make your own way off it."

Sigrid said nothing.

When they arrived at the nest the White Griffin was screeching like a wounded bear and beating her wings against the wave of Arimaspians jabbing their swords and spears at her. She desperately fought to shield her nest, snatching one of the men in her jaws and tearing into his soft belly, hurling another against the jagged ruins—and under her haunches the two women could see three large eggs, blue and white as slabs of sky.

"That's a very inefficient offensive, Oluwa. I thought you and your tribe were expert hunters! Clearly I was misinformed," Tommy hollered. The Griffin hissed at her, bright feathers flying. She was white from the tip of her tail to the crown of her head; even the fur of her lion haunches was pale as a glacier. Only her claws and beak were golden, the rest of her entirely blanched of color, pure as the sandy beach. Her eyes flashed, crackling with panic and despair. Oluwakim seemed to consider for a moment, then nonchalantly signaled to his men. They obeyed instantly, backing away from the rabid creature.

"What would you suggest, sea rat? Will you lend us your beast-cannons? A single broadside could have us a fine Griffin supper in a mere moment—and you your payment," he snapped.

Seeing her opportunity, Sigrid dashed past the adorned hunters and dove into the nest, while the Griffin roared her protests. She spread her skinny body as wide as she could, pitifully trying to block any spear's flight to the beast or the precious eggs. Of course the Griffin towered over her, entirely vulnerable.

"I won't let you kill her!" she screamed.

Both monarchs, the one of the sea and the other of the land, looked at her with amused impatience.

"You are a very bad servant, little girl," Oluwakim observed. He was quite calm—not at all perturbed by the notion of dispatching a child along with a beast.

"Do you really think a creature of that size needs you to shield it?" Tommy asked, grinning mischievously.

"Of course I don't," bellowed the Griffin, her voice echoing over the desolate beach like the flight of a single black bird. "But it's the gesture that counts." She nuzzled Sigrid roughly, a strange kind of reward for her bravery. "So you've come for me, have you, Oluwa? My brother told me you would, one day."

"Was that before or after he quickened your eggs, you barbaric half-breed? Even dogs don't deign to mate brother to sister," he scoffed.

"Don't try to shame me, ape. I know your nest is empty of roosters; what right have you to mock mine, which is not? We have no law against such things—and where was there another male to give me chicks? Thanks to you he was the last."

"I did nothing to him," sneered the Arimaspian. "He was torn into carrion, dumb meat and nothing more." She flinched and stared at the King with such hatred the rest of his companions stepped slightly away from him, expecting a furious attack. "I *saw* it, Quri," he taunted, tapping his golden eye with one dark finger. "I saw them devour your blue brother. They licked their lips and made a feast of him; they threw his bones to their dogs. Why don't you tell us the tale? We have time—I shall kill you before or after; I have no preference. I listened to the sire prattle on like a wind-up toy; I can extend the same courtesy to the dam. Everyone here *loves* to hear tales. Tell them how your brother died the day he lent his color to your eggs."

Quri bent her head in grief, staring at the iridescent colors of her unborn chicks. When she spoke, her voice was thick with anger.

"Not for your pleasure, little king of a little hill, but for the child who put her body between you and my eggs . . ."

The Second Griffin's Tale

I WAS BORN UNDER THE ROSE DOME OF SHADU-
kiam. Alone of all Griffin, a woman carried me in her
belly, like a human child, and from her my egg issued,
and from her I was born. It is a famous story—I will not
repeat it.

My Griffin-mother always told me not to return to
Shadukiam, the city of my birth. It is a wicked place, she
said, a man who keeps his knife hidden when others show
theirs plain. I wanted to obey; I wanted to be happy on the
heights of Nuru, happy as Jin was, nestled under our
mother's wing with the moon on his cerulean feathers.

But I could not. I was drawn back and back again to the

strange, sweet smell of decaying roses, to the mildewed walls which tapered into diamond turrets, to the dark gutters swollen with rain. I was drawn back to Giota, to the scent of her, which smelled more like mother to me than the soft golden straw of the nest. I followed that smell, the smell of blood and violets crushed underfoot, the smell of Giota's mouth. I did not remember, exactly, being inside her, but my heart knew that it had once beat beside another heart. I followed the memory of my heartbeat through the silver streets of Shadukiam, the lacy shadows cast by the diamond turrets, until I found her, the woman who gave me birth, sleeping on a rubbish heap outside a ramshackle inn. My throat was tight and I lay next to her, covering her body with my wings, weeping tears of gold into her hair.

I flew over the plains between Nuru and the city many times. Giota was always pleased to see me, though we rarely spoke. We pressed our heads together in the shade of wide-armed trees; we nuzzled each other and picked leaves, I from her ever-growing hair, she from my pelt. It was rarely necessary for us to speak, only to be together, in secret, mother and daughter who could never call each other by those names.

Jin did not understand, of course he did not, who never grew in the womb of a woman, but he never betrayed me, and my true mother thought me hers and hers alone until the day she was slaughtered and her beak cut from her face to decorate an Arimaspian head. We hid ourselves away in the blinding cliffs, for we were still young and could not defend ourselves against so many. Jin covered my face with his wings as the last screams of our mother echoed through the crystalline crater.

On that day I left him to the nest that was his, and went into Shadukiam to console myself on the breast of Giota. I could not stay under the Rose Dome—I was far too large to comfortably live in a city—but I built my nest of cedar and camphor outside that blooming arch, and each day one of us went to the other to hold our quiet communion. We were happy together, for a while.

I wept the day she forged her chain and beat the bolts into the wall of the great Basilica. I did not understand. I could not bear the thought of never sleeping again with her tiny heart beating against mine in my nest of red woods. She tried to tell me it would be no different, that I could still come to her in this strange churchyard—which was so near to the place where she bore me. But I knew, I knew it would be different, that something was ending before my eyes and I could not stop it. I stared into her dark eyes, my own lost in tears.

"Am I not enough?" I whispered hoarsely. "Can I not make you happy?"

"Oh, my darling," she answered, her mouth muffled by her rumpled, wet dress. She put her hands into my feathers as I longed for her to do. "You have always made your Giota happy. But I am not a Griffin; I have allegiances which are not to gold or egg. And I have this duty to perform."

"I have no gold to watch over. I have only you." I tried to press my head against hers, but she turned away, opening the hidden seam in her black frock so that the mouth in her belly—the mouth that bore me—could speak freely.

"You will, Quri. You will have a clutch of eggs and a nest of gold, as all Griffins do, one day. We must each tend to the talismans of our people— you to your gold and Giota to her wall."

"You have never told me the name of your people. I know nothing of you, of your ways and your blood. If you are leaving me for a wall and a chain, at least tell me why; tell me what burden calls to you from what tribe to do this thing. Tell me who you are!"

She grunted and leaned against the crumbling, moss-covered wall, holding her belly in her hands as she had done on the few days when she had spoken to me for longer than a few affectionate sighs—days I remember now like feasts, holidays, festivals of her voice. She turned her lipless face to the sky and shut her black eyes, and the tongue in her belly began to tell its tale . . .

THE ANCHORITE'S TALE

I KNOW WHAT YOU ARE THINKING. THAT SOME-where in the world there is a race of people who carry their mouths in their bellies; that somewhere there is a tribe in which I would seem unremarkable.

There is not.

I am only a woman, born from a woman, sister to women. Alas, women were rare in the wild, honey-colored expanse of my home—vast grass-swept expanses of land spotted with tree and horse. Thus, my caravan was always small. Sons were born easily, brothers quickly had, husbands too numerous for the few wives. Each woman had many—men fought for the honor of marrying into her bed. The women born were always powerful, almost to a girl a witch or a warrior. The birth of a daughter was celebrated by three nights of feasting on the meat of skinny hawks and blue-bellied lizards. The birth of twin daughters was considered a miracle sent by the blessed Stars.

Triplets occurred once in a generation, when the Snake-Star aligned with the Harpoon-Star, and the light of the Pierced Serpent fell on the yellow grass. These star-born triplets are the emblem of the caravan—we were known for them; they were prized; without these sacred births we were no more than a ragtag band of horse-traders peddling chicken feet as love charms from town to town.

The triplets are called the Sorella, and I am the youngest of mine—I was born a full minute after my sisters. We are special, we are sacred: The oldest of each triad carries her eyes in her belly, the middle her ears, and the youngest her mouth. The organs are erased from their right places, but not gouged out, not torn. It is simply as though some god passed her hand over our faces and washed away our eyes, our ears, our mouth. We were the Seer, the Listener, and the Speaker.

We were Pangiota, Legiota, and Magiota. We were sisters, and with one mind we guided the path of our caravan—for Legiota saw the path, Magiota heard the Stars' commands, and I spoke the path. We could not lie; we could not guide our people falsely. If the Sorella were consulted, only I could reply, and I could not fail to answer truly, to tell the tale of what my sisters saw and heard. We were more than an oracle: Our faces were the valleys on which the Star-gods walked. We braided our hair into sacred habits, for our bodies were the vessels of the Stars' light, and no woven cloth could be more holy. It was whispered that the Sorella were the same women in each generation, that the spirits of one set of sisters simply stepped into the bodies of the next. I know nothing of that—I am Pangiota; I have always been. More than that no one can tell.

I often envied my sisters. After all, I only reported what they told me, what Legiota saw and what Magiota heard. I, too, wanted to turn a secret ear to the sky and hear the white-hot words of the Stars pouring into me like burning honey. I, too, wanted to see the path of truth extending from my lashes like a golden ribbon. But I could only open my hair like a curtain and let my hidden mouth speak. The gods touched my sisters, they did not touch me. I used to pray that we could trade powers, that I could, just once, be the woman who laid out her body under the Stars and let their light spill onto her belly.

Children make prayers so thoughtlessly, building them up like sand castles—and they are always surprised when suddenly the castle becomes real, and the iron gate grinds shut.

One day, which was not unlike any other day on the steppes, when the honey cakes boiled in their pans and men shot lazy arrows at raccoons and voles who were little more than little bundles of dry bones, Legiota and Magiota called me to them in our secret place. We crouched in a cavern of black rock hidden in the flank of the orange-and-white-banded cliffs which marked the edges of the grassland, of our home. In the shadows, the sound of water dripping from the stone ceiling made us sleepy and calm—but that day my sisters were awake and nervous as foxes that scent a huntsman. They had unbraided their hair from crown to toe, and sat naked in the cave, their bellies displayed like jewels.

"I have seen a new path," Legiota whispered.

"I have heard the footsteps of the Stars diverting from their courses," Magiota added, clutching my hands in hers. I realized suddenly that they were frightened.

"There will be no more Sorella after us. The caravan is dying. There will be more daughters soon than ever were born to us, and mothers will no longer pray for them. There will be no more triple births. The Harpoon-Star has refused to pluck out the eyes, ears, and mouths of any other daughters, and the Snake-Star will not plant them in other wombs. They will give us generations of daughters as compensation, but all of them will be plain. They will not be born with power; they will have to wrest it from this cave, which is deeper dug in the earth than even we had guessed. We will be forgotten, and when the last gray-haired grandmother who remembers us bleeds her blackest blood onto the earth, the caravan will hunger, and thirst, and die."

Legiota spoke matter-of-factly, as though she spoke of the average rainfall on the flats. "A man has been born whose great-great-grandson will murder the Snake-Star, and there is no longer any path the Serpent of Heaven can take which will not lead to her death. She has told me this, and she mourns herself under the black veil of the sky. The Sorella were her handmaids while she lived; we cannot serve her when she is dead—she has told me that she will take other Stars as her own, little snakes to be her pallbearers, and remove herself to a temple far removed from the cursed city, to wait for her doom to come on heavy feet." Magiota's eyes filled with tears, and they dripped onto the shell-like ears in her belly.

"Pangiota, my sister, I am afraid of death," Legiota rasped.

"Why should you fear to die?" I asked. "If this will not come to pass until the prime of the grandson, we will not see the Serpent perish from the sky. We will not see the new handmaids take our place. We are safe, if no longer blessed."

My sisters exchanged glances, and Legiota passed her hand over the smooth expanse where her eyes might have been. "You do not understand. We two are her handmaids. We will go into seclusion with her, and give our strength to hers, our sight and our hearing to the little snakes, so that in five generations, her light will be so great that she will rise again from her own murder."

My eyes drooped and my shoulders fell. I touched my sisters' bellies with affection and sorrow. "And I am not to go with you."

"Pangiota." Legiota's eyes softened and creased their corners, trying to make her words as gentle as she could. "You are the least of us. Never has the Serpent-Star seen you or touched you; she only knows of you as our sister. You only speak, and she does not care for human speech. For the Sorella, you are vital; for the Serpent, you do not exist. And the Stars have determined that the Sorella should be broken."

These words hit me like a bellow of hot wind—but I knew them to be true. I was nothing, only a mouthpiece, a mute pipe into which my sisters' breath flowed. I bent my head and nodded, knowing how small I was in their presence. Magiota threw her arms around my waist and pressed her fluttering ears to my lips. It was an intimacy we three rarely shared, the touch of lash to lip and lobe.

"We will go; we love our god as we love you. But we have decided together that we cannot let the Sorella pass from the world. We have sat vigil in this cave, searching out a path which would allow us to stay with you, to stay Sorella, and to birth another three which will carry on our memory past the death of the Star. No caravan should be left blind and deaf, mute and helpless. And we have found a way." Magiota smiled and drew a small knife from her skirts, a curving silver blade with a handle of bone.

"What has been ours will be yours, Pangiota. We will cut out our eyes and ears and give them to you to swallow. The power will be passed to you, all the Sorella in one body. And you will leave the caravan, you will leave the horses whose smell you know like your own, and go into a city covered in a dome of roses, and there you will wait for the beast to cry out to you. I have seen this already; I have seen you walking under white petals." Legiota's eyes gleamed from her navel like green torches in the dark.

"You will swallow the child of the beast as you will swallow our flesh, and bear the creature within you like your own daughter. In this way two races will be saved, and the three of us will be always together, beyond the death of the Star. We will go into seclusion, and you will go into the wicked city, and give birth to us over again." Magiota stroked her ears quietly.

"I do not understand," I cried, unwilling to devour my own sisters, terrified of their strange words.

"Of course not, of course not, but you will. Prophecy is such a difficult thing, but we know that there is no other way to preserve the Sorella, and we will not refuse the call of the Serpent."

Oh, how I wept while I watched them! Naked as animals, they performed this surgery before my eyes: Magiota seized the knife and plunged it into her belly—it entered her with the sickening slick sound of a finger passed through running water—and slowly cut her sacred ears from her stomach, sweating and crying out quietly as she worked. She tried to keep her smile, so as not to frighten me, but I could not bear the sight; I retched in a corner of the cave while her whimpering sounded in my own ears. Legiota carved out her eyes next, never allowing herself to moan, but her breath was ragged as a torn dress, and her hands when I turned back to them were shiny and wet with blood.

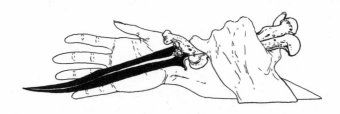

They placed the lumps of pitiful flesh in front of me like servants laying out an exquisite cake for their lady. Both still bled, yet they smiled and smiled, unbraiding my hair with almost maternal care, just as they used to do when we were girls together. They pulled the long sheaves of hair aside and put their arms around me, cradling my body with their own and stroking my face with sticky red hands, urging me to swallow them, to close my eyes and do it before the organs cooled and died. I screamed and screamed in their arms, my voice echoing in the rocky chamber until it seemed as though we were surrounded by a chorus of shrieking ghosts. They hushed me and held me close, and finally through my screams I seized the bloody clumps of my sisters and pressed them into my mouth, gagging, swallowing, gagging again. I forced it down my belly-throat, and my tears mingled with their blood until all I could taste was salt.

It was quiet afterwards.

I lay on the cool rock and they lay over me, blood drying on our skin like paint. We lay like lovers, tangled together in pain and sorrow. Legiota pushed the matted hair from my ear and said:

"Now we will never leave you; you are all of us, and you will go on. We will leave the world; you will go into its steaming heart. But remember that you are always Sorella. It is your duty to guide the caravan, the ramshackle train of kindred that crawls over the face of the earth, scrabbling at the dirt for fruit, scrabbling at the skies for revelation. When the beast has gone from the city and you have done your duty by her, you must be Sorella for all the caravans, and perform our duty for them. They will come to you, and you must see for them, and hear for them, and speak for them. Cut your hair when you go into the city, wear their threads and not your own, but when you have finished your maternity, when you are ready, braid it again into our holy dress. We will be with you, inside you, and we will love you for all the days of this body."

With these words, Legiota and Magiota laid their heads on my breasts like daughters and died, their spirits, their light, rising like steam to join the Serpent in seclusion.

I wept alone in the dark.

THE SECOND GRIFFIN'S TALE, CONTINUED

GIOTA'S EYES WERE DRY AND DULL.

"By the time I reached the diamond turrets of Shadukiam, I could hear their voices in me; I could hear the Stars singing in their choirs and I could see the path stretching out before me like a golden ribbon. I was not Pangiota any longer; I was only Giota, all of us and none of us. It is difficult to keep it straight—sometimes I seem to speak to them, sometimes to myself, sometimes to the dead air. I have done my duty by the beast, by the Griffin, and now I must do my duty by my sisters, I must be the Sorella of Shadukiam, the Anchorite, the Oracle."

I stared dumbfounded at her, humbled by the expanse

of what I had not guessed about her. "But why must you chain yourself to the wall? You can be an oracle anywhere; there are towers full of them! You could stay in my nest and the folk of the city could come out to you."

Giota looked at me with wild eyes, vulnerable as a lamb beneath a wolf's teeth. Though I knew her mouth was free and wide in her belly, the featureless skin where it should have been made it seem as though she was gagged with some terrible rope.

"I am so frightened, Quri. If I do not do this thing now I will not stay. I will go with you and I will abandon my sisters. All my life I prayed to have their power, and I am so frightened of it now. Do not begrudge me this: It is who I am; just as you will one day have your gold and your eggs to look after, I must look after them." She raised her hand to stroke my face—such a small hand!—and then lowered it to peeling off her dress. "Help me, my daughter. Help me braid my hair again."

I lowered my head to those long, coarse strands, their familiar smell overwhelming me, and lifted one bundle of hair over another with my beak, slowly, clumsily, weaving her habit down to her ankles. My tears fell onto the strange fabric, and left great golden stains on the braids.

"Mother"—and with the word a swollen river burst in my heart—"will I truly have gold of my own and eggs to tend? I cannot really believe it; I cannot believe that the race of Griffins will go on. If you are an oracle now, if you are the Anchorite, then you must tell me the truth; you cannot reassure me with lies."

"Quri, your brother lives, and while he does, you have a duty to perform as much as I do. He will quicken your eggs, and you will have three chicks to warm with the fur of your haunches. Go, return to the Red Mountain, and find him."

With this Giota clamped her chains around her wrists and took her place at the wall. I left her, though my bones mourned, and turned to the plains of Nuru, to find my brother's blue plumage again and obey my mother, as good children do.

In the Garden

IT WAS STILL DARK. THE SKY HUNG HEAVY ABOVE THEM LIKE A NOMAD'S tent, lanterned with stars and buffeted by quiet winds. The boy's head lay in the girl's lap—he had at first thought himself brave to lie thus, but she seemed to welcome it, and tousled his hair with a nervous hand.

"I'll be clever tonight," he whispered, "and I will not be caught."

The girl laughed like rain trickling through palm leaves.

"I will! I will not let your tale keep me until light breaks the sky like a pitcher! I will leave now, while the stars are still bright, and return to the blacksmith. Then Dinarzad will know nothing, and I will be able to come all the earlier tomorrow!"

The boy ran off happily, past the stately rows of cypress, back towards the minarets of the Palace, rising into the dark sky like a second grove of trees.

But the next evening found the boy not roaming free in the Garden, but curled in the corner of the stall, pouting. He drew his knees up to his chin and scowled. He had been lying that way for a long while when he saw a shape crawling towards him through the secret door. It was the girl, hay decorating her black hair like a crown of gold. He started in joy and dragged her with eager hands out of the passage and into his stall.

"I was not as clever as I thought," he confessed. "Dinarzad did not discover me, but the fat Cook saw me sneak in and swore to tell if she ever caught sight of me out of doors again. I could not decide whether to go out again—I was trying to think, trying to be brave as Sigrid on the pirate ship, to go to my Griffin no matter what. But I could not decide." He blushed, though he hated to do it.

"It doesn't matter. You are easy to find," the girl whispered, smiling with half her mouth. The two settled into the corner of the stall while the sorrel snorted and stomped softly, nuzzling at his salt lick.

"Now, the white Griffin was despondent for a long while after Giota embraced her wall," she began, her voice lilting like the sway of rushes in a summer storm. "She could not be consoled, and flew in circles around the Basilica, crowing in grief like an albatross. And this sound, though not so piercing as her mother's shrieks had once been, were carried gently on the wind to the red peaks of Nuru, and there Jin the blue Griffin heard his sister's sorrow echoing for years upon years. So when the Monopod climbed upon his back to go down into Shadukiam, Jin was glad, for the last two creatures he loved in all the world would be waiting for him under the dome of roses . . ."

THE SECOND GRIFFIN'S TALE, CONTINUED

I DID NOT KNOW MY BROTHER WAS COMING, BUT something in my lion's heart woke and began to stalk back and forth within me. Something in my eagle's heart rustled and tested the air with its wings. For days before his turquoise shape appeared, a blurry spot in the sky, I waited, though I did not know for what.

And then he came, carrying some misshapen creature on his back. We stood together before the Basilica, before the twisted roots of the high-arching door, dwarfing the parishioners who were so well trained to avoid looking at monsters while they passed in and out of the holy place. Monsters were part of the other Shadukiam, the shadow city which found its sacred space behind the church in the body of a twisted, mouthless creature. The pious Shaduki were very skilled at ignoring the other city.

The creature, which I could see was a Monopod with a rather unimpressive foot once he had extricated himself from my brother's feathers, stood awkwardly by while Jin pressed his head to mine, and we nuzzled each other in silence, stroking necks with our beaks and closing our eyes against the other's familiar scent. Unbidden, crooning, burbling cries rose from our long-separate throats. The Monopod cleared its hideous throat pointedly. Without looking at it, Jin barked:

"Go, Monopod. Bring the Yi-woman to me by midnight, and I will do your deed." His eyes stayed locked on mine, and the little man hopped away.

"Giota is not my mother anymore," I croaked, the sadness of it still able to break my throat in half. Jin only shrugged his azure shoulders.

"She never truly was, my sister. You ask so much from her."

"You haven't seen what she did to herself! Go to her and see it, see how she has beggared herself into filth and squalor! Go and ask her to tell your fortune—that's all she is now, a stupid gypsy reading the Stars for signs!"

And so we went to her together. Reunions are wearying to relate—they only matter to those reunited. The complicated embrace of two giants and a slight creature clad in her own hair is too delicate and careful to describe. We loved her; we still love her; we held her like a chick between us. She rolled her black eyes up to us, parting the hair over her belly to speak.

"I know you do not wish to hear it, but it is time—there are eggs waiting to be hatched, and my pretty blue boy will not live out the night."

Jin did not stir, but caressed Giota's cheek tenderly with a long ink-blue forefeather. I started, stricken. "I wish I had come only to see you, Quri," he whispered, "but I am here for the stump-leg, and I am meant to kill a thing tonight. Whenever you murder, you pay for it—thus do we pay for the Griffin who murdered horse and Arimaspian, and they pay for the Griffin they kill."

"Go now, into the sky," Giota rasped urgently. "If these can be called my grandchildren, so be it—but they must be born. There is no one else to quicken her." She climbed from our embrace back to her mossy wall, and turned her face from us, stroking her lips and muttering softly. Jin looked at me calmly, with shame or joy or despair I could not tell. But he rose up into the sky with a single stroke of his wings, and I followed.

How can I tell you of the mating of Griffin? We are not birds; we are not cats, but we spiral up to the bellies of the clouds as birds do, and we bite into each other's throats and shoulders as cats do. No one had told us how; no one had told us we should not. Our eyes blazed gold and black, our fur bristled and our hackles rose. We snapped at each other and growled deep in our chests; we wrestled in the air like angels. We circled each other in the blinding blue and white of heaven, and he sunk his teeth into the back of my neck, and I cried out like the sound of bells shattering, and we wept as we came together under the sun and the thousand roses of Shadukiam.

When we descended, the stars had broken the skin of the sky, and we were bloodied and bruised. The Monopod stood waiting at the great door of the church—at his side was another of his kind, a female. Its skin was pockmarked and sallow, almost translucent, like petals wilting. It leered at us, revealing tiny teeth, jagged and sharp. I sucked in my breath—it was clear that a Yi was lurking under that skin.

"Do I get the male or the breeding cat?" it hissed, grinning horribly at us.

"It was the only way," the first Monopod said pleadingly. "It would not come unless I promised it a body."

The Yi licked its cratered lips. "We have never managed a Griffin. You all fix it so that you die alone on wretched beaches and boil your blood in the desert. We are curious; what will it be like to fly with those wings?"

Jin looked at me for a moment and whispered thickly, "It is like dying."

Then his dark shoulders shifted imperceptibly. He moved so quickly I saw only a blue rush, and sunk his talon into the eye of the decaying Yi. It screamed with such violence my ears ached to burst, a terrible sound—metal grinding on metal or the squeals of pigs and rats. The eye-white around my brother's talon puddled and sagged, dribbling onto the polished courtyard like spoiled milk. Finally, there was little left but a pile of half-liquid bones, and these the Monopod gathered to his chest lovingly, weeping with thanks.

"I will bury them properly, I will say the words of the High-Growing Moss above her grave, and every year after on this day. Thank you, Jin-of-the-Red-Peak, thank you, thank you. You do not know how much you have given me." He bowed many times, bobbing ridiculously like a toy. I breathed relief; this horrible transaction was done.

And suddenly the courtyard was full of white shapes, panting like a pack of dogs and baring their teeth, yelping and snapping. I had never seen Yi, truly, only heard of them, and certainly I had never seen so many, and so many in the late days of their possession, when the bodies mirrored the surface of the moon—green-white, scarred, tight and shining like masks of bone. They had lost all semblance of the civilized demeanor they liked to affect, and stood around us howling and slavering like starving wolves. They clapped their cadaverous hands together with a gesture between menace and joy; bits of their fingers flew off the bone, thudding to the pavement like dough dropped from bakers' spoons.

Their speech was a terrible chorus of hissing and smacking of tongues, and they did not speak at once or separately, but their sentences floated from creature to creature, as though none could finish a thought without his brothers and sisters.

"How dare—"

"You touch us? You are—"

"Hated of Moon, we are her best—"

"Beloved children! We will gnaw your wing bones—"

"We will slurp the flesh—"

"From your knuckles! Half-breed mongrel—"

"You had no—"

"Right!"

Jin stepped slowly away from them, his hind paws clattering on the stone courtyard. But their slavering only increased, and a few—of shapes too strange to guess at—closed the circle behind him. The Monopod was pulling at my pelt, his great black eyes pleading.

"Come away, come away! They will never let him go now. If you run, they will not notice you."

"But his body! I cannot let them have his body—all this was for your own wretched woman and you would let it happen over again to my brother?"

"This is not a possession," he mumbled grimly. "It is a mob. They will not take his body; they will tear it into pieces. For them, to lose a single member of their tribe is like losing a leg at the knee. This is revenge, and when they are done, there will be nothing left but a few drops of blood for tomorrow's churchgoers to wipe off their shoes. I'm sorry, I'm sorry, I knew this might happen, but I had to help my Tova, I had to get her free. I promise, there is nothing you can do, even with all your strength. If you killed all of these, with their last breaths they would scream for their siblings—and they would come, from the deepest cracks and alleys of the city. There is no limit to their numbers. If you want to live to birth your chicks"—he blushed slightly and looked away, consumed, I surmised, by some tradition of propriety towards breeding females among his people—"the sky is the only safe place. Go, find some forgotten strand, and hide your young away. While the scent of my Tova is in the air, they will be frenzied, and forget you. When it has passed, they will calm again, and they will not give you the mercy of vivisection. They will take your body and your babes will be born gray and dead, their first cries mocking laughter."

I stared at the hateful little man, who had sold us to these scavenging horrors. I wanted to kill him. I wanted to put my claws through his eyes as he had begged Jin to do to that creature. It would have felt wonderful, I imagined, and his blood would be hot.

But Giota would be ashamed of me. She would turn away from me, and forget my name, and my children would never know her. She had known that Jin was near death—it must mean something, it must be more important than a mere balancing of scales after a murder.

I leaned into his face, and he did not blink. Quick as a tailor tearing her stitches, I snapped my head to one side and tore his left ear from his head and spat it onto the ground. His blood, hot as I had imagined, dripped from my beak, and I hissed through the red mess at our betrayer, before flapping my long wings—once, twice, three times, and lifting into the night.

I circled overhead, high enough to be safe from the pack of scarified Yi, who quivered with excitement and lust. There was no chance for my brother to follow my flight with his eyes, to know that I was safe before he died, a mercy that stories like ours always allow. It was not allowed to us.

I watched as they lunged forward and sank two dozen sets of diamond teeth into my Jin's flanks. He screamed, like a wind through broken glass, and kept screaming until one of the pale, bony things caught his perfect blue throat in its jaws, and he died with a wet, strangling whimper.

I watched as they ate him in the sickly light of their Moon.

The Tale of Saint Sigrid, Continued

QURI STROKED THE SAND WITH HER GLOSSY PAW.

"All my life, I never gave the Arimaspian problem any thought. How could I, when I was so busy adoring a human woman and bearing these poor eggs? I watched Jin die; I watched him become food for ghosts and wraiths whose blood was moonlight. I did not think about silly men who liked gold enough to kill an entire race for it. I came here; I laid my eggs all the autumn long in a dry patch of sand, and covered them with the fur of my body. Years passed—a Griffin's egg is a slow thing growing. Gold washed up in the waves, slowly, flecks and nuggets and slivers. It sparkled in the sand; it added to the sand. This island is half made of gold. Of course I didn't know that when I came; I only wanted a place to rest where no one would ever find me. The Boil would protect me. How could I expect that in the midst of boiling waters an island of gold would rise like a whale's fin? Slowly, I began to find it beautiful, and draw the larger pieces together to make a real nest for my chicks. Slowly, I began to see it as all Griffin before me had seen it—the color of the sun, burnished and burning, light and life and fire sparkling inside it so fiercely that it gives off a quiet heat that only we can feel. I began to love it. And still I did not think of the Arimaspians, the creatures who killed my mother, the reason we cannot hoard as much of the precious stuff as we wish, because it would draw the killers like bees to summer-honey. Until I saw a ship's mast, impossibly, on the roiling horizon, I never thought of it. Then I remembered; then I was ashamed at my naïveté. I wanted only to help my chicks break their eggs and teach them to fly; I wanted only to bring Giota under cover of night three perfect children, who would nuzzle against her neck, and press their warm heads to hers. I forgot that I am not a Griffin, I am only quarry—the last quarry."

Sigrid's eyes were full of tears, but they did not fall. She knuckled them away and fought the urge to touch the Griffin's beautiful fur, which glimmered coldly like snow over a silver statue. She just stared up at the fabulous monster, whose eagle head was silhouetted against the clouded sun. The gold of her beak flashed—and indeed, Sigrid could see answering flashes in the sand: Here and there and here again, a gold fleck gleamed among the grains.

Into her thoughts the deep drum-voice of Oluwakim burst like the flight of an arrow.

"Well. She's an abomination and a coward. I thought we'd come to find a real beast, and instead, we only find this poor heap of garbage, last bedraggled pigeon of a race of pigeons."

He shrugged, his great black muscles rippling like continents drifting in the night. His men had not moved, standing frozen as blocks of wood. In all this stillness, it would have been easy to miss the sudden rush of movement that snapped through the crowd, but Sigrid saw it: Oluwakim reached for his sleek, thin dagger and clutched it in his fist for only a moment before throwing it, almost casually, between Sigrid's arm and her ribs, directly at the heart of the White Griffin.

And as soon as the knife had left his hand, a second knife buried itself deep in his back, so that the dying cry of the King sounded in harmony beneath the last keening of the White Beast. Both bodies slumped forward and spilled the blackest blood of their hearts into the golden sand.

Sigrid cried out, and even in her mourning, she searched for the source of the second knife. Her eyes darted over the wretched beach, scouring it for an assassin. Finally, she seized upon black-haired Tomomo, who leaned casually against a skinny, starved palm tree, one muscled leg crossed over the other.

Standing next to her was a woman who might have been the twin of the dead King. Her hair was as long, and as braided with glowering gold. Her skin was as burnished black, the color of shadows within shadows. And where the King's golden eye had been, she carried an eye of beryl, green and blue, shot through with white. At her waist were at least a dozen knives, all of gold, hanging still as bells without clappers.

As Sigrid stared in wonder, Tomomo took the dark woman's hand in hers and kissed it in a genteel fashion. The two women smiled at each other, and the stranger took her hand from the captain, striding towards the corpse of Oluwakim with a grim face, her lips so tight that the thinnest thread could not pass between them. She stood over the body for a moment, her breathing harsh and ragged. Then, in one savage movement, she braced her sandaled foot against the King's massive shoulder and ripped the golden eye from his skull. The Arimaspians howled their outrage, but at a glance from the woman, they fell silent. Solemnly, she removed the beryl eye from its socket and replaced it with the golden one. The blood of the King dripped from the eye like tears.

"Tommy!" Sigrid cried, her limbs so frozen in shock and grief that she had not even left the great nest. "What is happening? What have you done?"

The captain left her tree and joined the other woman at the corpse of the King. She knelt and examined the body, plucking a few choice pieces of gold from his hair.

"Sigrid, this is what piracy is," she said ruefully, never looking up from the corpse, which she still combed for treasure. "Oluwakim gave us a great deal of money to chase down the poor Griffin. Oluwafunmike gave us more. We hid her away in the hold—not difficult. The *Maidenhead* is quite as remarkable belowdecks as she is above, as you've seen. She hoped, I think, that her father would only take an egg, and not kill the Griffin. It is sad that trust in one's parents is so often misplaced. But it is not our place to take sides in dynastic squabbles, even"—she raised her eyes to meet Oluwafunmike's, her gaze full of affection—"if one side clearly has the lion's share of virtue."

The princess scowled at her father's corpse and retrieved her knife. "Our people can no longer allow our entire race to be exalted by the murder of the Griffin. I take the Ocular now, and begin a new dynasty. This eye, this last of all eyes, will be passed from heir to heir, and never again will we rip our gold from the breasts of innocent beasts. The end to this sad circus was worth whatever I had to pay Tomomo—and worth bearing the presence of pirates." She jostled the captain's shoulder with a large and comradely fist.

"But this is who we are, daughter of the Oluwa," one of the Arimaspians protested. "Without the Griffin hunt, we are but nomads on the sea of the steppes. You will destroy our spirit! The Eye blessed *us*!"

"Can you not see? The Griffin are all dead. There is no hunt, whether I declare it or not. But if you would argue with me, or challenge my Ocular, you will find yourself as dead and rotting as my father. If I do not fear to sink my knife in his back, please believe I will not hesitate to bury it in yours." The man fell into sullen silence, and Oluwafunmike shook her head in sorrow. "They are all dead, son of the Ofira. Dead and cold as winter in the great desert. The Eye blessed us, yes, but we have not been worthy of its Gaze."

As if to answer her, a cascade of sound echoed suddenly over the beach. A quick, rustling noise could be heard, and it deepened into a cracking, clawing cacophony, like wood splintering under a silver axe. Tomomo and the princess started like pheasants in an autumn field, trying to discern the source. The Arimaspians looked suddenly ashen and fearful, as though they expected the ghost of their King to appear and punish them for submitting to his daughter. But Sigrid understood immediately: The eggs beneath her, still nestled in the golden nest, were hatching, and all at once, first of all the things which should not have been. Their marbled blue and white surfaces fractured like sapphire bones, and the last of the glittering golden yolk dribbled out.

Out of the cerulean ruins of the eggshells rose shakily three infant Griffin—two so deeply blue they were almost black, and one whose feathers shone whiter than the first snow in the first winter of the world. They were the size of wildcats, and power already rippled beneath their colored skins. They shook themselves like pigeons, spattering Sigrid's face with shimmering yolk droplets. There was no sound on the windswept beach, no sound but the wind battering the shoulders of a dozen people, none of whom dared to move or speak. The silence was unbroken, untouched, a block of obsidian.

Then the keening began. The newborn Griffin turned their delicate heads to the brooding sky and shrieked, their throats ululating with a terrible cry, like claws rending a mirror into ribbons. None could bear the sound—the Arimaspian horde fell weeping to the sand, scratching at their aching ears. Sigrid alone was not afraid, and the sound which to the others, even Tomomo and her princess, was a horror, was to her the simple and beautiful sound of birds singing up the sun. She crawled to the howling children and tentatively put out her arms to them. They quieted immediately and curled themselves into her small brown hands, snuffling at her to catch her scent, and still weeping softly.

It was then that Sigrid saw it, and her mouth hung open like a broken door in dismay and wonder.

The Griffin were deformed, misshapen. The larger of the two blue lionbirds had no eyes where they ought to shine—they blinked instead from his downy chest. The chest of the smaller creature bore two tiny holes: the ears of an eagle. And the white had no beak. Sigrid gently touched the pale bird's breast, in which a human mouth opened and closed weakly, its pink lips shining with golden tears.

"What's wrong with them?" Oluwafunmike asked, creeping forward to study the bizarre arrangement of their features. Tomomo inched tentatively forward beside her friend.

Sigrid shook her head softly, and for a moment, she seemed almost an Arimaspian, so coated was her long hair in golden yolk. She spoke in hushed tones, almost in the tenor of a prayer. "They are the Sorella. The new Sorella. Don't you see? When Giota carried the Griffin within her, she must have passed her sisters, and some sliver of herself, into the White Beast. And now the last Griffin are bound to the last Sorella—and Griffin are bound to humans."

The birds mewled helplessly and climbed into Sigrid's lap. The blue siblings began to pick at her vest, pulling at the rough stitches with their beaks. They tore at the cloth eagerly, in a fury, and soon Sigrid was left in the dead Griffin's nest with no more to hide her nakedness than the leather wrappings she had used to bind her breasts. She began to cry in shame, tears trickling down her sand-spattered face, trying to cover her deformity with her thin arms. But the Griffin were not satisfied. The white infant pushed her head under Sigrid's arms—patiently, without violence—and severed the leather straps with a single pass of her glittering talon.

Sigrid suppressed a wracking sob; her three breasts were suddenly exposed, and all the unfortunate spectators of the Griffin's beach were witness to her freakish body. There was nowhere she could look where she did not meet the eyes of a near-stranger gawking at her bare flesh. She pulled at the ruined wrappings uselessly. Yet even then, she was not afraid of the clustered birds. They pressed nearer to her, cooing affectionately, even purring with pleasure. Her breasts were suddenly heavy, and she could feel the skin which had never seen the sun stretch and tighten strangely.

The white Griffin laid itself against her and nuzzled her ear, clucking and chirruping gently. She wrapped her long neck around Sigrid's, and with infinite gentleness, her human mouth opened to suckle at the rightmost breast. Her blue brothers hungrily followed suit, fastening their beaks onto the second and third breasts. They were too rough at first, unused to human women, and bit her tender skin with their greedy beaks.

Sigrid put her arms around the three infants in awe, her tears flowing like streams from hidden mountains, falling to mingle with the blood the starving beasts had drawn, and finally with the milk which rushed freely from her body to feed the last of all Griffin.

Quietly, like a clock beginning to chime, Saint Sigrid of the Nest began to laugh.

The Net-Weaver's Tale, Continued

"THAT WAS THE FIRST MIRACLE OF SAINT SIGRID," the great bald woman said as the last red rays of the sun faded like drying blood into the horizon. The light seemed to slide along her tattoos and puddle on her broad face. "The others you will learn as you ascend the Tower—the Miracle of the Beard, the Miracle of the Waterless Sea, the Miracle of the Sacking of Amberabad."

"What?" I cried. "How can you tell me only part of a story? Did Sigrid stay to mother the Griffin or return to the ship with Long-Eared Tomomo and live her life as a pirate? Did Oluwafumike keep the Ocular? Was there war? Did the Griffin survive? I have heard they are extinct—are they not? Are they hidden in some aerie no man has seen?"

"Stories," the green-eyed Sigrid said, unperturbed, "are like prayers. It does not matter when you begin, or when you end, only that you bend a knee and say the words. And when we tell Saint Sigrid's story, we open ourselves to her—we cannot close ourselves, even if the story must continue on another day. Each miracle of the Saint is guarded by the women on one floor of the Tower. Should you choose to study with us, you will ascend physically as you become enlightened by the example of Sigrid." The great woman rose then and snuffed out the lantern at the door of the Tower.

"At least tell me how she died. Was it a very heroic death? Did she die saving the Griffin, or her shipmates? Surely a woman's death is a thing which all may know."

The Sigrid laughed. "A woman's death is the most precious thing she owns. But I will tell you, if you have decided that our Tower is to be your home and your mother for all your days."

"I have," I answered breathlessly. Surely these women who possessed such tales were the strongest and wisest of all possible women.

"Saint Sigrid of the Nest disappeared in her fiftieth year. Tomomo, though an excellent Captain, was not indefatigable. She eventually retired and passed the helm of her ship to Sigrid, her most beloved monster. Yet, some years hence, the *Maidenhead* was lost at sea, devoured by the Echeneis, a sea monster whose sheer size beggars the mind. It is said that whole cities could fit within its belly, and that its hide is like the shell of a turtle, impervious to all spears. It is the color of the sea itself, so that a ship may be swallowed before her captain is even alerted to the presence of the beast, though its girth mocks even the Griffin. This is the thing that swallowed the Saint of the Boiling Sea. All hands were lost."

I stood in the blue twilight, aghast. How could such a woman as Sigrid not have died crossing swords or defending the innocent?

I was very young.

The Sigrid rubbed her bald head thoughtfully, frowning at me, as if struggling with a secret. "Some in the Tower believe in a prophecy we refer to as the Heresy of the Lost. It is said by these women that Sigrid is not dead, but only lost, adrift within the cavernous belly of the Echeneis-whale, and that she lives still." She coughed, clearly thinking this particular tale nonsense not fit for the ears of novices. "They fasten their hopes to a fragment of an ancient song which was passed from mother to child in the north of the world, where the *Maidenhead* was lost."

She closed her eyes and sang softly:

> *O, sing of the ship with the mast of leaves*
> *And the maiden who stood at her wheel!*
> *Long ago, it is said, she was drowned until dead*
> *And her red ship was split at the keel!*
>
> *But she never went under, the old mothers know*
> *And she'll sail the brine another day*
> *An orphan will find her, a bear-cub will bind her*
> *And the wolf will lead them astray.*
>
> *And hand in hand they'll come whistling home*
> *The maiden, the bear, and the girl in gray*
> *Through the shining white foam,*
> *The red ship will roam*
> *And the wolf shall lead them astray.*
> *And the wolf will lead her astray.*

The Sigrid's voice was rough and low, like an oar pulling through dark water. When she opened her eyes, there seemed to be an odd light glimmering there, gentle and sad. I understood then that this Sigrid was a secret heretic, and I smiled to myself. But then, too, I began to believe the heresy, and worse, I began to believe that I was the one destined to find her—did not *The Book of Carrion* contain the same lines, and did not the dog-men whisper them as though they must refer to me?

Nothing in my life has birthed more pain than the faith I conceived in that moment.

There was no light left, then, and the Sigrid was silently replaced by another woman, as slender as she was muscular, but equally bald. The guard thus changed, the spice-skinned Sigrid took my hand in her huge palm, and I entered the Tower of St. Sigrid for the first time.

I did not leave it again for seven years.

The
Pale Girl's Tale,
Continued

"AND THAT IS ALL I CAN TELL YOU OF MY FIRST
years in Al-a-Nur," Sigrid said, fingering dark patterns on
the tavern table where decades of mugs had left their
marks. "The rest is secret, the province of the Sigrids, and
I could no more tell an uninitiated soul of the joys I suffered and the terrors I adored within those walls than I
could tell a deaf woman how the sea sounds before a
storm. I was accepted into the Sainthood—I received a
name. We are all Sigrids, but we have our own titles. The
Saint who is the Mother of us all is Saint Sigrid of the
Nest. The woman who told me that tale on the steps of

the Tower was Saint Sigrid of the Shallow Keel. I am Saint Sigrid of the Ways."

"Wait!" cried Snow. "That cannot be the end of the story! What about the Black Papess? How did you leave the city? Did you truly not see Bagdemagus for seven years? How can you stop a tale when so much of it remains, a meal half-eaten?" She was almost out of her chair with excitement—Snow had never known so many words laid next to each other at once, and all laid out for her. Sigrid laughed her languid, rough-hewn laugh.

"No, no, you're right. How impolite of me—there is a bit more to tell. But when I speak of the Mother and the Mast, I tend to drown in her story until I forget all the others. It is the way of religion. But Eyvind must fill up our cups again, and give us a plate of sweet bread and blackberry jam to strengthen the tale. I am not a small woman, and the stringing of stories like pearls on fishing line is not a task for the faint of belly."

Eyvind appeared more gracefully and with less commotion than Snow would have thought possible for a man of his size, and furnished them with fresh food and drink. To her surprise, he then dragged a heavy chair to the table and sat down himself to hear Sigrid speak, fixing her with his tired, drooping eyes. She seemed suddenly discomfited, like a bear caught scooping honey from a hive. But she drank deeply and swallowed a few mouthfuls of bread, and, eyes darting like fireflies between Eyvind and Snow, began again.

"It is the custom for novices, once their hair is shorn, not to leave the Tower for a full seven years. When they step outside it for the first time, it is not onto the soft grass but onto the deck of a small boat, and the acolyte then spends a circuit of seasons plying the river with her craft, never walking on dry land. Only after this is she allowed to venture into the Dreaming City itself. But I was not in seclusion for more than a few months when Bags begged an exception for me. I was not allowed to cross the threshold of the Tower, but he came to the gate, and I sat within it, my skull newly bare, and we talked, like old friends in need of succor. For the Black Papess had entered the Gates of Al-a-Nur . . ."

THE
NET-WEAVER'S
TALE, CONTINUED

"I SUPPOSE IT'S SIGRID NOW, IS IT?" BAGS ASKED, scratching his great furry ear.

I sat, legs crossed serenely, determined to act every inch the devout novice. "Of course," I intoned, as sagely as I could manage.

Bags smiled at me, his grin all teeth and silky muzzle. He leaned over the threshold and whispered huskily: "I've always thought it was a beautiful name."

I giggled, and held out my arms to be embraced over the awkward liminal law of the door I could not exit and he could not enter. He clapped me on the back several times and rubbed my shorn head gently where all my lovely hair had once been.

"And the sea-dog look suits you!"

"Oh, Bags, I've missed you!"

"No fear, lass, we've all missed you. We'd have looked after you in our own Tower, but we are glad for you here—sometimes a woman needs to be with her own. But I haven't come to tell you how pretty you look or dote on you like an old wolf nosing one of his favorite pups! Great things are afoot in the City, things you couldn't know about, cloistered away in your sail-slung Tower. I came to tell you how things fared with the Papess!"

"*Fared?* I've missed the battle?" I was furious, of course.

"In a manner of speaking." Bags nodded, suppressing a giggle himself. "But don't worry yourself, little whelp—I've come to tell you of the great contest, the great duel that Yashna fought with Ragnhild in the center of the City."

I remembered myself then, and took a step backward into the familiar shadows of my Tower. "But why should I know these things, Bags, when the other girls are at their studies and not called to the door like a princess to meet her suitor? If I am to know it, oughtn't I to wait until the Saints tell me in their own way, in their own time?" I dropped my voice to a whisper. "I'm a good girl; I don't want them to think I'm not."

Bags's brown eyes glittered. "You are a good girl, my young Sigrid. I would never doubt it. I have spoken to Shallow Keel and you are mine for the afternoon. And as for your right to know above all the other girls—if you were a worse student, you would likely know already, for the story has spread through the Towers like fire through a village of thatched roofs. But you earn the right to hear it firsthand because you came to the City with us, on the wings of our terrible errand. You are already part of this story—and you will be a part of its ending, before long."

Bags settled himself into the corner of the door frame and took my hands in his. He nuzzled my face a little with his sleek snout and growled slightly with the pleasure of a father who sees his litter grown, hunting swift and strong.

"Just listen, love, for I have a tale to tell which will be repeated in the alleys of Al-a-Nur as long as there are Towers to shadow the streets . . ."

The
Tale of the
Game

OF COURSE WE KNEW SHE WOULD COME, SOONER OR
later. We knew she would come leading all the hordes of
Shadukiam, all the horrors the Rose Dome could produce.
She did not disappoint us, and came riding a great black
antelope, whose slender legs were hooved in fire, and
whose baleful eyes seemed to look in all directions at
once. Behind her came her legions, Djinn with beards of
smoke and spells in their saddlebags, Monopods drafted
out of their ghettoes, their feet armored and bristling with
iron spikes, Centaurs and archers with a dozen arms, even
a few Manticore bred in who knows what foul cage. And
the humans screaming their war cries like frenzied ravens,

all those men with swords flashing, drunk on hatred of the Golden City, and adoration of the pale-haired Papess.

But she did not bring her damned army through the silver spires of the Salmon Gate. She bade them halt in the green fields outside the ringed Towers, and they halted. They quieted their cries and laid themselves out on the clover as though they had come to a country picnic—so completely were they in her power.

And Ragnhild, First and Second of her Name, the Black Papess of Shadukiam, entered the Holy City alone, without even a knife at her belt. She entered it like a postulant, with nothing but her torn dress fluttering in the wind, and her pale hair streaming behind her like a battle standard.

And alone she walked to the center of the City, to the Tower of the Papess, and no one dared to stop her, but all who could lay down their duties followed in her wake like a wave of flesh. Slowly, and without a sound, she seemed to glide over the blue-pebbled streets to the plain Tower with its deer-skin-slung windows, and strode through the door as if no one could contest her right to do so—as if it were her own house.

We were closeted with Yashna, in conference as we so often are these days. My brothers and I immediately growled; our hackles rose, ready to defend our Papess from whatever dank, filthy magic Ragnhild had brought with her into that sacred place. But the Apostate, her face as fair and terrible as it had been in the depths of our dreams, raised up her hands in a gesture of amity.

"Peace, my children! I have not come to fight with you, or to molest your poor Yashna. Smooth your venerable furs, and cool the blood in your veins. I have come on an errand of friendship. And we have seen, brave dogs, that you have no power over me. So I will say it again: Calm yourselves."

Yashna said nothing, but smiled imperceptibly, like a leaf rustling in a faint autumn wind. Bartholomew snarled in her stead: "An errand of friendship? With that band of creatures at your back?"

Ragnhild smiled coolly. "I have brought them for my own defense. Surely you do not expect me to breach the Gates of Al-a-Nur with nothing but my own skin to protect me against the Draghi. I know too well the fate of innocent maids when the ire of the Towers is raised." She lifted her delicate wrists and shook the golden manacles that still hung there like a dancer's bracelets. The high, thin sound echoed in the chamber.

Balthazar's fiery eyes narrowed into slits. "She cannot be trusted, Mother. You must call on the Draghi now, before she has unleashed whatever magic she is hiding."

Ragnhild laughed, a sound like glass breaking, or ice shattering over a running river. "Surely you do not think I could hide much in this, dear wolf," she said, gesturing to the wide tears in her violet gown. "But enough—I did not come to speak with those I have already welcomed in my own hall. I came to treat with my sister, and put all this misunderstanding behind us."

Yashna stirred in her chair and peered out at the Black Papess, whose smile seemed to glow with forgiveness and kindness.

"Very well, my child. Speak with me," she said, her voice steady and deep.

"The Caliph has declared me the rightful Papess, not once, but twice. He has declared Al-a-Nur a territory of the Caliphate and demands tribute. You cannot refuse these things—even a City of Heaven must bow to the Laws of Earth. Indeed, I was anointed long before you, sweet lady, in the days when Cveti performed her heresy. By rights this City is mine. I will take it by force, if I must, but I do not wish to. Abdicate in my favor and I will allow you to go into seclusion in the Tower of the Dead, your home. All will be peaceful, and the City will go on as it always has. Surely you must see how greatly I have been wronged by Al-a-Nur, and understand that I am not a wicked woman—I only ask for what is mine by the hand of the Caliph and the hand of Heaven."

Yashna rose from her seat, her yellow robes sighing behind her, and put out her hands to Ragnhild, taking those slim white forearms in her own withered brown palms.

"No one would deny that in your youth and innocence, you were wronged terribly, not only by Ghyfran, but by the Caliph himself. We know your sad tale, and we grieve for the gentle and bright-hearted girl you once were. If we could restore your life to you, please believe that we would do so, without a moment's hesitation. But it is not in our power—it would not even have been in our power to restore what strange and alien life you have taken for yourself in this body." Yashna paused, her eyes as full of pity as a well with water after a storm. "But you cannot believe I will simply hand this City to you. You know, in that stranger's heart, that what you ask is wrong. The child who came to Shadukiam innocent of the schemes around her is still within you, and she knows I will not give you what you want."

Ragnhild continued to smile in her bright, cold way, and her hands tightened on Yashna's arms. "Then I will burn it to the ground, and let my Centaurs piss on your altars and spill their wine over every holy text in this clutch of hovels. And when I have finished, the Caliph will send his men to rape your nuns and count out every stone of this carrion-town for the Treasury." Her smile deepened and grew even sweeter. Yashna's expression did not change.

"The Caliph cannot and will not touch us. Why do you think he has set up little girls in his bank vaults instead of assaulting us directly? Why has he never marched an army to the brink of our borders? He knows the Draghi are very charming and debonair, but they are decadent, and they are not a tenth of our power. The heavens themselves will crack and spill their mortar onto the heads of any soldier who dares touch the flesh of a priestess of this City. You will find the same if your monsters broach the Gate. Please believe that I do not lie to you—I am of the Dead, and the Dead have no need of fiction. You think we are at an impasse, and that to avoid bloodshed, I will surrender to your smile, or your kiss." Yashna released the Apostate's arms, her dark eyes flashing suddenly like iron striking stone. "We are *not* at an impasse, and the Dead care nothing for whether the blood of the living is spilled. Bring your army within the Salmon Gate, and I swear to you by the Seven Corpses of Heaven, not a shred of their skin will be left when the moon rises."

Ragnhild's smile faltered slightly; her eyes seemed to shiver within themselves, and for a moment, for only a moment, I could see the creature she must have been before the Caliph had her, and I pitied her, may the Bough bend in forgiveness. But it was a moment soon past, and the seraphic smile had returned, harder and brighter than ever.

"You cannot frighten me with the oaths of the Dead, old woman. I am dead—I am a wraith on the earth. I have crossed into shadow while you and your priests sit playing with toy gravestones in your Tower. Do not speak of what you do not know."

Yashna's gentle gaze returned, like spring returning to a thicket of pine boughs. "Stop, my daughter. You do not need to brag to me of your putrefaction—I believe you. But I have a solution, if you will hear it. In recognition of Ghyfran's mutilation of your first body, I will extend to you a single chance to take the Papacy in truth."

Ragnhild leaned forward eagerly, scenting her victory.

"You wish to rule the Dreaming City; you must excel in all its ways. Play with me, a single game of Lo Shen. If you best me, I will go into seclusion as you ask, and you will ascend to the Tower without the slightest argument, and without battle. No one will contest you, and you will rule as well as you are able. If you lose, however, you must disband your army, and take the vows of one of our Towers, enter it as a novice, and pledge yourself to our City for the rest of your days. In the Anointed City, this is the way disputes are settled. If you would rule us, you must behave as one of us. Show me that you are the rightful Papess. Show me that you exceed us in all things."

Ragnhild seemed to laugh, but no sound issued from her rosy mouth. Her eyes glittered like snowflakes catching the sun. "You cannot be serious. A single game to decide five hundred years of history?"

"Were it not that once my predecessor harmed you, I would simply kill you where you stand."

Ragnhild was silent for a long time, studying her opposite number. There was no sound but breathing in the Tower, the shallow, quick sighs of all of us waiting to learn what would become of this infant war. Finally, Ragnhild seemed to come to a decision, and leaned forward, her shimmering hair brushing Yashna's wrist. She cupped the older woman's face in her hand, almost as a sister might, comforting her sibling with a touch. She tilted her head and pressed her lips to Yashna's dry mouth, kissing her deeply, passing all of her murky magic through her lips and into the body of the ancient Papess.

When the kiss was ended, Yashna remained as she was, her smile, perhaps, a little sadder and a little more rueful than before.

"We are both creatures of the Dead, my dear. Let us not try to befuddle each other with these cheap glamours. It does not become us. Play my game, as I have now played yours, or go back to your army and see if the prancing Draghi are the worst we can muster to keep an infidel from our halls."

I thought for a moment that Ragnhild would cry. I cannot think why I would imagine that haughty face could break into tears, but I did.

"I will play," Ragnhild said quietly, with great dignity—the dignity, one might say, of a Papess. Yashna took her arm in a grandmotherly gesture and led her into the courtyard outside the Tower, and my brothers and I carried the vast ceremonial board into the sunlight, where the nuns and monks, priestesses and oracles, brothers and sisters, gathered to watch the greatest game in the history of Al-a-Nur.

How can I describe for you the spooling thread of a single game of Lo Shen, let alone the greatest game played in the annals of the Spheres? Should I tell you that the throng was hushed as grasses on a still summer day? How the Merchants and the Oracles and the Patricides gathered close in, how the Living and the Dead peered over their shoulders for one glimpse of the Apostate taking her place at the Board? That the light seemed to fall into Ragnhild's hair and pool there, so that her head was ablaze in a halo of light? That Yashna was ever Yashna, calm, quiet as the reflection of a star, her head solemn and gray, and never aflame? That the whole thing looked like a painting, and not like anything that was actually happening before us? Or shall I orate upon the nature of the game, its perfect complexity, the slide of stone pieces on a round stone board? What came first, the City or the Game? Surely it must have been the Game; how else could the Towers and roads be arranged in the patterns of the thousand combinations of Lo Shen? Yet the Game contains pieces called Pagoda-Towers, and Draghi, and Papesses, and Gods.

If the City came first, perhaps the Game is no more than a dumb imitation of Al-a-Nur in all its sapphire-paved glory. But if the Game existed in the shadowy years before the light of the Dreaming Towers, then perhaps there is some secret locked within its moves, some prophecy which would tell us, could we but read its meaning, the fate of all these roofs and doors. Perhaps the Papesses were made to defeat each other within the Game because one day there would be two Papesses to face each other in the City. Perhaps all our lifetimes of study of the Game were meant to culminate on that morning, in the sunlight thin as bones.

I do not know, little Sigrid, if they have begun to teach you the many formations of Lo Shen yet. If not, they will soon. We spend half our lives in study of this game; all our internecine disputes are solved with it—for the object is to topple the God of the opposing player: the single piece that rests at the center of the board, nestled within thirteen concentric Spheres, unable to move unless it is to defeat its opposite number. It is poetic, and it is political.

And so it came to pass that two women sat, quiet as nuns, at a great blue board the size of a giant's shield. Their hands flashed over the pieces like crow's wings waving, pale Triremes and dark Pagodas rising and falling, ranks of Draghi eradicated in a blow. Intricate combinations arose like glass webs, the Papesses as perfectly matched to each other as sisters: *Chang-O* and *T'ien Fei*, *Pa Na* and *P'an Niang*. For a long while, no one could see a clear advantage, the pieces merely circled the board like autumn leaves caught in a whirlpool. Ragnhild's hair curled around her hips as a cat's tail may around its haunches, and her soft smile never faltered, even as Yashna's exquisitely executed *Mang-Chin-I* combination swept her third Papess from the board.

I watched the sun move over their bent heads, cutting its path through the sky. The struggle for the city passed without a word, between grandmother and grandchild, and neither I, nor my brothers, nor the ranks of

Draghi with their silver helmets flashing, could affect a single slide of a Pagoda from Sphere to Sphere.

It drove us mad, of course, standing still at the sidelines. In the silence, my fur bristled as though it had been set aflame. But we are all of us, no matter what our Towers, accustomed to standing by while our mistresses perform their magic.

Finally, Yashna brought her Trireme forward in a quick slashing diagonal—just in the way a ship slips between the gusts of wind to stay on course. A ripple of caught breath swept through the crowd. The glistening piece, carved out of dark blue stone in the shape of a ship at full sail, completed her move: *Shun I Fu-Jen*. All four of her Papesses stood around the center Sphere, with a Pagoda-Tower, slim and gleaming, one ring behind them. It is an inescapable pattern, and Ragnhild's sea-colored eyes flickered in anger, seeing what we all did: that her God was trapped, and there was no move she could make to save it.

"*Sheng Mu*, my daughter. I have slain your God."

Yashna smiled in her way, a mother's smile which at once glows with pride in her child's performance and softens in regret at their shortcomings. She then stretched out her arm over the embattled Board and plucked the Apostate's God from the center Sphere. Holding the ends of the featureless blue column, pale as water in sunlight, in either hand, she bowed in the ritual fashion as she broke the piece in half. It takes great strength to end a Game in the old way, the way of the first Nurians, whose honor and shame were measured by the number of broken Gods their altars held.

Ragnhild, to her credit, took the severed pieces and bowed in her turn. Her face held no expression, but her cheeks burned, in rage, or in humiliation. I could not tell, for myself. She held her God at her side, fist tightening around the pieces until blood began to drip, thick and viscous, from her palm.

THE
NET-WEAVER'S
TALE, CONTINUED

BAGS STOPPED AND STRETCHED IN THE SUN, STROK-
ing his silky muzzle with strong hands. The snow of my
Tower swirled lazily around him, unaffected by the warm
sunlight.

"Is the army still at the Gate?" I asked breathlessly.

He just smiled toothily. "I can't say I understand her,
you know. My brothers and I, with a company of Draghi,
took her to the Gate, and the great army stood there, black
and red flags snapping in the wind. I thought she would
order them to flatten the City. I thought she would try to
kiss us again and madden us into joining her. I thought
she would conjure some terrible fiend and blow through

the blue streets of Al-a-Nur like a fiery wind. Where in women like her is the capacity to abide by an oath? But she did none of these things. She stared at her vast horde with no tear in her gray eyes. Slowly, she unlatched the golden manacles from her wrists and threw them to the dry earth. Her skin was red where they had chafed and rubbed her raw. She held out a white palm for a moment, and the air over it crackled silver and white, like a burning snowflake. Turning her hand over, the crackle of air shot down to the manacles, and they vanished, leaving nothing, not even dust."

The Cynocephalus shook his head, as if unable to believe what he was describing.

"The moment those chains disappeared, the whole army shimmered and disappeared right alongside them. In their place were a few starving lizards, feral cats, and one horse so old and mistreated that its ribs bowed like the bands of wine cask. The spectacle was nothing more than glamours and mirages. Ragnhild's jaw clenched.

" 'It is one thing,' she whispered, her rage barely suppressed, 'to command love and loyalty under the Rose Dome, where gold and beauty may buy any heart. It is another to bring them across the plains and pit them against a city they are certain is full of witches and messiahs—another to lead them in the body of a dead girl, to lead them when they knew I had stolen it, when they thought me a Yi, to be feared, but never one for whom they would risk death. They would not even risk dying in my presence, in terror that I would seize their corpses. They would not come.' She sank to her knees, and pulled at the ragged shreds of her gown. 'What was I to do? Five hundred years, and they would not come. I had to try, didn't I? For the child I was before all this, I had to try.' "

I sat back, stunned. All this had gone on while I was ensconced in prayer and study, with no notion of anything but icons of Saint Sigrid and nautical illuminations. Not for the first time, I burned to have done with contemplation, and witness those great deeds—the Game, the army, the fall of the Black Papess—for myself.

I was never a very good student.

But as I was rebelling against my Tower in my heart, a great commotion arose in the distance. A cluster of folk were moving up the path toward the Tower of St. Sigrid, kicking up dust like a ship leaving a white wake behind it.

In the center of the throng was a woman with hair of pale gold that lay over her brow like a crown, and she wore a deep violet dress.

My voice caught in my throat, and I stood, knees quivering, to greet them as they arrived. The Black Papess, Papess no more, wore a new set of manacles, plain iron, dull and gray. Her head was bent, in anger or shame I could not tell.

"She was given a choice, as you were, and she chose the Sigrids," Bags said, reaching across the threshold to touch my hair lightly. "If nothing else, she takes with grace the punishment the seed-scattered earth deals her. You must take her in."

"No! I . . . I can't! I'm only a novice. I cannot accept a new Sigrid!"

"Even a novice knows that she who guards the door is charged with the initiation of any postulant who appears on her watch. It is your duty, now."

Ragnhild raised her eyes to me, and I am not ashamed to say that I had never seen anything so beautiful as her silver gaze, the depth of feeling and sorrow and suppressed fury in her cool eyes. They searched me with a strange longing. When she spoke, the words were rote, taught to her by her captors, dead and empty, and forced. But her voice was rough, like silk torn by sharp diamonds, and I believed, truly, that she wanted nothing more than to disappear into the Tower and never emerge again.

"Please, Saint Sigrid, take me in from the storm and teach me to steer through darkness, for I am lost, and I cannot see the shore."

I did not move for a long moment. Then, slowly, I reached out my hand to her and whispered, "Come, Lady, I will cut your hair for you."

Her hand slipped into mine, hard and cool.

The
Pale Girl's Tale,
Continued

SIGRID SEEMED ENGROSSED IN PICKING THE DIRT
and bits of rope from under her fingernails. She stared at
them intently, avoiding Snow's pale eyes.

"And that, little love, is where I cease to be the hero of
my own tale. Seven years went by, and then my year on the
river currents. My time was not so very different from any
other Saint—I read, I prayed, I studied sky maps and sea
maps; I illuminated countless manuscripts with tiny
golden Griffin and their infants. My hair grew back; I did
not cut it, as many of the others did. They wished to be
humble before the Stars and their servant Saint Sigrid. I
believed that I was blessed, chosen. I believed"—the great

woman paused and grimaced, closing her eyes as if her mouth was flooded with bile—"I believed that I was the orphan of the prophecy—for I was alone in the world, was I not? My mother was alive when I left her, but perhaps by now she had died and her body was lying cold on a slab of ice in the Temple, tended by my sisters. This was my reasoning, my folly. I was more eager to believe my own mother dead than that I was not spoken of in some old ballad. I let my hair grow long, for I knew that the wolves had led me astray, and my destiny was to find the lost *Maidenhead* and her captain."

In one swallow, Eyvind drained the last of his mug and grunted softly, mockingly. Sigrid smiled ruefully.

"As soon as I was able, I left the Tower and the Dreaming City, and took to the sea in my little ship—for the last task of a Sigrid is to build a ship with her own hands, to perfect its lines and sails, and prove that it is seaworthy. On the day of my trials my craft performed beautifully, but instead of returning to receive my marks, I simply sailed away into the horizon. For years upon years I searched for any sign of the Echeneis, any tale of its passing. I scoured every sailor's haunt and foul-smelling tavern for someone who could tell me where this creature swam. How could something so vast hide itself from me? I found nothing. Not even a whisper of such a beast. Most had never even heard the word. Finally, I was forced to admit that perhaps I had been mistaken, that my mother lived, or that I simply was not the woman of the prophecy. And when this truth settled in me like a stone sinking to the bottom of a well, I died. I died to the world. I was despondent, and in my grief I sailed into a storm that my poor ship could not survive. It was dashed to pieces, and I was dragged from the sea by a Muireanner's fishing boat, seaweed clogging my mouth and my lips gone blue as sapphires. The fisherman rubbed life back into my limbs and cleared the ropy leaves from my mouth, and fed me a thin broth until I could stand on my own. Muireann is far to the north, the last part of the world graced by Saint Sigrid's ship and her crew. It seemed a good enough place to waste the last of my days."

Sigrid looked up at Eyvind, a strange cloud passing over her broad features.

"There were other reasons to stay. Things lying in the secret corners of this town I thought were long dead. But in my failure, in my shame and my hubris, I could not seek them out. Instead, I tied the knots of men's nets on the docks, and drank myself into dreams until I could forget that once I imagined myself a child of destiny, a heroine meant for the greatest task any Sigrid could wish for herself."

Snow thought she could see tears well up in Sigrid's tired eyes, but she could not be sure. She put her hesitant hand on the older woman's fingers, warm and brown beneath her icy palm.

"When my parents died," Snow said quietly, "and my hair went silver overnight, I thought it was a sign. A sign from the Stars that I was their special daughter, that they would be my mother and father. I thought I was meant for something more. But I do not even have nets to mend every day. I scrape in the street for a bit of fish and bread, I starve in the belly of a half-built ship most nights. It is not a grand destiny, but at least it is mine. And without it, I would not have known a real, living Saint." Snow touched her long, shimmering hair, in awe of it as she ever was, and as ashamed.

"I'm afraid I am a poor kind of Saint for you, my girl. Maybe the worst kind—"

Her words were cut off by a loud bang—the door of the Arm slamming open as a riotous group of three bizarre creatures burst into the common room, laughing raucously, like a pack of raccoons squabbling over a rubbish heap. Two enormous men, their muscles knotting under tattooed skin—not an inch of flesh showed which was not covered in colorful illustrations of battles at sea, mermaids with their arms trailing kelp, snarling tigers, lighthouses with beacons alight—carried between them a massive wooden tub filled to the brim with sloshing water. It spilled over the side onto the floor every time the men moved, and by the time they reached the bar, half the floor was swimming in brine.

In the tub was a woman with green gills opening at her throat, an inferno of green hair blazing around her head, and skin that held the sickly pallor of a fish. Her meaty hands were webbed as a frog's, her ears long and thin, like tiny fins. She was naked, and her ample breasts sagged heavily, tipped in blue nipples. From the waist down, her legs merged into a long, corpulent tail, silver-violet, with translucent tendrils flapping where her feet might have been. She took great pleasure in thrashing the tail about, spraying other patrons with water.

Snow stared in wonder. "Is that a mermaid?" she gasped.

Eyvind pushed back his chair with a loud screech of wood on wood. "If only! Mermaids are pretty as daisies, and they sing nice little rhyming songs all the day long, and they smell a fair sight better than that heap of dead clams. That's a Magyr, and she'll drink me into the street in an hour." He trundled over to the boisterous trio, his face a cold glower. After a moment, Sigrid and Snow followed, curious as a pair of kittens.

"Oy! Eyvind!" the Magyr hollered, her voice like a wave sluicing

through a tide pool cluttered with clapping mussels. "Fill my gullet with ale and my men's bellies with some of that foul bread you cook up in your back room! Have I got a story for you! You'll never believe it, not in a month of miracles!"

"I never believe any of your stories, Grog. And you'll show me your coin before you get a drop."

She ran a corpse-colored hand through her emerald hair, and when it came away, it was full of rough, filthy golden coins, so old that Snow had never seen their like. They were embossed—faintly, worn by countless hands and pockets—with the image of a single eye. Grog bit one of them with satisfaction. Sigrid stiffened.

"Aye, the great cow knows what these are! Coin from the Arimaspian Oculos! Two hundred years and more extinct, and yet I've got more of their coin than any collector in Ajanabh! Ask me where I got it! Go on, ask me!" Grog was crowing, stroking her shiny gills in delight.

"Where did you get it?" Sigrid asked, her voice icy and low.

Grog licked her bluish lips in anticipation and seized her tankard in one huge hand, the thin webbing between her fingers slapping wetly against the metal.

"My men—that's Sheapshank and Turkshead, you know, and it don't matter which one's which—had booked us passage on a sweet little schooner captained by a beast the likes of which a mother wouldn't even threaten her squalling brats with . . ."

The
Magyr's
Tale

SHE WERE SEVEN FEET TALL IF SHE WERE AN INCH, I swear it by my mother's fifth teat. All sweetness and light from the neck up—a regular princess, with hair like melting butter and starry eyes—but oh, those legs! A deer's legs, right down to the hoof, or would have been, if she had had hooves. Instead, she had great flapping frog's feet, and turquoise wings, feathers and all, tucked against her back. Her skin was all over tiger stripes, and her hands were furry as a wolf's, with great clacking claws. And of all things, a thick gray tail wagged through a slit in her skirts.

She was a perfect monster. But beggars can't be choosers! I can swim just as fine as a young shark, of course, but poor Sheapshank, he can't swim a stroke to save his throat, and Turkshead has a deathly fear of the sea. Anyway, I prefer to travel in style, with my tub full of warm water and a mug of rum in each hand. The ocean is cold as a witch's womb, don't you know, and it makes my tail peel to go wallowing through it week after week. A ship is far better suited to my taste, even if Turkshead retches like a pregnant wench every time a stiff wave washes the deck.

Now, my youngest sister had spawned not a fortnight before, and me being the maternal type, practically bursting at the gills with motherly affection, I wanted to see my little nieces and nephews whilst they was still wiggling little tadpoles—and enjoy a month's helpings of my sister's whitefish and squid pies. But the sea has spread my family far as the four winds would take us, and Tack's grotto is a full month's sail over the ice caps from Muireann. Muireanners don't take kindly to those of the maritime persuasion mucking up the berthing on their ships, so Sheapshank and Turkshead asked after the most desperate captain on the docks, one who wouldn't turn their dainty nose up at a paying fare.

And that was how we met Magadin.

Sheapshank and Turkshead carried my tub over to her fingerpier. I slapped the side of the old boat, fine old locust wood by the color, though more than a little dingy and worse for wear. I peered at the hull, where the ship's name appeared to have been carved into the wood by an inexpert hand. *Witch's Kiss,* it read, rather shakily. Just then her head appeared from behind the second mast.

"Are you looking for passage north, then? Old Man Glyndwr told me you'd be sloshing on by."

That woman's voice was like hot wine on a cold night. I gestured for my boys to set me down.

"What are you, woman, the City Zoo?" Sheapshank barked laughter at my little joke, but the lady just smiled.

"Hardly. There was a Wizard, some years back. He favored me with a change of costume." She scratched at the tops of her blue wings with a lazy claw.

"Ain't there always a Wizard, though? Bloody menace, if you ask me. No one cares for the likes of us freaks, but a whole stinking heap of us never caused the trouble of one Wizard in an ever-damned tower."

I thumped my tail in sympathy, but Turkshead leered at her and gnashed his teeth. I stroked his bald head to calm him—just like a pup my Turkshead is, can't stand the smell of a stranger. I traced circles on his painted pate as Turkshead moaned in pleasure. "So, pray tell, Lady

Menagerie, how did you come by a ship as big as all this? A captain all by
yourself and no one stabbing you in the heart in the depths of night to
steal it?"

The beast-maiden swung lightly down from the upper deck and fixed
her amber eyes on me. She moved faster with those mixed-up limbs than I
would have thought.

"If I tell you the tale, will you buy passage on my ship, and look
nowhere else? I'm hungry as a whelp without a dam, and I'd be glad of the
wage."

I gripped her hand in mine straightaway, flippers on claws—no one else
would have taken us, anyhow. "Aye, that I will."

"Well, then. Just as there is always a Wizard, there is always a hero ready
to rescue a pretty girl—and some do think me pretty, strange as it seems.
But that's not important. My life didn't begin, in truth, until I came to
Muireann . . ."

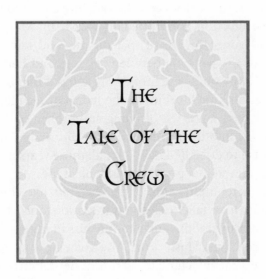

THE
TALE OF THE
CREW

BEING A MAIDEN, YOU SEE, IS NOT QUITE THE SAME
as being alive.

It is more like being a statue. The main skill of a maiden
is to stand very still and look very beautiful. Even when I
was a captive, I did little more than sit on my wooden
stool and try not to cry. I was nothing; I did nothing. Not
until I rode on the back of a red Beast through the ramshackle gate of Muireann did I ever take a step or utter a
word that was not planned out for me by folk in black
robes—whether those robes were those of parents or
wizards, it didn't matter much.

But Beast, kind as he was, could do little more than

leave me at the pier and suggest to the townsfolk that I might be a fair hand at sail-mending, or deck-swabbing, if one of them were to take me on. The throng of Muireanners stood stock-still in terror of the scarlet demon that had carried me to them, and a few nodded dumbly, praying only that he would leave, so that they could forget him all the sooner. Beast nibbled my ear with affection, and trotted off back to his Marsh and his King.

When he had gone, the crowd spat on me, and knocked me to the ground. They cut the webbing between my toes and half sawed my tail from my body. They would have broken my wings if they could have managed it, but I am no little bluebird in the hands of a child. My bones are strong, and they held. I was left bleeding and broken on the docks while they went laughing into their ships' holds for dinner, and night was coming on. What was I to do? All I knew, after all those years in my Tower, was how to stay very still so that people could look at me.

And so I lay there, utterly still, under the stars like chips of ice, until they came. I must have fallen asleep on the cold stones, for I awoke to a hand clamped over my mouth and a toothy hiss in my ear:

"Hush now, precious. Hush now." The voice's owner dragged me up into its arms like a cat snatching the scruff of her kitten's neck. In a whirl of shuffling feet, foul breath, and foul murmurings, I was carried to a creaking ship and lashed to the mizzenmast.

"Well, my mixed-up girl, you wanted to serve on a ship—I promise you'll serve now." The voice that had hissed in my ear on the docks belonged to a high-cheeked captain in a hat festooned with threadbare blue feathers and worn velvet. He was handsome as a duke—save that when he smiled his mouth was full of rotted teeth, yellow as a decrepit old wolf's.

"Now," he said, "we're going to sell you off at one southern port or another—if the mummers won't take you and the slavers won't take you, the fur traders will, and if they won't the meat markets will. But in the meantime you can put those mismatched parts to work scrubbing this ship splinter by splinter." He grinned, and tipped his hat. "And, well, it's a long voyage south. After a few weeks, you'll look downright fetching, and really, you're not bad from the chin up."

I looked up at him and my mouth watered behind my gag. I coughed politely, to let him know I wished to speak, and he obligingly removed the filthy rag. I made my voice as sweet and flutelike as a princess can. "You needn't sell me. I can be useful, and I won't fight you, or your men."

The Captain shrugged and stood straight, brushing the knees of his breeches clean. "This is what piracy is. If we took you willing, what kind of pirates would we be? You can be sweet and yielding as the first cream of the season with me, but try to put on a good scream for my boys. It keeps morale up."

I could not scrub the decks. My deer's legs would not bend, and my frog's feet slipped on the deck. I stumbled and fell, and a smart punch to the side would answer my clumsiness. I forgot, as the days went by, that I was a maiden, and then I forgot what a maiden was. The Captain told me each morning that he would expect me in his chamber that night; he told me each night that I was too repulsive for his taste, but "less ugly than you were yesterday, and uglier than you will be tomorrow."

One night, the crew was drunk on their last rations of rum, and they hauled me to their quarters. I remembered to scream. They jeered like jackals and pelted me with slaps and blows, until one of them thought it would be a fine trick to cut off my hair.

"We'll make her a real deckhand," he said, laughing raucously, "and no one goes to sea with a head of yellow curls! Cut it off!"

He came behind me and gathered up my hair in his hands, my dragon-fly wings fluttering in panic at the ends of the strands. Drawing his short blade, he sawed through the yellow locks, planting a slurping kiss on my bare neck.

I did not know what would happen, I swear I did not. He cut my hair, yes, but instead of silky curls falling to the floor, blood began to sheet from the severed ends as though he had cut into my heart, and my wings buzzed so loudly I could hardly hear the men's cries of terror and disgust. They backed away from me, staring, as blood soaked my shirt and the sec-ondhand trousers they had found in a dead sailor's trunk.

I stumbled to my feet, my vision a red blur. I felt very strange, as though all the creatures that had gone into my misshapen body were waking up, clawing for purchase on my soul. The wolf and the stag and the tiger and the bear, the frog and the dragonfly and the fish—all their many-colored voices begged to be heard, who had never so much as whispered before. My flesh was filled with howling, howling and baying and croaking and crying, roaring and shrieking, so much shrieking, like broken flutes thrown against a stone floor.

The wolf leapt first, I think, and then the tiger. I clawed out the throats of three sailors, and chewed through the ear of another before cutting into his eyes. The stag kicked at prone skulls, and the bear lunged into naked bellies. The frog and the dragonfly remembered to scream.

When it was over none of them were left; the room was empty as a prison cell. I wanted to feel sick. I wanted to delicately retch in the corner or feel faint, collapse in guilt. But I was not sick or faint, and the creatures in me exulted. Maidens stand still, they are lovely statues and all admire them. Witches do not stand still. I was neither, but better that I err on the side of witchery, witchery that unlocks towers and empties ships.

It was easy, once I had decided that, to slip into the captain's quarters and into that soft bed at last. The pillow was cool on my face, the blood of my hair dried and black against the fabric. I did not wait for him to wake, and I did not need a hidden knife. The bear opened him up like a beehive.

I sailed a ghost ship back into Muireann port.

THE
MAGYR'S TALE,
CONTINUED

THE BEAST-MAID CARESSED THE RAIL OF HER SHIP tenderly. "No one wants this ship, just as no one wanted me. They say I use no sails, but lash the ghosts of the crew to the mast and let the moon fill them up like wind. This ship is mine. I know it like my own body, and I am not sorry for what I have done. That is what piracy is, I suppose. I am not a maiden anymore, and I am glad to be done with that sorry state. I washed it off in blood and ocean. No one troubles me, and I do not trouble them."

"Well, that's a fish story and no mistake," I guffawed. My boys snorted derision along with their mistress, clapping each other on the back. "We've a real red-handed villain on our hands, boys! A hundred men at one blow!"

Magadin smiled patiently. "Not a villain. Not a witch, or a maiden. A captain, which is a little like being all three. But believe what you will. When a mermaid mocks a monster for telling a story too fantastic to swallow, who is to say which is the more ridiculous?"

I purpled, swelling up with rage like an overripe plum. "I am *not* a mermaid! Mermaids are skinny little fops with shells to cover their tiny tits! Mermaids do nothing but sit around on rocks staring into mirrors and teasing ships to their doom. Perfectly good ships! Galleons, even! Wasteful milksops, the lot of them, and you couldn't build half a brain if you had the whole race on a slab. I am a *Magyr*. I could crush your skull with my hands and drink this rat town under the table afterwards. And if I wanted to kill myself a passel of sailors, I'd bloody well do it with cannon, saber, and a fist in the teeth, not by batting my damn eyelashes. You'd be wise to remember it, Maggie, my love, and if we see a mermaid on our jaunt across the high seas, the best thing for all of us would be to let Sheapshank here put an arrow through her giggling head."

With that, I gave her a good splash with my tail and ordered the boys to take me aboard.

Now it were a week on the waves, and Turkshead vomiting over the side every morning like a fisherman throwing chum to the whales. Weren't nothing unusual that I could see: the ocean's blue no matter the day or the tide, and if I loved the great salt thing enough to describe it, I'd love it enough to swim in it, do you get me?

Maggie, for her part, sailed that ship like nothing I've seen. My boys are no layabouts when it comes to crewing a fine ship—I bought them at a bargain from the Ajanabh fleet when they were so poor they couldn't buy splinters. But she wouldn't hear of it, running up and down that deck like a dervish. You wouldn't have thought anyone could man a ship that size all on their own, but Magadin did it, and no lie.

Which is how it happened that Turkshead was the one to sight the monster first, while chucking his chum at dawn for the twelfth day. He came spluttering up to my tub like a baby who's discovered his thumbs, and dragged the old barrel screeching across the deck, spilling my brine everywhere, so that I could stare over the rail and see, horribly, the water breaking over a shell so enormous that at first I thought we'd hit land.

It was difficult to clap an eye on, a shell like a turtle rising up, but the color of the sea itself, so that it seemed like a wave or a reef, but too impossibly huge to be alive. Turkshead was crying, babbling that it was going to eat us—but I couldn't see a head to the thing at all. It was nothing but shell, rising and rising, water running off its back, slick tiles of shiny blue and black and green, repeating over and over like a puzzle. The ship was caught in a roil of froth and foam, the sea rushing into us as it rushed away from the beast.

"*Leviathan,*" whispered Sheapshank, and he mumbled a prayer so that I could not hear—the boys know I don't approve of their bloody damned Stars.

Magadin cried out to us, dashing from sail to sail, fighting to keep us arights. "It's the Echeneis! Don't you read books? That's not even half its girth you see! It can swallow us and not even feel the prick of the mast in its gullet. Man those lines, Sheap, or we feed the monster!"

The boys were so glad of something to do they fell over themselves trying to get to that flapping jib first. I just watched, frozen as a side of seal meat. The thing was still rising, so high now that it cast its shadow over us, and I shivered in the sudden cold. Goose bumps stood out green and blue on my arms, and soon there weren't no sea at all, only the ugly black thing, growing like a dead sun. I looked hard for the head, searched like a fish prodding through coral for a meal, for the littlest break in the giant shell.

Sheapshank screamed—I'd never heard my poor boy scream, I protect him so he don't have to—an awful, keening sound like iron sawing through iron, and suddenly the waves broke over the head, a whale's head, with a mouth that never ended. It stretched, all smiles, around and around until it seemed it would split the monster's head, with long, yellow-white curtains of baleen gleaming sickly. Its eye was the color of an old corpse. A stink wafted out, like rancid meat and soiled cabbage. As soon as it broke the salt scrim, Turkshead unlatched one of the thick-handled harpoons hanging on the sides of the ship and hurled it with all his not-inconsiderable strength towards the mouth of the Echeneis.

It glanced off like a hanky thrown at an iron door.

Magadin sighed heavily, as if she expected it. Her sad little ship was losing her battle with the wind, and sliding towards the black blot of the monster. Her face, such a pretty face, really, in spite of everything, settled into a grimace, and though her scaly arms did not loosen on the wheel, I saw her despair.

The Echeneis saw nothing. It only began the long opening of its mouth. Gray water rushed in, a wave crashing with a terrible noise like palaces falling, and the dark of its throat yawned, pulling us in. No matter how Maggie pulled at the wheel to swing us 'round, no matter how trim the lads kept the sails, we spiraled closer to the sloshing stomach of the sea-beast.

"Sheapshank, love!" I cried. "Your mistress is dumb as a team of cows. Bring me the harpoons!"

Always obedient, my Sheap gathered up an armful of spears and tipped them into my tub. "I swear, if my tits weren't screwed on, I'd have left 'em in a bar ten years ago." I grinned coyly up at his tattooed face. "Did I ever show you my gland, sweetheart? I don't show it to just anyone, but times being what they are . . ."

I lifted one of my heavy breasts and passed the sharp tip of a harpoon across the skin beneath. It parted, and a green ooze dribbled out onto my belly—Magyr, unlike those cretins called mermaids, are not defenseless dolls. We have sacs of poison in our chests, just like squid's ink. I stuck my hands into the mess of bubbling slime and told the boys and the beast-girl to do the same. Quickly, the four of us dipped the harpoons in my fluids and loaded Turkshead with the sopping sticks. He ran up to the prow, positively white with nausea, and hurled the first directly into the Echeneis's maw.

It disappeared, useless as a limp sailor.

He tried, again, and again it vanished into the black. Again, the monster didn't seem to grasp that it had swallowed enough Magyr oil to kill a herd of horses. Sheapshank sunk to the deck of the ship and began to cry.

But Mags, oh, Magadin—captain among captains, that one! She grabbed up the bundle of harpoons and kissed me smash on the forehead.

"See my ship gets home," she said, and winked at me. "The ship de-serves a harbor, whatever happens to her sailors."

"Wait! If anyone's to go overboard, it ought to be the lady with the tail, don't you think?" It's not that I wanted to leap off into the blue, you un-derstand. But I thought it was proper to offer.

Magadin laughed and thumped her wolf's tail against the rail.

"Absolutely!" she yelled. And with that, she leapt overboard, her frog's feet kicking up, bright green in the dull water. She was swept into the monster's mouth quicker than oil running downhill in summer—and as she passed the wall of baleen, she twisted, rode the swell of sea, and thrust her spears into the roof of its mouth.

The Echeneis roared in rage, and the sound bit at my ears, like rusty knives scraping the drum. It shook and pitched, the shell bulging bladder-full, and all in a rush, the hideous thing vomited, spewing a flood of gold coins onto the ship's deck, tearing through its wood like cannon-fire. The beast kept up its retching, showering the ocean with gold, and I saw Magadin's tail lift up soggily once, twice, before she disappeared into the black.

The Pale Girl's Tale, Continued

"THE BLOODY SHIP WAS FULL OF HOLES BY THEN, OF course. But full of gold, too! We steered out while the monster went under again—and a good thing we did! When the top of its shell sunk at the last, the sea washed in over it like a flood; we were almost caught. But my tub was at the wheel and the boys were patching holes for all they were worth, and we limped back into Muireann port with full purses! And not just gold, but antiques! Those are worth five times what a plain gold dime is! I'm only sorry I never got to see Tack's young-sters—and her pies." Grog looked sad for a moment, but drained her tankard and was all smiles again, her yellow teeth garish and bright. "That's a tale worth a meal, Evvy, wouldn't you say?"

But Sigrid's face had gone black and white at the same time, desire and hope and despair flitting like clouds across it. "You saw the Echeneis? You lost your captain to it?"

"Is this one deaf or feeble, Ev? Hasn't she heard what I said? Don't she got her hands full of dead men's gold?"

"Do you remember where, you soused dog?" Sigrid's eyes blazed like a fire in midwinter. "Could you find the place again?"

Grog looked at the woman pityingly. She ran her hands through her emerald hair, coifing the ratted heap.

"I know you're not from these parts, dearie, but you do see the tail, right? You do grasp the concept of a tail? It's for swimming and all? I may not like to dip my tender parts in it, but no one knows the sea like a Magyr. Of course I could find it again. But I have no mind to—I consider it a gift that I escaped with full pockets, and I'm not about to go skipping about looking for a nice big mouth to jump into. Now fill up my cup, Eyvind, and keep your woman nice and quiet while a body's having her drink."

Snow, unseen by all, as always, had crept closer to the wide tub of brine, and pulled a knife from the bar into her thin hands. She leapt like a feral cat onto the lip of the tub, and seized Grog by a tuft of bottle-green hair.

"Take us," she hissed. "Take us to the monster or I'll cut your throat."

"Snow!" Sigrid gasped. "What's gotten into you? If anyone's to threaten the sea-cow, it'll be me."

"Sigrid," Snow pleaded, "you know what's out there. You've spent all this time telling me about Saint Sigrid, and you think I'll let a chance to be in that story, to be part of it, slide by? Didn't you give *eight* years to a Tower because a woman told you a story you loved? All I want is a few days at sea! You *know* it was you in the song—but couldn't it have been me, too? *An orphan will find her!* I'm an orphan if you ever knew one. You've waited all these years to find the Echeneis and you're going to let this greasy old thing stop us? Let me come with you, let me help you find her—and let me cut this foul-smelling fish if she won't help us!" Snow pressed the knife into the rolls of fat around Grog's neck, and the Magyr squealed helplessly.

"Fanatics!" she screeched. "I tell you, there is nothing so dangerous in the world as fanatics! Sheapshank! Turkshead! Snap this one in half for mistress!"

The great hulks of men leapt forward to pummel the pale child, but Eyvind stopped them with a glance.

"Touch her and I'll bash mistress's face in with a bottle of rum," he growled. Sigrid gave him a grateful nod.

"All right! All right! I'll take you there, you stinking dogs. You used to run a fair bar, Eyvind, but look at you now! Groveling before some fat wench and her brat!" Snow released the Magyr's head and climbed nimbly down from the tub rim. Grog glared at her and spat out a hunk of green phlegm, which splattered across Snow's back. Sigrid smiled wanly and wiped it off.

"Thank you," Snow said stiffly.

"Mistress," came a soft, high voice. Turkshead had crept forward and was kneeling at the side of the tub, pawing Grog like a pup. "Not the sea again. Not the boat. Please. My stomach . . ."

"Not the sea again," agreed Sheapshank. "We've had enough. It's out there, waiting. We'll wait here for you—we love you—but we won't face the monster again."

Grog rolled her eyes. "Well, who will carry my tub, then? That waste of a girl couldn't lift a mug of rum!"

Eyvind coughed, spat, and gave the bar an affectionate swipe with his rag. "I'll go with you and carry your can of soup, you old sturgeon."

"Well, ain't that sweet of you, precious?"

"But I go for Sigrid. Not for you," he grumbled, and fixed his drooping eyes on the older woman.

"Fine. Everyone is so bloody loyal it stinks. Fanatics give me heartburn. Maggie's ship is lashed at the dock. Be sure you get a firm grip—I don't fancy spilling out on the street like a bucket of bluegill."

And so Sigrid, Snow, and Eyvind wrapped themselves in wool and readied themselves to go to sea. Sheapshank and Turkshead were given the back room to sleep in and the other customers gently shooed to the door.

"Bring a barrel of rum!" screeched the green-haired Magyr. "We'll want it, mark my words!"

In the Garden

"IF YOU'RE A SMART GIRL, YOU'LL GET OUT NOW," CAME THE BLACK-smith's voice like a hot iron through the silk night.

The girl jumped up immediately, accustomed to quick escapes, darting away from the blacksmith's shadow. She hardly looked at the boy as she dodged horses' legs and tin buckets, nimbly bounding out of the stable doors as the first drops of light seeped out of the East.

But though she found him safe and sleeping where she left him, Dinarzad kept the boy by her throughout the day, a torture worse than any she had yet devised, as he was made to copy her every action, and his fingers grew red and swollen from pinpricks, then black from inkstains, then blue with costly dyes. He could not do any of it properly, and so he was made to burn with shame under the disapproving stares of so many women. By evening, no matter how much he might wish to escape to the Garden, he was as exhausted as a deer which has stayed ahead of the hounds by the smallest of steps. Dinarzad insisted he sleep near her as well, and for once he did not protest, but fell onto the bed, sore and ashamed.

Past midnight, the boy woke to a pair of dark eyes peering through the stone arch, which was hung with soft violet gauze, thin as secrets.

Dinarzad lay still on her bed, covered in white furs, and the boy thought, not for the first time, that when she did not speak or move, she was beautiful. Her smoky black hair spread over the bed like a river of shadow, and her skin caught the moonlight just so. Her slim, elegant hands curled over the bronze keys which unlocked the bedchamber's proper door, and her breathing was slow and sweet as a flute.

The boy lay on a smaller spare bed, his own dark hair tangled, as though he had run his hands through it many times in anger. His eyes were wide and open, staring at the low window, and the girl's deer-poised form. He crept silently, a spider in a well, until he reached the windowsill and drew aside the lavender veils. Dinarzad's breathing continued, slow and rhythmic as a dance.

"You came!" he whispered. "How do you always find me?"

The girl smiled. "Magic," she whispered. "After all, I am a demon."

"You always come to the window, you come to find me and carry me away—that is not what girls are supposed to do. It is what the Princes do in all the stories."

"This is not that kind of story."

The boy tried not to look as glad as he was, a rabbit who knows that he will be caught, but cannot help devouring the carrot. He wished, fervently, that he could find her, and carry her off, like a proper Prince. But she was like air streaming through silk, and he could not touch her at all. They stood for a moment, separated by the low stone sill.

"I will be very quiet," she murmured, "so as not to wake your sister." She settled outside the window onto the deep, dewy grass, and closed her eyes.

"When the beast-maiden's ship had been bounding through the waves like a lioness through the grass for three days with Grog at the wheel, since no one would move her tub from that post, Eyvind found himself belowdecks with Sigrid, sharing a meager supper of seal fat and hard bread. They did not see Snow creep in behind them, as eager to hear their talks as a child who spies upon her parents . . ."

The
Pale Girl's Tale,
Continued

"WE'VE GOT A FARMER'S BUSHEL OF TIME, NOW, Sigrid," Eyvind said, settling into a chair with a grunt and a sigh. He sliced off the heels of a loaf for himself and spread it with the salted grease. "And it's been near ten years you've been making eyes at me and drinking my beer at the Arm, near enough to ten years that you've been looking like there were something you wanted to say to me—ten years that you haven't been saying it." He leaned in, his sandy hair flopping over his brow like a tuft of fur. "I'm thinking it's long past time you tell me whatever it is you've been keeping locked up tight behind those teeth."

She sighed, and stared at the grain of the table wood, unable to look the tavern-keeper in the eye.

"Eyvind," she began, her voice cracking like a frozen broom, "I'm not sure I should. There was a time, I think, when I first came to Muireann, when I might have told you, and it might have been the right thing. But now—so much time has passed, so many things happened, I think perhaps it is best that this stay dead, closed into a chest between us, fastened with locks."

"What are you talking about, woman? I've left my tavern for you; you might stop your shy-maid act—I know better than to think you're just a net-mender. You talk to that albino girl like she's your confessor, and you won't tell me why you watch me like I'm likely to grow a tail and start howling at the moon?"

Sigrid's face sagged, and she lifted her faded eyes to him, full of pity. She looked like nothing so much as a mother welcoming home a child who has gone far astray and become a stranger to her.

"Understand, please, understand that I never wanted to hurt you . . ."

THE NET-WEAVER'S SECOND TALE

WHEN I FIRST BECAME A WOMAN, THE LIMBS WERE as strange to me as the first taste of wine. For all my days until that one, I had been a bear.

I loved my mother and my Stars, and I loved a young bear with dark eyes, even after he left me. I was never strange, never different from my sisters.

The bear I loved disappeared, and the snow fell, the snow froze, the glaciers broke and re-formed without him. We knew nothing of where he had gone, and after a full turn of seasons without his tracking across our ice, mates were taken again, cubs were nursed. And life went on.

But one evening, when the blue lights of the heavens streamed through the prisms of the Temple, tracing shadows of cobalt and aquamarine across my thick fur, a vision came to me, glimmering on the ice altar with all the weight and depth of flesh. Laakea, the Harpoon-Star, stood before me, with his diamond spear slung over one shoulder, his skin whiter than light itself. His hair flowed over the altar like a frozen waterfall, and I trembled in his presence, terrified and exalted. I was a humble bear, not so very far past my cubhood, and the golden eyes of the Far-Flying Hunter were fixed on me. The honor was beyond bearing.

He told me, Eyvind. He told me that you had been made into a man, that you had sought to avenge the Snake-Star and been changed to keep you from it. It was not your vengeance to take, he said. But he also told me that you would never be bear again—or that it would be so long and at such cost that if you managed it, it would be worth less than ash. He told me, in a voice like snow, that I would never see you again, that you would never return.

And I wept, my love. I wept at his feet like an infant, and I could not raise my eyes to his beauty.

Laakea put his hands on my shoulders—the ecstasy of it!—and lifted me to his side. He said that if I wished, I could be made a woman myself, so that I could seek you out, find you again, find some happiness. Of course, I wished it! He drew for me a map in the ice, a map through the floes to a great wood at the othermost North of the world, where, he said, roamed a creature who knew something of trading skins.

And he told me nothing else. Not how to find you, or how to stand still while something unstitched my fur and lashed skin in its place.

Yet still, I loved you, and I believed you would want me to come to you. I could not stand the thought of you in misery, separated from your kind. So I went, into the far northern wilds, and I floated across seas so blue they chilled my bones, and frozen trees encased in sheaths of frost. And I came to a wood more vast than any I had ever heard tale of, darker than caverns in its paleness, and deeper, white with snow and terrible in its cold.

I wandered in it, I became lost in it. Perhaps it was an hour, perhaps it was a year. Perhaps it was ten. In the white, time is nothing, and I knew nothing but the winter, the scent of it, tracking it to its source. I followed the smell of ice over pine, over holly berries, of snowshoes slushing through drifts. I followed until I came upon a hunched figure in a frostbitten vulture cloak, whose feathers were gone to crystal and frost. I lumbered up to its silvery form.

"You came looking for Ghassan," the hunchback said. "But I'm not him. I'm Ghassan's girl, Umayma."

I frowned as best a bear can frown. "You don't look like a girl." And indeed, she seemed a wolfish, feral young boy with a cowl carved from a vulture's head, and leathery black legs with talons like a raven's. She stamped them in the snow and ground her pearly teeth, one against the other.

"The wonder of skins is that one need never wear one's own face. You must be weary of yours, or you would not have come looking for Ghassan and found me."

"Not weary, no, but I need another one."

"What sort?"

"A . . . a human girl."

Umayma pursed her lips. "That's a hard one to come by. Girls guard their skins very well. But I do have one." She pulled a bundle the color of good honey out of a fat leather satchel and held it up thoughtfully.

"Where did it come from?" I asked fearfully. "I wouldn't want to wear a murdered girl's body like a dress."

Umayma smiled and fluffed her vulture-skin. "A skin is a skin, but if you must know . . ."

The Skin-Peddler's Tale

THE FIRST THING I REMEMBER IS THE EGG. MY feathers were very black.

Ghassan told me, alone of all his children he confided in me, even when I was so young that yolk still clung to my beak, that he had been born nothing but a bird. A crooked old crow who wanted better for himself, he said. The first time he changed skins it was quite a surprise—he wrapped himself up in a snake's molting and the molting stuck, like a coat grown suddenly too small to take off. His feathers were a shrugged-off pile of soot on the forest floor, and he never looked back.

After a while he began to seek out skins, and not long

after that he developed a reputation—by the time he died he had not had to steal a skin in decades. Rich in skins, my father, which is all the wealth there is. Folk clambered to trade theirs over, and he always ran a brisk business. If a skin was troublesome, he could always get rid of it; if it was rare, he could always procure it. Some thought he was quite wicked, but in truth, he was no more or less than any other crow: enamored of bright new things, and too clever to get them by the usual path.

He taught me the trade. Most of his children were plain crows, dull as dandelions. But I was like him, he said. My heart was skinless, and therefore I could have any skin I wished. But I had no desire to steal skins, as he did, and which he believed was a vital skill, as vital as reading to a cleric. He chided me, yes, called me weak of will, threatened to teach one of his other crow-children if I could not sneak up behind that possum right this second and split it tail to crown. But I would not. A skin is a sacred thing, more intimate than mother and child, and I wanted to change, of course I wanted to change, to be like Ghassan, but I wanted each of those in whose bodies I nestled to desire the change as much as I did. I searched for a long time, asking this page and that potato farmer whether or not they would like to be a crow, and my father laughed each time they fled in terror or threw stones at me, or politely declined to eat worms and leaves.

But one day, as days will come, I met a girl in the forest, just the sort of girl black and taloned creatures meet in the forest: young and ruddy-cheeked, bright of eye and too curious to take the usual path.

"Hello," I cawed, hopping into her path.

"Hello, old crow," she said pleasantly.

"I'm not old at all, you know. I'm quite young, and my feathers have a lovely sheen."

"They certainly do."

"How would you like to wear them?" I asked, smoothing my voice into a hushed sweetness, like a pond lapping against its green banks.

The girl considered for a moment, twisting her brown ringlets in her fingers. "I think I would like that very much," she said softly. "I think it would be very nice to fly, and the life of a milkmaid is dreadfully dull. One always hopes such opportunities will befall one in the forest, but more often than not, one finds oneself an old grandmother with dragging dugs and a dewlap, her fingers numb from endless udders."

I hopped closer. "Would you let me wear your skin in return?"

She looked down at herself. "Oh, certainly, if you would not find it very plain, and prone to dragging and dewlaps. It is a beastly body in that way. I would not recommend milking cows. It's terrible for the knuckles."

"I shall remember that." I laughed, and we settled about the usual ceremony of stitching and unstitching, in which she was not at all experienced and I was barely adequate, so I am quite certain we made a mess of the whole procedure, but then, one's first time is always a bit awkward, is it not?

She was lovely, and smelled of milk and hay on the inside. She cawed happily and flew off into the pines.

And I began, each time seeking out accord, agreement, not because I thought it wrong to steal—I am still a crow, after all—but because I do not disdain the usual way. Still, I have fallen into my father's profession after all, as folk wish to trade and buy and sell, and I accumulated an excess inventory, and began to be sought after. I developed preferences, as Ghassan did—we both prefer a set of skins to one, and to maintain some of our crow shape in the set. I grew to enjoy wearing a boy's skin, as Ghassan often wore a woman's. Variety is important, you know, and it always pays to display the skins to best effect.

For all I know he is still crouching on his island, the island where I was born, the island where he squats and plays siren, but Ghassan has not been seen in the waking world for many years, and I am the only Skin-Peddler anyone speaks of these days, but they still call me Ghassan—who can tell who is who when our faces change with winter and spring?

The Net-Weaver's Second Tale, Continued

"THIS IS THAT FIRST GIRL'S SKIN. I HAVE CARried it with me as a kind of souvenir, but I will give it to you, because you are in need, and I would very much like a bear skin."

I pawed the snow. "Umayma, I'm scared."

"It's all right," she said warmly, putting a skeletal hand on my shoulder. "The first time always hurts a little, but it gets easier."

"This will be my only time," I said stiffly.

Umayma scratched her cloak of feathers. "A pity," she sighed.

And then she took me in her boy's arms. I do not

know how to say how it was. I felt myself splitting, like a nut in its shell, a fingernail carving the husk open, sugar-blood spilling out. I felt a star open in my chest, burning and searing, tearing the fur and flesh open as if along a seam, stitches popping and snarling. I cried out and my strong legs buckled beneath me, claws skittering on the ice. I could hear the ripping of my skin, then, a wet, sliding sound that brought with it a pain that clouded my eyes and blackened my brain.

And then, the Skin-Peddler was extending her hand to me, and wonderingly I extended my own to meet it—and it was not a paw but a slender girl's hand, with five fingers and dull, ineffective nails in the place of my proud claws. I stood naked before the vulture girl in her boy's skin, suddenly shivering without my fur. The cold was like a throttling—it clutched my throat and clawed my chest. I could not have imagined such a thing as this cold; I had always had my thick pelt to protect me.

And so I went home. My mother shrieked and would not speak to me; her despair coated the house like black honey. My sisters did not know me, and ensconced themselves in the Temple to pray for my soul, not believing for a moment that Laakea had bid me do this thing. Gunde called a Versammlung, but even they could not decide what to do with me. They resolved that I could stay—but if I could manage it, they preferred that I go.

When the wolves came, I went eagerly. There was nothing for me in the North. If I went south with them, surely I would hear word of you, or the Snake-Star. And in a city such as Al-a-Nur, what secret could not be discovered? I could make us both bears again; I could find you wherever you had become lost. Could it hurt if I stole some bit of excitement or adventure for myself while I searched? I set out with a heart high as hearth flame. And when I entered the Tower of St. Sigrid, I told myself, very reasonably, that such knowledge was as likely to be there as anyplace else, such histories, such magic. But in truth, I was enamored of the Saint, and the Dreaming City, and all that had come to pass in the world since you left me. You were already becoming a distant memory, a childhood love. The world had cracked open and shown me wonders—I knew I could not close it again.

I began to forget you, because I thought it best to forget. Another destiny awaited me, and it was not simply to be a bear-wife fishing through the ice.

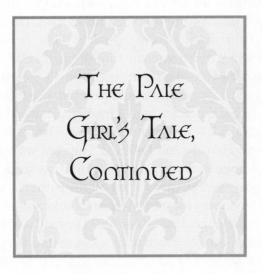

The Pale
Girl's Tale,
Continued

EYVIND STARED, STRICKEN. HIS EYES WERE FULL OF
tears, his stained shirt clenched in his enormous hands.

"So much happened, my love. I wore this skin until it
was so accustomed to me I don't think I could take it off if
I wanted to. I searched for years for the Saint, and when I
came to Muireann, destitute, in despair, there you were. I
knew you in a moment; of course I knew you."

"Then how could you keep this from me?" he blurted,
tears springing fresh and rolling down his great face. "For
years I waited for the change to come on me again, so that
I could be a bear again, and return to the ice, return to

you. All along you've been here and said nothing? You are cold, cold and cruel, Ulla."

Sigrid passed a hand over her eyes. "Do not call me that. It is not my name, not anymore. This is my name; this is my face. I am not her, I am Saint Sigrid of the Ways, however you may wish it were otherwise. I set out to find you—but it was truly for *this* I became human. This ship, coursing towards the beast that swallowed my goddess. This was my Quest, not you. When I saw you it only recalled to me all I had failed to do. If I had gone to you then, and tended a tavern with you all those years, perhaps you would have been happy, but it would have put a lie to all my training, all my life since the Skin-Peddler traded my flesh. It would have been the end to my story, and so it would have seemed that I had done all I did only for a husband. It was not the end I wanted. I am not your goal, Eyvind. I am an arrow shot towards Sigrid, and I must find my mark. The wolf led me astray, don't you see? The wolf led me off the path that wound to you, and into a place of whose jeweled mysteries I could not begin to tell you the first part. I am no longer Ulla—how could I dwell with Eyvind?"

The tavern-keeper's body seemed to dwindle, as if all the blood had run out of him. He put his head in his hands, his fingers in his thinning hair.

"My life has gone so far wrong I can't see the right for miles around. The Marsh King said I would be a man until a virgin was devoured, the sea turned to gold, and saints went west on the wings of henless birds. I believed the old stork—I thought it'd be a few years, no more. It went so fast; one day I was old and fat and the sea was still gray. I told a boy the story once; it seems like ages ago. I thought it would help, to tell someone. That it might hurry things along. But I couldn't tell, not one day did I even think on it, that my love was there, swilling beer in a dark corner. You should have told me, Sigrid." He took a deep, hitching breath. "If you are not my goal, what is?"

"I'm sorry, Eyvind. I truly am. None of this is how I meant it to be. I wanted to greet my captain young and beautiful; I wanted to be her savior. Now I can barely limp towards her on a leaking ship and hope I have the strength to throw myself in the path of the sea-creature."

In the corner of the hold, Snow wept silently, her tears wetting the wood of the softly rocking ship.

The silence between Sigrid and Eyvind was thick and dark as eel flesh for days upon nights. Snow hated the sound of it, echo of it in her ears. She was relieved as an ox without its yoke when Grog upended the last of her rum barrel into her blue mouth, belched forcefully, and bellowed.

"Shell off the port side!"

So it was—Snow could not breathe for her terror as the shell grew in size, black and green and blue and slick as a beetle's body, black and green and blue as the sea careening off of its dome. Its beady, baleful eyes crested the water, blinking their translucent eyelids in the dim sunlight. Grog put on a face of boredom, but beneath the brine, the pale girl could see her tail trembling. Sigrid's face was contorted in fear and ecstasy, and she was gripping Eyvind's hand with all her strength, whether trying to keep him at her side or anchor herself to the ship, Snow could not tell.

"Grog," Sigrid called out, her voice high and strong, "sail in! Into the mouth!"

The Magyr bolted upright in her tub, her violet tail thrashing. "Are you out of your mind, woman? I've gone this far, but knives or no, that's daft as an empty mug!"

"It's all right!" Sigrid laughed, throwing her head back, her hair streaming like a young girl's. *"Hand in hand they'll come whistling home, the maiden, the bear, and the girl in gray!"*

Snow patted the Magyr's shoulder, which glowed deep turquoise with fear. "I'll do it, Grog. It really will be all right. Probably. Anyway, the song says it will, and songs are usually right." She wrapped her slim fingers like candlewax around the wheel, and Grog lay back in her tub, her ample chest heaving.

"Fanatics!" she muttered, shaking her tattered green head.

The Echeneis's mouth yawned open, and the sea rushed in, past the forest of ivory baleen, the tiny ship buoyed on its crest like a toy boat.

The *Witch's Kiss* disappeared into shadow, like a lantern snuffed out.

In the Garden

"DON'T STOP!" THE BOY GASPED, HIS BREATH COMING QUICK AND
fast as a galloping colt. The girl frowned, creases forming in the inky expanse of her eyelids like constellations. Her glance flitted into the chamber, resting on the sleeping form of Dinarzad, whose hands moved
fitfully over the bronze keys.

"If I am caught here—"

"I will protect you! I am as brave as any Sigrid! Do you think I can't?"

The girl paused tactfully. "I think that's very brave. But you do not
really understand. Have you forgotten that you used to be afraid of me?"

The boy felt his cheeks burn. "Only a little," he mumbled, picking at
stray pebbles on the windowsill, trying to imagine that they were Lo
Shen pieces. The night was black as saddle oil all around, and only their
eyes gleamed.

"She is fast asleep," the boy cajoled, leaning across the window's
threshold, close to the girl, until he could smell her wildness, the scent of
tree and stone which clung to her. "Tell me the end."

THE PALE
GIRL'S TALE,
CONTINUED

WHEN THE SHADOW AND SPUME CLEARED FROM THE
eyes of the four creatures on board the little ship, the
world had changed around them.

This is to say, they had passed into a new world. The
belly of the sea-monster was vast, so vast that they could
only see the flank which was near to them, ribs curving
upward, taller than cathedrals—the other was lost in mist,
and the ceiling arched high above them, like a starless sky.
The stomach fluid of the beast made an inland sea, its
waves green and brown, noxious and steaming. The
schooner drifted through the oily waters, pushing aside
flotsam with its prow. The smell was of rotting fish

and kelp, and skeletons of unnamable things, things that had never seen the sun on the surface of the ocean, floated by as Snow stared over the edge at the hellish soup.

Sigrid did not lean over the rail to gawk at the accumulated trash of a life spent roaming the sea. She had taken the wheel and now looked straight ahead, eyes hawk-wide, at the wreckage laid out before them.

It was a city of skeleton ships, each bobbing in its own rhythm on the bile sea. Some were gray and crumbling with age, bones still gripping the wheel, skulls rolling back and forth over the decks in hypnotic repetition. Others were not so old at all; their paint was still bright in patches, and the figures slumped over the crows' nests and bowsprits were swollen and putrid, swarmed over with flies. The schooner passed without a sound through this necropolis, her crew agape. Eyvind finally covered his eyes when he could witness no more dead.

But Sigrid had fixed her eye on a ship, not far distant. Among all these ghost ships, one still had its lanterns lit, and the orange light spilled out over the brackish water, fire dancing on the slick of the monster's gluttony.

And voices could be heard—cheerful and raucous, shouts of glee and mirth. Snow's heart pounded within her. With aching slowness they drew closer to the mystery ship, and she dared to hope that it would be red, red as old dreams. But when they finally came within full sight of the galleon—for a galleon it was, and as beautiful a ship as had ever been built by hand or bough—it was not red, but white.

The surface of the ship—its beams, its sails and lines, even its figurehead, a woman with the head of a fox, arms extended high into the air to grip the prow in her fists—was caked with barnacles, glutted with them, like a flower in full seed. The living mast was coated in the white miasma, branches choked with it like some foul snowfall. There were not more than patches here and there where the stony shells had not fixed themselves, where the red sheen of the original ship shone through. It was nearly solid, like armor plating on a warhorse, and even Grog looked at the mass of creatures in dismay. Yet, on the deck of the ship many figures could be seen moving about, seemingly perfectly healthy and hale.

And from the bow, a woman's head appeared, a figure in leather breeches and a billowing white tunic, with skin the color of myrrh. Her tawny eyes were framed by dark hair which fell to her waist and gleamed like nothing so much as a great store of costly spices—and it was knotted through with gold, strung through ornate braids like beads. Just behind her stood a shadowy woman whose very skin seemed to be aflame, her fiery hand poised on the hilt of an enormous sword. But the dark-headed woman beamed at them, her face open and warm. She put her hand on her girlish hip and grinned at the newcomers.

"Welcome to the underworld!" she said with a laugh.

And it was then that Sigrid finally did begin to weep, brought face-to-face with her Saint at last.

"That *is* an odd reaction, if I may say so," Saint Sigrid remarked, and gestured for two of her women to lay a plank across the two ships so that the newcomers could come aboard.

"The *Maidenhead,*" Sigrid whispered, in awe as her foot rested on the famed ship's decks, encased as they were in stony white.

"Well, isn't that interesting? You must be one of the Sigrids." The Saint looked mildly disapproving, as if stepping delicately over a drunken priest slumped over in her path. Sigrid stared.

"You know about the Tower?" she gasped.

"Tower? No, I don't know of any tower, but that little cult was springing up even before I became a permanent passenger in this roving whale-turtle. They're tiresome, but what can I say to dissuade them? Whenever one does extraordinary things, someone is bound to try to repeat them for themselves. It's the way of the world."

Sigrid looked as though she had been slapped. "I have searched my life over for you, for the Saint of the Griffins, of the Boiling Sea, of the Red Ship. I have never tried to repeat your miracles. I have performed my own. I have only tried to be like you in spirit, to be brave, and noble, and to find my place in the world. To find you."

The Saint leaned in close to Sigrid, her face as round and ruddy as the day she vanished, and laid one finger aside her nose, her mouth spreading into a conspiratorial smile.

"Gods are always a disappointment," she clucked.

Grog whipped her tail noisily through her brine, demanding attention like a kid who cannot reach her dam for the suckling of her siblings.

"I don't rightly care who you are, you fancy sea dog. Your ship looks like it fell bow-first into a barrel of old cheese. Not what I'd call prime captain-ship, you know, Saint or not."

The Saint glanced dismissively at Grog's gesticulating tail. "Misadventures at sea are as common as apples in autumn . . ."

The Tale of the Captain and the Crone

LONG-EARED TOMOMO WAS THE FIRST CAPTAIN OF this ship—we carved that figurehead to remember her—but I'd wager at least one of you already knows that. She was a fine woman, and I loved her. But a fox's place isn't really at sea, any more than it's in a Palace. She gave the wheel over to me after we had been on the waves together for many a year, despite many other women being senior to me. She said that a lady should always leave her worldly goods to a daughter, not an aunt or even a sister. She touched my hair, just a moment's touch, and went into the forest when we made port, with a bag of gold under each arm.

I never saw her again, and the *Maidenhead* was mine.

And for a while, our lives were bright as moon reflected in black water.

I suppose it was my fault. I became convinced that we were charmed, that Tommy had gifted us with her fox-magic before she left our berths, and like that clever, black-nosed fox, we would never be caught. My first mate, Khaloud, was always the best of us when it came to finding treasure for us to plunder, and she usually tried to make sure that it was ill-gotten, so that we could sleep easy. It is a talent of the Djinn; they can smell gold like game in a wood. Unsurprisingly, it was a great number of Djinn, led by the great Kashkash, who founded the city of Shadukiam in all its jewel-drenched glory. Or so they claim. I have never heard the name of Kashkash except that Khaloud swore by him constantly.

It was night, after our dinner of roast pork and fresh apples plundered from the stores of some local governor or another, that Khaloud took watch with me. We stood in our customary place, smoking—I with my whalebone pipe and she with the little silver one she had brought with her from the Rose Domed city. In the evening, she cuts quite a figure, with her hair of smoke and spark, her fiery skin banked to a contented glow. Her eyes could still scald me like a pair of hot tongs, though—and so they did that evening when she told me of her latest scheme.

"It would be easy, Sigrid. Easier than stealing corn from a crow. There is no one to guard it but an old woman with a lame leg—she couldn't even hobble after us. And the stories I've heard about the treasure she keeps! A magic satchel, plain leather on the outside, but within, a supply of gold that never runs dry! By the beard of Kashkash! What madness it would be if we did *not* seek it out?"

I drew deeply on my pipe. "Khaloud, heart of my heart, I know your lust for coin has never failed us, but this sounds like a child's story. We have had a good year. Why go chasing after magic purses when our own, very real purses are full?"

"Do you believe that the purse which brims today will brim for all time? Perhaps you can sleep sweetly, believing it is summer. But my duty does not let me rest, and I must see after our purses in winter, as well. And as for magic and children, here we stand on a ship whose mast bears oranges and pomegranates for our pleasure, and a woman of fire speaks to the mother of Griffins."

"As ever, you are wiser than I, you old genie. May the Stars grant that you are always here to look after me."

"Are you taking up religion in your old age, then, Captain?"

"Hardly. Habit, my love, habit."

Thus it was that we set out for a small island in the midst of a murky, misty bay, as they all are, a rocky, barren place full of slate and basalt, festooned with silver clams and deep blue mussels clinging to the sea-worn stones. In the center of the island was a hut, and that was all that marked out this island from hundreds of other dead reef-shards floating in the ocean. Khaloud had traded a vial of her heartsfire for the chart, and when we saw the pitiful little house, we called that too highly bought. There would be hardly a need for blades; I took only my Djinn ashore. How foolish I was—but it seemed such a desolate place. The wretched hut was thatched in straw and leaves, and poorly thatched at that, as haphazard and tangled as a bird's nest. Its walls were wattle-and-daub, stinking of dung. It rested on splayed feet that seemed to be a pelican's or a heron's, the talons gripping slick rocks for purchase.

And sitting in its doorway was an ancient woman, her lap full of clapping mussels.

Her head was bent so that Khaloud and I could not see her face, a mass of ash gray hair snarling from the crown of her head to her heels. But behind her arms, the crone had long black wings; at their crest bunched small clasping claws which were something like hands, and at her calves began leathery black talons which were something like feet. The feathers gleamed in the sun and seaspray. Her clothes were ragged, falling apart, no more than a few strips of animal pelts stitched together with sinew. She grumbled as we approached, and slurped the orange flesh from a mussel, pitching the empty shell straight past my head.

"Old woman!" Khaloud announced, speaking before I could. She often did that, so that if some hapless soul were to become enraged with us, they would leap at her before they would cut my own throat. "We've come for the satchel. You can give it to us, or we can take it from you, as you like, but by the flame of Kashkash, we'll have it."

The old woman tossed another shell, which struck the Djinn directly between the eyes.

"Oh, yes," the crone growled. "Come and rob an old lady's chest of drawers, eh? So easy to do, is it not? Her bones are chicken-brittle, they'll snap so sweet it's almost music." She chuckled deep in her throat. "Only I am not such an easy mark, my beautiful peacocks, oh, no."

She straightened her hunched back then, the mussels spilling out of her lap and skittering across the rocks. She stood up and threw her head back, and we saw with horror that the face beneath was not withered with age or strung with spittle—it was not even middle-aged, but a hale and grinning man whose eyes flashed black and silver. The mass of hair streamed back over his shoulders, tumbling past his knees. He fluffed his wings impressively—and slung over one feathered shoulder was a fat leather satchel, bulging like a wineskin.

"Is this what you want, then? A couple of girls playing pirates come to take it from old Ghassan, eh, weak and helpless as he is? Yes, you and many others before you. And I'll give it to you, without even a fight, if you can match me drink for drink the whole night through. I'm a sporting man, after all."

I considered for a moment, sure that he had more tricks than simply costumes. "You'll swear to me that the purse is magical?" I asked.

"Oh, aye! It is at that. Now, are you coming in—and just you, mind you; I've no mind to go gambling with fire-demons—or are you going back to your ship to tell your crew you couldn't contend with a meek old woman?" He waggled the satchel mockingly from one of his three-fingered claws and strode back into his hut.

Khaloud looked sidelong at me with those coal-eyes of hers, and pulled a tiny vial from her belt. "Heartsfire," she whispered, her voice like the last wisps of smoke from a doused fire. "This very morning I bled it from my wrist. A drop in the drink and he'll fall like a rock dropped from a Castle tower."

I took the dusky orange liquid and slid it into my sleeve, sharing a familiar smirk. And, as full of folly as a maid who milks a bull, I followed Ghassan into his stinking house.

A low table was set with clay cups and a large pitcher the color of birds' tongues. Ghassan sat on one side of it, his wings folded neatly at his sides, beaming at me.

"Well done! Have a seat, my girl, and try my best vintage. Brewed from mussel shells and livers—best the islands have to offer."

I knelt and cast my eyes down in demure submission. "Among my people, it is customary for the female to serve. Will you allow me?"

For a moment he looked suspicious and I was sure he would refuse. But it is difficult for men to disbelieve a woman who insists that she wishes to serve them, and he nodded assent. I took the two glasses and filled them with the sickly liquor, which flowed out thickly, a viscous yellow slime.

And, letting my sleeves droop ever so slightly over them, I let three drops from the vial drip into his drink. He took it with pleasure in his stunted hand and quaffed it in one gulp.

"My appetite is famed the world over," he leered.

"As is the fact that you are an old woman with bad knees," I countered, and quaffed my own mussel brew.

We had drunk only three times before Ghassan began to reel on the floor, his eyes rolling in his head. I had not even begun to feel dizzy, and he appeared to be ready to vomit, or faint, or both.

"You cheated!" he gasped, clutching his belly.

I stood and laughed at him. "Even pretty girls playing at pirates know how to play them well."

Ghassan grunted, drooling a bit out of the side of his mouth, and lay down heavily, eyes drooping, his feathers crunching beneath him. "Take the satchel then, you lying wench. I hope you enjoy its fruits!" And with that, his body slackened and his great head with its crown of matted hair crashed to the floor. His snoring filled the little house like a storm beating at windows. I bent and slung the satchel from his body, pleased with my-self—a simple ruse, quickly accomplished.

I knew nothing.

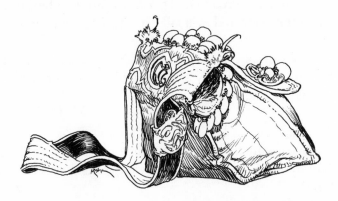

When I returned to the *Maidenhead* with Khaloud, the crew greeted us with cries of triumph. They crowded around, eager to see the purse per-form its magic. I held it over my head for all to see, then thrust my hand inside the thick leather to bring out the first handful of gold.

But when I pulled my hand from the satchel, there was no coin in my fist. Instead, my hand was fouled by a thick white ooze; it clung to my skin, my fingers, like a snail's body. A great clump of it had come away from the satchel, and now the leather sack was full of it, overflowing with pale sludge, splashing thickly onto the deck. I wiped my hand quickly on the wheel, disgusted by the stuff, which reeked of fish and salt. And then I saw—we all saw. The slime was hardening, wherever it fell, and spurting from the satchel like a fountain. It had already covered half the ship as thick as snowfall, bubbling into strange egglike shapes and stiffening into the familiar gray-white rocks of barnacles.

Of course I ordered the girls to get the decks clean of it, but nothing they did was of any help, even when they fell to hacking at it with their swords. We were halfway out of the bay by the time the red ship was red no more, and all of us in a panic. Halfway out of the bay when Ghassan woke—too strong, it seemed, to fall beneath Khaloud's fire for long—and came screeching out of his hut.

"Go! Go! You stupid hens! Carry them as far as you can, carry my babies until they use your ship as a nursery and foul it with their first dung! Fools! Steal from an old woman and see what you get! Thieves! Villains! I hope they tear open your livers for their birthday breakfasts!"

Sick with dread, Khaloud and I stood at the bow of my once-beautiful ship, and stared after the bird-creature, who cawed and flapped his huge black wings, cackling in the stiff wind.

The Pale Girl's Tale, Concluded

"It was not long after we left Ghassan that we encountered the Echeneis—that is not a very interesting story, no story involving a sea-monster is. A ship meets the monster; it either escapes or is devoured. We were swallowed whole, and found ourselves on this strange sea. But somehow, time is stretched here, and it has been hundreds of years. Hundreds of years and the barnacles have not hatched, we have not aged much, nothing has changed. We have eaten the creatures the Echeneis eats, and you would be surprised how many seals and sharks it has swallowed. We have never wanted for food. And from time to time, there have been other ships. But none who sought us out, as you did."

The shadowy woman sidled up to the Saint and kept her hand on the hilt of her sword. Snow knew her immediately by her fiery skin: Khaloud.

"Your timing," she said throatily, in a voice like flames rippling, "could almost be called providential. Can you not see the creatures stirring in their eggs? The birth is coming; I would swear it by the lamp of Kashkash."

"Indeed, it is. Within the day, I think—I do have some experience with hatching birds. The barnacles have never been so large, and we can see blackness fluttering within." The Saint looked critically at the four strangers. "We have decided to attempt our escape. Will you help us or hinder us?"

Sigrid seemed to stifle the urge to fall to her knees. "Anything I can do, I will do, my lady."

Grog belched. "Well, we haven't got any choice, have we?"

"You old trout!" a voice came from belowdecks, quickly followed by a body—a woman with the tail of a wolf, the haunches of a deer, and bright blue wings. Magadin strode across the ship to the Magyr's tub, her gray eyes blazing.

"I thought I told you to see my ship safe home! You brought her back here to get chewed to pieces?" she bellowed.

"What? Look, this lot kidnapped me!" Grog looked away, nervously, picking at the scales of her violet tail. "I was going to take it back, I swear. But they made me come back, and shouldn't you thank me for keeping her bow and stern attached as well as I have? And besides, I hardly expected you to survive, did I? And dead women don't complain."

Khaloud frowned. "We fished her out of the bile half dead, but taking on monsters is a sacred duty left to us by old Tomomo—we pressed her into service, and she is with us now."

Magadin hooked her shaggy arm around the Djinn's smoky waist. "It is pleasant to be part of a crew, and not manning every sail yourself. Part of a crew and not a prisoner, not a maiden, not cargo. I died in the whale and washed up on the deck of paradise. This is the best death I could have asked for, and I hope to stay dead for a long while." She smiled, and her tail wagged, and there was no weariness left in the lines of her face.

"Now that we're all family," growled Eyvind, "hadn't we better see about getting ourselves retched out of this beast?"

"An excellent suggestion," the Saint said.

———

Within a few hours, both ships had drawn back through the sea of bile, close to the mouth of the Echeneis. Eyvind and Grog had stayed aboard the beast-maid's ship, while Sigrid and Snow were huddled close with the pirates. Baleen hung in the distance like a glossy door, and they could hear the sea crashing outside.

"First we must raise the monster," said the Saint in a hushed voice. "Khaloud?"

The Djinn drew a dark, curved bow back almost into the shape of a full moon, and lit the arrow from her belly. She fired it directly up into the whale-turtle's mouth—and for a moment, it simply disappeared into the mist and there was no sound. But then—a dull clunking noise echoed through the mouth and the creature moaned in pain, ascending through the waters to destroy whatever had troubled it.

"How can we be sure they will hatch?" Snow whispered, clutching Sigrid's hand to calm her heart.

The Saint looked grim and glad all at once, drawing a dagger from a sheath bound to her thigh. "We aren't going to let them dawdle. The eggs should be weak enough now for them to break out—or for us to break in. Get yourself a knife, girl."

Grog hollered at Eyvind to drag her to the side of the ship and began to smash the barnacle-eggs with hurled harpoons. Every creature on the *Maidenhead* was slashing, clawing, cutting, crushing the eggs. Khaloud flicked her fingers at one after the other, engulfing them in little orange flames. The sickening crunch of it made Snow gag, and the smell was worse, like overripe meat. At first it was slow, just a few black infants hopping out of their shells—but then the roaring sound of thousands of wings filled the mouth of the Echeneis, doubled and tripled with echoes.

It was the Saint who laughed first—and then the Djinn joined her. They saw, and soon all could see, a great flock of crows rising from the ruined barnacles, their huge wings flapping noisily, like pages turning. More and more of them shattered their eggs of their own accord, eager to join their siblings. Countless wings beat against the wall of baleen, the arched roof, the cheeks of their prison. The mouth was filled with them as if with a draught of fouled wine, and the monster began to roar in rage, a guttural sound like the earth opening.

And it did open. The Echeneis's jaws cracked slightly, and a blinding sliver of light seared across the two ships. The sliver became a wash as the mouth opened wide and the sea rushed in, sparkling blue and gray and white, buffeting the ships on its waves. There was a great cheer from the crew of the *Maidenhead,* and the sails were drawn tight. Eyvind wrestled

the rigging of the other vessel, and when the sea flowed out again, they rode the crest of the foam out into the sun and the world again.

With them, thousands upon thousands of gleaming black crows streamed out of the mouth of the Echeneis, heralding the ships and following them, soaring up and out of the whale like an exhalation of dark angels. The sound of their flapping wings was like grapeshot; the sunlight caught their feathers and glowed deep violet against the pale sky. The monster groaned, almost a whimper, and sank again below the surface as the ships sped away from it with taut sails.

And so, as quickly as the birth began, it was finished. The red ship and the brown floated together in the broad light some space away from the place where the monster had submerged, lashed together so that farewells could be made. A few lingering crows circled overhead.

The sun was setting over the sea, its light pooled over the water, unfurling itself like a glove, staining the water a perfect shade of gold, as if a lady had dropped her best necklace into the depths. The golden light flooded over the deck of the *Maidenhead,* and Eyvind's eyes filled with tears.

"The virgin was devoured," he said wonderingly, gesturing at the red ship, "the saints will go west with henless eggs, and the sea," his voice tightened, "has gone to gold."

Eyvind seemed to shimmer and to wriggle, like a worm spasming on a hook—and then there was no Eyvind at all any longer. A great white bear stood in his place, tears streaming from its large black eyes. Its fur was smooth and snowy, illuminated with light and sea spray. The timbers groaned under the sudden weight. Sigrid cried out and crossed the plank from the red ship to the *Witch's Kiss,* sinking to her knees and touching his furry face.

The bear closed his eyes, and laid his head heavily in his lover's lap.

"It's happened." He sighed, his voice changing to something deeper and rougher now that it was his own again, more growl than tongue. "And now we can go home. At last, we can go home. We will go to Skin-Peddler, and you will ask for your skin again, and we will go back to the snows and the wilds, together. It's over."

Sigrid took her hands away slowly. "No, Eyvind. I cannot. I am not Ulla, and I will never be again. I go with my Lady, as I was meant to. *The maiden, the bear, and the girl in gray.* You must find your own way now."

"Do not leave me, Bear-wife. All I have done has been for you." He lifted his limpid eyes to her, stricken.

"All you have done, you have done for yourself, so that you could live again as you thought you should. I cannot be a part of that dream—all I have done I have done by instinct and desire, save for what I have done for *her*. She is the object of my Quest, and I cannot reject it now. I feel as though I am being split apart again, my skins warring with each other. But I'm sorry, my love. There is just no getting any of it back."

She stood and stroked his coarse white head, bent and kissed it, her tears wetting the fur through. He begged her, and clutched at her uselessly with his clumsy paws.

"Where will I go? What will I do?" he whispered hopelessly.

Sigrid shook her head, unable to give an answer. She crossed back to the red ship with its carpet of broken shells. The Saint embraced her, and Sigrid came away from that embrace glowing like a new bride.

"Come on, then, Bear," Grog said with a sigh, sprinkling a bit of brine over her chest. "Seems you and I are going home lonesome. Snow, get on the boat, child. I've no taste for blubbering send-offs."

But Snow, her pale hair catching the last light of the sun, stepped backwards into Sigrid's arms. "I'm staying," she said uncertainly. "Muireann is not my home. There is nothing for me there. If the captain will take me, I will call this ship mother and father. Perhaps some morning I will wake up and my body will have flushed dark and rose again." She smiled, and the smile warmed her face like a swinging lantern.

"Of course we'll take you," the Saint said. "Tommy bade us never turn away a recruit—we are a family of monsters, and the birth of new beasts is a cause for joy. There is so much for us to do—the sea and the tide are ours again."

The planks were unlashed and the ships separated like twins within their mother's womb. The *Maidenhead* sailed west, her sails blazing with light. Grog and Eyvind remained on the dilapidated *Witch's Kiss*, turning east, away from the sun and into the gloomy twilight. The Magyr looked after the bear, who stood on the foredeck, staring after the red smear of the receding ship, his great shoulders slumped in grief.

"Come on, love," she said, feeling strangely tender suddenly, "I'll take you home."

"Muireann is not my home, either. But I am not monster enough, it seems, to be offered a place at sea." Grog searched for a grain in the boards, uncomfortable with his mourning.

"Then I'll take you north, Evvy," she said brightly, her voice like buttered rum. "To your real home. You can go back now, right, and rest with your own people? That's something, don't you think? Don't you miss the Stars a-shining on the glaciers, like a thousand candles?"

Eyvind turned his ursine head towards her. "I do," he admitted.

"Then I steer north, old bear. And when you've felt the snow beneath your paws again, the world won't seem so black. At least, that's my guess. Who can tell with your lot?" Grog ran a hand through her green hair.

The white bear walked gingerly over the decks to her tub and settled his bulk down next to it. He laid his head on the wooden rim, and, as the last ribbons of day unwound from the sky, slept.